THE BATTLE OF FORT ROCK

GOD'S BATTLE FOR KENT STATE IN 1990

BY KEVIN L. MOODY

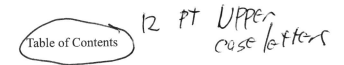

Table of Contents

12 Pt UPPer case letters

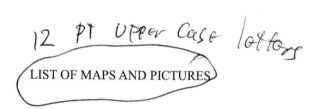

12 Pt Upper Case letters

LIST OF MAPS AND PICTURES

LIST OF MAPS

LIST OF PICTURES

Fiberglass Air Bubbles

LIST OF LETTERS

Letters

1 space (204 PX)

ACKNOWLEDGEMENTS

I thank God for my best friend and adviser, Mike Kaplan. I thank Chris of the Glass bubble project and Mike Kaplan for inspiring me to write this book. Chris gave me the original inspiration, and Mike Kaplan supported me as I finished the book. I thank Chris of the Glass Bubble Project, Mike Kaplan, Mike's friend Bruce Grossman, my niece Kortney Rockwell, Dave Learn, and the crew of the Glass Bubble Project for valuable feedback concerning this book. I give special thanks to Chris for giving me the tough criticism necessary for writing a good novel. I thank Dan Eaves for drawing many of my maps and illustrations. I thank Mike Kaplan and Dan Eaves for being my friend through thick and thin. I thank Josh Faunce for telling me that setting the record straight at Notre Dame was God's will.

Right and left Justified

10 pt letters

INTRODUCTION

This novel is based on a true story. This story is fiction mainly because I changed the names of many characters, changed the names of some of the universities I attended, and changed the name of my hometown and locations associated with my hometown. These names and locations were changed to protect the privacy of the individuals involved. I also used literary license to depict a few events that I theorized or did not witness. There really was a Project Texhoma, a crisis with the US Dollar, an extremely bad influence in the fiberglass industry, the rock band Kritikal Kondishun, a vicious hex that felt like Pearl Harbor, or striking coincidences appearing to be that hex, and a May 4th controversy that almost caused a riot or an illegal protest in Kent in 1990. This is the story of how God used my attempt to build a perpetual motion machine to help me to become a good friend of Kent State's hippies. This friendship helped them to protest the scaled back memorial and strong disrespect concerning the memorial in a peaceful and legal way in 1990.

[handwritten marginalia: Ten point Lines at each chapter Heading]

CHAPTER 1

THE GAINESVILLE DREAMS

[handwritten marginalia: Ten point lines at each chapter heading]

In 1973, I was an 'A' science student at Gainesville High School. I predicted the weather almost as well as the best meteorologists in Dallas. My brains and casual businesslike appearance made up for my moderately plump and uncoordinated body. My way of choosing friends had to make up for my defects. I introduced myself by explaining who I was including my non-conformity; such as my non-athletic body, my scientific brain, or my resulting mundane personality. If a person accepted these things, I accepted him because he likely would prove to be a friend over time. If he did not prove to be a friend, he was at least a friendly acquaintance for the time. Though this way of choosing friends proved to be imperfect, I always seemed to have friends, despite my interest in primarily intellectual things.

In the fall of 1973, The Arab Oil Embargo began. This caused a gasoline shortage throughout the United States and Europe. This shortage was called the energy crisis. Hoping to find a solution to the energy crisis, I studied physics in the library. There, I found a contradiction between the inverse square law in magnetism and the law of conservation of energy and matter. The law of conservation of energy and matter states that energy is neither created nor destroyed. This law implies that perpetual motion is impossible. The inverse square law, in magnetism, states that the force of attraction or repulsion between two magnets is proportional to the product of the pole strengths of the two said magnets divided by the square of distance between the two magnetic poles in question. The inverse square law implies that a perpetual motion electric motor would work with the right distance between the magnets comprising the motor.[1] I thought, "This perpetual motion motor could be the solution to the energy crisis." I proceeded to make a crude model prototype, but I could not make it well enough to test the theory. I was a tenth grader in Gainesville High School and did not have the resources to make a good prototype. With the resources of a student, I could make straight 'A's, but I could not get a valid test of my proposed perpetual motion machine.

I feared that my idea would fall into the wrong hands. This idea could change the balance of world power. Maybe, one of America's big companies would simply steal my idea. Maybe, the oil companies would buy my idea and throw it away. Or maybe, the Soviet Union would find out about my idea. I feared the Soviet Union the most because it was a rotten country. The Soviet Union was an enemy of the United States with thousands of nuclear missiles pointed at America. Tensions between the United States and the Soviet Union often ran high. The KGB was their secret police and their spy agency. The KGB often tortured scientists with inventions such as mine. I needed to keep my invention out of the hands of the Russians. I needed somebody I could trust to help protect my invention. I appointed my best friend, Jimmy Woodman, to run security and to protect my invention.

This new organization, charged with building my perpetual motion machine, was called US Physics. I made all of my prototypes at my house. I called my house Gainesville Security Central. My effort to build a perpetual motion machine was called Project Texhoma. Jimmy Woodman, my best friend of three years was Security Chairman. He appointed a committee. This became the Board of Judges of Texas. The Board of Judges of Texas was the Board of Directors of US Physics. I was the President of the Board of Judges and could appoint any officer of the Board. Jimmy was the Vice President and committee Chairman of the Board. This committee chairman is a Head Justice. He appointed a committee. Members of this committee were called State Justices. He appointed Brian Fogman as First State Justice, Larry Waterman as Second State Justice, and John Ferro as Third State Justice. Jimmy was a loyal, feisty, in your face kind of friend. He laughed when I felt good. This caused me to like him in spite of his short height and long haired youthful appearance. Consistent with the peaceful ideals Jimmy represented, he advised me, "Cry wolf concerning your perpetual machine, but hide the goods. Keep your credibility low until you have the goods." This represented the policy of wolfcry. Brian, Larry and John were normal teenagers of 1973. Then, we had a club called the Council of State Justices. This club consisted of officers of the

---

1   See picture 1 The Workings of an Electric Motor on Page 198 at the end of book.

Board of Judges of Texas and their friends and of officers of US Physics and their friends.

While I was getting my 'A's and investigating a possible perpetual motion machine, Dad ran three plants for White Fiberglass. Dad was a person with a businesslike demeanor. He was thin, tall, and neatly dressed. One of his plants was in Plant City Florida, another plant was in Parsons Kansas, and another plant was in Gainesville, Texas. Dad's office was located at the Gainesville plant. The company called Dad's plants the southwest zone of White Fiberglass. White Fiberglass was a company which made fiberglass tubs and showers for various wholesale customers. This company had its corporate headquarters in Middlebury, Indiana with eight other plants in Elkhart County, Indiana; a plant in Plant City, Florida; another plant in Parsons, Kansas; and another plant in Gainesville, Texas. When White fiberglass would have a corporate meeting, Dad would take his family to South Bend, Indiana. I looked forward to those trips because I could see an old grade school best friend. He was a lot like Jimmy Woodman. He was Jimmy's cousin, Tommy Woodman.

My scientific brain gave me a theory concerning perpetual motion and the organization to develop it. This scientific brain also made me an Atheist. God seemed unscientific. I asked God to show me that He existed if He did. To prove his existence, God gave me several dreams which would predict some of my future. In one of these dreams, an angel of The Lord took me to Parsons, Kansas. This angel showed me a calendar and a clock. It was October 18, 1978 at about 8:00 am. I was standing at White Fiberglass on US 400 in Parsons, Kansas (Map 1). All of a sudden, Communist airplanes started to bomb White Fiberglass and the surrounding areas. I got into my car and fled to US Highway 59. As I left Parsons, I woke up back in the present year of 1973 to get ready for my day at Gainesville High School. Every time Dad stopped at Parsons, Kansas on the way to South Bend, I thought of seeing Tommy. Parsons, Kansas seemed to be a symbol of Jimmy and Tommy. I feared that something bad was going to happen to my best friend Jimmy Woodman, Tommy Woodman, or somebody like one of them on October 18, 1978.

Another 1973 dream took me to Big RV International in 1979. There, I saw a short, scruffy, but well-built old man with a limp. He was the final finish foreman, Ted Monsterman. He was a conniving and mean foreman. If you were not his friend, he would nit-pick your work and spread vicious rumors about you and all of your friends. He hated Jason Shoemaker, but Jason was a fun loving, long blond haired, skinny, tall, and bearded person who would give the shirt off his back for a friend. Ted would persecute Jason worse than any bully in fiberglass. Ted would call Jason names and spread vicious rumors

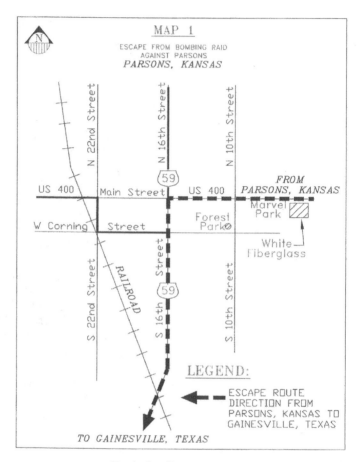

Map by Dan Eaves

about Jason and all of his friends. While Ted was causing his havoc, a deep recession set in. During this deep recession, Dad, the general manager, ran the company. It made 30% profits. Dad believed that people should be rewarded on the basis of merit. In this dream, Jason Shoemaker became the best pattern maker on the face of the earth. This company was so greatly blessed. I was the richest mold repairman in the history of fiberglass and the worst worker in the plant despite flawless mold repair work and perfect attendance. Jed Pugent, the plant manager, had a medium height, skinny, but neat appearance. He told dirty jokes and forced some women employees to have sex with him and some men to drink with him outside of the plant. He was good friends with Ted Monsterman, the final finish foreman. Other than his damning major sins, he seemed to be a great plant manager. In February of 1980, Ted Monsterman called the corporate office of Big RV International and lied about Jason. He said that Jason Shoemaker sold him heroin. Jason Shoemaker was fired and blackballed. On April 10, 1980, Ted Monsterman convinced the cooperate office that Dad, the general manager, should be fired because he was friends with Jason. Ted lied again! Ted called Dad lazy and said he really made the profits. They fired Dad. I warned Jed and Ted that God would judge Big RV. I explained, "When Joe Sinc the glamorous baby brother of the Pee Weas, shall come to Elight Island, Big RV International will face the wrath of God. Flee the plant on that day." After Dad was fired and blackballed, I woke up back in 1973 to face a day at Gainesville High School. I had an English test that day.

A later 1973 dream took me to Big RV International in 1980. Big RV Plastics fell apart after Dad was fired. The company did not make a dime. The fiberglass parts they made were junk, and the customers were mad. These parts were paper thin, dull, and full of air bubbles. Pollution and dangerous chemicals abounded. At noon every day, The dust and fumes stank and burned the neighbors' eyes from California Road to the south, to the Red River on the north, to Farm Road 678 on the east, and to I-35 on the west (Map2). Paul Chrispeace, father of Tom Chrisgood's best friend Gerard Chrispeace, lived a block and a half south-east of the plant and suffered daily from the noon pollution. Tom Chrisgood, Gerard Chrispeace, and Paul Chrispeace were all devout Christians and good friends. They all had a neat but natural appearance. They were committed to remaining good friends for life if possible. This pollution and the blackballing of me, of Jason Shoemaker, and of Dad outraged a chapter of the SDS from a famous university. The SDS was a student organization of hippies actively protesting the Vietnam war. Their protests sometimes were violent or illegal. Jason was their brother in the liberal culture. The SDS members arranged a protest march outside of Big RV Plastics. The SDS remained peaceful but was viciously accused of trying to burn down the plant. The SDS members would get arrested for this protest. They paid their fines and sued Big RV Plastics for polluting the air. Big RV Plastics bribed the judges. As a result, their case was thrown out of court, in spite of an almost perfect case. All of the SDS members were warned to leave Texas forever. To seal this ruling, Ted Monsterman ordered five barrels of radioactive resins and placed them in his one hundred barrel inventory. He illegally removed the labels from the radioactive resin barrels and warned that he would spill these resins in the creek next to the plant if the SDS protested, if the police tried to arrest him, or if the government tried to shut down the plant. This creek, Wheeler Creek, drains into the Pecan Creek. Pecan creek drains into Elm Creek. Elm Creek drains into the Trinity River. Dallas gets some of its drinking

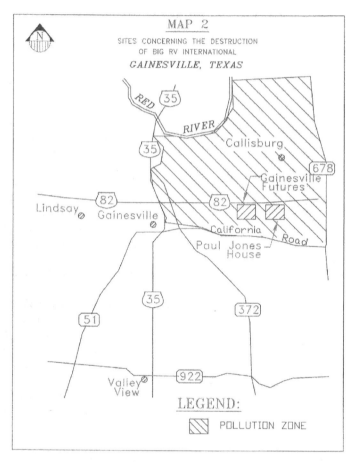

Map by Dan Eaves

water from this river, so nobody dared to challenge Ted Monsterman, also known as the Monster of the North. Little did I know, every rock star in Hollywood wanted to defend the honor of the SDS. Even the conservative administration of the famous university from which the SDS came marveled at the wickedness of Big RV International. They resented Dad's blackballing and the slander of their students and alumni. They publicly rebuked Big RV asking, "Why do you mock our students and our alumni? Why did you blackball our conservative brother in the plastics industry?" Everybody associated with this famous university turns on Big RV. This university embraces their hippies, Dad, and all of his blackballed employees. Despite this healing, Big RV hardens their hearts and continues in their wickedness. As a result, Paul Chrispeace and his neighbors were oppressed daily by the plants pollution at noon for over a year. Then, I woke up back in 1973 to face a day at Gainesville High School. I had a French Test that day.

I was talking to my Mom laughing at this dream. I said, "I will never be friends with those hippies in the dream or even any hippies from Kent State. I am too smart for them. Besides, Dad would kick me out of the house for being their friends." Mom replied, "If you say you will never be friends with those hippies, you will some-day be their friends." I replied, "God does not exist. I will never be their friends."

In the final dream, my friend Jimmy Woodman went to the Joe Sinc's record company, to see if he could restore the honor of the SDS. Jimmy was the same loving liberal that he was in real life. Every rock star in America wanted to stand up for the SDS, but they feared the Monster of the North. After a long and inspiring talk by Jimmy, Joe Sinc, little brother to the famous Pee Weas, volunteered to restore the honor of the SDS. Joe's strategy was to visit Elight Island on a Monday at noon (Map 2). Jimmy Woodman routed Joe's Car down California Road at the border of Ted Monsterman's pollution zone. Robert Elight objected. He said, "We are unnecessarily risking Joe's life." Joe said, "Those hippies risked their life to end the war in Vietnam! As a fellow peace activist, I defy the Monster of the North in the name of the Lord and take California Road." Robert was a body builder with a tanned body and a short and neatly trimmed beard. He was my friend. Robert, Jimmy, Jason, and I met Joe at the Denton Airport. I took Joe out to eat and get to know each other while Robert, Jimmy, and Jason went to Elight Island to celebrate Joe's friendship. At 11:45 am, Joe and I left for Elight Island. At about the same time, Jed Pugent came to Elight Island to flee the coming wrath of God. He warned Jimmy and Robert of Ted's plans to stage an industrial accident and to kill Joe Sinc. Jimmy rushed to try to stop Joe from coming down California Road. Joe and I walked right into Ted's trap. Just after my car reached the intersection of California and Grand, a thick cloud of fiberglass dust and fumes came from the north. I started coughing and feeling my eyes burn. I was forced to pull my car over to the side of the road. As I pulled my car to the side, Jimmy Woodman arrived with a dust and particle mask for each of us. We each put on the masks. Jimmy took us to the hospital. I was treated and released. Joe was hospitalized for fiberglass poisoning and possible exposure to the radioactive resins. While I was in the hospital, Jimmy went to Big RV Plastics to bust Ted in the teeth. Luckily for Jimmy and Ted, Robert stopped the fight. Jimmy had good reason to be mad. This "accident" killed twenty-five workers at Big RV Plastics and injured forty-one people in Gainesville including Joe Sinc.

In this same dream, on the next day in the afternoon, our group visited Joe in the hospital. I said to Joe, "God is with you. I had a dream concerning your future against Big RV International. I saw three demon angels fly over that plant. The first demon angel flew over the plant. This symbolizes your record company's leader, Jim Doe, giving his approval for you to stand for the SDS. The second demon angel flew over the plant and was grabbed by a rope and pulled into the fire. His head was stamped with the word "homosexual." After God destroys that evil plant, Big RV will call your brother in the Pee Weas, Barry Sinc, a homosexual. You are the third demon angel. This demon angel was singed by the fire. That is your injury now. God will heal you. This third demon angel flew north, flew back, and smote the plant off of the face of the earth. You will perform a free rock concert north of town that will make the pollution zone a ghost town when God destroys that evil plant. After your brother is slandered as a homosexual, you will cry out to America. Your cry will make it un-American to own a Big RV product. Everybody will try to sell all of their Big RV products. This will destroy Big RV.

Here's Mitch Angelman, Gainesville High School's great man of God." Mitch joined us to pray that God would heal Joe Sinc. God healed Joe! God told Robert through Mitch, "Stop praying for Big RV and Ted." He commanded, "Robert, go to the Big RV corporate office and tell Big RV, "In ninety days and ninety nights Big RV International is going to be destroyed.""" He did this and was arrested. The judge in Dallas was not sympathetic toward Big RV. He said, "I believe that you monsters at Big RV had better repent of your sins. Big RV is lucky that this case is not about the accident in Gainesville. Twenty-five people are dead and forty-one are wounded. You monsters are lucky that I don't issue a bench warrant for your arrest. Leave Robert alone before I change my mind. Case dismissed."

In this same dream, preparations were undertaken for the coming wrath of God. Joe arranged to give a free rock concert, in Marietta, Oklahoma, on the day of God's judgment. Marietta is due north of Gainesville. The First Apostolic Church arranged for a show of its young people's choir to get the older people out of the neighborhood. These people's preparations made the pollution zone a ghost town. At 10:10 pm of God's judgment day, the local weatherman came on and told of a very severe thunderstorm that was 20 minutes away from the plant. The lightning burned everything it struck. This weatherman said, "Big RV International had better repent, or the plant in Gainesville will be destroyed, as Robert Elight predicted." Meanwhile, Big RV executives mocked the weatherman saying, "This is only a summer storm. God can't touch us." Twenty minutes later, lightning struck the north gable of the plant! Then, lightning struck the south gable! Suddenly, lightning struck the air compressor! The building started on fire! The earth quivered and quaked! Fire arose from the center of the earth! As the earth quaked, Gerard Chrispeace, who did not know of God's judgment of Big RV, was hit in the head by a vase on the mantle of the fireplace at Paul's house a block southeast of the plant. The smoke from the fire killed Gerard. Ten miles to the north, in Marietta, Joe Sinc and all of his fans heard the explosion, felt the earth shake, and saw the Big RV fire on the south horizon. This fire was so hot that its smoke rose 50 miles. The Big RV Plastics plant was completely destroyed. Despite the radioactive resins, no detectable radiation fell to the earth. Despite this earth shaking explosion, no other buildings were damaged! The Gainesville Fire department marveled at God's judgment. They said in astonishment, "Fire and brimstone came down from heaven and could not have been man-made. Only God could have protected all of the other buildings. God destroyed Big RV Plastics." They knew that God destroyed the plant and rejoiced in Gainesville's deliverance.

In this same dream, Big RV did not repent of their great sins. Big RV slandered the Sincs as homosexuals. Suddenly, Americans took their Big RV products to the dealers for trade-in. Lines at every dealership were at least a mile long. People who could not get to the dealerships sanded the name of Big RV off their vehicle. It became un-American to own a Big RV product. Big RV's banks and stockholders wanted their money back. This bankrupted Big RV in 1 hour. After this bankruptcy, I told Joe, "You went north to play a concert that saved many lives in Gainesville. Your cry bankrupted this evil company." After my talk with Joe, I woke up to face report card day at Gainesville High School. My grades were all A's!

About two and a half years after these dreams, eight events caused my friendship with Jimmy Woodman to end. One of these events had Jimmy making fun of a fellow student named Frank. Frank was an intellectual, straight 'A' student who looked the part. I criticized Jimmy for this, and he was mad. This event happened during the full moon. Another event had his best friend Eric joke around about becoming a communist. Eric was a medium height, dark complected, long hired hippie. I actually thought Eric may have been a communist. This occurred during the new moon. Six other events coincided with the phases of the moon. These events destroyed our friendship and caused Jimmy's resignation as security chairman in 1976. His whole committee also resigned.

CHAPTER 2

THE BATTLE OF AMERICA

In June of 1976, near the end of Gerald Ford's term of office, I found a new friend. His name was Tom Chrisgood. He was a neat appearing, tall, skinny, and short haired Christian who knew how to handle guns and who seemed like he would be a loyal friend. I appointed him as the Chairman of Security, Vice President, and Head Justice of the Board of Judges of Texas. His family's house headquartered security operations. It was called Fort Riblet Security Central. He appointed his own committee to replace the one that quit with Jimmy Woodman. He showed me how to use guns to protect the project. Gerard Chrispeace was his assistant and First State Justice. Gerard was a medium height, stocky friend of Tom. Tom also appointed Brian Todwink Second State Justice, and Jimmy Raker as Third State Justice of the Board of Judges. The new state justices were normal, and clean cut Christians of the day. He took me to church at The Second Apostolic Church. There, they taught the plan of salvation. In August of 1976, I enrolled in classes at Denton State University. In September, I did what would have been the unthinkable three years ago. I repented, got baptized in the name of Jesus, and started praying for the infilling of the Holy Ghost. On Easter of 1977, I was filled with the Holy Ghost.

Between September of 1976 and Easter of 1977, Tom Chrisgood faced a bad tribulation. This tribulation started when Tom and I visited Booktrash on I-35. We were visiting Booktrash to buy identification badges for US Physics. At

Booktrash, I ordered the ID badges. While I was ordering the badges, Tom saw some pornography. While Tom was looking at the pornography, the store's owner, Antwan, stared at Tom and psychically put a hex on him. As Antwan stared at Tom, Tom felt an eerie feeling. Antwan was a short, skinny, and wrinkle faced warlock. He hated Christians. He was the most powerful warlock in North Texas. Tom was a vulnerable young Christian. After this encounter with Antwan at Booktrash, Tom became wild. He missed church regularly and acted silly with Gerard in front of his Mom. He even tried pot. His Mom noticed his strange behavior. On Christmas Eve, Tom's Mom talked Tom into going to the First Apostolic Church in Gainesville to get prayer about his situation. That night, Lester Winterman of The Christian Church in South Bend, Indiana was preaching at that church as a visiting evangelist. Tom went to the altar for prayer. There, Lester Winterman laid hands on Tom and said, "I command the demons of rebellion and fornication to leave this person, Tom, in the name of Jesus!" Immediately after Rev. Winterman said this prayer, Tom said, "Praise the Lord, Jesus." He spoke in other tongues as God gave utterance. Rev. Winterman said, "Praise the Lord. Tom is delivered of demonic oppression." Demonic oppression is a sophisticated term for a hex.

A Christian Marine recruiter worked in a place close to Booktrash. He visited Booktrash on Good Friday of 1977, and he was strongly tempted to look at pornography. He plead the blood of Jesus and left. He returned a few weeks later with all of his Christian friends. He told Antwan about the saving grace of Jesus. Antwan rejected Jesus. The Marine recruiter warned Antwan, "Repent and get baptized in the name of Jesus for the remission of your sins. If you do not repent, you will face God's judgment for those sins." Antwan did not repent. Tom heard a rumor that a Christian Marine recruiter broke Antwan's power and warned him to repent. Three weeks after Easter, Tom and I visited Booktrash. There, we found witchcraft books, voodoo dolls, and pornography. We left and enjoyed the rest of the day. The next day, I thought, "Booktrash will face God's judgment. I fear for the safety of all young people in Gainesville."

In July of 1977, I was angry with Booktrash. Antwan hexed Tom Chrisgood and maybe another good friend, Jimmy Woodman. I lost my friendship with Jimmy through a union of events coinciding with the phases of the moon. I prayed for God to protect Gainesville from this warlock. I prayed for the young people who were lured into crime or hexed by this operation. I prayed for God to help Tom and Jimmy. On my way to church, I spoke in tongues, and asked God to burn Booktrash to the ground. I left this matter in God's hands. Nobody else knew of my prayer or anger with Booktrash. Three days later, while I was in church, Booktrash burned to the ground. I vowed that no more of my friends would fall prey to sorcerers. Thus began the tradition of the Occult Defense Command. The Occult Defense Command had one weakness. I and the other officers assigned to pray needed to stay right with

God to pray effectively for the Council of State Justices Members. Sin to us was what kryptonite was to Superman. If I or my other prayer warriors committed sin, those praying needed to repent to keep their prayers from being hindered. I would serve this position alone for about two years.

In September of 1977, Tom Chrisgood would return from Europe with a damning indictment of the Soviet Union. Late in August, He and two other new-found European friends like him would attempt to smuggle Bibles into the Soviet Union. The KGB caught them at the border crossing at Kishinev. The KGB kept Tom and his friends in jail for four days. During those four days, the guards told Tom and his friends that neither Jesus nor President Carter could get them out of this prison. Tom and his friends drove the guards crazy by showing them kindness and talking about the love of Jesus. This caused the authorities to take their money, stamp their passports "persona non grata," and kick them out of the country. Tom and his friends arrived at the US embassy in Bucharest, Romania. There, they had the opportunity to tell their story to Time Magazine. They declined because they thought that bad publicity about the Soviet Union would only make it harder for their Christian brothers and sisters in the Soviet Union. From there, they returned to their countries. Tom returned to Gainesville. I responded with outrage. I said, "These rotten Soviets broke the Helsinki Accords they signed. Build more bombs. They break treaties at will. They want war." Tom replied, "We need to love the Russian people. They think Americans are monsters because their government told them so." I replied, "Please forgive me for falsely thinking that all Russians are monsters. Washington told me so." Tom and I had three months of quality friendship. In December, Tom joined the US Army. He requested to be stationed in Germany, so he could be with his European friends. The Army honored his request. He reported for duty in mid-December.

In April of 1978, I discovered that I needed $5000 to do a good prototype of my perpetual motion machine. Any job I could have would be inadequate to raise this kind of capital, so I sent in to a mail-order company ran by a famous importer, Mr. Meillinger. Meillinger sent me a course on running an import company. I studied his literature for the summer and decided to try a party plan for selling imports. In September, I booked two parties and sold $200 worth of imports. After that, I failed to book any more parties.

Also, in April of 1978, I also realized that the Apostolic Christian community was in a state of near panic. Inflation roared through the economy at nearly 20%. This caused many Christians of my faith to fearfully struggle. Rumors of Satan worship abounded. Some of these were true. Last year, God burned down Booktrash. Antwan, the owner of Booktrash, put a hex on my best friend, Tom Chrisgood and perhaps Jimmy Woodman. Many people of my faith thought that the Russians were coming. There was a minister at a famous radio church who quoted a general in the army as saying, "The Russians are coming and we (America) had better be ready." In addition, the US Dollar plummeted daily. These things made us fear the coming of the Anti-Christ.

I loved America and lived through these fears. As my country seemed to be headed toward an almost certain fall, I started to pray for it. When the US currency plummeted, I prayed that God would help to lift the US Dollar and save this country from ruin. When I heard that the Russians were coming, I prayed. When witchcraft was practiced publicly, I asked God to destroy the covens (witches dens). Through this type of prayer, I grew to love America greatly. After months of hearing daily about the fall of the Dollar, I decided to pray. For this prayer, I became discouraged, as the Dollar continued to fall.

Little did I know, Currency Trader, George Moneyrat, was trying to cause a depression. This depression would make George Moneyrat filthy rich. In New York on October 16, 1978, George Moneyrat, said, "If the Dollar continues to plummet, we will have a depression in a month. I don't care because I will be filthy rich." Paul Stare replied, "There are Christians praying for the Dollar." George replied, "Make them hurt until they quit." Paul replied, "I will look into my crystal ball to see if any Christian can stand up to my pressure." George Moneyrat was a middle aged, neatly dressed currency trader. His friend was a powerful warlock named Paul Stare. Paul was a neatly dressed and well-built body builder. He was a mean and powerful warlock. Later that day, Paul told George, "There is a church in Gainesville powerful enough to pray for the Dollar and stand the pressure. One guy in that church rebuked the most powerful warlock in North Texas." George asked, "What is that guy's name?" Paul told George, "My crystal ball says Kevin Moody, President of the Board of Judges of Texas. Stopping him is not that easy. He has one weakness. He wants to make right with a former best friend, Jimmy Woodman." George asked, "Can't you put a mean hex on Jimmy Woodman?" Paul replied, "Kevin and all of his friends are praying for Jimmy, but I know a future best friend of Kevin's a lot like Jimmy that I can hex. He is a reckless teenager in Ardmore, Oklahoma. His name is Johnny Oilstring. I can stage a terrible accident on US 77. Johnny will be in the wrong. I cannot stop his prayer, but I will cause him enough pain to keep him from praying for America again." George replied, "Thanks for warning me. I will sell my currency positions tomorrow." Paul went to his crystal ball and hexed Johnny Oilstring. He sprinkled his magic dust on his crystal ball and chanted the incantation, "In the name of earth, air, fire, water, and the spirits, let Johnny have an accident on US 77 which kills three children waiting for a school bus. Let one of these children have a politically powerful father, so Ardmore, Oklahoma would want to hang Johnny. Let Bobby Weakleg of Kevin's church become Johnny's friend and fall under this hex. Spirits punish these Christians who pray for America and keep the Anti-Christ out of power." Paul called George and said, "Kevin will never pray for America again."

On Tuesday, October 17, 1978, I attended a revival meeting held at First Apostolic Church in Gainesville, Texas. This preacher was a fiery preacher. I prayed for my starting import business, my research project concerning perpetual motion, and the US Dollar. Fellow Christians from my church, Second Apostolic Church, were there. Among these Christians was the Martian *Martin* Family. This preacher gave his sermon and made an alter call after the service. At the Altar, the Martian Family prayed for their son's infilling of the Holy Ghost. That night, Jimmy Martian received the gift of the Holy Ghost. As Jimmy received the Holy Ghost, God told me to pray and fast for the US Dollar starting Sunday for a day and then to repeat every 3 days until the Dollar went up. That night, I visited the Chrisgood's and declared prayer and fasting concerning the Dollar.

On Wednesday, October 18, 1978 at about 7:30 am in Ardmore, Oklahoma, my best friend to be, Johnny Oilstring, was entertaining two of his friends, Scott and Frank. Johnny and his friends were normal fun loving sixteen year old children of the day. Johnny was a tall, long black hired, and skinny hippie a lot like Jimmy Woodman, but unlike Jimmy, his high school grades were low. All of his friends had a reckless and long haired appearance about them. Johnny showed them his dogs, Christian and Meagan. Johnny commanded his dog, Christian, to lay down and roll over. Christian laid down and rolled over. Johnny gave Christian a bone and petted him. Christian playfully licked Johnny. Scottie commanded Christian to sit and roll over. Christian sat and rolled over. Scott gave Christian a bone. Johnny commanded Meagan to sit. Meagan sat, and Johnny gave Meagan a bone. Christian and Meagan both licked Scott. Frank gave Meagan a piece of bacon. Meagan licked Frank. Johnny and his friends had a good time with the dogs for fifteen minutes.

At 7:45 am, Johnny and his friends left to pick up another friend like Scott or Frank, Hank. The roads were more slippery than usual due to the light rain mixing with the oil on the roads. At about 8:00 am, Johnny took a curve on US 77 too fast. He hit three children and pinned them to the side of a ditch. Scott and Frank had minor injuries. Johnny bled from the back. The three children died. The police took Johnny to the hospital and arrested him. They tested his blood for drugs and alcohol. They found nothing. They tested him again and found nothing! His lawyer threatened to sue unless the police stopped harassing him. Later that day, Jimmy Wolfman, brother of one of the children killed, tried to kill Johnny. The police stopped him and placed him under arrest. The police asked Johnny, "Do you wish to press charges?" Johnny replied, "Forgive him." It was later shown that Johnny Oilstring was guilty of a tragic accident and nothing more. This accident occurred the day immediately after I declared fasting and prayer concerning the US Dollar. In 1973, I had a dream that Communist airplanes attacked Parsons, Kansas on October 18, 1978 at 8:00 am. In that dream, Parsons, Kansas symbolized Jimmy Woodman. Johnny Oilstring would later prove to be a friend with many similarities to Jimmy, and something bad happened to him that day. These coincidences and dreams make me believe that Johnny Oilstring was innocent because he was operating a motor vehicle under the influence of witchcraft. After all, witches, working for currency manipulators in New York or Europe, may have learned of my prayer and fasting for the Dollar through telepathic means and retaliated against this prayer by hurting a future friend like Jimmy. If I am correct, the witches responsible for staging this accident are terrorists. For this awful act, they should be executed or put in jail for the rest of their lives.

On Friday night, I went to the First Apostolic Church to listen to the young people's choir. There, they sang the chorus, "For if my people who are called by my name shall humble themselves and pray, then I will hear from heaven and heal their sick nation." I prayed for America and its Dollar. I also prayed for KLMoody Importers-Exporters, my import business, and Project Texhoma, my research project concerning perpetual motion. After my prayer, I asked Mr. and Mrs. Chrisgood to fast for the United States on Sunday. They said, "We are not medically capable of fasting, but we will pray." I replied, "Thanks for helping to save the US currency."

Later that night, I heard about the tragic Oilstring accident on the eleven o'clock news. I prayed for Johnny, and God told me in a still soft voice, "Go visit Johnny at the hospital, and make him the head of the party plan at KLMoody Importers-Exporters. I shrugged this leading of God by saying to the Lord, "I am shunning evil companions. I refuse to see Johnny."

On Saturday night, I went to The Second Apostolic Church and requested prayer for the Dollar. The Church prayed for the United States and encouraged me to love America. After the service, I bought a dozen doughnuts and shared them with the Chrisgoods. Mr. Chrisgood, Tom's father, is also known as Myron Chrisgood. He trained Pentecostal missionaries in the word of God and was Tom's father. I said, "My calling from God is to pray for America." Mr. Chrisgood said, "You do not stand alone concerning your prayers for America." I replied, "There are many people praying for America." Mr. Chrisgood replied, "God will answer our prayers even if we stood alone." I added, "That is because two people gathered together in Jesus' name can pray for any honored prayer, and God will answer." Mr. Chrisgood said, "God will save our currency because his people prayed." After we beseeched God to save our currency, we thanked the Lord and enjoyed our doughnuts.

On Sunday, I started to pray and fast for the Dollar. In the morning, I went to the Chrisgood's to pick up Tom's sister, Gloria, to go to Sunday school. On my way to Sunday school, Gloria told me about a revival service at Brother Joseph's church at 3 in the afternoon. I took her advice and went to the service. On my way to the service, I heard the Pee Weas on the radio and prayed for God to show me a sign. I prayed that God would cause Joe Sinc's song "Dogbratlove" to play next on the radio if He was going to stop the collapse of the American currency. Joe Sinc's song "Dogbratlove" was the next song to play! I went into the church to rejoice for the victory God promised. I finished the 1 day fast successfully. I turned on the radio at 6 am the next morning. The Dollar still plummeted. I yelled back to the radio, "Satan get out of the European money markets!" I prayed throughout the day and turned on the radio at 6 am the next morning. The Dollar fell again. I yelled back to the radio, "Satan get out of the European money markets!" I added, "If you are not gone tomorrow, I will fast again, and God will throw you out!" I prayed again throughout the day and into the next morning. I prayed to God that this currency would go up just before I turned on the radio. On the radio, I heard the good news. The Dollar soared by 2%! Later that day, I heard that President Carter had ordered the Federal Reserve to buy Dollars in the Foreign Exchange Market. The Dollar then rose for a month straight. God had given President Carter guidance and saved the country. Perhaps I was not standing alone for my country. Others probably bugged the President, and some others likely prayed to save our Dollar, but I was there to fight for my country through prayer and fasting. I was happy to see the results. If the Dollar had continued its fall, an economic collapse equal to the Great Depression could have resulted. This depression could have caused the rise of a dictator, perhaps the Anti-Christ. The Dollar's fall was contained, and our democracy continued. Was The Anti-Christ thwarted for a generation? I was happy for the moment, but Johnny Oilstring and his three unintended victims seemed to suffer for this same country because of currency manipulators in New York or Europe. Little did I know that God had plans for me and Johnny in Kent a decade later.

CHAPTER 3

THE BATTLE OF BIG
RV PLASTICS

Despite the fact that I knew of none of the people or companies of the Gainesville dreams in 1973, some of these dreams seemed to describe 1979 and early 1980 at Big RV Plastics. I tried really hard to start my import company. I tried the party plan. I booked two parties and sold $200 worth of goods, but could not book another party. I tried to sell my imports by mail using display ads. I got only one response and spent $500. I tried to recruit wholesale distributors by direct mail. I got none. With my resources exhausted, I called the import business quits. "Perhaps, I should have made Johnny the head of sales," I thought. Because I failed at the import business, I decided to pursue my physics and math degree at Denton State University and make Project Texhoma a secondary priority for the moment. To finance my degree and project, I needed to work at Big RV Plastics.

Big RV Inc. was a big and diversified conglomerate. It had an automotive division, an appliance division, and its RV division. Big RV employed thousands. Big RV Plastics was a small division of this company. My dad, Murray Moody Jr., was the general manager in charge of this division. He made all of the decisions concerning the division. This includes sales, financial, and manufacturing decisions. His businesslike appearance, attitude, and knowledge of the fiberglass manufacturing process made him well qualified for the job. He believed in rewarding people on the basis of merit. He employed Jed Pugent as a plant manager. The plant manager handles all manufacturing decisions concerning the plant. He looked like a young business professional, but his immaturity was a tragic flaw. He liked sex and his alcohol. Ted Monsterman was the final finish foreman. His job was to supervise fiberglass repair in the plant. Jed and Dad were his bosses. He acted like a company man, but he was a conniver. Tony was the mold shop foreman. He also lied when convenient.

On the Monday after July 4, I had a friendly conversation with Jason. He was the same fun loving, tall, skinny, and bearded person I saw in the dreams, but he was the fastest pattern maker in Texas. He talked about his four wheel drive truck and asked me to see him at lunch someday. We had several conversations. He talked about his family, cars, and work; and I told him of possible land deals in Duluth, Minnesota. I told him that I may be able to buy land at $6 an acre. Then, Jason would have mood swings. In one conversation, he said, "I am not a final finisher. I feel like quitting." I replied, "You don't need to quit. You will learn if you try. It won't be that bad." Jason replied, "You don't know the final finish foreman, Ted Monsterman." I asked, "What is wrong with Ted Monsterman?" Jason replied, "You have to be his friend to work for him. If you are not his personal friend, he nit-picks your work and lies about your private life. He has gotten many people fired this way." I replied, "Dad better not catch him playing these games. He rewards people on the basis of merit. This kind of politics makes him mad." Jason said, "You don't know Ted." I replied, "He had better be cleaver. Dad is the boss."

Ted started by grilling Jason until he admitted, maybe falsely, to smoking pot at the lunch hour. This depressed Jason for a half week. Ted nit-picked Jason's work far above company standards. In fiberglass, nit-picking was often done to make a person look unproductive. A boss would complain about aspects of quality which would take a long time to correct, but these things would not make the product much better if corrected. If an employee responded to this nit-picking, he became a very slow worker. Ted's nit-picking made Jason unproductive. He then called Jason sloppy and unproductive. My cousin, Melissa Rose, also worked with Ted. She was a plump but good looking, blond haired, and clear complected woman with a friendly smile and personality. She became friends with Jason. Ted slandered her reputation. He called her a pot head and picked on her work. She stood up to Ted but to no avail. Her stand gave her Jason's bad name. Then, Ted's friend, Tony, nit-picked Jason's work in the mold shop. Ted harassed Jason like a high school bully. Every time he saw Jason, he said in a loud voice, "There he is!." On one Friday before Labor Day, I saw Jason a distance when Ted said, "There he is." I was scared. I thought he said it about me! I still continued my friendly relationship with Jason but kept it secret because I wanted to keep my job. I feared that Ted Monsterman would slander or fire me if he found out about my new-found friendship with Jason.

On the Friday before Labor Day, a dream that I had in 1973 came to remembrance. Jason asked, "Do I have a future at Big RV Plastics?" I replied, "As long as Dad in control, it will depend on your work." Jason replied, "Your Dad does not seem to know that Ted is lying about me." I replied, "I had a dream in 1973 which may describe this situation. In this dream, I saw a blue building, like this building, with the name of Big RV Plastics. Four great powers ruled. The first great power was a German Shepherd. His technology was great and he was the legal authority of the company. This first power is me, Dad, and Melissa. The second great power was a bearded hippie. He howled like a wolf and was a friend to the first great power. That second great power is you and all of your friends. You howled for the sake of fun and humor yesterday, and we are all friends. The third great power was named the King of Sodom. He promoted adultery, drunkenness, and forced it on many workers. God will render this power harmless and to eventual repentance. This great power is Jed Pugent and his friends. He promotes adultery and drunkenness with the employees, but seems to otherwise be a good plant manager. The fourth great power was a gargantuan monster seeking whom he may devour. He had teeth like razor blades and bit in the back. God said of this power, "I have cursed him. My wrath will be against him. He will be a reproach to every nation on the face of the earth. He will bring down Big RV." This power is Ted Monsterman. The third and fourth great powers will drive out the first two. If Ted Monsterman is unchecked, Ted Monsterman will eventually fire and blackball me, you, Dad, Melissa, and all of our friends. I don't know how to check Ted. I believe that God will keep us through this coming trial. Pray that God checks Ted and stops this potential problem." Jason said, "I am glad to hear God is with us. I am glad you and your friends are praying about this situation." I replied, "I will understand if you find another job and quit because this may be a bad situation for us." Jason said, "Gotta go. Time for work."

After Labor Day, the bottom fell out. Jason was chewed out for some bad work. He seldom produced bad work, but the harassment pushed Jason to a breaking point. As a demoralized worker, he was reprimanded, but his work did not improve. He was so depressed that he did not even talk to me. After two weeks, Jason quit Big RV Plastics. One week later, Dad, the general manager, had a massive heart attack. This was unfortunate because my dad, the general manager Murray Moody Jr., rewarded people on the basis of merit. This meant that Ted Monsterman destroyed Jason's reputation hopelessly because Dad was the only sincere professional on the staff.

Meanwhile at the Chrisgood's House; Tom's sister, Gloria Chrisgood, was appointed Chairman of the Board of Occult Defense Analysts and Strategists. She was a clear complected, black haired, skinny, good looking, shy, and intelligent Christian woman of her day. Her duties were helping me to understand how to handle Jed and Ted according to Biblical principles, and helping me to solve moral dilemmas that come up during Project Texhoma. Gloria appointed Myron E. Chrisgood, her Dad, as an Occult Defense Analyst.

His duties were also applying Biblical principles to the policies of the Board of Judges. Ted Monsterman, final finish foreman, and plant manager, Jed Pugent, were the most powerful evil influences in fiberglass. Ted Monsterman was everything evil that Jason said about him. He was a short, but well-built old man who walked with a limp. Jed Pugent told dirty jokes regularly. He was medium height and well-built and understood some about business. He forced young women to have sex with him. If they refused, they were fired and blackballed. If you were a man, you had to party with him on your own time, and you had to work more than 60 hours a week on many occasions. If you refused, you were fired and blackballed. They came from Fiberjunck in McKinney, Texas. Fiberjunck had a reputation for lousy work and immorality as bad as Sodom and Gomorrah. God wiped Sodom and Gomorrah off the face of the earth for forced sex outside of marriage, ruthlessness, and greed. Ted and Jed were management at Fiberjunck before God bankrupted this evil company. Fiberjunck corrupted every Christian entering the company. Willie, a friend of Jason from Fiberjunck, gave this account of an event at Fiberjunck, "An ordained minister of God worked in this company. We got him drunk, and he had sex with a girl from production because we influenced him." With Dad in the hospital from his heart attack, these former Fiberjunck managers were operating at Big RV Plastics unchecked. Gloria's job was really to help protect the spirituality of me and my friends at US Physics by applying Biblical principles. Her strategy was to encourage me to focus on the job and preach fire and brimstone to Jed and Ted.

Gloria's strategy seemed to work perfectly until the first of November. About the first of November, Jason Shoemaker and his friend, Tim Skullman, came to the Big RV plant to work for Jed. Tim Skullman was a long haired and rough looking person with a tough motorcyclist's personality. They were friendly to me all day long. At first break, Jason asked, "How are you doing?" I replied, "Fine." Jason asked, "How are your courses at Denton State University?" I replied, "I am making straight 'A's." Tim asked, "Having a good time with your other friends?" I replied, "I am having a good time with my church life, and I have a new friend named Gloria Chrisgood." Jason said, "I would like to see you sometime." I asked, "How do I get a hold of you?" Jason replied, "My number is in the phone book." I said, "Break's over. Gotta get back to work." During that week, Jason, Tim, and I would have six friendly conversations at the plant.

On that weekend, Jed told Dad about Jason and Tim's presence in the plant. Jed said, "Jason and Tim caused trouble in the plant." Dad asked, "What did they do?" Jed said "They slowed down production by talking to the employees during company time." Dad said, "Keep these people out of the company."

Next week, I arranged to see Jason Shoemaker on Saturday. Up to this time, Gloria's policy of fire and brimstone preaching seemed to hold Jed and

Ted in check. I was able to live a Christian life without interference from Ted and Jed up until this time. On that Friday, Ted told Dad that Jason smoked pot. Because Dad thought that Jason smoked pot, Dad asked, "Are you friends with Jason Shoemaker or Tim Skullman?" I did not answer, so he said, "If you are going out with Jason Shoemaker or Tim Skullman, get out of the house." I did not want to get kicked out of the house. Doing so could mean dropping out of college or giving up Project Texhoma. To save face with Dad, I canceled my plans with Jason and put the friendship on hold. Ted Monsterman proved he could use Dad to control friendships. Ted Monsterman won round one.

At about the same time that Ted forced my friendship with Jason into hiding, Ted showed his ruthlessness to everybody at big RV Plastics. Ted disrespected Dad, the boss. Dad got mad at Ted. Ted put his feet on Dad's desk. Dad angrily ordered Ted, "Get your feet off my desk now!" Little did Dad know, Ted left the office and told everybody, "Leave Murray for dead if he has a heart attack." I replied, "If Dad dies that way, I will prosecute you and sue Big RV Plastics! I can't follow this ungodly order!" I made the mistake of not taking Ted seriously. I did not tell Dad because I quickly and unwisely forgave and forgot.

After hearing this ungodly order, I finished my semester at Denton State University and made contact with Jason Shoemaker immediately after Christmas. In that conversation, I asked Jason, "Could you help me draw plans for the armature of my new motor?" Jason replied, "I would be honored to help with your project." I said with shame, "I am sorry that Dad disapproved of our friendship. I did not know that Ted Monsterman could turn Dad against our friendship. I have hired my cousin and your friend, Melissa Rose, to spy on Ted and Jed. If they say anything affecting me or Dad, she will let me know." Jason replied courteously, "I am sorry that Ted slandered me and tried to stop our friendship. Ted Monsterman is not your fault," I replied, "He is lucky that Tom Chrisgood is not in town. God's judgment would be upon him. Wicked rulers are an abomination unto the Lord. I need to get going. I will call you in about a month." Jason replied, "Think highly of you. See you later."

I enrolled for classes at Denton State University and worked normally at my job and at my classes for about a month. On the second Friday of February, I called Jason Shoemaker and arranged to meet him at a pizza place in Ardmore, Oklahoma on Tuesday at 7:30 pm. The next day on Saturday, I worked ten hours at Big RV Plastics. During that shift, Ted threatened to trick Dad into firing me. I placed this matter into the hands of God. When I got home, Dad said, "Ted seems to be my friend at Big RV." When I heard this, I asked God to give Dad guidance. I feared Ted would blackball all of us. I placed this matter in the hands of God. Perhaps, I should have told Dad about Ted's back-stabbing of Jason or his ungodly order concerning his possible future heart attack. I feared that he would not believe me and get mad.

At about 6:30 pm that night, I arrived at the Chrisgood House, "Dad thinks that Ted Monsterman is his friend," I told Occult Defense Analyst Myron E. Chrisgood, "The Gainesville Dreams imply that Ted will be one of the worst back-stabbers in the history of The United States. In the dreams, Ted Monsterman is a gargantuan monster seeking whom he can devour. There seems to be a danger of me and Dad being blackballed." Occult Defense Analyst Myron Chrisgood replied, "Perhaps God will resolve this situation before it gets way out of hand." He added, "Mrs. Chrisgood and I will pray that God gives your Dad and any or all who may be concerned guidance so that God's anger will not hit Big RV International and put thousands on the streets." I replied, "Let's pray that God spares Big RV and gives Dad guidance."

After we prayed for God to give Dad guidance, I asked Occult Defense Analyst Gloria Chrisgood, "Would you want to go with me to meet Jason Shoemaker this Tuesday at our favorite pizza place in Ardmore, Oklahoma?" Gloria replied, "I would love to meet your friend Jason Shoemaker." I then proceeded to give Gloria instructions for meeting Jason, "I will tell Dad that I am taking you out to eat in Ardmore," I instructed Gloria, "Dad will not know that we are meeting Jason Shoemaker. Me and Jason will discuss the drawings that he is to do concerning my prototype, and you will also have a chance to have fun eating pizza and getting to know Jason." Gloria asked, "What time will you pick me up?" I replied, "At about 7 pm on Tuesday." Gloria and I bought doughnuts and shared them with the Chrisgood parents. We all had a good time until 11 pm.

On Tuesday, I attended my math class at Denton State University. Afterward, I met Gloria at 7:00 pm, and I headed toward the pizza place in Ardmore. On the way to Ardmore, I told Gloria, "You are helping to protect a friendship from Ted Monsterman." I further emphasized, "We must stand behind our friends no matter what other people think or do." Gloria said, "I am looking forward to meeting Jason." I replied, "He is a friend you will like." We arrived at our restaurant and ordered Cokes. At 7:30, Gloria asked, "Where is Jason?" I replied, "Jason is a hippie, and they are sometimes fashionably late." Gloria asked, "What if Jason does not show up?" I replied, "We can have a good time ourselves eating a pizza and remembering the good times with her brother Tom." We talked for fifteen minutes and Jason arrived. I greeted Jason and said, "This is Occult Defense Analyst Gloria Chrisgood." Jason said, "I am Jason Shoemaker. I am glad to meet you, Gloria." We ordered our pizza, and I presented Jason with the rough sketch of the prototype drawings. I said to Jason, "We will be friends no matter what Jed Pugent and Ted Monsterman do." Jason said, "I think highly of you, and I am glad you will stand behind me." Gloria said, "When my brother, Tom, gets back from Germany this September, Ted and Jed will pay for forcing Kevin's friendship with Jason into hiding." I said very seriously, "Tom Chrisgood is a good security man with training in the US Army's Military Police Unit. Ted will wish he never crossed him. Tom may do surveillance or undercover security against Ted and Jed." We ate our pizza and talked. We all had a good time. At about 9:00, Jason said, "It was nice to meet you, Gloria." I replied, "I am glad we can be friends under these bad conditions." Jason said, "See ya later." Gloria and I wished Jason good luck and said, "See you later." Gloria and I returned to Gainesville hopeful and victorious. We could be friends with Jason no matter what Ted Monsterman thinks or does.

That night, I got sick. I vomited twice and could not show up for work. I laid in bed feeling like I would die and prayed that God would heal me. At about 9:30 am, Dad came into my room and asked, "Was Tony, the mold shop foreman, giving you a hard time?" I replied, "He yells at me for a lot of stupid reasons, but that is normal for him." "Tony and Ted got together to badmouth you, Melissa, Jason Shoemaker, and Tim Skullman!" Dad angrily declared, "I will not put up with this crap! I pay these managers to look out for the company and treat the workers fairly! I saw those scratches on fiberglass parts that Ted polished and shined! He needs to watch his own step. Tony is behind in his work. He needs to work lots of overtime to catch up. If their conduct does not improve, I'll replace them. Don't worry about Big RV. Just get well. Take the rest of the week off. See you tonight." Ted Monsterman got caught stabbing employees in the back. Dad now knew that Ted was a back-stabber. Ted's game was stopped for the moment. Gainesville Security Central and Dad won this round.

That next Sunday, at Pastor Lion's church, Brother Weakleg and Sister Goldman requested prayer for Bobby Weakleg and his rebellious friend Johnny Oilstring. Sister Goldman said with a serious tone, "Bobby Weakleg found a new bad influence of a teenage friend. This friend goes on trial for an accident he had two years ago. This concerns Bobby greatly. Bobby and his friend need our prayers very badly." Pastor Lion replied compassionately, "God can help Bobby and his friend through this trial. The church will pray that God will show love towards Bobby and his friend. Pray that the judge has compassion on Bobby's friend." The church prayed for Bobby and Johnny that Sunday and at prayer meetings for the next two Tuesdays. The judge went easy on Johnny.

Over the next two months, Jason and I had two more undercover outings. One was a short fifteen minute visit to a fast food restaurant down the street from his house. The other outing, I met Jason Shoemaker at that same fast food restaurant There, we left for Denton. He showed me a machine shop there, and we had a good time talking and joking around. When we arrived at his house, Jason said, "I will be busy this summer." I asked, "Will we see each other this summer?" Jason replied, "Just have a little patience." I replied, "See you later." I went home with a good feeling, but Jason would avoid me for the summer. Jason did not like hiding from Dad. Ted Monsterman's slander of a few months ago forced a choice of losing Project Texhoma or hiding Jason's friendship from Dad. I could no longer be an effective friend to Jason and pursue project Texhoma. Ted Monsterman won this round.

Just as Jason gave up being an under-cover friend, I contacted my old friend Gerard Chrispeace. He was a loyal and fun loving Christian hippie. He was also one of Tom Chrisgood's best friends. We rekindled an old friendship. He introduced me to his roommate and half-brother, Robert Elight. Robert Elight was Gerard's half-brother. He was a backslid Christian of my faith. He was a wild, fun loving, friendly, and stylish body builder. His neatly trimmed beard and his dark tan complexion attracted many women. I liked his friendly personality, so I became friends with him. I told everybody, "I am a spirit-filled Christian from Second Apostolic Church in Ardmore Oklahoma." I told Robert, "Jesus requires me to accept your group as friends because he requires me to love my neighbor." Robert said, "The older people at the First Apostolic Church got mad because I partied like a hippie of old." I said to Robert, "You and your friends will get to heaven before any of your critics who did not show you good friendship." Robert's kid brother Rodney was a tall, skinny, and very friendly person. He wore his long and curly hair in the style of an Afro. He asked, "What do you think of Kent State?" "I will never see any of those liberals at Kent State," I replied. "Oh-oh! I should have said that by the grace of God, I will never see Kent State. If I ever run into those liberals, I pray that I would treat them like I am treating you tonight." After this conversation with Rodney, I asked Gerard to see *The Empire Strikes Back* with me the following Monday and left.

Meanwhile, at Big RV, a rumor surfaced that Ted Monsterman was lying about being hurt, and cheating the company through insurance fraud. That night, Gerard and I saw the Star Wars sequel and discussed under-cover military action against Ted. I said, "Gerard, We must have the freedom to choose our friends and appoint people to assist me at project Texhoma. We need to retaliate against Ted Monsterman for interfering in my friendship with Jason Shoemaker and to promote my freedom to choose those assisting on project Texhoma. I heard that Ted was working while claiming to be disabled." To investigate that rumor, we arranged to map Ted's hometown of Valley View in two days.

That Wednesday on the way to Valley View, Gerard and I discussed old times and both talked of how we missed Tom. I told Gerard "I hoped to see Jason Shoemaker again." Gerard said, "You may bring Jason to George Elight's house on Wheeler Creek and take him to our private island." I said, "You, Tom, Jason, and I will have a lot of fun together on the creek." We talked about the movie we saw two days ago, and how we enjoyed popcorn and pop. As we arrived in Valley View (Map3), we went downtown and called telephone information to get Ted's address. We drove by Ted's house. We discovered that we could spy on Ted by playing basketball at a school across the street from Ted's house. We also found that we could quickly leave town on old US 77 or farm road 922. Afterward, we headed for Gainesville victorious. We now could spy on Ted and find dirt on him if he harassed us. Gainesville Security Central

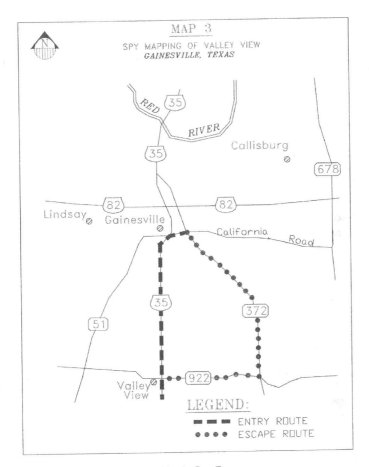

Map by Dan Eaves

won this round.

Thursday night, I talked with Jason's wife, Pat. I said, "Under-cover security chairman Gerard Chrispeace is going to Valley View to find dirt on Ted Monsterman this Monday morning at 6 am. I have heard that Ted is working while collecting disability on Big RV's group insurance policy. I also heard he drinks like a fish." Pat asked, "Is using under-cover security this way ethical?" I replied, "With project Texhoma, I must have the freedom to choose my friends and those assisting with the project. I need Jason's help concerning some mechanical matters on my machine. Without this freedom, I cannot solve these problems. Project Texhoma could be doomed. Because I am working on a perpetual motion machine, this could be bad for national security." Pat replied, "You don't send an army after Ted. Perhaps, God has another way." I replied, "Maybe you are right. I will pray that God will stop this mission if it is not his will." Pat said, "Got to go. See ya" I prayed, "Lord help me concerning the mission I am assigning Gerard. If you don't want him on this mission, please forgive me and cause Gerard not to carry it out. If you stop Gerard, let nobody be hurt. In the name of Jesus, I ask. Amen."

Next Monday night, I called Gerard. I asked, "How did the mission go?" Gerard replied, "I had to work a construction job this morning." I said with a sigh of relief, "Ted worked at Big RV today. He was demoted out of management. The mission is off. Besides, I asked God to stop the mission if He did not want it. He stopped it, so we will abort the mission. We now have the advantage. We can find dirt on Ted. We can spy on him at will. For now, let's leave it go at that." Gerard said, "Let's have a good time for the rest of the summer." I agreed. Gainesville Security Central won this battle.

In September of 1980, I went to Gerard's apartment. Gerard was not there, but Robert and all of his friends were there. They all gathered together at the kitchen table to smoke pot. They offered me pot, and I said, "No thanks." They offered again, and I refused again. Robert said that I needed to fit in. I left and said, "If you are a good friend, you will understand."

The next night, I came back to Gerard's house hoping that I could salvage my friendship with Gerard. I feared that my argument with Robert about pot may have destroyed my budding friendship with Gerard. Gerard was not there, but Robert was. Robert said, "I am sorry for last night." I said with conviction, "The definition of a true friend is a person who accepts me for who I am without regard for money, popularity, or intelligence without consideration of circumstances involved." I added, "I can be a good friend if you understand that I do not smoke pot." He replied, "I understand." He added, "I would like a chance to be your good friend." This began a great and historical friendship with Robert.

Robert and I had 3 weeks of quality time together. One example of that quality time together was a Sunday in early October. On that Sunday, I went outside and helped Robert wax his car. Robert asked, "How are you doing?" "I am doing fine," I replied, "I am just taking an afternoon off during my busy schedule of studying." Robert replied, "Nice to see a good friend this afternoon." I asked, "How does the waxing look on that trunk hood?" Robert said happily, "The waxing on that hood looks fine." Robert asked, "Do you wax professionally?" I replied, "I wax molds for a living when I am not studying." Robert said, "You must wax molds really well." I replied, "I need to wax molds perfectly to keep fiberglass parts made off them from sticking to the mold and damaging it. I assume that we need to wipe off all of the wax on the car to get a perfect shine." Robert replied, "Exactly." Robert asked, "I have heard that you are working on a research project concerning alternate energy." I replied, "I am working on a perpetual motion electric motor. I am investigating a contradiction between the inverse square law of magnetism and conservation of energy and matter. The inverse square law, in magnetism, states that the force of attraction or repulsion between two magnets is proportional to the product of the pole strengths of the two said magnets divided by the square of the distance between the two magnetic poles in question, This inverse square law implies that perpetual motion is possible with the right distance between the magnets of an electric motor. Both laws are explained in a high school physics book. If you are interested, I can write a derivation. If I am right, there will be no more energy crisis." Robert said, "I believe you." I asked, "Am I shining this car up real well?" Robert said, "This car is looking real nice. I will proudly show this car on the strip. Maybe, I will pick up a foxy chick." For the next half hour, we waxed the car and had a friendly talk. As we completed the waxing job, I said, "I enjoyed our afternoon together." Robert said, "I hope we will have many more good times together." I happily said, "I have many good friends at Gerard's apartment." Robert replied, "That is how we want you to feel." I replied, "Must go. See you later." Robert replied, "Hope to see you soon."

Some nights, I would stop at Kathy's apartment to see Robert. Kathy was a clear but dark complected, good looking, and friendly Greek nursing student at Denton State. Kathy was Robert's girlfriend. Kathy and Robert were always happy to see me. One such night, Kathy, Robert, and, I had a real good time. Robert asked, "How are you doing?" I replied, "I just completed an optics exam." Robert asked, "How do you think you did on the exam?" I said, "I likely made a 'C' on the exam, but I am averaging a 'B' in the class. Robert said, "I bet you would like to forget that exam tonight." Kathy asked, "Would you dance to the music with me?" I danced with Kathy for a half hour and had fun. Kathy, Robert, and I had a friendly conversation for an hour and parted company.

After three weeks of partying together, Robert sensed that I was distressed about Ted Monsterman. Robert said, "I respect your strength at serving God." I replied, "At Gerard's apartment, serving the Lord is easy. Serving the Lord at Big RV Plastics is another story. I am still pure, but the management from Fiberjunck manages Big RV Plastics. At Fiberjunck, every Christian working there was corrupted and backslid into gross sin. I fear that I will also backslide. Ted Monsterman is very ruthless and dangerous. He slandered Jason Shoemaker and all of his friends. He made them look unprofessional when they weren't." Robert replied, "Let me at Ted Monsterman! He won't push me around without a fight. Pray for strength. If God be for you, Ted Monsterman will face defeat. Ted cannot face the power of God and win." I replied, "We can have victory through the power of prayer."

He convinced me that the Board of Judges of Texas could beat Ted Monsterman of Fiberjunck. I appointed Robert W. Elight Chairman of the Board of Occult Defense Analysts and Strategists and let go of Gloria Chrisgood.

While I had my quality time with Robert, Tom Chrisgood returned to town from three years of service in the Army and a failed Bible smuggling operation into the Soviet Union. Tom and I went to Dallas on the bus to sell some gems that I bought at bargain basement prices. While we were on the bus, we saw the ranches of Valley View and Denton County, Texas. Tom commented, "The buses in Romania are more efficient than those of this bus line." I replied, "America was once the best country in the world." Tom replied, "America needs to replace its outdated modes of transportation." I replied, "Europe gained the advantage over America when they replaced their factories and machines that were destroyed in World War II. The new machines and factories are more modern than the old American factories. Maybe we should have left Europe rot." Tom replied, "World War II hurt America in the long run." Tom emphasized, "Nobody benefits from violence and arrogant pride." The bus pulled into Denton, and we saw more empty land. After the bus cleared Denton, Tom fell asleep, and I watched the scenery. I saw the farms of and the ranches of the countryside. I was most impressed with the highways of Dallas. After we passed through the city, Tom woke up and asked, "Are we there yet?" I replied with joy, "I can't wait until we get to Dallas and sell these gems." A few minutes later, we arrived in downtown Dallas.

In downtown Dallas, Tom and I went to two jewelers. The gems were not worth what we paid for them. Tom said, "Let's go and see Dallas." We went to a restaurant and ate hamburgers and French fries. The hamburgers really tasted good to us. We toured downtown and went to a Socialist bookstore. There, I found a book about the KGB. This book said that the KGB entrapped American men by having woman KGB agents seduce and blackmail them into spying for the Soviets. I commented, "No secret is safe in America." Tom replied, "That is why I fear that the Soviets will conquer this country." I replied, "God will destroy the Soviet Union." Tom asked, "How so?" I replied, "The Soviet Union will attack Israel. When the Russians attack Israel, God will rain fire and brimstone on their army. Five sixths of their army will be wiped off the face of the earth. What's left of their army will flee to Siberia. Praise the Lord!" Tom said, "I hope that it never comes to that." I asked in response, "Is there any such thing as a nice Russian?" Tom replied, "The Soviet Government is pure evil, but Russia's people are like you or me. The Russians think that Americans are monsters. They want to nuke America. We need to love and pray for the Russian people." I replied with broken pride, "I should love the Russian people, but I need God's help." Tom said, "I understand." After our good time in Dallas, we returned to Gainesville to rest.

On the next Friday, I went to Ada, Oklahoma with my friend Tom, to visit his sister Esther. Esther was a plump but very friendly person. At Esther's house, we bought pop and potato chips and asked Esther, "How are you doing?" Esther replied, "I am doing fine." Tom asked, "Would you or Maggie like any pop or chips?" Maggie was Esther's plump and friendly eight year old daughter. Maggie asked, "Would you like some candy to go along with your pop and chips." I replied, "Thanks. I will be glad to help you eat your candy and share the pop and chips." Maggie turned on the TV, and we snacked on the good food. While we were snacking, I asked Maggie, "Do you remember when you were little and I spent the night at Tom's house?" Maggie asked, "What do you remember exactly?" I answered, "The time you said to Brian Todwink, "Get up Brian. Time to get up."" Maggie answered, "I miss Brian." I replied, "We sure had a good time with Brian." Maggie said, "I wish he were here." We talked and snacked all night long. Tom and I had two more such parties in Ada.

On Halloween night of 1980, Gerard and Robert had a party. Robert, Tom, Gerard, and I were there. We all danced with the women and had a good time. Robert wore a superman suit, and I dressed like a ghost. At about 10:30 pm Tom Chrisgood interrupted our good time to propose that Robert be made the Executive Vice President of the Board of Judges of Texas. Tom thought that Robert knew the Bible and the goals of US Physics really well. We all accepted Robert as second in command. We enjoyed a great party which gave US Physics Robert Elight as a leader.

For the next month, Robert, Tom, Gerard, and I partied together about every night. Robert taught me how to have a good time without sex, drugs, drinking, or rock and roll. Robert and Gerard liked to drink and mess with the women. Gerard's girlfriend was Darlene. She was a shy but good looking woman. Robert's woman was that beautiful and very friendly Kathy. Kathy, Robert, and I were real close friends. Kathy and Robert almost got me to drink a beer, but I did not drink that beer because I feared that Robert would not respect me anymore. I thought that Robert was testing my Christian character to see if I was real. I would see Tom, but we would only talk for short periods of time.

The next month would be the moment of truth. I would start the month studying for finals at Denton State University. Then, Tom decided to confront Ted Monsterman. Tom said, "We must show ourselves inside his Valley View neighborhood." Then, we started to drive toward Valley View, Texas. On the way to Valley View, Tom told me about his days in the Army. Tom said, "The Russians will take the Rhine in two days if we go to war with them." He added, "After the Russians take the Rhine, they will nuke the United States and make America a communist country." I asked, where did you hear this rumor?" Tom said, "I heard this rumor from my Christian friends in Germany. They feared that the Russians would then nuke America." I said, "I thank God that you heard this rumor from an unreliable source, but you may be right, so I will pray that America can defend itself." Tom also said that I was a good friend to him and that he appreciated our friendship. Then, we arrived in Valley View and drove by Ted's house twice. We then drove downtown and headed east on farm road 922 (map 3). The police followed us to farm road 372 and left us alone at that point.

The next morning, I came to Big RV half asleep from the night before. Ted probably saw my car near his house and likely wanted to confront me concerning this matter. Ted started this conversation by pushing quick mold work on me. He said, "Grind the edges, and rough up the chipped areas of the door mold sitting next to you." I ground the edges and roughed up the chipped areas of the Big RV door. Ted said, "Patch the mold with this mixture of tooling gel and production gel on my bench." I asked, "Why use your patching material?" Ted replied, "It will harden in fifteen minutes." I patched the mold with his materials, and it was ready to sand in fifteen minutes. I sanded the mold. I buffed, glazed and waxed the mold. Ted said, "After break, I will run this mold." I said, "It is break time." We went to the break room. There, Ted told me that the police were watching his town. I said, "They must obey the law." He said, "They will put you in jail for turning corners too sharply or moving one mile per hour over the speed limit." I told him, "I will use a rental car, and the police will never find me." He said "The police will hunt for Gainesville license plates. They will put you and your friends in jail." I said, "We will go to Denton to rent the car. The police would not know that car." Ted said, "Let's agree to stop this fight and shake hands." I said, "I do not want this conflict either." We shook hands and made a shaky peace. We had a potential fight over my right to pick and choose my friends. Under-cover security or slander could have been used. This fight was prevented by talking. Eight months later, Jed and Ted would leave Big RV Plastics for good. Gainesville Security Central stalemated the war and won the peace at Big RV Plastics. Perhaps, the only thing that saved Big RV was the fact that God provided for my needs. I would not have needed Big RV if I had obeyed God about making Johnny Oilstring the head of the party plan at my import business. I heard that Johnny Oilstring was the top salesman at Rainbow. He quit because he did not like to sell these expensive machines to old ladies who could not afford them. Maybe, he could have made my import business work.

Two weeks after the peace at Big RV Plastics, Robert and I got together twice a week to lift weights. Robert liked the role of teaching me physical fitness. The first session, he introduced me to the system. I started out benching 60 pounds. Robert said, "I will have you in shape in one year." I replied, "I will be diligent and do my best." After the first workout, we talked for a half hour, and I went home. Two sessions later, I could bench 70 pounds. Robert said, "Good work. You will be in good shape sooner than you think." I replied, "Thanks. Maybe, I can still have a good body. Perhaps, you could learn math." Robert replied, "Thanks. I am doing well as a mechanic." Three months later, I could bench 110 pounds, but Robert was not doing so well. Robert said, "I hurt because Kathy no longer wants to see me." I replied, "I care, but don't understand women. I am too busy learning physics and math and working on my perpetual motion machine to have time for women. I guess the feeling is a lot like losing a best friend." Robert replied, "That is part of the feeling, but even best friends cannot fill the void left by losing Kathy." I replied, "I care, and I am still your friend." Robert replied, "I hope you will understand that I won't have time to work-out with you because I need to find a new girlfriend." I asked, "Will we still see each other?" Robert replied, "We will still get together. Just call me." I went home disappointed that Robert could no longer work out with me, but he was still my friend. However, when Robert stopped working out with me, I got discouraged and stopped exercising.

In early June, Robert, Tom, Rodney, and I went to the apartment swimming pool to get a tan. We laid beside the pool and relaxed for a half hour. Then, Robert met a beautiful girl. Robert flirted with the girl and said, "Hey beautiful, my name is Robert." The girl said, "My name is Sally. You must be a body builder." Robert replied, "I am a body builder, and I want to have a good time." Sally replied, "I would like to get to know you." Robert agreed, and they talked for two hours. They liked each other. After two hours, Robert asked, "Would you like to go out tonight?" Sally replied, "I would love to go out tonight." Robert had found a new girlfriend for the moment. Tom and Rodney quietly tanned while Robert found his new girl. Happy for Robert, we all headed home.

The peace was won at Big RV Plastics. Robert, Tom, and I partied, and I studied at Denton State. That summer, Robert and I went to ~~church~~ Pastor Lion's church. There, Robert and, I met Bobby Weakleg. Bobby said, "Hi, my name is Bobby." I replied, "My name is Kevin." Robert said, "My name is Robert. How are you?" Bobby replied, "I am doing fine." I said with conviction, "I believe that God instructs us Christians to love all people including those hippies who like to party." Bobby replied, "I accept anybody who will accept me." Bobby said, "We accept you." The voice of God said in a still soft voice, "Bobby will change the course of history at Kent State University." I shrugged it off by thinking. "This is not the voice of God. Bobby is a backslider." I said, "Church is about to start. Nice talking to you. See you later." Little did I know that Johnny Oilstring was his best friend, and Bobby was there for Johnny in his hour of need. Johnny would change the course of history at Kent State University.

Over the next year, I concentrated on getting my degree at Denton State University and preparing for graduate school. I received an offer for an assistantship at West Virginia University. I accepted this offer, but wanted to tour Morgantown, West Virginia. Tom and I agreed to go to Morgantown for a couple of days in June of 1982.

On the first Tuesday of June, Tom and I departed for Morgantown. We took interstate 70 through Indianapolis to Ohio (Map 4). At the 50 mile

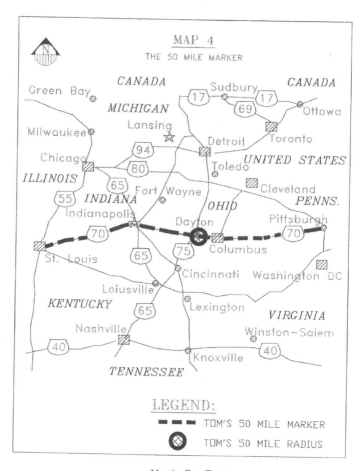

Map by Dan Eaves

Marker, Tom said, "I feel an evil presence here." I asked, "Do you really feel something evil?" Tom replied, "This is really evil." I asked, "What is this evil presence?" Tom replied, "The National Guard killed four students at Kent State University on May 4, 1970." I replied, "This may be sin, but what can I do about it?" Tom replied, "Pray for Ohio." We headed for Morgantown.

At Morgantown, Tom and I toured the city. We saw the mountains and the city. Tom looked at the University. He saw many buildings in need of repair and thought the school was having financial problems. I visited with the

Physics Department Chairman and felt good about the University. Tom had his doubts but encouraged me to pursue my degree at West Virginia University. We ate dinner, watched TV, and slept so that we could head for Gainesville the next day.

CHAPTER 4

THE COMMISSIONING OF JOHNNY OILSTRING

I completed my degree at Denton State University. I wanted to go to graduate school in physics to further my education in physics and continue Project Texhoma. If I started my career in physics at this time, I would have had to give up any possibility of patenting any perpetual motion machine that I could invent. Most companies employing physicists require their new employees to give any new inventions to them.

I received an offer of an assistantship at West Virginia University in Morgantown. In late August of 1982, I quit Big RV Plastics and started Graduate School at West Virginia University in the Physics Department. I enrolled in three courses. They were Electricity and Magnetism, Mechanics, and Quantum Mechanics. Electricity and Magnetism is a course dealing with how electricity interacts with matter, and how magnets interact with matter. Mechanics is a course dealing with the laws of physics concerning observable matter in the universe. Quantum Mechanics deals with how atomic and molecular sized matter interacts with the universe. As a graduate student, I needed to make a 2.75 GPA on a four point scale. That is three 'B's for every C or better. I taught 3 freshman Physics labs. I also tried to find a church home in Morgantown. The first church did not seem to respect me. I found no friends there.

Meanwhile, I struggled to make the grade at West Virginia University. To keep my hopes for Project Texhoma alive and further my future career in physics, I needed to make the grade. In my Mechanics class, I made a 50 on my first three homework assignments. I was discouraged and prayed for God's help. On my 4th assignment, my grades improved. In my Quantum Mechanics class, I made 70's and 80's on my assignments through the first four and a half weeks. I felt good about the class until I took the first test. I made a 50 and thought I flunked the class. My Quantum Mechanics professor said it was a 'C-'. In my Electricity and Magnetism class, all of my assignments were good. I was averaging a 'B' in that class. I did poorly on my Mechanics test. I made a 65 which was a 'C+'.

In the seventh week of my Wednesday evening lab that I taught, I found somebody I thought may prove to be a friend. His name was Steve Horseman. Steve was a friendly, dark complected Christian with short curly hair. Steve was one of my better students. He consistently made 95's and 100's on his lab reports. In the seventh week of my Physics 201 lab, my students had trouble with an air cart experiment. Steve helped me to figure out the problem. I thanked him, and we talked about the class. I asked, "How well do you understand the material?" "I understand the material pretty well," replied Steve. "Some of my friends in your class are having difficulty. I think they understand because you are a new teacher." I asked, "How can I best help these students?" Steve replied, "Give these students individual attention and have patience with them." Steve asked, "Are you a Christian?" I replied, "I am a Christian." Steve asked, "Would you come to the First Apostolic Church in Saberton with me on a Sunday morning?" I replied, "I will come sometime in the next semester after I give you your final lab grade."

On Friday of that week, I took an exam in my Electricity and Magnetism class. On Monday, I found out that I made a 49 on my exam. That was a 'D'. I returned to my apartment ready to quit. I laid around the apartment depressed all afternoon. At about six O'clock, I called my friend Robert. I said, "No matter what I do, I can't seem to make a 'B' on any exams." I added, "I think that I will flunk out at the end of this semester." Robert replied, "I will be your friend even if you flunk at West Virginia University, but I think you will find a way to pass." Robert asked, "How is everything going other than your exams?" I replied, "I am learning how to use my TRS 80 computer, and I should soon learn to program it in Basic." Robert asked, "When are you coming to Texas?" I replied, "I am coming to Texas on Thanksgiving break and look forward to seeing you." Robert and I talked for an hour, and he inspired me to study harder and try again.

On Wednesday, I made a 60 on my Mechanics exam, but I decided to study very hard on my Quantum Mechanics for two weeks until my next exam. On that exam, I made a 50 which was a 'C+'. I felt good about that exam, but needed greatly to improve on my other exams. Nonetheless, I called my friend Robert to rejoice, "It looks like I may pass the first semester after all," I told Robert on the phone. "I made a 'C+' on my Quantum Mechanics exam. I may be able to improve to a 'B' in Quantum Mechanics. With luck on my next Mechanics exam and on my next Electricity and Magnetism test, I will be averaging a 'B' in both classes." Robert said, "Good luck." I replied, "Pray for me and be my friend." After Robert and I talked for an hour, I returned to my stressful studies.

On the day before my Electricity and Magnetism exam, I was stressed out concerning this exam. The week before, I had done my homework and studied every problem and concept in my book, until I was exhausted. "Lord Jesus please help me to do well on the exam coming up tomorrow," I prayed to the Lord, "If ever I needed to do well on an exam, I need a good grade tomorrow. If I fail to make a 2.75 average, I will be without a job and my dream of being a scientist ruined. Please help me with my Electricity and Magnetism exam tomorrow. Amen." I took the exam and felt good about it until Sunday. I had a panic attack and thought I made an 'F' on the exam. On Wednesday, I found out I made a 69 which was a 'B'. I was averaging a 'B' in Electricity and Magnetism. Thank God for my success. I have a hope for continuing Project Texhoma and pursuing my degree.

I studied my Classical Mechanics exam for 1 week straight. I reviewed all of my problems and concepts until it worried me sick. I called Robert on the night before the exam to try to forget my worries. We had a good conversation for an hour. I got a good night's sleep and prayed to God that I would pass the exam. I made an 82 on the exam, and I knew I was averaging a 'B' in Mechanics.

On the last day before Thanksgiving Break, I rejoiced through my Quantum Mechanics class, my Mechanics class, and my Electricity and Magnetism class. My bags were packed, and I was ready to go to Texas. I said in my Electricity and Magnetism class, "When this class is done, I will hit the interstate to Texas." The Electricity and Magnetism professor said, "I will stay off the interstate." At the end of the class, I started toward Texas. I was so enthused about Texas that I failed to watch my speed. I got a speeding ticket at the 43 mile marker on Interstate 70 in Ohio for doing 72 in a 55 mph zone. This fine was 55 Dollars on the Visa Card. After that ticket, I drove for a day, and I arrived safely in Texas.

My Mom and Dad were happy to see me. I was happy to have a break with a reasonable chance of making it through my first semester. On Sunday, I arranged to see Robert on Tuesday. Between Sunday and Tuesday, I worked on my new TRS 80 computer. I was writing a program to optimize prototypes of my perpetual motion electric motor of Project Texhoma. I made good progress and contacted Robert on Tuesday. We made arrangements to see each other on Friday night. On Wednesday, I worked on my computer. On Thursday, our family celebrated Thanksgiving. On Friday, I studied physics until the evening and headed to Robert's house.

At Robert's house, I embraced Robert, and he introduced me to his new girlfriend, Jeannie. Jeannie was a clear but light complected, medium built, long blond haired, attractive, and friendly young woman. We ate potato chips and drank pop. We had a good time for two hours. As I was leaving his house, I said, "Back to Morgantown." Robert said, "Good luck, "I hope you make all 'A's!" I replied, "Back to PRT cards and long physics lectures." I greeted Robert, "See ya later." I headed back to Morgantown to face three weeks of hell.

In Morgantown, I studied all of my physics in anxiety about what I had learned early in the semester. I wondered whether I learned the first three chapters of each subject and struggled to learn the last two weeks of material. On the Sunday before finals, I was stressed out. I bought a big bottle of pop and a big bag of potato chips and ate the whole thing. On Monday, I studied like crazy for Tuesday's Mechanics exam. I struggled through my Mechanics exam and thought I made a C but made a B in the class. On Wednesday, I bombed my Quantum Mechanics test. I Thought I made a D in Quantum Mechanics. On Friday, I did really well on my Electricity and Magnetism test. I thought I made an A or B in Electricity and Magnetism. To my relief, I made a C in Quantum Mechanics. Although I did not know my other grades, I left for Texas with a good feeling.

In Texas, I worked on my computer programs concerning perpetual motion until Christmas. On Christmas, our family went to my Grandma Esther's house. There, we celebrated Christmas by eating a feast and exchanging gifts. After Christmas, I visited Robert three times and had a good time each visit. I also worked on my computer programs. Throughout the period, I anxiously awaited my report card to see if I flunked out of West Virginia. On the last day before I left for Morgantown, I visited Robert. Upon arriving, I greeted Robert, "How are you?" Robert replied, "I am doing fine, but I am busy at work." I said in a depressed tone, "Tomorrow, I leave for Morgantown. I will find out if I flunked out of West Virginia tomorrow. I will likely find my report card in the mail when I get back to Morgantown. Pray for me." Robert replied, "You won't flunk out of West Virginia tomorrow, but I will be your friend if you do." I replied, "I am glad to know you will be my friend through thick and thin." Robert and I had a good time for two hours, but then it was time to say goodbye. I told Robert in a depressed tone, "It is time to say goodbye for three months or so." Robert replied, "That three months will go by fast. We will talk about every two weeks, and you will be busy. I wish you luck, and I know you are a good friend." I replied happily, "I will be glad to see you spring break." Robert replied, "See you later." I replied, "See you later." I headed to Morgantown feeling good. I received my report card in Morgantown. I was in good standing at West Virginia University.

I enrolled in Electricity and Magnetism II, Mechanics II, and Computer Programming. I started out with 'A's and 'B's in each class. For the first five weeks everything went well in these classes. I even did well on my exams. In spite of my good performance, I felt lonely. My only close friends seemed to be Robert and Robert's new girlfriend, Margie. I decided to try to make friends in Morgantown.

About six weeks into the second semester, Robert proved not to be so perfect. I called Robert at his Chesgas Station on Monday. He was grouchy and told me to call tomorrow. I called him on Tuesday, and he told me to call tomorrow. I called Robert on Wednesday, and he told me to call on Sunday. After Robert pushed me off on Wednesday, I called his girlfriend, Margie. Margie, like Robert, was dark complected, friendly, and very attractive. I asked Margie, "Is Robert mad at me?" Margie asked, "Why are you concerned?" I replied, "Robert pushed me off three days straight and told me to call back on Sunday." Margie said in a reassuring tone, "Have patience. Robert is very busy, and he is stressed out from working until 10 pm for the last week. I know that it does not look good, but Robert talks good about you. Just have patience, and call back on Sunday. While waiting, just work on your classes." I thanked Margie for her reassurance and earned good grades for the week. On that Sunday, Robert talked with me. He explained that he was tired and burned out. We talked for an hour sharing dreams and experiences. This quality time made me feel good.

About seven weeks into the second semester on Wednesday, I met Steve Horseman at his Baptist church, The First Apostolic Church in Morgantown. This church was friendly. Pastor Brown taught everybody to be good friends and to love their neighbor as themselves. I attended church there every Sunday and met new people. I worked hard on my studies and did well until spring break. I went back to Texas for spring break. I worked at my family's new business, Family Fiberglass, for the business week. I had a good time with Robert two nights. I returned to Morgantown ready to finish my last five weeks. I finished them successfully.

I returned to Gainesville for the summer. I spent this summer socializing with Robert Elight and helping to build Family Fiberglass, the new family business. In the family business, I worked overtime to help make it work. On one Tuesday, I worked until 6:30 pm and went home tired. Lots of overtime frequently was necessary. When I socialized with Robert, I often helped with his front yard. One Sunday, I carried tree branches to the fire all afternoon with Robert and had a good time. At the end of the afternoon, I ate hamburgers with Robert's family. Get-togethers like this were common with Robert.

Upon my return to Morgantown, I enrolled in Math Physics I, Classical Mechanics, and Solid State Physics. I joined Rushing Wind, A Christian

Organization run by Pastor Brown's Church and Steve Horseman. On the Tuesday of the fourth week, Hurricane Alicia formed in the Gulf of Mexico, and headed for Houston. I prayed that God would protect Houston and the oil industry there. Much of Houston and its refineries were safe after the storm. That Friday, I went to Rushing Wind's picnic in the mountains. There, I rejoiced that Houston was safe and enjoyed the picnic with Steve and all of his friends. For the next three weeks, I did well in all of my classes and saw Steve at the Rushing Wind meetings on Friday nights. In the eighth week, I earned a 'C-' on my Solid State Physics Exam. This worried me for the weekend.

On Wednesday of the ninth week, Iran threatened to block the Strait of Hormuz. Much of the world's oil flowed through the strait. Iran was backed by the powerful Soviet Union. President Reagan said, "The United States will keep the Strait of Hormuz open." I feared that this could cause Armageddon. I prayed and fasted all day Thursday concerning a possible conflict in the Strait that could cause World War III. God answered my prayer, but I had a small doubt concerning the security in the Strait and ultimately the US security.

On the ninth Saturday of my second year, I met Brian Nehjer at the Agape House. The Agape House was a Christian nightclub in downtown Morgantown started by Steve Horseman and Pastor Brown. Brian was an average looking student of his day. We picked up our cider and cookies and talked about our dreams and lives. He said, "I am a youth minister in a church in Pennsylvania during my summer vacation. I asked, "Did you sing in the Choir?" Brian said, "Yes. I sing in the choir and play Christian rock at places like this Agape House." He asked, "What do you do?" I replied, "I am a physics graduate student at West Virginia University." He asked, "How do you resolve the conflict between science and the Bible?" I replied, "God, The Devil, the demons, and God's angels are all free to move freely through at least one dimension more than mankind. The beings of heaven can freely move through time and possibly through parallel time. This freedom of movement explains most observed miracles of God and acts of witchcraft. I arrived at this idea by doing a few derivations of my own, but I could be wrong. I have also found a contradiction between the law of conservation of energy and the inverse square law of electromagnetism." He asked, "Is this a new source of energy?" I replied "Yes. If my understanding of this contradiction is correct, perpetual motion is possible by choosing the right distance between electromagnets comprising an electric motor." Brian said, "If this machine works, the oil companies will buy your invention and throw it away." I asked, "Won't America's big companies or the government be interested?" He said, "All of the big companies are controlled by a big world-wide organization, and the oil companies would be protected from the competition of your invention. I asked, "What is this world-wide organization?" Brian replied, "This world-wide organization is a committee of national leaders and corporate leaders around the world. Many of these leaders are rich enough to own a small

American state or an entire third world country. Dad developed a new drug that would make chemotherapy obsolete for cancer. He submitted results of his research to the big company. His idea was thrown away." He gravely warned, "Lives have been threatened over good inventions." He added this warning, "You will need God to market yours." That night, I left the Agape house discouraged. Little did I know that this discussion would lead to my friendship with Johnny Oilstring and change the course of history at Kent State.

On the tenth Sunday, I went to Pastor Brown's church. I prayed rejoicing that the straight was safe. Pastor Brown taught that day to speak your prayers, and God will answer them. I talked with the church people about the sermon after the service and started to drive home. I took Saberton Road. As I arrived at the Intersection of Saberton Road and State Road 7, the Devil gave me a thought that the Strait of Hormuz was not safe. While I was waiting at the stoplight, I prayed to God. While I was praying, God caused me to get mad at the Devil. I spoke in tongues and said with the arrogance of a tenured professor, "Satan get out of the strait of Hormuz before I ask God to throw you out!!!" God gave me peace concerning this situation. Iran stood down. There was peace in the Strait for nearly four years.

Until Thanksgiving break, I would socialize at the Morgantown's Christian nightclub, the Agape House, and study physics while school was in session. My Solid State Physics would improve to a 'B' over the next two exams. I would maintain a 'B' average in Classical Mechanics, and maintain an 'A' average in Math Physics I.

During Thanksgiving break, I would socialize with Robert six nights. On that sixth night, I sensed that Robert was upset with me. I would return to Morgantown and maintain my grades until finals week. I would try to call Robert at the end of two weeks. He was short with me and seemed grouchy. I took my final exams. I blew it on my classical mechanics exam. I made a 'C' in Mechanics, 'B' in Solid State Physics and an 'A' in Math Physics.

I returned to Texas for Christmas break. Our family celebrated Christmas and gave me a printer for my TRS 80 computer, but this Christmas was bittersweet. From the time I returned to Texas until December 30, Robert avoided me and made me depressed. On December 30 at about 8:00 am, I confronted Robert. At first, Robert told me to get lost. Then, I explained that I was his friend, but I wondered why he was avoiding me. Robert explained that he was busy, and he apologized.

Robert and I went into his office at his Chesgas station, and we talked. Robert said, "I am leaving Margie, and I am dating another woman." I asked, "Who is she?" Robert asked, "Will you keep a secret?" I replied, "You can trust me because I am your friend." Robert said, "The name of my new woman is April." I asked, "When can I meet her?" Robert replied, "You can meet her at Rodney's party tomorrow night." I replied, "I will be at Rodney's party tomorrow night." Robert said, "Thanks for understanding and forgiving me." I replied, "You are my best friend, but I have a question concerning the Occult Defense Policy of US Physics and the Board of Judges." Robert asked, "What is the question?" I replied by asking, "Should we have a qualifying exam for new Occult Defense Analysts when we need them in the future?" Robert asked, "What would be on that exam?" I replied, "I will ask for a person to relate two commandments such as thou shalt not steal and thou shalt not kill to the golden rule and to loving Jesus." Robert replied, "This is a good idea." I replied, "This will ensure that a person understands how to think about the word of God. We will call this exam the Biblical Scholastic Aptitude Test or the BSAT" Robert and I talked for two hours and I returned home. Little did I know that this exam would help to change the course of history at Kent State University. I attended Rodney's party and got together with Robert one last time before my return to Morgantown.

I returned to Morgantown to enroll in Graduate Quantum Mechanics, Math Physics II, and Electrodynamics. In my Electrodynamics class, they used the toughest textbook in physics, *Classical Electrodynamics* by J.D. Jackson. About a week into the class, my electrodynamics professor said, "Your math skills need development." He warned, "If you stay in this class, you will fail, and I will give you an 'F'." I asked, "What should I do?" The professor replied, "See if you can withdraw from this class and get into a vector calculus class."

On the next day, I approached the chairman of the department to discuss this problem. The chairman said, "You are not making good progress toward your degree, but I must let you withdraw from Electrodynamics." I asked, "Should I also withdraw from Graduate Quantum Mechanics?" The department chairman replied, "Stay in Quantum Mechanics, and make a 'B' in that class." I asked, "What happens if I fail to make a 'B' or at least a 'C' with an 'A' in Math physics?" "If you fail to make a 'B' average this semester, you will lose your assistantship," The chairman replied.

I went back and studied like mad to understand Quantum Mechanics and made a 'C' on my exam. I went back to the chairman to discuss this situation. The chairman said, "I am glad to hear that you are averaging a 'C' in Quantum Mechanics and an 'A' in Math Physics." I asked, "Will I save my assistantship?" The department chairman said, "Check back with me in two weeks." Two weeks later, the chairman replied, "I will let you know at the end of the semester concerning your assistantship."

After this stressful eight weeks in Morgantown, I arranged to meet Robert at Martz Fast Food in McKinney at 2:30 pm, so we could talk about spring break (Map 6). Because Robert was staying with Rodney, and Rodney did not have a phone, I feared that missing this appointment meant that I would never see Robert again. I should have realized that I could call Robert at work as long as necessary, but I was not thinking straight. At about seven o'clock, I left for Gainesville. As I approached The Kent State Exit on the Ohio Turnpike, God told me to head to Kent and to talk with the Kent State hippies. Fearing I would miss my flight from Cleveland and would lose my best friend, Robert Elight, I proceeded to The Cleveland Airport. I flew to Dallas and drove to McKinney, Texas in defiance of God. In McKinney, I met with Robert at Martz Fast Food at the intersection of US 75 and US 380. I arranged to see Robert the following Tuesday.

On Tuesday of spring break, I met with Robert at Martz Fast Food Mart. "God told me to take the Kent State exit and talk to the hippies last Friday," I told Robert, "Fearing that I would lose contact with you, I disobeyed God and came to visit you." The spirit of God came over me and caused me to say, "Robert, there is going to be a major occult war. Its final battle will be at Kent State University. Its hero will be a Kent State hippie. The name of Billy Glassman comes to mind. Some guy with the first name of Freddie also comes to mind. He shall be a major friend like you." Robert said, "Everything will be all right." I humbly replied, "By the grace of God, I hope that you are right."

Robert and I continued to keep contact through the rest of the academic year at West Virginia University. I studied like mad but did lousy on my final exam in Quantum Mechanics. In spite of my 'A' in Math Physics, my performance was not good enough to keep my assistantship at West Virginia University. To re-instate my assistantship, I needed to pass my qualifying exam in the physics department.

During the summer, I worked on a program to simulate my version of electromagnetic theory on various electric motor designs. I worked on debugging parts of the program to calculate magnetic field strengths due to the armature and field electromagnets. I found many typos and needed to correct them. I spent many long nights finding these errors. On Thursday nights, I would visit Robert at his station in McKinney. We would talk and play arcade games many of these Thursday nights. In mid-July, I made my program calculate the armature field strengths and field magnet field strengths. One week later, my program calculated the speed and torque correctly. I wrote the program for energy losses, but started to study for my qualifying exams in Morgantown. I went to the Denton State University Library and studied every weeknight for about three weeks. Feeling that I was not ready to pass the qualifying exam, I arranged with the Physics Department to take the exam in January.

This process bored Robert, so he had little time for me. He got mad at me and allowed me to call only once a week on Sunday. If he was not there, or he did not want to talk, I had to try him again next week. This situation made me feel lonely. Even though Robert was probably still my friend, I decided to make a new friend.

Meanwhile; at Family Fiberglass, I met Johnny Oilstring. Johnny was a fun loving tall skinny person with long scraggly black hair. His aggressively friendly personality gave me the impression of very loyal and fun loving friend, though his long hair and his bad reputation made me think he was a little reckless. Johnny Oilstring was developing a rock band. One day, I was working on rear caps for RV's. Johnny said "Hi, How's it going?" I replied "Fine. Just fixing these fiberglass parts." Johnny said, "These parts are junk." I replied, "Production cracks these parts and leaves lots of air in them. We fix these parts so well that they are perfect when the customers get them." Johnny complained, "I know that this job is tough. I wish they paid me more than $4.75 an hour." I said, "I have no control over management. You need to talk to them. See you later." Johnny said, "Best of wishes. See you Monday."

Little did I know that Johnny was the hippie like Jimmy Woodman, symbolized by the dream of the Attack on Parsons. He was hexed in retaliation for my prayers concerning the US Dollar in 1978. This hex helped to cause Bobby Weakleg to backslide. Though this hex may have been intended to hit me or my church, it failed to harm the church or me because the church and I prayed for Bobby and Johnny. In spite of these prayers, Johnny still suffered from the accident and hex though I thought he was just a normal bad kid with no accident or hex.

On that summer Monday at 6 am, the plant manager and the production manager were late. I told Johnny, "I am going to call Dad, the owner." Johnny plead with me, "Don't call your Dad because he will be in a bad mood all day long. He will yell at us for every little mistake." I replied with haste, "I can't listen to you. You are just a peon! Sorry Johnny, you are better than a peon because you are my friend. All of the others are just peons!" Johnny asked, "How do you know that the others are worthless?" I hastily and unwisely said, "None of them make good friends." The production manager then arrived and opened the plant. As the production manager opened the plant, Johnny asked, "How do you know? What gives you the right to judge?" I replied, "Sorry to hurt your feelings." Johnny said, "That's OK. I forgive you." I thought, "Good thing that nobody else was in the room to hear me call them worthless. I would have needed to apologize to the entire plant to remain right with God."

A few days later, the plant was busy and Johnny brought in a friend for me to train. Johnny said, "Kevin please make sure you train him right." I replied, "Don't worry. I care about the company. I will train him right, so the job will get done." Johnny said, "This is Tim Coleburn, my guitarist in the band." Tim was a tough looking, well-built, but attractive person. I shook Tim's hand and said, "Watch what I do to fix this bumper." Tim asked, "What are you doing?" I replied, "I am banging a rod against the edges and corners of this bumper to check it for air bubbles between the glass and the paint, [2] "Production loves to leave air because they do not care about their jobs. They like to party, and some miss every Monday." I warned Tim, "Don't associate with production, or you will be blamed for their mistakes." Tim asked, "What are you doing?" I replied, "I am grinding out all of the air bubbles, so the

2   See pictures 2a and 2b on pages 200. 210

patches will stick. Now, I will show you how to patch. You mix some gel-coat, paint for fiberglass parts, of the same color as the part you are trying to fix with some Cab-o-sil. Cab-o-sil is a paint thickener used in the fiberglass industry. Stir until you have a paste with no lumps. Then, you mix this paste with a little catalyst so this paste will harden. Then, you use this paste to fill the holes left from grinding the air. Then, you sand all of the patches with 220 grit wet or dry sandpaper until they are smooth. If the colors match, sand these areas with 320 grit, 400 grit, and 600 grit as I am doing. After you 600 sand, you buff this part until it shines. If the colors of the patches do not perfectly match the rest of the bumper, or you sand through the paint, paint the spots and repeat sanding and buffing. This is how you do final finish on these bumpers." Tim asked, "Will you tell me how to handle tricky situations as they come up?" I replied, "Yes. I will work with you until you master the job." Tim said, "It is nine O'clock." I said, "Oh my gosh! It is break time."

On Friday before Labor Day, I told Tim, "We need to finish eighteen bumpers today. I will try to make the job as much fun for you as possible. The main thing is to do as many bumpers as possible." As I was doing bumpers, I asked Tim, "How is your band doing?" Tim replied, "We are doing fine. Practice is going well, and we hope to be playing at parties and in bars." I told Tim, "I am busy with research concerning a contradiction between the laws of electrodynamics and conservation of energy. If my interpretation of this contradiction is right, I will build the first perpetual motion machine. If this machine works, it will solve the energy crisis, but big companies may try to suppress this machine. After I complete the computer program to optimize the design of my machine, I would like to see you and Johnny play." Tim said, "Come see us. Check us out." Tim and I finished twenty Heritage RV bumpers, and we had a lot of fun doing them. I declared, "I will come and see you."

On the following Tuesday, I met Johnny in the break room. "I will talk to Occult Defense Analyst Robert Elight about approving my friendship with you and Tim," I told Johnny. "This approval is necessary because you work in fiberglass. Approval by a Scriptural Analyst will help to weed out people like the evil Jed Pugent and Ted Monsterman." Johnny asked, "What are the most evil jobs?" I replied humorously, "Witchcraft and fiberglass manufacturing in that order." The time clock buzzed. Johnny and I went back to work.

The next day on Wednesday, Johnny and I met in Family Fiberglass's break room. I told Johnny, "Robert approved our friendship, and I am free to see you." Johnny asked, "What about your Dad?" I replied, Dad is overprotective, and his disapproval of Jason shoemaker made the situation with Jed and Ted worse. I must obey God." Johnny asked, "Why can Robert judge me?" I replied, "Robert helped to solve a bad situation with Jed and Ted. If I run into a moral dilemma concerning this friendship, Robert has a better chance of resolving it." Johnny said, "I am busy seeing Virginia this weekend. Talk to me next week about getting together." I correctly thought that Johnny was upset that I needed Robert's initial approval to be his friend.

The following Tuesday, Johnny and I talked again. I asked Johnny, "When is a good time for me to see you?" Johnny replied, "Come over any time. My house is your house. The band practices in the garage. Come and check us out." I replied, "I will try to be down tonight because I look forward to seeing you."

That night, I drove to Johnny's house, knocked at his door five times, and went to Johnny's garage. There, I heard the loud sound of his band playing loud music. Tim said "Hi! How are you doing?" I replied, "Fine. How is the band doing?" Tim said, "Nice to have you party with us and see our band." Johnny said, "How are you doing?" I replied, "Fine. I see a band that knows its music." Johnny said, "Kevin. This is my wife Janie." Janie was a clear complected, blond haired woman who seemed friendly. I replied to Janie, "Nice to meet you." Johnny said, "We are going to play some Ozzy." He added hurriedly, "Talk to you in a little bit." The band then loudly played *Paranoid*. Then the band played *Ironman*. Then Johnny introduced his drummer. Johnny said, "This is my drummer, John Wildkid." John Wildkid's wild but very friendly personality and his long and clean hair gave the appearance of a care free young adult. Tim said, "This is my girlfriend, Penny Peacechild." Penny was a plump, but very friendly woman. The band then played *Stairway to Heaven* by Led Zeppelin and *I Can't Drive 55* by Sammy Hagar. Johnny asked, "Do you want a drink?" I replied, "A Coke or a Mountain Dew." Johnny said, "I'll get you a great big glass of Mountain Dew with ice." Janie asked, "How do you like our band?" I replied, "They know their music. Johnny and Tim are really making me have fun." Johnny came back with my pop and asked, "Are you having a good time?" I replied, "Yes. I will try to make it here twice a week." Johnny said, "I bet you like it here better than you like it with Robert." I replied, "I don't know about that, but I am having a good time tonight." Johnny's band then played two more Ozzy songs. I said, "You make these songs sound good, but Van Halen is of the Devil. Steve Horseman gave me a list of Christian rock stars. Rock is not all evil, just some music and some artists." Johnny said, "Van Halen is not of the devil. Look at this record cover. The lyrics say that he found no true friends by running with the Devil. Running with the Devil made him lonely. That is hardly devil worship. Van Halen bashed the devil!!!" I replied, "Sorry. Van Halen is not of the Devil. I came up in the church and was taught to downgrade rock music." Johnny replied, "That is all right. I will teach you how to have a good time. You will like me better than Robert." I replied, "I stand behind all of my friends. I figure that Robert is my best friend. If I have a good time like I am having tonight, you can equal him." Johnny said, "I am glad you are having a good time." I replied, "I need Robert to figure out what the word of God says when US Physics faces a moral dilemma. I have had to fight witches as well as doing my research project." Johnny asked, "What is your research project?" I replied, "I am attempting to build and optimize a perpetual motion machine." Johnny said, "I will play a song that reminds me of you." Johnny played *Last in Line*. The lyrics contained this line "We're after the witch. We may never never never come home." This song was called *Last in Line*. "Fighting witches is part of my life on this project," I said. "That is why I must stand for the principles of God and be loyal to my friends." Johnny replied, "I bet you had more fun tonight than when you were with Robert." I replied, "I will try to see you once or twice a week." I said, "I had a good time." Johnny said, "My house is your house. You are welcome any time." I replied, "I have to be going. See you later." Johnny said, "Hope to see you soon!"

On Saturday September 22, 1984, I stopped in to see Johnny and Tim. They were playing their loud music and partying. Johnny brought me to his friend and introduced me by saying, "This is Calvin." I replied, "Nice to meet you." I asked, "How are you doing?" Calvin said, "Just fine." I asked, "What are you working on?" Calvin replied, "A heater for the garage." I said, "Let's listen to the band." Calvin replied, "I'll join you in a few minutes." Calvin was a street-smart, tall, long blond haired, and friendly young adult from the neighborhood. As I walked into the garage, Johnny met me and asked, "How are you doing?" He added, "Hope you are having a good time." I replied, "Your friends are interesting and fun." Johnny asked, "What is that book in your hands?" I replied, "This is a Quantum Mechanics book. I need it to study for my qualifying exam at West Virginia University." Johnny said, "Go ahead and study while the band plays its music." The band proceeded to play *Ironman* and *Paranoid*.

After the first round of music, the band took a break. During that break, Johnny asked, "Can I run security for your research operation?" I asked, "What makes you qualified to run security?" Johnny said, "You are smart with books, but I am street smart." I asked, "What strategy do you have for defending me from the Soviet KGB?" Johnny replied, "We will act like a bunch of street smart teenagers. We will dress in tee shirts and jeans. You will have no credibility as a project leader with anybody except the people you are working with." I asked, "How will you guard the lab during the test run?" Johnny said in response, "All but two guards will double as lab technicians. Those two guards who are not in the lab will be posted at the door as greeters. They will turn all of the people away who are not with the lab by telling them that the band will be back in two hours." I asked, "What uniforms will the guards wear?" Johnny said, "They will wear T-shirts and jeans like other teenagers of the day." I replied with curiosity, "You seem to believe in Jimmy Woodman's policy of wolf cry. Wolf cry, for US Physics, is a policy that requires US Physics to make its credibility low until it has the goods. With the goods, US Physics will show its credibility. You have solved half of the problem." Johnny asked, "What is the other problem?" I replied, "America's own big companies may try to suppress this machine. What can you do to counter this?" Johnny

THE BATTLE OF FORT ROCK

said, "We can contract a rock band to run an entire rock concert off of your perpetual motion machine." I asked, "How can you contact a rock star?" Johnny replied, "Look at this record cover." I replied, "This is a Pee Weas album." I asked, "What do I look for?" Johnny said, "The lead singer's name is Joe Sinc. My Uncle's name is Jimmy Sinc." I said, "Wow!" I asked, "Can I meet your uncle?" Johnny replied, "He lives in Ada, Oklahoma and he is very friendly. When your project is complete, I can contact Joe Sinc through the Sinc family reunion." I said, "You are a great criminal defense man."

Johnny said, "I also can run the Occult Defense System because me and God are real close." I replied, "To become an analyst you must pass an exam demonstrating that you know the basics of the Bible." Johnny said, "I am ready for that exam." I replied, "This exam will be a two question oral essay exam." Johnny said, "Ask the first question." I asked, "How do you relate the commandment "Thou shall not kill" to Jesus' first two commandments of loving God first and loving your neighbor as yourself?" Johnny said, "I cannot kill because I do not want to die. I would not kill my fellow man if I loved him." I asked, "Will a man go to hell?" Johnny said, "Jesus died on the cross, so no man should go to hell. I cannot kill because Jesus does not want me to take a chance on sending my fellow man to hell." I replied, "Now the second question." Johnny said, "Bring it on." I asked, "How do you relate the commandment "Thou shalt not steal" to the golden rule?" Johnny said, "I would be mad if somebody stole anything from me, so I disobey God by stealing anything from my fellow man." I replied, "You scored a 100 on your exam." Johnny asked, "Do I need to be sworn in?" I asked, "Johnny, do you swear to God to defend the interests of The Council of State Justices, of the Board of Judges of Texas, and of US Physics to the best of your ability?" Johnny said, "I will look out for all of our friends." I said, "I then commission you as a Criminal Defense Commander and an Occult Defense Analyst of the Board of Judges of Texas."

Little could anybody know that Johnny Oilstring's passing of the Biblical Scholastic Aptitude Test (BSAT) would give Johnny the capacity to change the course of history at Kent State University a half decade later. I prophesied at the Fast Food Mart about six months earlier, "Robert, There is going to be a major occult war. Its final battle will be at Kent State University. Its hero will be a Kent State hippie. The name of Billy Glassman comes to mind. The name of Freddie also comes to mind. He shall be a major friend like you." Nobody could predict that Johnny's knowledge of scriptural basics would help this prophecy to happen.

I asked, "If I put you in Robert's place as an Occult Defense Commander, how would you handle the Church of Satan?" Johnny replied, "I will ask you to calculate the dead center of the United States and put your Occult Defense Command headquarters there. This would scare the Church of Satan into respecting the Board of Judges of Texas." I replied, "You have an excellent plan for challenging America's big Companies." I added, "I am naming you as Chairman of the Criminal Defense Security Administration (CDSA) and Chairman of the Gainesville Wheeler Creek Security Council." Johnny Asked, "What is my compensation?" I replied, "If you stay with US Physics until the day of the test run, you will get 5% of US Physics. If you carry out the protection, you will get another 5%." Johnny said, "That is good." I replied, "If you have no questions, I will let your band play." Johnny said, "I must start singing."

Two days later at about 6:30 pm, I visited Johnny again. I saw him and the band play *Ironman*. After *Ironman* was through, Johnny came over and asked, "How are you doing?" I replied, "Fine." Johnny asked, "What is that book in your hands?" "That is a Quantum Mechanics book," I replied. "I need to study this book while you are playing." Johnny said, "Go ahead and study while I am playing. This way, you can pass your qualifier in Morgantown." I replied. "Thanks. I will study with your group while you are partying. I have one more order of business. I need to know what code name to give the garage regarding my research project named Project Texhoma." Johnny said, "Name my facility Fort Rock. This is to symbolize that rock music shall play here and defeat America's big companies." I replied, "I shall name this place Fort Rock Security Central."

Two days later on Wednesday, Johnny's band was playing *Paranoid*. Johnny was following the music perfectly, but his voice was cracking on the high notes. After he completed the song, Johnny asked, "Would you like to be part of the band?" I replied, "I have no musical talent." Johnny said, "But, you know about business." I replied, "You will have to teach me about the music business." Johnny explained, "That is no problem. I just want you to be part of my dream. You are a good friend." I said "Thanks." Then, I asked, "What can I do to help the band?" Johnny said, "Just listen to us and tell us how we sound. We have to sound good on October 22 to play Peggy's party." Johnny then went back to play *Ironman*. The band sounded good on that song. The band then played Sammy Hagger's song *I Can't Drive 55*. The band sounded all right but not ready to play a party. Johnny's band then played *Paranoid*. The band sounded terrible. Johnny's voice cracked, Tim hit a wrong note on his guitar, and John's drums went out of beat. I asked, "Why don't you guys take a break?" Johnny said, "Good idea." I asked, "Were you playing any other parties?" Johnny said, "We are working on an opportunity to play Cowboy's Place in Lindsay." I replied, "Good luck. I am with you." I hung out with the band, as they practiced all night long.

One week later, Johnny got mad at Family Fiberglass. He was irritated because Murray, Dad, told him one thing and Joe Featherman, the other partner, told Johnny another thing. Furthermore, Johnny was really wrought because Joey Featherman, Joe's son got to leave early for lunch, but Johnny had to follow the schedule. This anger caused Johnny to quit. Work in a fiberglass factory can be stressful. Perhaps, this was the little thing that caused Johnny to quit a job which he did not enjoy. That night, I went to visit Johnny. I knocked at his door, and his wife Janie told me he was asleep, but I saw him go into the kitchen through the window. I came back 15 minutes later to see if Johnny was back. He was back, but he was asleep. Janie let me in, and Johnny awoke. I said, "I am your friend even if you quit the plant." Johnny replied, "I am not coming back to Family Fiberglass." I said with conviction, "You do not have to work at Family Fiberglass to be my friend." I added, "I stand by my good friends no matter where they work." Johnny happily said, "Good. I am happy to hear that. I am burned out, but be here for practice tomorrow night." I replied, "I'll be glad to see you. I put my good friends first." Johnny said, "Love you. See you tomorrow."

Two weeks later, the band still had its problems getting a good sound. Sometimes, Johnny's voice would crack, Tim would play stray bouts on his guitar, and John Wildkid would mess around on the drums. When they tried to play a song, it turned out all wrong. Johnny admitted, "We are not ready to play Peggy's party." I replied, "To have a good name, the band must play well together." Johnny replied, "The band should play on the night before Thanksgiving at a big party at my house. We should order a pony keg of beer and have everyone get high. We will advertise this party everywhere we go. Let's make this party the mother of all parties." The other members of the band agreed. I proposed, "We should invite Robert ~~and Margie Elight~~. The band could play at the Council of State Justices party celebrating the completion of the computer program to optimize the perpetual motion machine of Project Texhoma." I asked Johnny, "How much will you charge United States Physics to play this party?" Johnny said, "One hundred Dollars." I replied, "I will be glad to make this band part of Project Texhoma." Johnny proposed, "I think that we shall call this band "Kritikal Kondishun" because our state of practice is in bad condition." The members of the band agreed. Johnny said, "Starting tomorrow night, we must practice every night, so we are ready to play the big Thanksgiving party, but let's party hardy tonight."

[handwritten margin note: Eight and his Girlfriend Margie]

Kritikal Kondishun practiced every night for a month straight. Tim's guitar and John's drums worked in synch, and Johnny's singing seemed to get better. One week into the month, a new guitarist joined the band. His name was Doug Richland. His businesslike demeanor and neat appearance commanded the respect of the band. His guitar made the band sound better. He was considering a career in engineering. For the next two weeks or so, Johnny, Tim, John, and Doug practiced together and became close. It was the Sunday before the big Thanksgiving Party. Johnny called the Party Store to order a keg of beer. I bought three giant 2 liter bottles of Mountain Dew and five big bags of potato chips. Johnny made up posters advertising his big party and sent me to the Public Library to copy 200 posters. Johnny had me post one at Family Fiberglass and took the rest to post at nearby stores in Ardmore and Marietta.

Johnny was hoping for a big turnout. Johnny arranged for me and the other band members to meet him at 5:30 pm on Tuesday.

That Tuesday, Johnny came down with a cold and a hoarse voice. I asked, "Will you be all right for tomorrow's party?" Johnny replied, "I will be all right for tomorrow's party." He emphasized, "Be sure to be there at 5:30 pm to help us set up and make sure we have all of the refreshments." I asked, "Do you need me to pray about your cold?" Johnny replied, "I do not need you to worry about my cold. Just be sure to be there to support our party. Our neighbors, most of whom are friendly acquaintances to me, will like us even if we are not perfect." I said, "I wish for you to get well and for your band's success. See you tomorrow."

Thanksgiving Wednesday, I met Johnny at 5:30 as he requested. "Put the pop and potato chips on the table," Johnny said, "You can go get something to eat." I asked, "Do you want me to order something for you?" Johnny replied, "Just get me a large Coke and an order of fries." About an hour later, I returned from the fast food restaurant to help the band set up. Johnny asked me to vacuum the living room floor. I vacuumed the floor clean. Johnny sent me to the Party Store to pick up the pony keg. I went to the Party Store to wait 1 hour and to finally pick up the pony keg. It took them 15 minutes to find the tap for the keg and 5 more for the cashier to ring up the sale. By the time I returned, it was 10 minutes until the party was to begin. Johnny had me greet the guests for the first hour of the party.

One interesting guest I met was a hippie from across US 70. His name was Steve Hammon. Steve asked, "How are you doing?" I replied, "Fine, How are you? I said, "My name is Kevin." "Steve is my name," Steve said, "I am interested in electronics and music. I like Def Leppard and Van Halen. I help people with their stereos and love to party." I replied, "I am interested in physics and Johnny's music. Johnny's music will help me market an energy source that I am working on." "I came to get drunk and listen to Johnny's band!" shouted Steve. I replied, "I will let you listen to Johnny's great band."

The neighbors at the Thanksgiving party liked Kritikal Kondishun. They played songs such as *I Can't Drive 55* and *Ironman*. The people at the party even liked Kritikal Kondishun with Johnny's hoarse voice. At about 10:00 pm, my little brother Kris came to the party. Kris was an attractive, friendly, and mechanically inclined body builder who carried the authority of Dad that night. I fearfully asked, "Will Dad kick me out of the house?" Kris said, "Everything will be all right." I asked Johnny, "When will Robert and Margie be here, or will they even come?" Johnny said, "Have patience. The night is still young." The band then played continuously until about 11:30 pm. Then, everybody went into the living room to visit and talk. Then seemingly from nowhere, Robert and Margie knocked at Johnny's front door. Johnny said, "Come on in." I said "Johnny, This is Occult Defense Commander Robert Elight and his girlfriend Margie." "Nice to meet you, Robert," said Johnny,

"Make yourself at home" For about the next half hour Johnny, Tim, John, Doug and Calvin got to know Robert and had a good time doing it. Afterward, Robert and I went home to prepare for Thanksgiving.

Our families had a good Thanksgiving. Most of the Thanksgiving weekend was spent studying for my qualifying exam. Sunday night, I stopped in to see how the band was doing. I watched our band practice until 10:00 pm. I left at 10:00 pm for home. At about 10:05 pm the police came to Johnny's house to give the members of Johnny's band a ticket for disturbing the peace. All of the members were told to appear in court ten days later.

Throughout the next week, Kritikal Kondishun prepared for the big Council of State Justices party on Saturday of that week. Posters were set up all around Sherman, Texas and Ardmore, Oklahoma. This grand party could make the band. Everything was going well until Johnny came back down with laryngitis on Friday before the big party. I asked, "Johnny will you be all right for tomorrow?" Johnny said, "Don't worry about me. I will be fine." I replied, "If your voice is not better, you can lip synch the records if you want." Johnny said, "I can sing." I said, "I am the President of the Board of Judges of Texas, and I can let the band play instrumentals if you cannot sing." Johnny said, "Dag nabbit, I want to sing!" I replied, "I am your friend, and you have the choice." Johnny said, "Thanks for your respect." I said, "Get well soon, and see you tomorrow."

Meanwhile, on Tuesday of that week, I met Robert and discussed Johnny's position at US Physics. I told Robert, "I appointed Johnny Oilstring Chairman of the Gainesville Wheeler Creek Security Council." Robert asked, "What makes Johnny qualified to head security." I replied, "He has a plan to get my invention past America's big oil companies." Robert asked, "What is that plan?" I replied, "Johnny proposes that we have a rock band from the recording industry run a rock concert off of my machine. He has a member of his distant family who is a lead singer of the rock band, "Pee Weas" Robert said, "I have my doubts about Johnny." I asked, "What are they?" Robert replied, "Johnny's house is in poor repair, and his friends are bums." I asked, "Can we get help marketing this invention without Johnny?" Robert replied, "We will likely face political opposition concerning Johnny." He added, "We are not ready to be activists." I replied, "God will help us in our weak areas if we are diligent in business." Robert replied, "We will need God's help handling the politicians because we do not have the resources to handle them ourselves." I said, "I will pray that we will never have to handle the politicians." Robert and I agreed Johnny was the best man for the job. He provided hope that we could market the perpetual motion machine against America's big energy companies if necessary.

The band met at 1:00 pm on that Saturday. Johnny told me to meet Robert at his house and get the party hall. I went to meet Robert at his apartment complex only to wait a half hour. The band arrived a half hour earlier than Robert. Johnny began to lose his cool. He asked repeatedly, "Is Robert standing you up?" I replied repeatedly, "We should wait patiently. Robert is coming." At about 5:00 pm Robert arrived. Robert apologized and let us in to set up the party. The setup went well, and the party started at 8:00 pm as planned. At the party, Johnny and Robert became friendly. After Johnny and Robert became friendly, the band started to play instrumentals. They sounded good. After about five instrumentals, Johnny came to the mike to sing. His first song, *I Can't Drive 55* sounded good. Then, Johnny's voice cracked on *Ironman*. His voice got progressively worse, as the band played through the night. One competing manager told me to keep the instrumentalists and dump the singer. He also talked to Tim. Robert said, "We all had a good time, but the band needs to improve." I let the band socialize at about 11:00 pm. Loren, Robert and Margie Flight, and the band members all became friendly. Loren was Robert's young, popular, and charismatic cousin. While this night was bad for the band, Robert's friends and family had a good time.

On the following Monday, the band regrouped. We all decided that the band needed more practice before they went on the road. We decided to practice every other night. We also decided to find good songs that Johnny could sing easily. Then, the bottom fell out. Wednesday, Ardmore, Oklahoma's judge put the band on probation. They could not play for six months. Johnny plead, "Kevin could you get a lawyer to appeal this sentence?!" I said, "I will call a lawyer and see what I can do." Johnny said, "I hope we can win this appeal." I replied, "The lawyer will tell us that. I am your friend either way. See you later."

I made an appointment with an Oklahoma lawyer for that Friday. The band presented their case to her. The woman lawyer had a professional demeanor and seemed to know her job well. The lawyer said, "I will study the case, and I will get back with Kevin on Tuesday." That Tuesday, the lawyer said, "There is little chance of appealing this sentence successfully. An appeal of this sentence will cost $30,000." I told Johnny that overturning this sentence was impossible. Johnny suggested that the band would play on a ranch owned by John Wildkid. They played there a week later and did not like the 50 mile drive. Johnny then suggested that the band put styrofoam over the basement windows and play in the basement. Kritikal Kondishun tried that suggestion the following Sunday. It worked fairly well but not good enough. The band could be slightly heard at the property line. We all decided to get together and practice in the basement during the day on weekends. We needed to respect our neighbors, so the band could stay out of jail. If we had not been so reckless, we could have practiced more openly. We all regretted our mistake because we were wrong and got caught. We all tried to continue in disrespect for this harsh sentence, though we acted more responsibly to stay out of trouble.

On Friday December 21, 1984, Johnny offered to take me out to drink a strawberry daiquiri. I replied, "My church teaches that drinking is a sin."

Johnny said in a friendly manner, "What does the word of God say?" I unwisely replied, "The Bible says that Jesus turned the water into wine. The Bible allows moderate drinking to show friendship. Where do you want to go?" Johnny replied happily, "The Ace Hi Bar on Main Street. They have good chicken and French fries. They also have a train that runs around the room on a ledge near the ceiling. You will have a good time there."

At Johnny's house two hours later, Johnny drove me and Janie to the Ace Hi. Johnny said, "Order anything on the menu." I ordered a chicken dinner with two large orders of French fries and a chocolate pie. In addition, I ordered a Coke and a strawberry daiquiri. Johnny and Janie ordered a T-bone steak and a baked potato. They also drank a strawberry daiquiri. After I drank the daiquiri, Johnny asked, "How did that drink taste?" "This drink was good," I replied. Johnny pointed out, "There is the steam train!" I exclaimed, "That train looks like an authentic scale model!" I liked looking at the train with a steam locomotive and three passenger cars, as it went around the room. Johnny and I enjoyed talking about the band and eating our good meal. Johnny told me of a song he had written. He figured that he could sing it well. The name of this song was "Evil Street."

The next day, the band practiced together. Johnny said, "This is a song that I wrote and I can sing. The band asked Johnny to sing this song. He sang the song and the band did the instrumentals. After about three or four times of practice, the band did a beautiful sounding rendition of "Evil Street." The song went:

> I was walking down the streets of Dallas.
> I was walking down the streets of LA.
> I was walking down the streets of Detroit.
> I was walking down the streets of Miami.
>
> The streets were full of evil.
> Women were full of fear.
> The laws are full of bullshit.
> The cops were full of evil.
>
> Evil Street! Evil Street!
> We're walking down Evil Street.

The second verse was not complete. Kritikal Kondishun sounded very good playing this song.

Our families celebrated Christmas, and the band met next Saturday, "Tim is talking bad about me again," said Johnny, "Doug, Tim, and John are butchering up my song. They play it all wrong. Tim is hurting my feelings. The band cannot make it without me." I tried to reassure Johnny that the band would stay together. I was wrong. Two days later, the band moved out of Johnny's basement without telling Johnny or me that he was out of the band. I went with the remnants of the band promising to see Johnny later that night. Tim told me not to go see Johnny that night. I kept my arrangement with Johnny and found that he needed a friend. Johnny and Janie cried on my shoulder all night.

Two days later, Johnny and Janie would have a party because I had to go to Morgantown to take my qualifying exam. Johnny and Janie invited me to a night club in Lindsay. I met Johnny in the parking lot, and I was happy to see him. We went inside and found a table. I ordered my favorite, chicken and French fries. Johnny and Janie then ordered. After the orders were placed, Johnny gave me my going away present. It was a computer disk drive! I thanked Johnny, and we had fun conversation throughout the meal and desert. Then, the hard part came. I had to say goodbye. I hugged Johnny and made arrangements to keep contact. I did not know that I would fail the qualifying exam at West Virginia University and be back in two weeks.

CHAPTER 5

THE BATTLE OF SHERMAN

Two weeks after I left for Morgantown, I failed my qualifying exam in the Physics Department of West Virginia University. I called Johnny. Johnny asked, "What are you going to do?" I replied, "Get a job in my field or attend a masters granting university." Johnny emphatically asked, "Can't you continue at West Virginia University?" I replied with a sense of hopelessness, "The electromagnetism professor does not recommend it. I cannot continue as a student in good standing. He recommended that I go to a masters granting school such as Denton State or Arlington State University." Johnny suggested, "Why don't you contact Arlington State University as soon as you get back from Morgantown? I know that you can pass if you have a good chance to study." I replied, "I think I can get my master's degree from Arlington State University. Pray my parents see it my way and let me try." Johnny said, "Your parents love you and will forgive you." I said, "See you later."

The next Tuesday, I visited Johnny and talked about my future plans, "I called Arlington State University and learned that I will easily be admitted and could qualify for an assistantship in the Physics Department," I told Johnny, "I sent for an application and literature from Arlington State University. I will also call Denton State University tomorrow. I will also work on Project Texhoma. I may need to go to the Public Library in Dallas to do patent research." Johnny replied, "Let me know which Saturday, so we can go to Dallas together. I happily replied, "We will go in about three weeks." Johnny and I spent the evening in friendly conversation.

Although it is normal for a man to reap what he has sown, bad things coinciding with the phases of the moon are not normal. Neither are bad things being predicted by horoscopes. They smack of a hex.

That Thursday, Janie came down with the Asian flu. Johnny's friend Calvin and I came to visit him. Johnny said, "I think that I am hexed because I am having all kinds of bad luck." I replied in a professional tone, "Get me the calendar. I need to check your luck against the phases of the moon. I take it that your bad luck started when you got your hoarse voice before Thanksgiving. That occurred on November 20, 1984, two days before the new moon." Johnny added, "Then, the court stopped the band from playing on the Wendsday after Robert Elight's party. I replied, "This event occurred on December 5, 1984, three days before the full moon." Johnny said, "My truck blew a rod, and Janie got mad at me two weeks later on the Friday." I said, "This event occurred on December 21, 1984, one day before the new moon. The use of styrofoam in the windows failed two days later. This dashed the hopes of the band completely and occurred on December 23, 1984, one day after the new moon." Johnny said, "The Sunday after Christmas, my Plymouth did not start for two weeks." He explained, "This ended my job at Terra Glas." I replied, "This firing occurred two days after the new moon on January 9, 1985." Johnny said, "Janie got the Asian flu." I replied, "This occurred three days after the new moon on January 21, 1984." Johnny's Dad asked, "Why are you marking the calendar? Are you some kind of psychic?!" Calvin responded, "He is using this information for good." I replied, "I am trying to figure out if Johnny is hexed. Johnny does not look hexed in spite of this 2-3-1-1-2-3 pattern of bad luck. That is Johnny has one major bad luck experience two days before a major phase of the moon on November 20, 1984. This is the first two in the bad luck pattern. His next bad luck event, the court date, occurs three days before the next phase of the moon on December 5, 1984. This bad luck event corresponds to the first 3 in the bad luck pattern. The next bad luck event, Johnny blowing a rod on his truck, occurs one day before the next phase of the moon on December 21, 1984. This event corresponds with the first 1 in the bad luck pattern. The next event, band couldn't play because Styrofoam over the window did not work, occurs one day after the new moon on December 23, 1984. This corresponds with the second 1 in the bad luck pattern. The next bad luck event, Johnny Oilstring's firing, occurs two days after the full moon on January 9, 1985. This event corresponds with the second 2 in the bad luck pattern. The final event, the Asian flu, occurs on January 24,

1985, three days after the new moon (see Calendar). This pattern of bad luck is symmetric concerning the phases of the moon with only one exception. Although this probability of this union of events forming this almost symmetric 2-3-1-1-2-3 pattern of bad luck concerning the phases of the moon is about one in 2 million, I think this is coincidence[3]. It is about the chance of

**November
1984**

				1	2	3
4	5	6	7	8	9	10
11	12	13	14	15	16	17
18	19	20 Got Laryngitis	21	22 New Moon	23	24
25	26	27	28	29	30	

---

3 Morris and Degroot. *Elements of Statistics and Probability*; Reading, Massachusetts: Addison-Wesley Publishing Company, 1975, pp.19-28, and pp. 39-45.

**December
1984**

						1
2	3	4	5 Court Date	6	7	8 Full Moon
9	10	11	12	13	14	15
16	17	18	19	20	21 truck blew rod	22 New Moon
23 Styrofoam didn't work Band stopped	24	25	26	27	28	29
30	31					

January 1985					
	1	2	3	4	5
6	7 Full Moon	8	9 Got fired	10	11	12
13	14	15	16	17	18	19
20	21 New Moon	22	23	24 Asian Flu	25	26
27	28	29	30	31		

me or you getting struck by lightning in a given year. These events look suspicious, so I will pray for God's protection. I will also pray for the salvation of Johnny, his friends, and his family just in case I am wrong." Johnny asked, "Does this mean that the band is not to blame for these circumstances?" I gave this lecture in response, "Although this coincidence is suspicious, I am not blaming the judge. The case just happened to come on his docket on the right day for this coincidence. He did not control this luck any more than you or I. He was doing his duty, though we may dislike his harsh sentence. What a man sows, he will reap. A way to fight a hex is to do good works. If you had respected your neighbor by keeping the band quiet after 10 pm, this coincidence fails, the band is still legal, maybe together, and back to the drawing board for Satan concerning this possible hex. Service to God and country will defeat a hex every time."

On the following Monday, I visited Johnny. Johnny and I got into a discussion about each of our good friendships. I said to Johnny, "Robert helped me solve a serious moral dilemma at Big RV plastics." Johnny asked, "How so?" I replied, "Fiberjunck had a record of corrupting every Christian entering the company. Big RV Plastics was run by the same people who ran Fiberjunck. If I lost my job there, forget Project Texhoma. Robert reminded me that God will keep me even with those managers in control. God kept me."

Johnny got each of us a Mountain Dew and told me about his close friend Bobby, "I practically lived with my good friend Bobby Weakleg," Johnny said, "He was there for me during the aftermath of my 1978 accident. We did everything together. We went fishing together. One time he caught a big trout, and I caught only seaweed. We drank together. He was even my best man at my wedding." I asked, "What happened to him?" Johnny replied, "After I married Janie, we went our own ways. You are now my good friend."

The following Thursday, I did 1 hour worth of patent searching at the Denton State University Library. At Denton State University, I found that I needed to go to Dallas to complete my patent research. I asked, "Would you like to go to Dallas with me to do patent research with me?" Johnny said, "I would like to go with you two weeks from this Saturday." I asked, "Would you like to party while you are there?" Johnny said, "I would like to leave Friday night to go to the WWF fights." I replied, "We will also need a hotel room. I will call Holiday Inn." I called Holiday Inn and reserved my room in Fort Worth, Texas. Johnny called the ticket office to buy the fight tickets. Johnny and I talked about the upcoming party in Dallas. We both looked forward to our weekend in Dallas.

On a Friday night in middle February, I met Johnny at his house. We talked about the coming night in Dallas. I said, "I hope to eat a bunch of fried chicken and French fries." "I hope you get wild with me and my friend, Doug," replied Johnny, "I would like you to get drunk and high with us and meet a foxy chick." I replied, "I doubt that I can party that hard, but we should have a good time." Johnny found the WWF tickets for the match at the Dallas Gymnasium. He said, "We do not want to forget these." I replied, "We want to see Andrea the Giant beat up Hulk Hogan." Johnny replied, "Hulk Hogan will find a way to beat Andrea the Giant. These matches are rigged, and Hogan is the good guy." I said, "I hate to interrupt you, but we must get going if we are to make the match." Johnny said, "We will take your car, but Doug will drive. Dallas is a dangerous place, and Doug knows how to drive there." I handed Doug the keys, and we left for Dallas.

After we left for Dallas, we decided to get gas in Lindsay, Texas. We all wanted refreshments. I took Mountain Dew brand soda and cheese crackers. Johnny took Mountain Dew and pretzels. He checked to make sure we had plenty of pot for the night. Doug took Mountain dew and potato chips. He went next door to buy vodka. I filled the tank with gas. Afterward, we left for Dallas. On Interstate 35, we talked about the night of fun. We ate and drank some of our refreshments. "Our hotel in Fort Worth has a weight room and a swimming pool," Johnny said. "You can work out and look at all of the pretty women after the wrestling match. Perhaps, you can find a beautiful woman." I replied, "I would like to eat a good chicken dinner then figure out what to do next. If I am not tired, I may party with you guys." We entered the city of Dallas. On I-20, we got caught in a traffic jam. Doug said, "We will be out of this traffic jam in fifteen minutes." Doug maneuvered by zig-zagging through the traffic. As the traffic started moving, a car passed us to the left and almost hit us. Doug said, "This is normal during rush hour traffic in Dallas." We got on I-35W and drove to our hotel room in Fort Worth.

At the hotel, I checked in. Johnny said, "If we are to get to the fights on time we must get going." We all got into the car and headed for the gymnasium. When we got to the gymnasium, we paid $3 for a parking place. We walked two blocks to a line another half-block long. After we got into the match, we watched the fight. "Ain't that Bad!" Johnny shouted, "Andrea the Giant body slammed the Hulkster." Johnny meant that he was having a good time watching Andrea The Giant beat up Hulk Hogan. I replied, "They staged this match to be exciting. I am rooting for the Hulk." Doug said, "Hey look, the Hulk has the Giant in a painful, arm twisting, arm bar." The Giant got out of the hold and walked around in a daze. As the Giant walked around in a daze, the Hulk jumped the Giant from the top rope of the ring and pinned him for the three count. After the Hulk's victory, we went to the refreshment stand. I got my chicken and French fries and over-ate them. Johnny and Doug got popcorn. While we were eating, Johnny's favorite cousin, Timmy Oilstring met us. All four of us went to see the remaining WWF matches. Afterward, we went to the hotel.

At the hotel, we went to our room and watched TV. Johnny got out the pot and vodka. He lit the joint and mixed the vodka with pop. All of us talked and partied in our own way. After fifteen minutes, Timmy fell asleep. Johnny got high, went out to the pool, and looked at all the pretty women. He went swimming and met a few of them. Johnny came back into the room and said, "There are a lot of foxy chicks out there. Why don't you come out to meet them?" I replied, "The wrestling match tired me out. I just want to talk." Johnny asked, "Do you want to puff this joint?" I replied maybe later." Johnny said, "I'll let you rest and talk to you in an hour." Doug and Johnny went to the pool. A half hour later, I met them there and almost puffed on that joint. We went back to the room, and I almost hit that joint again. Doug asked, "Do you want to work out with me. I told Doug, "I am tired and feel like sleeping." Doug and Johnny partied for two more hours, and I went to sleep.

The next morning, we slept in until 10:00 am and needed to check out at 12 pm. We packed up, ate breakfast, and checked out of the room. The opportunity to party was over. We proceeded to the Dallas Public Library to do our research. I looked for perpetual motion machines. I was happy to find none patented. I then looked for designs on electric motors. We found no data we could use with my optimizing program. While I looked for electric motors, Johnny and Doug looked for alternate energy sources in "Popular Mechanics" and "Popular Science" magazines. Johnny found a solar powered car that could be made for $100,000. Doug and Timmy found nothing. From this trip, I did a complete patent search and decided to take apart and measure armatures and field magnets to get the data for our computer simulations. The trip was successful, though it was disappointing concerning our research.

We departed from the library to return home. I asked Johnny, "How are you doing?" "I am doing awful," replied Johnny. "I am disappointed that you did not puff that joint with me." I replied, "We had a good time overall. Didn't we?" Johnny replied, "Yes. We had a good time, but I just wished you would have puffed a joint with me, got laid with one of the beautiful women we met, or got drunk." "I almost puffed that joint and got drunk," I unwisely replied. "The next time I will puff that joint and get drunk as a show of our friendship. It is better for a friend to smoke pot than not to show his love for that friend." Johnny said, "I'll get over it and feel better, but not tonight." Doug said, "I like you, and knowing Johnny, he does too." We discussed Johnny's disappointment all the way to Denton, Texas. In Denton, we said goodbye to Timmy and headed home. Johnny slept all the way to Ardmore. When Johnny woke up, he was in no mood to talk. When we arrived at Johnny's house, Johnny in his disappointed mood said, "See you Monday or Tuesday."

The next Monday, I met Johnny at his house, and he was still hurt. I asked Johnny, "Do you want to help me set up the motor measuring lab in your garage?" Johnny asked in response, "Will you party with us that night?" I replied, "Yes. I will get drunk and high with you if you want." I said, "I will even pay you $50 a month in lab rent." Johnny asked, "What night would you like this party?" I said happily, "I would like this party three weeks from this Friday." "I feel good again," Johnny replied, "At least you trust me." I replied, "I will let you influence me again. We will have a good time." For the three weeks after this discussion, we enjoyed our good times together.

On that mid-March Friday, I gathered my tools for my research project and took them to Johnny's house. When I arrived at his house, Johnny asked, "How are you?" "I am fine," I replied. "When are we going to get started setting up the lab?" Johnny said, "Give me ten minutes, but we can talk until I am ready." I explained, "This lab will be used to measure the dimensions of electric motor armature and motor field electromagnets. From these dimensions, I will run my program to simulate my perpetual motion motors and generators. I will simulate thousands of machines on my computer. This way, I can have a good machine when we enter the market." Johnny asked, "Will this machine run my house?" I replied, "This machine will run your house with no outside electricity or fuel if it works." I asked, "Would you like to have one for your house?" Johnny said, "I will let you test the first motor-generator on my house. It will save me money." I said, "We had better get out to the garage if we want to set up the lab tonight." Johnny said, "I am coming."

I said, "Johnny, we need to sweep and organize this garage," Johnny asked, "What do we do with the wood burning heater we used with the band?" I replied, "Keep it. I will buy it for $25. We need heat during the winter months. This heater will be a cheap source of winter heat." Johnny asked, "What about the bikes and toys?" I replied, "Put them against the wall. You can store your things if they are organized, and if my property is respected. I see a green shelf case. May I use that for storage?" Johnny replied, "Yes." I asked, "Would you put my toolbox on the bottom shelf?" Johnny said, "Hand me the toolbox." I handed him the toolbox, and he put it away. I asked, "Could you sweep the dirt into a pile while I put the motors on the shelf?" I put the motors away while Johnny finished cleaning. Johnny and I picked up the dirt and began to party.

After we finished the cleanup of the garage, Doug, Johnny, and I began to discuss the big party. Johnny said, "This is the big day you party with us." I replied, "This is the day that I drink and get high with the group." Johnny said with great joy, "We will play some bad tunes by Led Zeppelin. Let's turn the volume up as high as it will go. We want our neighbor, Denny, to know about this party. Denny was a massively overweight, long haired, bearded person. He was an unemployed computer programmer. He could barely walk around the block. He said he would be here in a half hour." We waited for an hour for Denny to show up. Afterward, we all decided to take a ride in Johnny's truck. We went to Denton to get good weed. We listened to Led Zeppelin and Kiss all the way to the south side of Denton, Texas. In Denton, Johnny bought the weed. The dealers described the weed as the best in North Texas. They said that this weed could corrupt even the best disciplined Christians in America. Johnny asked how much would this weed cost. The dealers would sell 5 ounces of weed for $25. After Johnny met with the dealers, we headed back to Ardmore anticipating how much fun we would have.

When we arrived at Johnny's House, we all sat in the living room, and Johnny gave me a beer. I drank it as I ate a bunch of pretzels. Then, Johnny gave me two other beers. I drank them as I ate potato chips. Then, he passed the joint around the room. I took four hits on the joint. Each time I took a hit, I inhaled deeply and coughed. After Johnny got me drunk and high, he noticed that I was less talkative than most nights. He seemed to like my high state. I told Johnny, "I am tired and burned out. I want to lay down on the couch." Johnny said, "Go ahead and lay on the couch and watch TV." After about 15 minutes, I fell asleep in front of Johnny's TV. After about an hour of sleeping, Johnny awoke me and asked, "Do you want to sleep on the couch?" I groggily replied, "Yes. I want to sleep right here. Pot only makes me tired and burned out. I can get the same effect studying JD Jackson's book *Classical Electrodynamics* for ten hours. If I study this book, I will learn a lot about physics and spend a lot less money." Johnny said in a reassuring voice, "You can dislike pot. I'm glad you at least tried it. This shows you at least trust me. Well, I will let you get to sleep." The next morning we went out to get coffee and doughnuts. After we had breakfast, I returned to Gainesville.

A few days later Tim Coleburn came to Johnny's house with two electric motors. I bought them for $30. I visited Johnny two days later, and Tim brought two more motors. I bought them for $25. Again three days later on a Thursday, Tim brought 3 motors. I paid him $30 for them. I told Tim that I had enough motors for my research. Tim took the initiative and got me a big electric motor. He offered me this motor for $30. I accepted this offer, but Johnny did not allow this motor in the lab. Johnny warned me that this motor may be stolen. I gave Tim the $30 for his effort and told him to return it to its owner. He gave me and Johnny an argument and tried to make us feel guilty. Johnny prevailed, and Tim took the motor away. After our argument with Tim, Johnny, his family, and I went out to dinner at My favorite Gainesville restaurant. At that restaurant, Johnny told me, "Tim Coleburn is trying to steal money from you." "How much?" I asked, "As much as he can get from you," Johnny replied in a concerned manner, "He is not a good friend to you. I am a good friend to you. I am trying to protect your money. It is hard to support a family, and money is tight for me. It must be valuable to you" I replied, "I don't have a lot of money to spare, but I care about you." Johnny replied as a good friend, "I also care about you." I said, "It is time to order." I ordered fried chicken and French fries. Johnny and Janie ordered spaghetti and meatballs. Hank ordered chicken and noodles with mashed potatoes. While we ate, we discussed the future of US Physics. After our meal and discussion, we said goodbye for the night.

On Tuesday April 16th, I went to visit Johnny like any other night. I saw cars belonging to Tim, Steve, and two other friends. I knocked on his door and nobody answered. I left to drive around for another half hour and came back to see if Johnny and his friends were back. I knocked on the door, and nobody answered, but it looked like his friends were hiding. I knocked again. I saw two people moving around. "Johnny may not like me anymore," I thought, "I'll drive around for another half hour and see if I can talk to him." I drove around for twenty minutes, saw the cars of Johnny's friends in the driveway, and knocked at his door. They still avoided me for the night. I drove home with doubts about my friendship with Johnny.

The next day I visited Johnny at 5 pm. I asked, "Are you mad at me?" "I am not mad at you," replied Johnny, "Why do you ask?" I replied, "I saw cars belonging to four of your other friends, but they did not answer the door. They chose to hide from me and avoid me." Johnny replied, "Some of my friends may have been there, but I was not at home. I still like you as a friend." I replied, "I am glad to hear that there is no problem. If there ever is a problem, please talk to me about it without avoiding me. I will regard this friendship as if last night never happened." The newspaper horoscope for April 16th said that this would be a bad day for close friendships. The same newspaper horoscope for April 17th said that this would be a good day for intimate relationships. The horoscope for April 18th said nothing about relationships and nothing happened. April 19th was supposed to be a good day for social life for both me and Johnny. We got together and spent two hours of quality time together playing euchre with Doug and Janie.

Although I normally did not look at newspaper horoscopes because I did not believe in them, I looked at my horoscope by chance and got correct results concerning my friendship with Johnny for four days straight. This seemed strange to me, "Could this be the hex Johnny is complaining about?" I thought, "A few months ago he had strange events concerning the phases of the moon. I only wish I knew that I was not losing a good friend.

The next Sunday and Tuesday, Johnny and I spent more quality time together. We played euchre both days with Janie and Doug. The horoscopes said that Sunday and Tuesday were good days for intimate friendships. Sunday and Tuesday were good days for me and Johnny. The horoscopes for last Saturday, Monday, Wednesday, and Thursday said nothing. Our group did nothing on those days even though Johnny and I had plans for Monday, Wednesday, and Thursday. That Friday, I caught Johnny at home. I asked, "What happened?" I added, "We were supposed to get together on Monday, Wednesday, and Thursday, but we didn't. It seems like you are upset at me about something." Johnny said, "We are good friends, but I can't tell you because you can't understand." I replied with worry, "I may not fully understand, but I will continue to be your friend if you give me a chance. First, you hide from me, and now, you keep avoiding me. If there is a problem, please tell me. I stand by my friends." Johnny's sister Melody said, "You and Johnny both are acting like kids." I replied, "I am only trying to protect my friendship with Johnny." Johnny said, "You have nothing to worry about." I asked with grave concern, "When do you want to see me again?" Johnny said in a stern voice, "Call before you come. If I am busy, I will let you know. I must get going. See you later." I headed home concerned about the future of my friendship with Johnny. On that Friday, my horoscope predicted a disaster for my social life and a day for Johnny to watch his social life. Johnny made me wonder if he liked me. The next day, Doug had me come and visit him. Johnny was not there. Doug and I had a good time for two hours, but he could say nothing about Johnny. I did not see Johnny that day. My horoscope predicted a good day for my social life, but it was neutral for Johnny.

I was afraid for the future of my friendship with Johnny. Thirteen newspaper horoscopes in a row and a six event coincidence of bad luck coinciding with the phases of the moon do not occur in nature, but rationality did not rule with me at that time. In the passion of my fear, I looked to the horoscopes to learn of my future friendship with Johnny. I should have prayed a little harder, but I loved Johnny as a good friend. I fell apart under the pressure concerning my friendship with him. I prayed to God for guidance concerning Johnny. I did not know what to do. I should have suspected a hex.

Sunday and Monday were neutral days for Johnny and I, and we did not see each other, even though we needed to talk about recent avoidance, resulting suspicion, and poor communication in our friendship. On Tuesday at about 5 pm, I called Johnny to see if it was all right to come over. Johnny said he was too busy to even talk with me. He said try me tomorrow. I said all right. Worried about the friendship, I went to Johnny's house to see if he was busy. He had other friends over, and I was not invited. I knocked on his door, and he let me in. Johnny asked, "What are you doing here!?" I asked, "Why did you avoid me tonight!?" Johnny angrily replied, "You don't trust me! You are here when I told you I was busy. That proves you don't trust me." I replied angry and concerned, "You don't give me a chance. You avoid me like I am not a friend and expect me to trust you when you do not keep your word with me. You said you were busy, and you have time for other friends. I will trust you as soon as you make and keep a few commitments concerning our friendship. If you make and keep a few commitments and stop avoiding me, I will trust you again." Johnny replied, "You are not going to come over all of the time." I asked, "Then what do you expect?" Johnny replied, "I need time with Janie. She is mad at me and may divorce me if I don't give her some time of her own." I replied, "Don't use your privacy as a weapon against this friendship! I will respect your phone and house if you treat me like a friend and keep your word with me." Johnny said, "I should be free tomorrow, but call me to be sure." I replied, "See you tomorrow." The horoscope for Tuesday said that Johnny and I would have a bad day socially. Wednesday was predicted by our horoscopes to be a bad day for relationships. On that Wednesday, I called Johnny. He was busy and did not want to talk with me. He said, "Call me Friday." He added, "I will be free for sure." I asked, "Are you sure? I really need to know you are still my friend." Johnny said, "You're still my friend." Johnny said, "See you on Friday." I respected his wishes, but Wednesday was a bad day for my friendship with Johnny, as predicted by my horoscope. My horoscope for Thursday was neutral, and nothing happened that day. Friday was predicted to be a bad day socially. I laughed at that horoscope. The horoscope was right. Something came up. Johnny had no time on Friday either. I was beginning to wonder if Johnny still liked me. He told me to call him at noon on Saturday May 4, 1985. I Thought, "Twenty newspaper horoscopes in a row correct and six bad luck events coinciding with the phases of the moon smack of witchcraft. I will pray concerning this situation. If that does not work, I will call my Occult Defense Commander, Robert Elight!"

On May 4, 1985, I woke up at 8:30 am and feared the worst. I read my horoscope, and it predicted the end of an important relationship. Johnny was my best friend until this problem started three weeks ago. For close to a year, we would see each-other at least three times a week, share dreams, and work together. My relationship seemed to be in jeopardy. I turned to the Lord in prayer and cried out for God to spare the friendship. I wept in desperation that

God would hear my cry. The spirit of the Lord came over me, and I told Satan, "Get out of Johnny's house, or I will ask God to throw you out!" I felt better for about three hours. At about 11:30 am, I began to worry about my friendship with Johnny. I turned to God, and he helped me get through that long half of an hour. I called Johnny at noon. He told me, "Come over at 4:00 pm. I will be glad to see you." God had spared Johnny's friendship, I rejoiced in the blessing of the Lord, but almost knew that this was a hex. Twenty correct predictions in a row from a newspaper horoscope and six terrible days coinciding with the phases of the moon reek of witchcraft or other Satanic intervention.

The probability of twenty consecutive newspaper horoscopes coming true can be estimated by assuming that the probability of a horoscope predicting a good day for a friendship that is active three or four times a week is 1 in 3, a bad day in 1 in 3, or a neutral or inactive day is 1 in 3. Under this assumption a good model is a spinner with three spaces. Space #1 corresponds with the number 1, space #2 corresponds with the number 2, and space #3 corresponds with the number 3. The probability of spinning a 1 is 1 in 3. The probability of spinning a 1 two consecutive times is 1 in 9 or 1 in 3 multiplied by itself 2 times. The probability of spinning a 1 three consecutive times is 1 in 3 multiplied by itself three times or 1 in 27. Similarly, the probability of spinning a 1 twenty consecutive times is 1 in 3 multiplied by itself twenty or about 1 in 3.5 trillion. Half the world's population would have to perform 400 spins to have 1 person get twenty consecutive 1's. Similarly, half of the world's population would have to perform 400 spins to have one person predict twenty of them consecutively. For twenty consecutive horoscopes to correctly predict good, bad, or neutral days for friendships, the probability is about one in 3.5 trillion under this model. Other alternative probability models give probabilities of one in a billion to one in a quadrillion. The probability of the six bad luck events coinciding with the phases of the moon in a 2-3-1-1-2-3 almost symmetric pattern a few months ago is one in 2 million. Since it must be assumed that the twenty consecutive horoscope predictions and the six bad luck events coinciding with the phases of the moon do not influence each other, these events are independent for probability calculating purposes. This means that the probability of the phases of the moon coincidence and the twenty correct horoscopes both occurring is the probability of the twenty consecutive horoscopes occurring times the probability of the phases of the moon coincidence. This probability is at most one in a quadrillion [4] or one followed by fifteen zeroes. This will happen in nature to one person out of six

---

4   Morris and Degroot. *"Elements of Statistics and Probability;"* Reading, Massachusetts: Addison-Wesley Publishing Company, 1975, pp.19-28, and pp. 39-45.

billion once every two-hundred years. This union of events looks

Calendar of Events Concerning My Friendship with Johnny Oilstring

April 1985						
1	2	3	4	5	6	
7	8	9	10	11	12	13
14	15	16 horo bad friend bad	17 horo good friend good	18 horo neutral friend neutral	19 Horo good friend good	20 Horo neutral friend neutral
21 Horo good friend good	22 Horo neutral friend neutral	23 Horo good friend good	24 horo neutral friend neutral	25 horo neutral friend neutral	26 Horo bad friend bad	27 Horo* neutral friend neutral
28 horo neutral friend neutral	29 horo neutral friend neutral	30 horo bad friend bad				

Notes: Horo=Horoscope   Friend = Friendship
* This is for my friendship with Johnny Oilstring. I had a good day with Doug. My horoscope predicted a good day for my social life.

May 1985

			1	2	3	4
			horo	horo	horo	horo
			bad	neutral	neutral _bay_	bad
			friend	friend	friend	friend
			bad	neutral	neutral _bad_	prayer #
5	6	7	8	9	10	11
12	13	14	15	16	17	18
19	20	21	22	23	24	25
26	27	28	29	30	31	

Notes: Horo = Horoscope   Friend = Friendship   # = Prayer answered friendship good
Calendar of events described on pp. 64-69 76-79

supernaturally engineered by witches! Little did I know that Johnny's hex started with an "accident" staged by a warlock involved in currency manipulation in New York or Europe.

"Kevin, are you going to Gerard Chrispeace' wedding at 1 o'clock?" asked Mom, "Yes, I am," I replied, "I was so worried about another friendship that I nearly forgot. Maybe Robert's Mom can pray for my friend. I will get dressed real fast and meet Gerard." Gerard Chrispeace was an old friend who was a short and stocky in appearance. At Gerard's wedding, I gave Gerard best wishes and asked his old friend, Jimmy Raker, to pray for Johnny, "Would you pray for my new friend, Johnny?" I asked Jimmy, "Johnny appears to be a victim of witchcraft. Twenty horoscopes concerning Johnny all predicted disastrous problems for our friendship and his life. If Johnny is not hexed, he is rightly very discouraged." Jimmy replied, "You should not read horoscopes. I replied, "If I would not have read those horoscopes, I would not have known to pray for Johnny. Please forgive me Lord Jesus. Jimmy please ask Jesus to help Johnny." Jimmy replied, "I will definitely ask Jesus to help Johnny. Let's find a seat, so we can watch Gerard get married." The bridesmaids and the groomsmen came into the room and took their seats. The church organ played the "Wedding March" as the bride and groom came into the room. Gerard's wife to be is named Kerri. Kerri is a medium height, clear complected, and friendly woman worthy of Gerard's hand in marriage. Bishop Stern gave a brief sermon and asked, "Gerard, do you take Kerri as your wife? To love her in sickness and health, rich or poor till death do us part?" Gerard said, "I do." Bishop Stern asked, "Kerri, do you take Gerard as your husband? To love him in sickness or health, rich or poor till death do us part?" Kerri said, "I do." Bishop Stern said, "I now pronounce you man and wife. Gerard, "You may kiss the bride." The wedding party and all of the guests went to the front of the church and threw rice on Gerard and Kerri. Everyone went to the church kitchen for the reception. Robert's Mom said, "Look at all that chicken, potato chips, and smashed potatoes. Eat away." While I was gobbling down the food, Gerard came to me and asked, "How are you doing?" I replied, "Fine. Would you be interested in meeting my other best friend, Johnny?" Gerard said, "I live by the Junior College and would love to see both you and Johnny." I said to Gerard, "It is about 3:45. I told Johnny that I would see him at 4:00. I need to be going." Gerard said, "Thanks for coming to my wedding. I was glad to see you. I wish you luck with Johnny."

I met Johnny at 4:00. Johnny asked, "How is my good friend doing?" I replied, "Fine. I am glad to see that we are still friends. You seemed mad at me. When I am respected, I trust you. I just need you to treat me like a friend. This hostility only causes me to doubt you. I honestly hurt when you hurt. Give me the chance." Johnny replied, "I am sorry. I really like you as my friend, but Janie and I need time to ourselves. I am glad you respect my wishes concerning my wife. I am sorry to ask you to read my mind." I gladly said, "I look forward to seeing my good friend and like you as a best friend." Johnny asked, "Do you want to go with me to pick up my truck?" I replied, "Yes." As Johnny drove to the mechanic's garage, he asked, "Do you want to take Dawn to the prom and have sex with her afterward?" Dawn was a medium height, pleasingly plump teenage friend of Johnny's band. I replied, "I will gladly take Dawn to the prom, but I must think twice before having sex." Johnny replied, "I am glad that you are dating Dawn. I hope you will get romantic and have sex." Doug said, "I will also have a date," Doug declared, "I will corrupt Kevin. He will enjoy it." Johnny picked up his truck, drove it home. He arranged to play euchre with me and Doug on Monday.

Later that day, I was watching the ten o'clock news on channel 8. I heard on the news that Kent State University's hippies were happier at this moment than the Board of Judges of Texas. I wondered how Johnny Oilstring fell under the occult. God answered my prayers as far away as Kishinev, Russia. I successfully prayed for God to stabilize the US dollar in 1978 out of fear of a Great Depression. In 1980, Robert Elight and I defeated one of the worst satanic influences in the fiberglass industry. In October of 1983, I prayed and fasted for peace in the Strait of Hormuz. Iran threatened to close this strait and block much of the free world's oil shipments. Iran was backed by the powerful Soviet Union. Like an arrogant professor, I commanded Satan to leave the Strait of Hormuz. Perhaps other Christians prayed for the same thing. There was peace in the strait until 1987. Then, the Soviets were too broke to help Iran. I thought that the board of Judges was invulnerable to an occult attack. The Board of Judges faced a hex that felt like Pearl Harbor. This hex involved manipulations of time and chance against my friendship with Johnny Oilstring. It smacked of retaliation against my prayer concerning the US currency in 1978. The hippies and Kent State officials seemingly were at peace. President Michael Schwartz and his executives seemed to be friends with the hippies. This was a happy time for the Kent State hippies. "I could only wish I were friends with those hippies." I thought. "I rejoice in their present joy. I wish Johnny and I were closer. Perhaps, someday Gainesville Security Central and the SDS could be friends. Lord please forgive me for having such an idealistic dream. It never will happen." The Lord replied in a still small voice, "I will give you friendship with these hippies." He added, "It shall make you happy." "Thank you Jesus!" I replied, "Just help me understand Johnny and his friends. Perhaps this will make me worthy of Kent State." "Have patience," the still soft voice of the Lord said, "Those hippies will be your best friends. I love them too. I will give your friendship with Johnny my guidance and support." I said with great joy, "Thank you Jesus! Amen!"

I met Johnny at his house on Monday May 6, 1985. There, Johnny, Doug, Janie, and I met to play euchre. Johnny and I played on one team, and Janie and Doug played on the other team. Johnny said, "Your turn to deal, Kevin." I dealt a winning hand to my team. My team won ten out of fifteen hands to win the first match. Then we played a second match. During the fifth hand of the second match, Johnny said, "I am going on nights at Texhoma Box and Crate, so I will only be here on Sundays." I asked, "How do I contact you on these Sundays?" "Call me at about two in the afternoon," Johnny said, "I should be here." Janie said, "You will not see Johnny as much as he says you will." I asked Johnny, "Is everything all right between us?" Johnny angrily asked Janie, "Why do you act so poorly towards my friends?" Janie said, "I think some of your friends are gay." I angrily replied, "I will do my best to respect your marriage, but I need a little respect! Tell me what you can do. If it is reasonable, I will understand." Johnny said, "Janie apologize to Kevin." "I am sorry," Janie said. "You can see Johnny on Sundays." I said, "Apology accepted." We all played four more hands of euchre. On the fifth hand, I said, "This move at Texhoma Box and Crate looks like a move to cover up this hex against you." Johnny asked, "What hex?" I replied, "This bad luck you were complaining about follows some predictable patterns. A few months ago you had six bad luck events which coincided with the phases of the moon. Just recently, newspaper horoscopes predicted the good, bad and do nothing days for our friendship twenty times straight. The probability of these things both happening in nature is estimated at less than one in a quadrillion. This seems to establish a hex. Once a hex is established, any bad luck is suspicious." I warned, "I will be watching for signs of this hex." Johnny said, "I told them that I cannot work nights, but they made me work nights anyway." I replied with sympathy, "I understand your situation. I suggest that you start looking for a job in case this one does not work. I suspect this job change is connected with your hex." Johnny said, "I will go on days as soon as possible, but I must make a living." I asked, "Is my date with Dawn still on?" Johnny said, "Doug will help you with that date to the prom." Doug said, "Go to the Tux Shop to order your tuxedo tomorrow." He added, "Meet me at Johnny's at five o'clock Friday." We finished our euchre match. I said, "I must be going." Doug said, "See you Friday." Johnny said, "Ill see you Friday or Sunday."

I met Doug at Johnny's house on Friday at five o'clock sharp with tuxedo in hand. I put on the tuxedo and Doug helped me look sharp in it. He straightened my tie and combed my hair. He put on his tuxedo and we both looked sharp. We headed to Dawn's house in Gainesville, Texas to pick up Dawn and Jill. When we arrived at Dawn's house, Dawn introduced her friends to us. She said, "Kevin and Doug, This is Jill." I said, "Pleased to meet you, Jill." Doug and I talked as Dawn and Jill got ready for Gainesville High School's prom. Dawn was glad to go to the prom, but I was a lousy date. The Oilstring hex was on my mind. This bored Dawn to tears. After the prom, Doug still wanted me to sleep with Dawn. We proceeded to Johnny's house. We waited for an hour, but did not see Johnny. Doug, Jill, Dawn, and I proceeded to I-77 and went through Marietta, Oklahoma. As we headed towards the cabin where we were to spend the night, I prayed that God would not let me and Dawn have sex. Doug arrived at the cabin to find it locked. We proceeded to Johnny's house. It was three in the morning, so I headed to Ardmore without having sex with Dawn. God had delivered me. I never put myself in that situation again.

On Sunday at two o'clock, I called Johnny. Nobody was home. We fought so much in the last month, I wondered if we really resolved our problems. I tried him at three. I got no answer. I tried at four. I still got no answer. Tried at five ten times in an hour and got a busy signal every time. I called Denny. Denny went to Johnny's house and got Johnny to talk to me. He had me come over and play euchre. When I arrived, I asked Johnny, "Am I trying to see you at the right time? It seems like you are still mad at me." "Janie left the phone off of the hook," said Johnny, "I am sorry this happened. I will try to do better. Want a couple slices of pizza?" I replied, "All is forgiven." Johnny said, "We will normally get together on Sunday afternoons and evenings if you are free at these times. In two weeks me and Janie are spending the weekend at a hotel to get away from it all." I said, "That is all right. At least you are telling me what to expect and avoiding hostility. Let's eat pizza and play euchre." We played euchre until ten o'clock at night and had a good time.

On the next Sunday at five o'clock, we got together to play euchre. Johnny and I had a good time beating Janie and Doug. Johnny and I won 10 out of sixteen hands of euchre. Doug proposed that Johnny be on his team and Janie be my partner. Johnny and Doug beat Janie and I 10 out of 18 hands. This contest seemed to prove that Johnny and I were good euchre players. Some would say that Johnny was the winner.

After those two euchre matches, Johnny, Doug, and I went upstairs to the family room in the attic to talk about the apparent hex and have a good time afterward. There, we held an informal security meeting concerning the Oilstring hex, the future of US Physics, and the Board of Judges of Texas. The meeting started with me saying, "These twenty consecutive horoscopes concerning our friendship are serious evidence of a hex against you by the occult community of Ardmore, Oklahoma. I suspect that these sorcerers planned your night shift at Texhoma Box and Crate. The Occult Defense Command at Elight Island Security Central is watching because we think that an occult attack is going to hit when Gainesville Security Central and Elight Island are not watching." Doug asked, "What do you propose to do about this situation?" I replied in a military fashion, "I propose as the President of the Board of Judges of Texas that we do a Jericho run around this neighborhood. We will drive around this neighborhood seven times and order Satan and his demons to leave this house by praying to Jesus Christ. We will start at the intersection of US 199 and US 77 (Map 5). We will proceed down US 199 to state road 142. We will follow state road 142 north to state road 142 west. We will turn left on state road 142 west and proceed to US 77. At US 77, we turn left and drive to US 199 and turn left. We repeat this route six more times. While driving this route we will be fasting and praying for Johnny Oilstring. After this Jericho run, Johnny will be free of this hex." Johnny replied, "Let's wait to take action. I do not want to chase witches unless it is absolutely necessary." I replied, "I respect your wishes, but I think you are taking a big chance with your soul and your freedom." Johnny said, "Just wait. I will be all right." I replied, "I will respect your wishes. Just call me if you need me." Johnny said, "I will be there for you. Thanks my good friend! By the way, you are invited to eat with Janie and me at Hacienda Restaurant on Friday before we go to our hotel." I replied, "Thanks for inviting me and treating me like a friend. I will gladly see you at your house at five o'clock on Friday afternoon."

At Gainesville's Hacienda Restaurant, Johnny, Doug, Janie, and, I met to eat a good dinner. We met in the lobby and waited for twenty minutes. While waiting, Johnny asked, "Will you take care of Janie if something happens to me in the course of duty, such as marketing your invention against America's big businesses?" I replied, "I cannot marry Janie, but she will inherit your

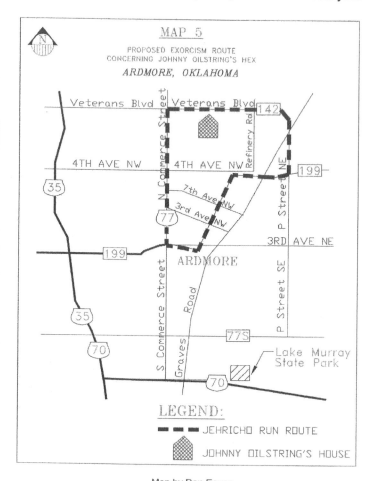

Map by Dan Eaves

share of US Physics. You will be rewarded if you die or become incompetent. I know that you love your three year old son, Hank, and your wife, Janie." Johnny said, "Time to get our table." We proceeded to our table and ordered our drinks. We all ordered Cokes. Then, it came time to order our meals. Johnny ordered tacos. Doug ordered a burrito with a fajita. Janie ordered a taco and all you can eat chili. I was the oddball. I ordered chicken, French fries, and corn in place of salad. "You are ordering chicken," said Johnny in a surprised voice. He added, "The Colonel makes chicken. You are at a Mexican restaurant. Be adventurous. Order Mexican." I replied, "Being with my friends make this outing fun." Johnny said, "I am not mad if you eat chicken, but you should try tacos." I asked, "May I order my chicken if I try a piece of your taco?" Johnny replied, "You may order chicken and try a piece of a taco." I replied, "Let's have a good time and enjoy ourselves. We will not see each other for a week." We all had a good time for an hour, and I returned home.

On that Tuesday, I was to see Robert Elight at his house. I said, "I am seriously concerned about the events at Johnny Oilstring's house." Robert asked, "Why?" I replied with great concern, "First, Johnny loses his band, blows a rod on his truck, and has his family get sick in accordance with the phases of the moon. Then, the events of my life and Johnny's life are predicted accurately by the horoscopes in the newspaper twenty days straight. Just one week ago, Jim Ratman, one of Johnny's neighborhood friends, pretends to be the devil in Johnny's neighborhood. I think that this neighborhood may be hexed. Should we consider military action against the Occult Community of Ardmore, Oklahoma?" Robert asked, "Are you sure that this is witchcraft?" I replied, "The probability of this union of events is conservatively estimated at less than 1 in a quadrillion." Robert asked, "Can you further analyze the moon and horoscope data?" I replied, "I could investigate further if we had time, but Johnny may be dead if we don't help him." I asked, "Can we have another meeting one week from tonight?" Robert replied, "Let's get together next week to discuss this possible hex. Let's be safe concerning Johnny."

Five days later on June 2, 1985, I was running late returning from my normal Sunday drive, so I proceeded to the pay phones at the mall. There, I popped a quarter in the machine and called Johnny's house. Doug answered the phone. I asked, "Is Johnny there?" Doug answered, "Johnny is there, but he cannot come to the phone because he is having family problems." I replied with great anxiety, "I must have contact with Johnny. Johnny and I can only talk once a week, and I need to talk to him. There could be a problem with an occult attack, and I must speak to him to confirm that he is all right." Doug replied, "I will see what I can do." I replied, "I pray for Johnny that God protects him and blesses him." Doug said, "I need to see you. Please come over." I replied, "I will be right over."

I left the mall. I rushed over to Johnny's house, and found Johnny waiting for me on his front porch. Johnny came to my car and told me that he needed to talk with me. I picked Johnny up and went for a ride. "I had a bad night last night," Johnny said, "My wife's aunt took her away for no reason. I tried to stop Janie's aunt, but the police came in force. I had to give in to them. My wife is not home with me. She is mad at me, and I don't know what to do." As we headed north on I-35, I asked, "What can I do?" Johnny said, "If you are going to do something, do it now." I was surprised to learn that Johnny and his wife Janie were about to get a divorce. I replied in a serious and assertive manner, "I am going to start with immediate protective prayer. It will take me 48 hours to mobilize. I am going to conduct a defensive exorcism raid on your house. This raid will commence when I leave for an occult defense meeting at Robert Elight's house in McKinney, Texas (Map 6). On this exorcism route, I will pray for God to stop your ungodly bad luck. By my faith in God, I say this. When I hit (arrive at) the US 75 bridge in Sherman, Texas, thus Saith the Lord, God of Israel, "This ungodly hex shall cease to exist and judgment will fall on these sorcerers who dare to hurt the least of my people." By the time I get to Robert's house, this hex shall be history. You will only feel trials relating to its aftermath." Johnny asked, "What can I do to help?" I replied, "Do not tell anybody about this exorcism raid until you hear from me. Nobody knows about this military action, not even Robert Elight. The board of Judges of Texas will surprise and defeat the Occult Community of Ardmore, Oklahoma through the power of Jesus Christ and the element of surprise. This is why you must keep this secret." Johnny replied, "It is nice to know that you are looking out for me." I replied, "I hurt when you hurt. Jesus loves you and wants to save your soul." As we arrived at Johnny's house, Johnny said, "Doug also wants to see you."

I picked up Doug. He wanted me to drive to Dawn's house. On my way to Dawn's house, I said, "Johnny appears to be under a hex. Horoscopes, this ridiculous separation, and his accident of seven years ago point to a very viscous but subtle hex. This hex at times haunted Johnny's friends and even some of his employers. Within 48 hours, the Board of Judges of Texas will be involved in a major occult war. Over a year ago, God told me to talk to some Kent State hippies. Fearing that I would lose contact with Robert Elight, I went to see him instead. When I confronted Robert about this, God came over me and caused me to say, "There is going to be a major occult war. Its final battle will be at Kent State University. Its hero will be a Kent State hippie. The name of Billy Glassman comes to mind. The name of Freddie also comes to mind. He shall be a major friend like you." Final victory may go through the Kent State hippies." We arrived at Dawn's house. I sat there praying for Johnny and talking to the friendly women. Doug tried to get a date with Jill. Doug and the women talked for two hours and I prayed for Johnny and Janie. Doug asked, "Do you want to get going?" I replied, "The sooner we get to Johnny's house, the sooner Johnny and I can eat." Doug said, "Hey girls, I must get going." On my way to the car, Doug asked, "Why don't you ask Dawn out for another date?" I replied, "There may be a major occult war in 48 hours. I must pray for Johnny and his wife." We arrived at Johnny's house. There, I invited Johnny to a dinner at the my favorite Gainesville restaurant. Johnny and I temporarily forgot about our problems as we ate chicken, French fries, and smashed potatoes. We went home and to be with our families.

On Tuesday June 4, 1985 at 6:30 pm Central Daylight Time, I called Robert. Robert answered saying, "How are you doing?" I replied, "Fine. Just calling to find out if it is all right to come over." Robert said, "I will be looking

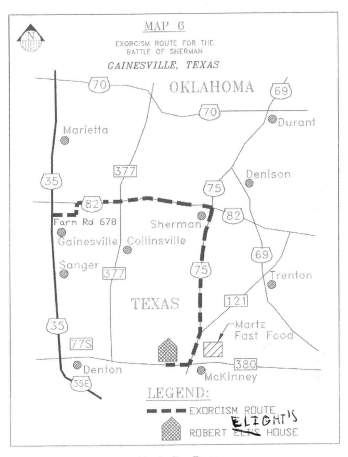

Map by Dan Eaves

forward to seeing you." I replied, "See you in a half hour. Bye!" I left for Robert's house to embark on a very dangerous occult defense mission. I was backslid and needed to ask God for forgiveness in order to be effective. When I hit California road at Rosewood Lane, I could have been intercepted by the occult community of Ardmore and hexed because I was not right with God. I prayed that God would give me the right attitude for repentance all the way to the first gravel road (Map 6). After I passed the first gravel road, I wept and cried for the Lord to forgive my sins, such as smoking pot, drinking, and almost having sex with Dawn, for the sake of Johnny Oilstring. As I hit the second gravel road, I began to rejoice that the Lord had forgiven my sins. I rejoiced all the way to the high tension power lines, to the north bend of Farm Road 678. At the north bend, I followed the curve. As I proceeded toward US 82, A still soft voice said, "I will deliver Johnny and his household from this hex. This hex is a stench in my nostrils." When I hit US 82, I began to rejoice that Johnny was about to be delivered of this hex. Meanwhile, in Marietta, Oklahoma, the Occult Community of Ardmore, Oklahoma happened to be together on Presto Avenue. The four sorcerers of the Occult Community of Ardmore, Oklahoma, were named Antwan, Mar, Dogfish, and Monster. Antwan and Monster put the hex on Johnny years ago and were about to face the judgment of God for their sins. As I hit US 82, I began to pray in tongues for Johnny Oilstring and his household. As I proceeded east on US 82, I believed that the hex against Johnny and his household was removed. As I hit the US 75 overpass, the hex was gone. Meanwhile, in Marietta, Antwan and Monster cried out an incantation and said, "Abra cadabra, let Johnny Oilstring be hexed again." They tried to put the hex on Johnny again. God had enough. He cast the demons out of Antwan and Monster and broke their power to commit witchcraft. Antwan asked Mar to check his crystal ball to determine what hindered Antwan's hex. Mar looked into the crystal ball, and he saw the God of Israel. God was mad! Mar said, "I saw the God of Israel in my crystal ball. He means business! We had better back off of the Oilstring hex before God breaks our power, or worse before He strikes us dead!" The warlocks took Mar's advice seriously and gave up on the Oilstring hex. Back in Sherman, a still soft voice told me that the sorcerers planned to put the hex right back on Johnny as soon as I stopped praying. I asked God to break the power of those sorcerers who hexed Johnny. After I hit the next exit on US 75, The Occult Community of Ardmore was defeated, and their power was broken. I rejoiced all the way to Robert's house in McKinney.

On Tuesday June 4, 1985 at 7:00 pm Central Daylight Time, I asked Robert, "How are you?" I replied, "Fine. I rebuked the occult community of Ardmore, Oklahoma and broke the power of the witches responsible for the Oilstring hex. The God of Israel has delivered Johnny from a bad hex." Robert said, "Let's celebrate the victory." Robert gathered everybody in the family room for a cookout. Robert made enough hamburgers to feed a big army, potato chips to feed ten pigs, hot-dogs to feed a navy, and enough pop to feed everybody three times. Robert talked about his girlfriend and the party. Everybody had a good time until 10:00 pm when they went home. I would see Robert about once a week throughout the summer.

On Thursday, Dad received a call from a man claiming to be a bail bondsman. He claimed that I posted bail for Johnny Oilstring, and Johnny skipped bail. After work, I went to the Gainesville Police to check out this warrant. A clerk in the police department checked this warrant and found nothing. This clerk said that collectors were harassing and there was nothing to worry about. I returned home to be asked about my relationship with Johnny. I told him that collectors likely were harassing about Johnny's past due credit card payments. Dad disapproved of my friendship with Johnny. He said that I was never to see Johnny again. I secretly disobeyed my father and saw him anyway that same night. He asked for me to give him and Janie an Anniversary present. They wanted a weekend away from home together in a hotel. As an Anniversary present, I paid for their hotel room. They wanted to have a good and romantic time together. I gave them this present and they spent the next weekend together.

On Tuesday, Johnny surprised me with a terrible call. To my surprise, Janie left Johnny. She left him to see her evil aunt. She took all of the pictures of her and Hank and even took Hank. Hank cried that he wanted to see his daddy. Janie did not care. Johnny and I took a drive around Gainesville and cried. When I was driving down US 82 west of I-35, Johnny cried with great passion, "She is gone! She is gone!." I cried for Johnny, prayed to God and said, "I am your friend even if Janie does not love you. I pray that Janie comes back to you. Do you want to come to a Bible study at the First Apostolic Church? There, the church can pray for the marriage." Johnny replied, "I will go to church unless Janie gives that all important call." Johnny and I returned to Johnny's house and Johnny immediately called Janie's aunt and asked to speak to Janie. The aunt of the family did not let Johnny speak to her. Johnny was hurt. Johnny asked, "Do you think Janie will ever come back?" I replied with great sympathy, "Janie will come back if you show her that you love her. Try to be Janie's friend. No marriage has a chance unless the partners are good friends." Johnny replied, "It hurts now. I just need a friend until my marriage is healed." I replied, "I am your friend until that happens." Johnny went to the church on Wednesday. Johnny and I prayed for his marriage. Johnny told me to meet him Friday at his house. I met him Friday at his house. He wasn't there. He was back with his wife at her aunt's house. He was bringing Janie back home. Johnny was happy.

One week later, Johnny would tell me of the anxieties he faced concerning Janie. Johnny said, "I try to love Janie, but I cry when I remember that she cheated on me." I replied, "Try to remember that you forgave her, and she loves you." Johnny replied, "I just seem to lose my feelings for her every time I see her and remember that she cheated." I asked, "Why don't you ask God to help you get over the hurt?" I added, "Maybe you should take her out to dinner and have a good time together." Johnny replied, "Prayer and dinner are a good idea. I'll do just that." Throughout the summer, Johnny cried on my shoulder concerning Janie and showed her love. His relationship with his wife improved greatly through that time.

We also had our times of talking about my dreams and hopes that summer. One such time we went to the my favorite restaurant to eat dinner. There, we talked about the progress on Project Texhoma. I asked Johnny, "How are you." Johnny replied, "Fine. I am getting along with my wife better. Prayer and quality time seem to be working. How is Project Texhoma coming?" I replied, "I am glad to hear you and your wife are getting along better. I have just run my first computer simulation of my perpetual motion motor on the computer. It was a ten horsepower version. It was 700% efficient. I need to do thousands of simulations on my ten horsepower version, thousands of simulations on my one horsepower version, thousands of simulations on my one hundred horsepower version, and eventually thousands of simulations of my ten thousand horsepower version, thousands of simulations of my one hundred thousand horsepower version, and thousands of simulations of one million horsepower version. How much power is needed to run a rock concert?" Johnny replied, "Probably about one hundred kilowatts. Maybe it requires a thousand kilowatts." I replied, "That will be a motor of one hundred and fifty horsepower to fifteen hundred horsepower. What kinds of rock groups would be interested?" Johnny replied, "Look to the idealistic hippies. Some modern heavy metal bands are good. These modern bands have name recognition and have acts which use a lot of power." I replied, "These are all good ideas. It makes me anxious to work on the project." The waitress came in and took our orders. I ordered fried chicken and mashed potatoes. Johnny ordered meat-loaf and a baked potato. We enjoyed our food, talked for an hour, joked around some, and returned home.

Little did I realize, fears concerning Big RV foretold in the Gainesville dreams were the reason that Robert was there to help fight the Oilstring hex. If The Board of Judges of Texas had not prayed for Johnny concerning his marriage or drove the exorcism raid in Sherman, Johnny may have been dead or had his marriage and life ruined by this vicious hex. Gainesville Security Central stopped this hex in Sherman, Texas. Needless to say, it would have been impossible for us to share our dreams or to have Johnny's assistance on Project Texhoma if this hex prevailed.

CHAPTER 6

THE BATTLE OF ARLINGTON

After a summer of being a friend to Johnny and Robert, It was time to study physics at Arlington State University. My academic adviser assigned me to work-study tutoring in the department's study room and picked out my classes for me. My academic adviser was a moderately plump, middle aged conservative who wore a cowboy hat. After I registered for classes, I headed for my dorm-room. In the elevator, I met Ron Christman, a geology graduate student. I said, "Hi, my name is Kevin." Ron said, "My name is Ron." He added, "I am a geology student with a bachelor's degree in architecture." I said, "I am a physics graduate student and an accomplished Christian." I asked, "Can I help you move in?" Ron said, "I am already close to being moved in." He said, "I am tired from moving." He asked, "Can we talk tonight?"

Ron was a conscientious graduate student. His medium build, clean shaven, short haired, and neat appearance made him look the part. Later that night, Ron and I talked in his dorm-room. Ron asked, "Would you like to see my drawings of an earth sample from Colorado." "Yes. I would," I replied. Ron got out his pictures and showed me the various soil layers. Ron said, "This top layer is topsoil, this middle layer is subsoil, and this bottom layer is bedrock. I took this sample on a field trip with the department last summer." I said, "I have a good friend named Johnny Oilstring. I prayed for him all summer. It started with a prayer I said on June 4 of this last summer while I was on US 82 driving near the Sherman city limits. I asked God to stop a string of bad luck that looked a lot like a hex. God stopped this string of bad luck and broke the powers of the guilty sorcerers. I am happy God was there for Johnny. I transferred from West Virginia University because I failed my qualifying exam. I am committed to graduate from this school with a master's degree."

After one week at The Arlington State University, I had perfect scores on all of my physics papers and was averaging straight A's. My academic adviser called me in his office to give me a much needed assistantship. I signed the papers and rejoiced all day long. That night I would get a call from Johnny Oilstring. "Could you please give me $600?" Johnny said in a fearful voice, "Unless I get the money to pay the mortgage on my house, the bank will foreclose tomorrow. I am scared." I Asked, "How do I get this money to you?" "Wire it to me," replied Johnny. I asked, "How do I know you have it?" Johnny replied, "I don't know." I asked, "Could I drive it to Ardmore?" Johnny said, "If you can get it here in four hours, it will be appreciated." I replied, "I'll get on the road right now, and you will have it."

I proceeded to my Arlington bank and withdrew $600. As I started on I-20 west, I asked God in prayer, "Why should I deliver this money to Johnny? Johnny was told that I had no more money." About then, the still small voice of God said, "I will provide for you if you help Johnny." As I proceeded to I-35 north, I started to pray for Johnny. I knew that God led me to help Johnny, but I was afraid of not having enough money for college. I continued to pray. As I reached US 82, I got some potato chips and gas. Then, I proceeded to Denny's house. Denny said, "Johnny will pay you back this Sunday. Thanks for helping Johnny in his hour of need." I drove back thankful that Johnny's house was safe. In my dorm-room bed that night, I asked God, "Will Johnny pay me back?" A still soft voice of God said, "I will provide for you even if Johnny never pays you back."

That Sunday, I was to meet Johnny at his house. I waited for three hours and did not find him there. Denny was upset that Johnny did not show up. I just asked Denny to tell Johnny that I am still his friend even if he does not pay back the $600. I went back to Arlington hurt that Johnny did not even talk to me. The next Sunday, I returned to Johnny's House. He was fixing his bathroom. I asked Johnny, "When can you pay me back the $600 that you owe me?" Johnny replied, "It will be a month before I can even begin to make monthly payments. This bathroom unexpectedly gave out. It is going to cost more than $600 to repair. I am sorry for this emergency. I was scared that you would not forgive me." I was relieved, "I will be your friend even if you do not pay," I replied. "I will not loan you money for a while, but I am your friend even if you can't pay me back." I went back to Arlington very happy that Johnny still seemed to be a good friend. Two weeks later, I returned to Johnny's house to ask if he could start payments. Johnny said, "I am completely wiped out financially." I replied, "We are still good friends. I will need God's help to make it through school. I may need to return home for one semester to earn money. Pray for me that I can get that assistantship next semester. I like you Johnny. Just pray for me." Johnny said, "I will pray for you, and God will bless you for helping me." Though Johnny never paid me back in cash, God provided for me. Johnny will have repaid me by doing some drawings for me a few months later.

On my way back to Arlington, I prayed for God to provide my needs, "Work at your Dad's company every weekend," the still soft voice of God said, "If you repair molds every weekend, I shall provide your needs and fix your family life. Your Dad is in trouble, and he needs you just as much as you need my help. Through work at Family Fiberglass and your assistantship, I will provide for you." I trusted God and began to live from day to day. I paid the rent due for October and had enough for the rest of the month.

On the last Friday of October, something horrible happened. A newspaper of local interest brought up Johnny Oilstring's 1978 accident. I was outraged. With the help of students from Arlington State University English department, I wrote a letter to the editor rebuking the newspaper. The newspaper published my comments and those connected with haunting Johnny apologized.

The next weekend, I came back to see Johnny. I drove by his house three times on Saturday and Sunday, But Johnny was not home. I drove to Steve and Melody's house. Johnny's truck was there. I knocked at the door. Steve answered and said, "Johnny is not here." I replied, "Johnny's truck is here. I know he is here." Steve replied, "No he isn't!" I replied, "I'll drive around and check back later." I drove around for an hour and returned to Steve's trailer. Steve again insisted that Johnny was not there. I drove around for another half of an hour. I drove up and finally saw Johnny. I asked Johnny, "Is everything all right between us?" I said," You seem to be avoiding me." Johnny replied, "I was just running errands when you came to see me earlier." Johnny asked, "Would you come to my birthday party this Saturday, at 8 pm?" I replied, "Yes. I will gladly come." Johnny and I talked for a half hour. Afterward, I headed to Arlington to study for my Thermodynamics and Quantum Mechanics exams.

I studied hard for my Quantum Mechanics exam on Monday night. I reviewed Hamiltonians, commutators, basic equations and concepts, potential wells and definitions. Tuesday at 1pm, I took the exam. At first the exam seemed hard. After a half hour, It all came together. I knew that I made an A or B on the exam and probably had an 'A' in Quantum Mechanics. That Tuesday night, I celebrated by eating at the local restaurant. Wednesday, I graded my final batch of papers and studied for my thermodynamics exam. I reviewed the differential, partial derivatives, Gibbs functions, and problems early in the book. I took the exam at 1 pm Thursday. I struggled with it for an hour. The exam came to me after an hour. I set up all of the problems and completed half of them. I thought I had a B in thermodynamics, and I was stressed out. I left the exam and headed for my dorm-room to pack my bags for Gainesville, Texas. As I approached the entrance to the residence hall, Ron Christman came to me panicked. "Some sorcerers came up to me and told me of the June 4 exorcism raids in Sherman," Ron said in a fearful voice. "They asked where you were. I told them that I did not know and would not tell if I knew." I replied, "I will pray that God protects you. You should be all right through the break. Don't worry. God is with you, and he is more powerful than those warlocks." Ron replied, "Thanks for your help. See you next quarter!" I replied, "See you Later." I headed to Gainesville with my last $10. God had provided for my first quarter.

This show of terrorism by the Occult Community of Ardmore, Oklahoma was a warning of things to come for the next three weeks. I worked at Family Fiberglass Friday and Saturday morning. I earned enough to get through the week. That Saturday night, I showed up for Johnny's party. I asked Johnny, "How are you?" Johnny replied, "Fine." Johnny said, "There are potato chips and pop, so dig in." Later that night, we played monopoly, and Johnny offered me a drink of wine. I slowly drank the wine. When I finished, he gave me another. After I drank the wine, I fell asleep. I woke up at 11:30. Johnny drove my car to the gates of Wheeler Creek. There, I said goodbye to Johnny and drove my car safely home down the side streets of Wheeler Creek. On that Monday, I tried to see Johnny. His truck was there, but the person answering the door said Johnny was not home. I tried again to see Johnny on Tuesday, Friday and Saturday afternoon only to see his truck and be told he was not home.

That Saturday afternoon, I met with Occult Defense Commander Robert Elight. I told Robert, "Johnny seems to be avoiding me for no apparent reason. Every time this happens, it can be explained by him being stressed out or an outright hex. It looks like demon oppression." Robert replied, "Johnny is acting strangely. Are there any other signs?" I replied, "Ron Christman, a friend from Arlington State University, said that witches from Marietta asked him where I was because of a prayer for Johnny in June concerning his hex. This scared Ron. He thought that he was in danger." Robert said, "This looks bad." I asked Robert, "Should we encourage Johnny's friends to boycott pornography from Marietta and Ardmore or declare a day of fasting and prayer?" Robert replied, "A day of fasting and prayer is the only solution to this problem." We declared this day on the second Friday of the new quarter at the university.

At 8 pm that evening, I tried again to visit Johnny. I knocked at his door three times and got no answer. I came back five minutes later and knocked again. They were home, but nobody answered. I thought I heard Johnny invite me into the house. I walked into his house. I was wrong. His Dad told me, "Leave, or I will call the police." I left, parked my car one block away, and knocked at his door one more time. I proceeded to leave. About the time I walked one half-block, Johnny's Dad called me back. Johnny met me, and I asked, "Are we still friends? Johnny told me, "Do not come back for two or three weeks." I asked, "Are we still friends!?" Johnny replied, "We are still friends, but I would not come back for two or three weeks. Dad may call the police." I left doubting that Johnny still liked me.

On Sunday, I left for Arlington with a painful doubt concerning Johnny. I prayed to God concerning Johnny and my assistantship. The Lord gave me a peaceful reassurance concerning both. That Sunday night, the house council had a meeting. Their student senator resigned. I volunteered to take his place for the year. On Monday, I met with my academic adviser. I had my assistantship for the Winter Quarter. Praise the Lord!!! God had provided for me after helping Johnny Oilstring. I enrolled in Solid State Physics and Quantum Mechanics. The first assignments in these courses were easy A's. This helped me deal with the pain of the situation with Johnny. On Thursday, I attended my first Student Senate meeting. At that meeting, one student senator said, "I wish to make a motion for a faculty appreciation day." Another senator said, "I second the motion." Another senator said, "Our professors need to be shown appreciation." I asserted in debate, "This appreciation day will cause students to compete for favor from their professors by polishing the apple for them. This will lead to professors showing favoritism to some students. This undermines the academic integrity of any university." The motion failed because I made the senate think.

Meanwhile, in Ardmore, Oklahoma, communication with Johnny's friends was severed, and it was painful. I called for Denny on Thursday, but he was not there. I returned to Gainesville on Friday. On Saturday, I asked God for a sign. I prayed, "Lord Jesus, If Johnny is still my friend, let me see his truck in the driveway." I drove past his house to see his truck in his driveway. That Monday, I returned to Arlington State University in pain concerning Johnny. I tried to call Denny's house. The line was busy all afternoon. I left for my Solid State Physics class in pain. The Solid State Physics lessons relieved the pain because the lessons presented a chance for an easy 'A'. At the end of my Solid State class, I tried to call Denny. His line was still busy. The next day, I worked on my easy assignments and tried to call Denny in the afternoon. His line was still busy. My Quantum Mechanics class relieved my pain. My Quantum Mechanics professor talked about Clebsch-Gordon coefficients. This reminded me of Morgantown, West Virginia, before I was to depart for spring break to see Robert Elight in McKinney. I also felt victory over this material was nigh at hand. After my class, I tried to call Denny. His line was still busy. I was thinking all of Johnny's group had abandoned me. That Wednesday, I worked on my assignments and grading papers. At 2 pm, my work was done. I called for Denny. His Mom finally answered. She said, "This weather shorted out my telephone line." She added, "Denny should be here tomorrow night." I felt like God was going to save my friendship with Johnny.

My fast concerning Johnny started midnight Thursday morning. I prayed unto the Lord that he would show me how to be a friend to Johnny. As I skipped breakfast, Jesus gave me peace that I would resolve this situation with Johnny. I went to work on my hardest Solid State problems and solved them, skipped lunch to praise the Lord for the pending victory, came back to serve my office hours, and ended my day by calling Denny. His line was busy all night, but I felt peace because God was about to make peace between me and Johnny.

On Friday morning, Dad called and suggested that I should leave early because a storm was coming. I left at 9:30am for Gainesville. As I left, the snow fell and blew. As I got on I-20, the road started to become slick. When I arrived at I-35, the snow let up. I-35 was in good condition, and the snow was light. I rejoiced that God would bring me safely to Gainesville to resolve my problems with Johnny. When I arrived in Denton, on I-35, The snow started getting heavy, and the roads were slick and snow covered. North of Denton, the snow was heavy, and I could barely see the road. I felt like turning back when the still soft voice of the Lord said to keep going. I obeyed the voice of the Lord and carefully drove to Gainesville, on I- 35. At Gainesville, the snow had stopped. My drive from there was easy. I arrived at Save Mart across the street from Johnny's house at 12:15pm. At about 12:30pm, I left to go south on US 77. I arrived at State Road 142 (Map 7) to spot Johnny's truck. I followed this truck to The Texgas Station and parked my car. As Johnny was filling his tank, I asked Johnny to forgive me for aggressively invading his privacy. He forgave me, and he asked me to forgive him for his avoidance. The hostility was done. I arranged for Johnny to do some drawings that would otherwise cost me about $600. He called me at Arlington State University that Monday and arranged to see me on Friday. Our friendship was restored.

This Friday was the start of a three week Christmas break at Arlington State University. Johnny, my family, and I enjoyed Christmas break. Johnny and I got together five times during Christmas break. One of these times, we went to the my favorite restaurant. At my favorite restaurant, I asked Johnny, "How is my good friend doing?" Johnny replied, "I am doing fine. How is your schooling going?" I replied, "I am averaging Straight 'A's. Quantum Mechanics reminds me of Morgantown in 1984 when I was struggling to learn the same material. My Solid State Physics Class seems to be an easy 'A'. How are you doing?" Johnny said, "I am doing fine with my job. I just got a raise of $1 an hour. I am getting along with my wife. I replied, "Glad to hear that. How are the drawings coming?" Johnny replied, "I just got started with them. Let's discuss them on your spring break." The waitress came and took our order. I ordered a Mountain Dew, chicken and French fries. Johnny ordered a plate of turkey and mashed potatoes. Johnny said, "In about a year or so, I hope your machine works. Maybe we can get a famous rock band to play a concert off of

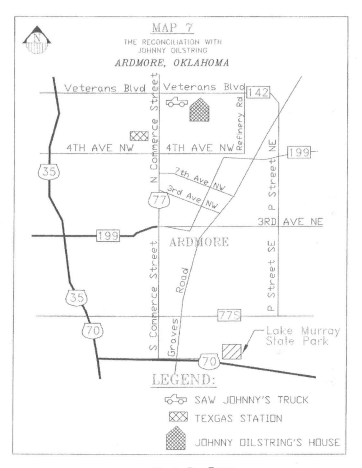

Map by Dan Eaves

this perpetual motion machine." I replied, "We first have to make this machine work, but I am glad you are sharing my dream." Johnny replied, "I like to be there for my friends." We ate our food and talked for an hour and returned home. We shared our dreams, talked about our lives and had good times through my Christmas break and the next quarter.

Upon return from Christmas break, I studied my Solid State Physics and Quantum Mechanics with the hope that I could go back to get my PhD. upon graduation. I sent for ten catalogs and looked through them. The four that got my attention were Notre Dame, Kentucky, Cincinnati, and Kent State. At Notre Dame was a professor with the last name of Wolfman. After careful thought, I figured that this professor had no association with Johnny's accident, but it did concern me. At Cincinnati, I figured this school to be a lot like Arlington State University. Kentucky seemed to be a good school like Notre Dame. Kent State was likely a school a lot like Arlington State University, but I had one question about Kent. In Kent State's Graduate School catalog was a statement about May 4, 1970. This statement implied that all of the problems with the May 4th shootings were solved, and that there were only a few protestors of the memorial. I asked God, "Why did Kent State write the May 4th statement if all of the problems were solved there?" Then, an intelligent thought came to mind. I thought, "Maybe the problems at Kent State were not solved." I began to fear, "The problems at Kent State were not solved. To keep the hex from coming back on Johnny, I must obey the commandments of God. To obey God's commandment of loving my neighbor as myself, I need to be friends with the Kent State hippies if I attend Kent State University. This may mean joining them." I prayed to God and decided to make Kent State my last choice. I thought with a sense of relief, "This way the Kent State hippies won't be my neighbors, and May 4th will not be my problem." Little did I know that God was setting the stage for Billy Glassman's heroics at Kent State University.

I studied hard until the end of the winter quarter, made an 'A' in Quantum Mechanics and an 'A' in Solid State Physics, and enjoyed spring break. Spring break was especially fun because I saw my friend Johnny Oilstring three times. One time, we discussed the drawings and arranged to discuss them again if necessary. The second time, we went to the my favorite restaurant and had a good time. At that restaurant, I asked Johnny, "How are you doing?" He replied, "I am doing just fine." Johnny asked, "Would you want to go with me on a fishing trip on Lake Michigan this summer." I replied, "I would like to go with you." Johnny said, "We can stay with my brother, Jimmy Oilstring. He lives in LaPorte, Indiana, near Lake Michigan. I will enjoy my vacation with you and Jimmy this summer." The waitress came. I ordered chicken and French fries. Johnny ordered Ham and a baked potato with Cole slaw. We ate our meal, talked and laughed for an hour. Then, we returned home.

After spring break, I returned to the University. I enrolled in Electricity and Magnetism I and Solid State Physics II. I visited Johnny once a week throughout the spring quarter and the summer. I talked about my schooling or my project. He talked about his job or his wife and his son Hank. We were good friends and had a good time together.

On Tuesday March 14, 1986, Ron Christman came to me saying, "A group of four warlocks from Marietta, Oklahoma, met me on the elevator and asked where was Kevin. I told them that I would not tell them. They said that they had a green bag of dust which could blind me and threatened to use it. The elevator opened, and I ran." I told Ron, "Do not fear those witches because God will protect you. I am praying for you. Jesus will protect you." Ron replied, "I fear that those witches will separate us and kill us both." I replied, "God will not allow it! In retaliation for this attack, I will drive an exorcism raid through Denton, Texas, this Friday to rebuke those sorcerers. I will call a meeting of the Occult Defense Command in McKinney, Texas. If those witches harass you between now and next Monday, The Board of Judges of Texas will declare a day of fasting and prayer to place these witches in the hands of God and possibly put them out of business. They will not prevail." Ron said, "Thanks for the encouragement and prayer."

Wednesday and Thursday passed without incident. On Friday, I drove to Gainesville starting on I-20 and on I-35 to Denton. Between Arlington and Denton I reflected on the love of Jesus and began to count my blessings. I thanked the Lord for my assistantship, my grades, my friendship with Johnny, and my job at Family Fiberglass. As I counted my blessings, God said in a still soft voice, "I will defeat those witches and make Ron safe." Between Denton and Valley View, I rejoiced in the victory God had wrought. When I arrived in Valley View, I knew Ron was safe for now. Although I felt that Ron was safe, I proceeded to Johnny's House. On my way to Johnny's place, I heard a rock song called "Armadas." This song made me feel that we would defeat those witches in a classic and decisive manner. About fifteen minutes after hearing that song in Gainesville, I arrived at Johnny's house. I told Johnny, "We rebuked a band of warlocks in Denton." Johnny asked, "Did you really knock them out of commission?" I replied, "We rebuked some of them." Johnny said, "You had better find out what is going on." I replied, "Every time they pop up their ugly heads, we will rebuke them." Johnny asserted, "I think The Occult Defense Command needs to head straight at them." I replied, "Just in case, you had better warn Steve and Melody about the possible occult attack." Johnny said, "You warn them yourself." I replied, "I will drive by Steve's house and pray for God to protect him from those sorcerers. Praying for Steve will protect him from the sorcerers and save Steve much worry. I have to be going now. See ya later."

That Saturday, I worked a half day at Family Fiberglass. There, I met Jim Ratman. He looked tough but was a very friendly person. He asked me to take him home. On the way home, Jim asked, "How is Johnny doing?" I replied, "Johnny is doing fine. He is the chairman of security of US Physics and a very good friend." I asked, "How is Jason Shoemaker doing?" Jim replied, "He is doing well. He is the head of the Mold Shop at Quality Glass. He is really making good money." I replied, "I am glad to hear the good news about Jason Shoemaker." Jim said, "Turn left here and drop me off at Jason Shoemaker's house." I dropped Jim off at Jason's house and doubled back to pray for God's protection of Jason and Jim. After I prayed for Jason and Jim, I headed up to

Oklahoma to pray for God to protect Steve and Melody from the warlocks attacking Johnny in Ardmore and us Christians in Arlington.

After my prayers for my unsaved friends, I headed for McKinney to meet with Occult Defense Analyst Robert Elight. I told Robert, "Ron Christman was harassed by Marietta's witches in Arlington." I asked Robert, "What should we do." Robert asked, "Did you pray for all of your local friends?" I replied, "I prayed for Johnny and his friends and family. I prayed for Jim Ratman and Jason Shoemaker. All of my other friends are protected by the promise of God." Robert replied, "Check with Ron on Monday to see if he was harassed over the weekend. If Ron reports that he was harassed by these witches on Monday morning, let's declare prayer and fasting, and pray for Ron. Call me if your friend was harassed over the weekend." As of Monday, Ron was not harassed again, and the crisis was over.

Meanwhile, in Ohio, former Governor Rhodes declared his candidacy to become governor again! He was responsible for the Kent State shootings on May 4, 1970. Many hippie culture students in Kent and other areas of Ohio opposed re-electing former Governor Rhodes to the office of Governor. A Kent State student, Kathy Peacegood of Beckley, West Virginia, founded a student organization to oppose Governor Rhodes called Students United Against Rhodes. She was a friendly and loving liberal woman who practiced Christian basics. These students claimed that Governor Rhodes was not fit to govern Ohio because he ordered the Kent State shootings and never apologized. They feared their rights would be trampled.

Back in Arlington early in April of 1986, my academic adviser was giving a lecture in his Solid State Physics II class. My academic adviser was one of Arlington State University's most conservative professors. He expressed his anger at Arlington State University administration for making his job hard. He said, "All leaders in the AD buildings seem to have the same bad attitude." He added, "They expect teachers to make geniuses out of dummies." A fellow student, Stan asked, "What school did you graduate from?" My academic adviser replied, "I graduated from Kent State University in 1970. I remember the shootings that occurred there on May 4th. These shootings occurred because a few trouble causers disrupted the campus. I wanted to complete my dissertation, but the campus was closed due to the shootings. Finally, the campus reopened. Since then, the Kent State administration tried to minimize publicity about the May 4th shootings. At least Arlington State University administration is honest, but they aggravate me sometimes," Hearing this, I prayed that God would spare me attendance at Kent State, so I would not need to be friends with those Kent State hippies. The government classified some of them as communists, so I feared losing my future career in physics!

In mid-April of 1986, the caucus chairman approached me to debate for maintaining the Arlington State University graduation tradition. The caucus chairman approached me because I successfully debated many issues concerning Arlington State University students. My success started on my first day. On that day, I debated against a proposal for a faculty appreciation day. I said, "This bill will undermine the academic integrity of the university." The bill was voted down. Toward the end of the second quarter, the Student Senate tried to remove the academic standards for Student Senate membership. These standards required a 2.5 GPA on a 4 point scale, in other words, a 'B-' average. I argued that participation in student government required good knowledge and general intelligence. A GPA of 2.5 is indicative of this knowledge and good sense. The Student Senate kept the 2.5 GPA requirement. After the vote was taken, a student named Chuck Smith withdrew from the Student Senate because he had a 2.4995 GPA. The meeting ended on that note. The politically motivated Student Senate seemed to make a fool of me. They seemed to demonstrate the folly of a GPA requirement, but I would get the last word. At the next meeting, Chuck Smith's candidacy was debated again. I argued that Chuck had the needed 2.5 GPA. I said, "The rules do not require a 2.5000 GPA. They require a 2.5 GPA. If we round 2.4995 to three significant figures, we get that Chuck has a 2.50 GPA and is qualified to run. This argument is also an example of the need for student senators to learn their courses. I learned this reasoning in a physics course." Chuck was allowed to enter the Student Senate. The Student Senate tried to impeach the president of the Student Senate, Stacy Peacelove, over a small mistake with a small amount of money. "The student Senate should penalize her appropriately by making her return the money and asking her to apologize," I argued, "She should still be president." That is exactly what the Student Senate did. It was incidents like these that made me worthy to argue for maintaining the tradition of the graduation ceremony. They wanted to save time by ending the tradition of letting the salutatorian speak. I argued successfully before the Student Senate, graduation traditions should be honored as a time-tested tradition and changed only by the student body or the Faculty Senate. In spite of the fact that the Student and Faculty Senate bodies voted to keep the tradition of the graduation ceremonies, the university no longer let the second ranked student in the graduating class speak. That argument marked the close of my career in the Student Senate. The quarter also came to a close. I made an 'A' in Electricity and Magnetism I and a 'B' in Solid State Physics II.

In Kent, Kathy's organization, Students United Against Rhodes, was actively supporting Dick Celeste for Governor. Former Governor Rhodes ordered the Kent State shootings of May 4, 1970 and wanted to be governor again. There were many protests against Gov. Rhodes. These protests were staged at Kent State University and other college campuses in Ohio. Some high school students joined the protests. One of the participants was Stew Bushman. A future friend of Billy Glassman and myself, he was a normal long haired, friendly liberal teenager of the day with high ideals. He and two other students skipped school to attend a protest at Kent State University. Stew's English teacher admired Stew and his friends for fighting the evil Governor Rhodes.

Back in Gainesville, I worked at Family Fiberglass and saved money during the summer. I saw Johnny twice a week throughout the summer. The first Saturday of the month, Johnny and I went to the my favorite restaurant. There, he asked, "How are you?" I replied, "I am doing fine. How are the drawings coming?" Johnny replied, "The drawings are nearly complete." I replied, "Let me see them." Johnny showed the drawings. I said, "These look good. I will take them. You no longer owe me $600." The waitress came to take our order. I ordered chicken and French fries. He ordered roast beef and mashed potatoes. We ate our dinner and he told me about his family. He was getting along with his wife, and his son was doing poorly in school. We talked and joked around for an hour and went home.

Another good time I had with Johnny was a fishing trip on Lake Michigan near Jimmy Oilstring's house in LaPorte, Indiana. We went to St. Joseph, Michigan. In St. Joseph, we went to the pier, at the mouth of the St. Joseph River. There, we bought bait, talked, and laughed. It was cloudy and about 70 degrees. The fish were not biting. Jimmy cast his hook and line into the lake. He caught seaweed. Johnny and I cast our lines into the water. Johnny said, "Start to reel the line back. If you feel a tug on the line, jerk the pole back and reel it in." Johnny felt a tug and started to reel the line in. The hook broke free of the rocks at the bottom. He said, "I caught a rock-fish" Jimmy pulled up some seaweed and said, "I caught seaweed." I reeled my line back and threw it back in the water." This time I caught seaweed." Johnny said, "You're catching on. You caught seaweed." I replied, "Though we have not caught a fish, I am relaxing being near the lake and watching the birds and the waves." Johnny replied, "Getting away from the city and watching nature is half the fun of fishing." Jimmy said, "I think I may have caught a big fish." Jimmy caught a bunch of seaweed. For the rest of the day, we caught rock-fish and seaweed, but we enjoyed the lake and each other's company.

At the end of the day, we went to a restaurant in Michigan City to eat. There we discussed our dreams. Jimmy Oilstring said, "I heard that Kevin was working on a perpetual machine, and that you Johnny were going to have a rock-band run their show off of one of these machines if the invention works." Johnny said, "If this machine works, it can change the world." I said, "It will be a couple of years before the test run. If this machine works, we can all be rock stars." Johnny said, "Even if this machine does not work, we can have a good time as friends and enjoy life together." The waitress came and took our order. I ordered chicken and French fries. Jimmy ordered turkey and gravy. Johnny ordered chicken and noodles. We talked and laughed for an hour until we returned to LaPorte. We hiked, camped, and fished for three days of similar enjoyment before Johnny and I returned home to the Red River Valley.

I also saw Robert once every two weeks. One such time we got together at a big nightclub in Sherman. There, I asked Robert, "How are you." I replied,

"I am doing fine. I look forward to eating a bunch of fried chicken and French fries." Robert replied, "I look forward to seeing the show after dinner." I asked, "You mean the local rock band." Robert replied, "They will play lots of Elvis Presley songs." I said, "They even have an Elvis Presley look alike singing." The waitress came and took our orders. I ordered chicken and French fries. Robert ordered the same. We ate our food and talked for an hour. The show started. Robert drank wine, and I drank Coke. We had a good time.

After my summer with Johnny Oilstring and Robert Elight, It was time to enroll for classes in Arlington. I took Electricity and Magnetism II, and Graduate Classical Mechanics. I studied these classes intensely, I and was averaging A's in these classes. I saw Johnny Oilstring once a week on Saturdays. We discussed my grades, Project Texhoma, his family, and his job. We sometimes joked around. Sometimes I would see Robert and do the same.

Meanwhile, my brother Kris was getting ready for his marriage he was planning in October. His wife to be, Jean, was a production worker at Family Fiberglass. She was an attractive, friendly, and clear complected woman. Dad was leery of the marriage. He thought that Kris should marry another girl. I agreed. I said, "Marriage is tough, and it is for life. He really needs to think this out and seek God's will." Dad talked this out with Kris. Dad asked, "Are you sure you are in love with her?" Kris replied, "I love her and want to marry her." Dad said with great worry, "Think this out for a month. If you still want to marry Jean, I will support you and respect Jean as part of the family." One month later, Kris decided to marry Jean. Dad and Mom got to know and like Jean. They figured that whether they liked or hated Jean, she was going to be part of the family. They learned to love Jean out of love for Kris.

Now that Kris and Jean were getting married, Mom and Dad had to prepare for the wedding. Kris, Mom, and Dad arranged for the wedding to be held at Epworth Methodist church in Gainesville, Texas. They arranged to have the reception party at the downtown party hall in Gainesville. Mom, Dad, and Kris sent out wedding announcements and invitations. It was going to be a grand celebration.

About a week before the wedding, I went with Dad to the post office. Dad asked, "What am I going to do with those employees who say that they want to work and then quit one hour after they are hired?" Dad said, "We treat these employees well, and they walk all over us." I replied, "I really don't know. Sometimes, I honestly think that we should not pay them a dime for their services." Dad angrily replied, "You can't do that! It is against the law!" I was speechless for 30 seconds. Then, I replied, "It may not be against the law to pay such workers minimum wage for the hours they worked." I paused for 30 seconds and said, "To make this policy work and to make it legal, we should give it to them in writing and make sure they know this policy." Later, Mom told me, "The company had been paying people, who quit without notice, the minimum wage for three years." I replied, "I guess that Dad was teaching me a little concerning the business by making me think about it."

With all of the wedding preparations made, it was time for rehearsal. We all went to the church and slaved over the details. The ushers were told to seat the bride's family in the front three rows left of the aisle, and the groom's family in the front three rows right of the aisle. Then the bridesmaids and groomsmen came into the room side by side and marched to their appropriate positions in front of the alter. The groom came up to the altar. Then, the organist played *Here Comes the Bride*. The bride marched up to the altar. Dad gave her away. The organist then played *Sunrise Sunset*. Dad went down the left center aisle singing that song happy for Kris and Jean. After the rehearsal, everybody went to a restaurant in Gainesville to eat. I ordered shrimp and French fries. We all filled up with the foods on the buffet.

The wedding went as planned. Now, it was time for the wedding reception. Wedding receptions are always fun. When I arrived, I drank three tall glasses of Coke. Then dinner was served. I ate three plates full of green beans, fried chicken, and mashed potatoes. Then, they cut the cake. Kris and Jean took the first pieces. I ate two servings of cake. Then, it came time to dance. Jean danced with every male family member. First, she danced with Dad and Uncle Larry. Then she danced with my brother-in-law, Lefty. Finally, she wanted to dance with me. I replied, "I am full and do not feel like dancing." Dad replied, "It won't be that long, and it will be all right with Kris." I replied, "OK." I danced with Jean for one song. Afterward, I sat out until everybody formed a circle and started to polka. When this polka was finished, the party broke up.

Meanwhile, back in Kent, Stew Bushman went to Columbus to hand out literature supporting Dick Celeste. They aggressively pointed out that students' rights were in jeopardy if Rhodes were elected. They did not want a governor who ordered students shot in Kent on May 4, 1970. They handed literature to everybody on the streets. They talked to Christians. They even talked to members of the state legislature. They were united in an effort to keep a potentially ruthless candidate for governor out of office. If I would have known, I would have come from Texas to help their cause.

A few days later at my dorm-room, I was watching the six o'clock news on TV. There was a story of the Tarrant County sheriff watching the school for kidnappers. These kidnapers intended to sacrifice children in Satanic rituals. When I heard this story, I asked God to help the sheriff to catch these child killers. I told Ron one day later, "I heard that a Satanic cult in Fort Worth was looking for children to sacrifice." Ron replied, "What an awful thing." I replied with disgust, "I prayed that God would help the sheriff catch these criminals before one child died. Frankly, I hope that the judge locks these criminals up and throws the key away. Then, I pray that Jesus saves their souls while they are in jail." Ron replied, "They should make sure that these criminals never see the outside of a jail as long as they live. Sacrificing children is a horrible crime."

Back in Kent, Kathy and her friends were celebrating the defeat of Governor Rhodes. Her organization made the difference. Protests were tough and aggressive. They involved some of the nation's best politicians. Robert had no plan for handling politicians opposing Johnny's rights. Perhaps Kathy kept the nation's best politicians from hurting Johnny Oilstring in Ardmore. What if Richard Nixon or Governor Rhodes tried to bring up the 1978 Oilstring accident!? What would Robert have done to protect Johnny from this onslaught from both witches and politicians!!? The Kent State shootings and the Oilstring Hex have high ranking connections in the occult. Richard Nixon was The President of the United States. Nixon had access to the best witches in the country any time he wanted them. The Oilstring hex may have had a connection to currency manipulators in Europe or New York. Perhaps, the hex and the shootings are connected. Praise the Lord that Kathy and her friends defeated Governor Rhodes and may have helped to keep the witches on their own in the Red River Valley!!!

On that same day, witches from Marietta harassed Ron. Ron came to me and asked, "What do you think of somebody who says, "You're going to hell?"" I replied, "Only God can judge you. They are hypocrites. Jesus says in Matthew 7:1 "Judge not lest ye be judged." If you have sinned, ask Jesus for his forgiveness, and you will not go to hell." Ron asked, "Could this man be one of the witches harassing me." I replied, "He is not likely to be a warlock, but more likely to be a Christian hypocrite. Even if he is a warlock, he has no authority to judge you. Jesus Christ is your judge. He will forgive you if you repent of your sins." Ron said, "Thanks for your encouragement. Please pray for me." I said a brief prayer for Ron and shrugged it off as Christian hypocrisy. I did not truly understand Ron's peril.

Back in Arlington on the very next day, I made major progress on my thesis and returned to my dorm. When I arrived there, I found written on my door in red paint or blood, "Death to Johnny Oilstring." I looked at this writing on the door in disgust and anger. I thought, "I will always pray for Johnny until I die or Johnny gets saved." I told Satan, "If you want Johnny, you will have to kill me. Even that is no guarantee that Johnny dies. God may raise somebody else to pray for him." Satan gave me a thought, "I will kill you and Johnny's Mom." I replied angrily, "If you want us, come and get us! You will have a fight. You will catch me only if God allows it. As for me and my house, we shall serve the Lord, Jesus." I proceeded to the bathroom to get water and some rags and wash this filth off of my door. As I got half of this filth off of my door, Ron came to my door and said, "I did not put this stuff on your door. They painted pentagrams and other satanic symbols on my door too. They even came into my room, lit candles and drew pentagrams on my dorm-room floor, in chalk." I replied to reassure Ron who felt threatened by the visiting witches, "I know that you did nothing of this kind. I am mad at the Devil. One more false move, I will rebuke him and the offending witches. I am tired of these witches subtly threatening you." Ron, in a somber voice, said, "If these witches approach me one more time, I will have to tell them where you are. That may cause a confrontation or endanger your life, but I am scared." I replied, "Fear them not. Have a little patience. I am praying for God to give you strength." Ron replied, "I am happy to know that you are praying for me." I replied, "They will probably not see you ever again. It is only six weeks until you return to St. Joe. There, they will not bother you again. They want me or Robert because we are challenging their power. God is protecting you. Do not be afraid." Ron fearfully asked, "Can I see you tonight?" I replied, "I can see you at 8:30 tonight. We can get a pizza then. Meet me at my room." Ron said, "OK, See you at 8:30."

After Ron talked with me, he visited his Bible Teacher from Intervarsity Christian Fellowship named Tom. Tom was a well-built and neat appearing Christian going for a PhD in Psychology. Ron asked, Tom, would you please pray for me?" Tom asked, "What is the problem?" "Witches are chasing and harassing me," replied Ron. "They are retaliating against my friend Kevin's prayer for his friend Johnny. They met me in the elevator and threatened to blind me unless I told him where Kevin was. I am scared." Tom asked God, "Lord, please protect Ron, Kevin, and his friend Johnny. Please give Ron a sense of peace and Kevin courage. Cause peace between the spirits on this campus. In the name of Jesus we ask this. Amen." Though Tom prayed this prayer in earnest, Ron was still scared.

At 8:30pm, a frightened Ron met me at my room. We ordered pizza and talked about how life was treating us. Then, Ron asked, "Are you afraid of those witches?" I replied, "No, I am not afraid of those witches. I am mad that they harass you because of Johnny." Ron asked, "What if they try to kill you?" I replied, "These witches will do me a favor. They will send me straight to heaven. I will not have to worry about getting an 'A' in nuclear physics, my thesis, or paying my car payments. There are benefits when a person dies in service to God. God will call me a hero in heaven if that happens. These witches will not likely be so lucky because God must first allow these witches to kill me. God is on my side, so they will likely face defeat." We ate our pizza discussing this incident further. Ron asked, "Would you give into these witches if they tortured you." I replied, "God will give me the strength to endure such torture and keep me until I die or help arrives." Ron asked, "What if they threatened to kill your mother?" I replied, "That matter is in God's hands. He will likely stop such a disaster." We finished our pizza and talked about school for a half of an hour.

After we completed the pizza, Ron and I got the munchies. We went to the snack bar on the first floor. I bought a tall glass of Mountain Dew and a five ounce bag of potato chips. Ron bought a taco and a Coke. We gulped down our food and drink. I told Ron, "If we meet those witches, I am going to tell them that Jesus saves." Ron asked, "What will you say about Johnny?" I replied, "Bottom line, you will leave Johnny alone, or God will be against you. If you do not like it, you can lump it. As long as I live, you cannot hex Johnny." Ron somberly said, "You had better be careful. You may see those witches." I replied, "What do you want me to do, hide my salvation under a bushel basket? Can't do it, especially for these witches. They need to know that Jesus saves." Ron said, "There are the witches!" I turned around to face them, and they fled. I asked, "Where are these witches?" Ron said, "I do not know." Though I did not see the witches, I believed Ron, and I replied, "We do not need to fear them because they ran away from us." Ron said, "Let's search the basement." We looked in the basement and the witches were nowhere to be found. I told Ron, "These witches ran, so we have nothing to fear." We looked for them until 3 am and found nothing. We gave up and felt safer. We scared those witches away and beat them by the grace of God.

In January of 1987, I decided to stay in Arlington for a weekend. Two friends from Intervarsity Christian Fellowship invited me to church with them. One was named Bob, and the other was named Stan. Stan was my prayer partner a year ago. I went with them and worshiped God with them. After the service, I talked about how God protected Johnny. Stan had a scary experience with demons or possibly criminals. He said, "I arrived at my dorm after a long day at school. I closed the door and the room suddenly was dark and suddenly felt colder and colder. It was almost freezing when somebody put a knife to my neck and started to choke me. I cried out to Jesus. With every ounce of strength, I broke free and ran." "Through the grace of God, you are free and alive," I replied, "I must get going to study. See you later."

Finally, it was the end of the winter quarter at Arlington State University. After eight years, Ron's academic career at Arlington State University was finished. He earned a bachelor's degree in Geology. Ron needed a ride home to St. Joe. Ron took me to his dorm and loaded my Chevy to the brim. He loaded all of his clothes, all of his drawings, all of his comics, and the rest of his stuff until I had only the use of the front seat of my station wagon. After Ron loaded my car to capacity, we proceeded to St. Joe. "This is the last time you will ever deal with those witches that harassed you," I said, "God kept you through the hard times, and you are safe and through with school." Ron said, "It is only three hours until you get to my house. When we get there, we are going to have a cookout to celebrate my graduation and to thank you for taking me home." All the way to St. Joe, I could taste the baked beans, hot dogs, hamburgers, and potato chips. Finally we arrived in St. Joe, had the picnic, and headed to Gainesville.

Meanwhile, back in Kent, Kathy and her friends formed the Progressive Student Network from the group of students opposing the election of former Governor Rhodes. Her student organization kept many of the nation's politicians busy supporting Governor Rhodes. This and Johnny's more down-to-earth lifestyle may have protected Gainesville Security Central from fighting a deadly alliance of witches and politicians. Both The Kent State shootings and the Oilstring Hex have possible connections high in the occult. Richard Nixon had access to the best witches in the country, and the Oilstring hex may have had a connection to currency manipulators in New York or Europe. Gainesville Security Central's fight for Johnny's soul may have helped protect the Progressive Student Network from witches into black magic. Robert Elight and I kept some them busy chasing Johnny and fighting us in Texas. Kathy's Progressive Student Network also would be a proving ground for many of my life-long friendships. I will have met my future best friend, Billy Glassman, there.

CHAPTER 7

THE SURVIVAL OF
FAMILY FIBERGLASS

At Arlington State University, I completed my research, so I could write my master's thesis. I headed home to Gainesville. On the Sunday after my arrival in Gainesville, Dad and I toured the Family Fiberglass plant. There, Dad pointed out the mess in the production room. He said, "Look at all of that glass on the walls and the floors." Dad said in a serious tone, "What a mess, and what a waste! The chopper should get more of the glass on the part he is making. He should at least clean up his mess every night." I replied, "I am at least more concerned about my job than that." Dad said in a serious voice, "I have no more money to put into the plant. It needs to run well, or it will be shut down." I replied, "I will do my best to make sure that does not happen. I will pray that God will provide for our needs."

On that Monday, I arrived at Family Fiberglass and began to repair every mold in the most efficient way possible. I worked this way from 6:00 to 4:30 every day for six weeks until the mold repair station was caught up. While I worked hard to catch up the molds, the rest of the plant also worked hard. The production room did quality work, and final finish repaired the fiberglass parts with efficiency. The plant became a profitable place for the moment.

Out of mold repair work, I started to assist Tom with mold and pattern work. Tom was a party loving, long haired, pot smoking, but deceitfully friendly hippie who secretly held a grudge against the establishment of the fiberglass industry. Tom would complete the patterns through prototyping and the final painting of the surface. I would sand and buff the same surface. After this surface shined, I waxed this surface and completed my work on the pattern. I assisted Tom for two weeks this way and performed well. On the third week, I would be asked to complete a sanding job on an RV skirt. This skirt was 25 feet by three feet. They wanted this job completed by the end of the day. This was a job that would take at least three days if done by normal procedures. I proceeded to use shortcuts to get the job done. I used a dual action power sander with 80 grit sandpaper and sanded the skirt thoroughly in a half of an hour. Then, I used a dual action sander with 220 grit sandpaper to remove the eighty grit scratches. As I completed the 220 sanding, another mold shop employee, Vern, said, "You are going too fast. We need quality." I replied, "The company needs speed on this piece. Our quality will be good." Vern disgustingly said, "We'll see!" After our argument, I used 320 sandpaper on a dual action sander to remove the scratches left by the 220 grit sandpaper. Then, I sanded with 400 and 600 sandpaper and buffed the skirt. The skirt shined at 2:30 that same day. It was completely waxed at 4:30.

I worked aggressively throughout the summer to protect Family Fiberglass. Johnny and I got together once a week to have a good time sharing dreams and talking about problems like we did for all of the last academic year. I also saw Robert occasionally during the summer to do the same. In the last weekend of August, Johnny and his friend Denny invited me to go to Tulsa, Oklahoma, to pick up Denny's girlfriend Rebecca. Rebecca was an attractive, clear complected, poor, but friendly woman. Johnny told me, "Bring a six pack of pop and prepare to party hardy. We like to laugh and have a good time on our trips." I replied, "I look forward to seeing you and hope to show you a better time than I did in Dallas." Johnny said in a charming fashion, "I hope you will get high and drunk with us." I replied in a respectful fashion, "I enjoy pop and potato chips. I hope we will eat a nice greasy chicken dinner complete with French fries and a lot of ketchup. I love greasy food and plenty of it." Johnny replied, "Greasy food is just as bad as pot or booze, but I will let you have a good time your way. We will be glad to see you. Be here at noon Saturday." I replied with excitement, "Look forward to seeing you at noon on Saturday!"

On that Saturday, I met Johnny at his house. We proceeded to the nearest gas station. There we bought pop, potato chips, peanuts, beer, crackers, and gasoline. Johnny said, "Better get all of the refreshments you need for the first 100 miles because we want to get to Tulsa as quickly as possible." We all gathered in the car with all of our refreshments and proceeded toward I-35. On our way up US 199 to I-35 we munched on our snacks and listened to Led Zeppelin tunes on the radio. As we arrived at Oklahoma City, we entered I-44 East. A few miles down I-44, Johnny asked, "Kevin, How are you?" I replied, "Fine." Johnny asked in a friendly manner, "What kind of music do you like?" I replied happily, "I like Def Leppard." Johnny proceeded to put on Def Leppard's song *Animal*. I enjoyed the Def Leppard album all the way to the 30 mile marker. At the 30 mile marker, Johnny said, "You are awful quiet." He asked, "You having a good time?" I replied quietly, "I am enjoying the scenery and the trip." Johnny asked, "Do any of you want to stop to eat?" We all decided to stop in at the 60 mile marker. There, we decided to spend the night in Rebecca's apartment and to eat at Sonic Drive-In. At Sonic, we all ordered chicken and French fries and ate hardily. After we stuffed ourselves to the gills, we all proceeded to Rebecca's apartment.

At Rebecca's apartment, we introduced ourselves and started to party. Rebecca asked Johnny, "What is your favorite rock group?" Johnny enthusiastically replied, "Led Zeppelin." I interjected, "I like Def Leppard." Rebecca played Led Zeppelin's "Stairway to Heaven" album and Def Leppard's "Animal." Rebecca asked, "What would you like to drink?" I replied, "Mountain Dew pop." Johnny replied, "Michelob beer." Denny replied, "Jack Daniel's whiskey." Rebecca brought out our drinks, a 30 ounce bag of potato chips, and a 30 ounce bag of pretzels. We ate, drank, and watched Saturday Night Live. After Saturday Night Live, Johnny and I went to sleep on the couch. Denny went to bed with his girlfriend. After a good night's sleep, Denny, Johnny, Rebecca, and I headed back to Ardmore, Oklahoma. We dropped Rebecca and Denny off and headed to Johnny's house. From Johnny's house, I headed to Gainesville.

A week later at the Chrisgood's house, Mrs. Chrisgood said, "The State police caught a whole coven of witches sacrificing children in St. Joe, Texas. There were 144 witches, wizards, thugs, and kidnappers in the ring." I replied, "Thank the Lord that it was not Gainesville!" Mrs. Chrisgood replied, "You have to be on guard against Satan all of the time. Perhaps you need to go to Pastor Lions' church and fellowship with them!" I replied, "St. Joe is near Ron's house. Perhaps God avenged Ron's harassment at Arlington State University. Witches harassed Ron three times. You may be right about my church attendance though. It certainly will not hurt my relationship with God." "Is Ron all right?" asked Mrs. Chrisgood. I replied, "By my faith in God, I believe Ron is all right, and he is being protected by God as we speak." Mrs. Chrisgood replied, "Let's praise the Lord that Ron is fine, and play a game of scrabble." We played scrabble until midnight, and I headed home.

Next week, Family Fiberglass needed extended overtime to complete vital mold and pattern work for Pallard. I worked until 6:30 pm every night for three weeks and made great money. We completed the patterns on time and in good quality.

Thursday, after Family Fiberglass completed their vital patterns, I stopped to visit Johnny. His truck and all of his cars were in the driveway, but Janie said, "Johnny is not here." The same thing happened on Friday night and two times Saturday night. I saw Johnny on Sunday night. Johnny said, "I am going to start worshiping Satan. I sat there and avoided you because I am broke, and you are a Christian." I asked in a serious and hurt fashion, "Johnny, what is the problem? How did I hurt you?" Johnny replied arrogantly, "You have done nothing to hurt me. I am just very depressed because I am broke with no hope." I replied, "I like you a whole lot, and Jesus loves you. May I pray for you?" Johnny replied, "You may pray for me, but I will still serve the Devil. You can be my friend as long as you tolerate my new love of the Devil." I replied, "I will tolerate your religion, but I will pray that you will change your mind. I still love you. See you next Saturday." Johnny replied, "If you catch me."

That Saturday, Johnny got mad at me because I did not pay his Radio Shack bill. Johnny said, "I need for you to give me $40."I replied, "I cannot give you the $40 and wish you would stop demanding me to lend you money." Johnny replied in a mean manner, "I need that money more than you! I am no longer there for you!! See Ron or Robert. I am no longer there!!!!" Timmy Oilstring stood in the background. He asked, "Could you take me home to St. Joe?" I replied, "I can." Timmy said, "I can get Johnny to be your friend again." I asked Timmy, "How can Johnny be my friend again?" Timmy said, "Give me Johnny's Radio Shack Payment. I will give this payment to him and he will be mad at you for a week and get over it. He is depressed about his bills. Help him, and he will love you again." Timmy gave Johnny the $40, and we drove to St. Joe. Timmy was still my friend. He reassured me that Johnny was my friend.

One week later on Sunday, I stopped by Johnny's house. I brought Johnny two Radio Shack payments totaling $60. Janie answered the door and gave Johnny the payments. Johnny received the payments and took a little time to talk to me. Johnny said, "Thanks, I am glad to know that you care about me." He asked, "Will you come over tomorrow night?" I replied happily, "I will be glad to come over." Johnny said, "Come over at 7:00 tomorrow night." I said to Johnny, "See you later." Then, I drove home to Gainesville.

On that Monday, I saw the news. The local news reporter told of a cult of Satan worshiping teenagers in Valley View, Texas. These teenagers painted pentagrams on the side of homes and businesses. They painted graffiti on many more stores in Valley View and Denton. They threatened to kill anybody who would try to stop them. Many people in Valley View thought that their children would be next to be offered to the Devil. I prayed for the people of Valley View and thought, "Robert's brother, Rodney, is only eight miles from this cult." I prayed for Rodney and headed to Johnny's house.

At Johnny's house, I told Johnny, "I paid two months of Radio Shack bills amounting to $60. Hope you have forgiven me for being mad at you." Johnny said with a smile on his face, "I have forgiven you, and we are good friends again. In a few months, I may be able to pay you back." I replied happily, "I am glad that we are good friends again. I forgive you for avoiding me." We ate, drank, and chatted for an hour and enjoyed every moment. Then, Johnny asked, "Would you like to come to my Halloween party a week from this Saturday?" I replied, "I would like to come, but I will be busy." Johnny asked in a disappointed tone, "What will you be doing on Halloween?" I replied, "I will be in Valley View on an occult defense raid. These witches are a threat to all of southern Cooke County. It is the policy of the Board of Judges of Texas to rebuke all witches who pose a threat to the public." Johnny asked, "Are these witches a threat to Gainesville Security Central?" I replied, "Their central command is only 8 miles from Rodney Elight's apartment in south Gainesville, 10 miles from Robert's house, 15 miles away from Gainesville Security Central, and 50 miles from Fort Rock Security Central." Johnny said in a spiteful I-told-you-so manner, "These witches threatened us from San Francisco and Liverpool two years ago, Fort Worth a year ago, and now they are even closer in Valley View. We had better show them we mean business." I said in a business-like manner, "I have declared next Friday a day of fasting and prayer concerning this matter. On Saturday Night, I plan to do a Jericho run seven times around Valley View on the highway system." Johnny asked, "Shouldn't you do this run on Friday night instead?" I replied, "You are probably right. The witches will probably do their damage the night before Halloween." Johnny asked, "Do you want a drink of pop?" I replied, "Yes. I want a Mountain Dew. When you get back with our drinks, I want to discuss the plans for the exorcism raid against the occult community of Valley View." Johnny returned to the room with the drinks. Johnny asked, "What are the plans for the occult defense raid in Valley View?" I replied, "I will pray for God to deliver Valley View of this cult while driving a Jericho run around this city. I will start the Jericho run on the intersection of Grand and California (Map 8). I will take Grand Avenue which is also farm road 372 and proceed to farm road 922. I will take 922 past Valley View to farm road 51. I will take farm road 51 to Grand Avenue and repeat this route seven times. On the eighth time down farm road 922, I will enter Valley View and break their power in the name of Jesus. These teenagers will learn that Jesus Christ is Lord."

Johnny asked, "Why don't you go straight down I-35 from Gainesville (Map 8)?" Johnny said, "This will show those witches you mean business." I replied, "The route I take in praying for Valley View should make no difference. God answers prayer anywhere in the universe. These witches are no match for God. This proposed Jericho run around Valley View will help me to complete preparations for the attack against those witches. I will have time to be sure that I am submitted to the Spirit of God. This way, I will be more effective in Valley View." Johnny emphatically replied, "You may think you are well prepared, but these witches will know that you have a lapse in faith." Kim, one of Janie's friends from the nursing home walked into the room and replied, "These witches are very powerful and seem to form a big coven." I emphasized, "God can take down one witch or one hundred witches. They are

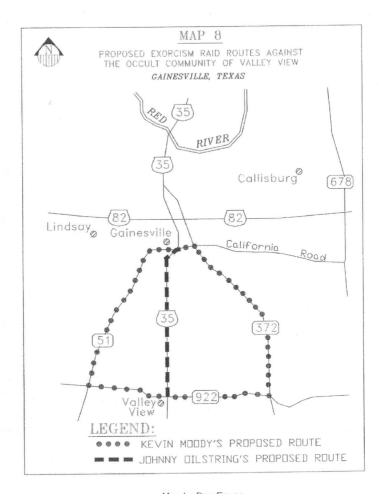

Map by Dan Eaves

no match for God. I know how to communicate with God. I pray to him regularly." Kim replied, "I am a Baptist-trained Christian, and I urge you to start your preparations at least one week in advance of the attack." I replied in a friendly manner, "I will take your ideas under advisement. I will consider them when I have my occult defense meeting with ODA. Robert Elight this next Wednesday. Johnny, I must be going home now. See ya later." Johnny replied, "Good luck on your occult defense raid."

On the Wednesday before the proposed occult defense raid in Valley

View, I had my meeting with Robert. I said to Robert, "Those teenage witches in Valley View have vandalized property, produced graffiti, threatened lives, and terrorized all of Valley View. These witches are within an eight mile striking distance of Rodney's apartment in Texas Hills. Do we need to drive an exorcism raid into Valley View?" Robert replied, "The chances of the Valley View witches of reaching our unsaved people such as Johnny or Rodney are extremely small. To be safe, we should ask God to protect them this coming week and make this our long term strategy." I asked, "Should protective prayer be our top strategy in occult defense?" Robert replied, "An ounce of prevention is better than a pound of cure. God promises that he will protect us if we ask him." I asked, "Does this also include our unsaved friends such as Johnny or Rodney?" Robert said, "This approach will include our unsaved friends and will be more peaceful than the policy of retaliating against witches for hurting our friends. This retaliatory policy is obsolete and should be used only as a last resort." I replied, "I will declare the occult defense raid for now, but I will seek God's guidance about whether he wants me to show his power in Valley View or stay put in Gainesville."

On the Friday of the proposed occult defense raid, I fasted breakfast and prayed for strength and guidance from God. I worked the morning shift and fasted lunch. At about 2 o'clock of the afternoon shift, Tom Smith, our company's painter, asked, "What are you doing this weekend?" I replied, "Lord willing, I am going to Valley View to rebuke a big coven of witches who are terrorizing that city tonight." Tom asked, "Are you ready for such an undertaking?" I emphatically replied, "If God wants me in Valley View, I am ready." Tom asked, "Are you sure? See ya later."

At the end of my day, I arrived at home. There, I checked my rough draft of my master's thesis before mailing it to my research adviser for evaluation. Just as I was about to leave for the post office, my Mom and Dad came home. Dad asked, "Could you get chicken on the way home?" I replied, "Yes. I can pick up chicken at Chicken Dump on US 82." I started on my way to mail my thesis at the downtown Gainesville post office. As I was driving toward the post office, I started to pray. I asked the Lord, "Should I drive the Valley View exorcism raid?" I waited patiently and asked the Lord, "Should I continue my fasting even if Dad knows that I am fasting? Isn't prayer and fasting supposed to be done in secret?" At that time, I arrived at the post office and mailed my master's thesis at the post office window. I started back home. I proceeded down Broadway to make a right turn on Lindsay street (map 9). I took Lindsay street to California Road. On California Road, I started to ask God the same questions concerning the Valley View Raid. I proceeded past the Railroad crossing and past Kroger's. Between Kroger's and Grand Avenue, God gave me a thought that I should drop the fast and the raid. The still soft voice of the Lord then said, "Eat chicken with your family." God said firmly in a still soft voice, "Stay home with them tonight because your family needs you." I asked

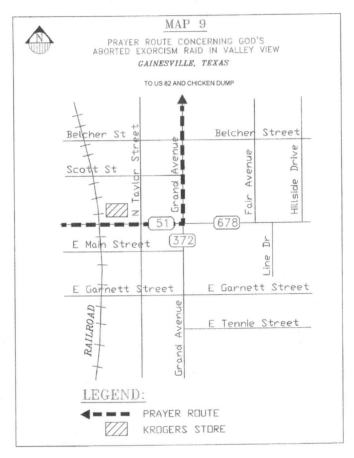

Map by Dan Eaves

prayerfully, "What about Valley View?" God replied in his still soft voice, "I am mad at these witches, and I will take care of them better than you can. Valley View is in good hands. Go home and eat chicken with your family." I replied in prayer, "I will go to Chicken Dump and eat with my family. Thank you Jesus. Amen." I thought, "God does things his own way. He answered my prayer and told me to spend time with my closest neighbors, my family. Loving my family is also my duty to God. This matter is in the hands of God."

I went to Chicken Dump on 82. I ordered my normal order. They took 45 minutes on my order, and it was cold and wrong. I angrily said, "You stupid idiots! You never get my order right!" The woman manager angrily replied, "We are not idiots! I will give you a new order, and it better be right. Do not come back to the store again, or I will call the police!" I replied, "I won't be back! Your service and attitude stink!! If this order is not right, I will humiliate you in the newspaper!!!" The order was correct but cold. On the way home, I asked God for forgiveness. God forgave me and assured me that Valley View was safe. When I arrived at home, I told my Mom and Dad that I had their chicken. I told Mom and Dad, "I was kicked out of the store because they got mad about my complaining about their wrong order." My Mom and Dad were furious at Chicken Dump, "They never get our order right!" Dad angrily said, "I am going to give the owner a piece of my mind after dinner." We enjoyed our dinner. As we finished dinner, my sister, Kim, came to the house. I told my sister about my experience at Chicken Dump. She went to Chicken Dump and placed an order. She got the same wrong service and told the woman manager in front of five customers, "You gave me and my brother a wrong order and kicked my brother out of the store because he got mad about your mistakes!" Kim said angrily, "Give me my money back and the order too!" The manager in a nasty voice said, "Here is your stupid money and your order!" The five other customers left with Kim. This made our family a little closer and Valley View was safe. I would find out that the Texas Rangers caught the teenagers comprising the coven and took them home to their parents. God did it his way.

Throughout the month of October, Family Fiberglass thought that they were making good money. Their income statement indicated a profit of $41,000.00. As of the end of October, business had slowed down drastically. Much of the $41,000 was used to pay bills. Twenty thousand of the forty-one thousand was owed by a struggling RV company known as Pallard. Pallard could not pay $10,000 of its debt until spring. The slow month put the company in a financial bind. On the Sunday of Thanksgiving weekend, Dad asked, "How much money do you have in the bank?" I replied, "I will have to look it up." Dad angrily said, "If you do not have two thousand Dollars in the bank, get out of the house!" I replied, "I have close to that amount in the bank, but I don't know exactly the exact figure." Dad replied in a fearful manner, "The company is out of money and sales have stopped. The only thing we have going for us is six weeks worth of supplies in inventory. It will be a miracle if we make it through Christmas." I replied in a serious but reassuring fashion, "I will pray that the Lord will provide for the company. Just pray and do your best to manage this company. The Lord will do the rest."

Meanwhile, Johnny and Robert continued their pattern of quality time. One such time was with Johnny was at his house in the middle of November. I asked Johnny, "Can you read some of my thesis and tell me if you understand what I am doing?" Johnny said, "I can read part of your thesis and ask you about anything I do not understand." I replied, "I am trying to make my thesis understandable to any common man who can read. You will be a help." Johnny asked, "When can I help." I replied, "I will have my thesis ready for you about two weeks before Christmas." We talked and joked around for an hour. Then, I went home.

On Monday, Dad followed my advice. He laid off everybody except the mold shop. The mold shop completed a large cap and Texas Coach paid their bill. Family Fiberglass made it through the first week. On the second week, Family Fiberglass received an order for three sets of bus parts to be shipped to a company in Dallas. The mold shop completed these parts on Thursday, and the company was paid on Friday. The company made payroll for two more weeks. Then, Christmas week came. The company started the week broke. Tom and I worked on a pattern of a Tontau Cover. On Monday, we completed the pattern. On Tuesday, we started the mold. On Tuesday night, Dad said, "We must get that Tontau cover mold completed tomorrow if we are to make it as a company." I replied, "I will do my best to get that mold done." On the next day, I told Tom, "Dad demands us to complete this mold today before we go home." Tom asked, "Will the company go broke if we don't complete this mold?" I replied, "If we complete this mold today, the company will make it through these bad times, and it will prosper." Tom said, "All right. we will get this mold done." At noon, the mold was completed. At 1:00 pm, the company was paid. Dad breathed a sigh of relief. The company made it through Christmas. Money was tight for the next month, but the company survived according to Dad's plans until sales resumed to normal levels in late January.

Just after Thanksgiving, my research adviser returned my thesis to me and wrote, "After this round of corrections, we will defend the thesis." I checked the thesis for typing mistakes, misspelled words and edited it for content for an hour a night until Christmas. I also let Johnny read it. He understood it. At Christmas dinner, I asked my sister, Kim, to critique my thesis. She took the rough draft home and read it. She corrected a few style mistakes and told me that it sounded good. I made the corrections on the word processor and sent the thesis to Arlington. It was completed. The next step was to present the results of the research behind my thesis to the physics department. Three professors comprising my thesis committee were charged with grading my effort. This process is called defending my thesis. If I passed, I graduated.

Meanwhile, Johnny invited me for a Christmas Party at his house. Johnny gave me a new watch for Christmas. I gave Johnny $50 towards the $100 he owed me for bills that I paid three months ago. Johnny paid me the other $50. His wife cooked ham and all of the fixings. Johnny said, "Your advice of spending quality time with Janie paid off. She helps me run my house and seems to love me." I replied, "Christian principals pay off in the long run. They make a person's life better in ways a person may not think about." Johnny asked, "How is your thesis going?" I replied, "I am about to

submit its final draft. Hope to defend this thesis and graduate this year."
Johnny asked, "What are you doing then?" I replied, "I hope to try for a PhD at
The University of Cincinnati or Kent State University." We ate the ham meal
and had fun talking for two hours. Then, I returned home. We got together
about once a week until I left for Kent in August.

On Friday March 19, 1988, I defended my thesis. At about Ten o'clock,
my research adviser asked, "Are you ready to defend your thesis?" I
responded, "I am as ready as I will ever be." We proceeded to the study room,
and the audience from the department entered the room. This audience
consisted of physics majors, some professors, and my thesis committee. I
explained my research, answered a few easy questions, and completed my
defense. After my lecture, I awaited the answer from the thesis committee. My
research adviser said, "These fifteen minutes are the longest fifteen minutes
you will ever experience." I replied, "I pray that I pass this exam, so I may go
to Kent State next year." My research adviser asked, "Would you like a pop?" I
replied, "Yes." My research adviser gave me that pop and wished me good
luck. Twenty minutes later, my research adviser returned with the good news.
She said, "You passed!!" I replied, "I will graduate with a master's degree." I
returned to Gainesville victorious.

On my return from Arlington, Dad had bad news. Family Fiberglass had
just learned that they just lost the Trashy Van Account. Next week, Trashy Van
continued to order. They clarified, "We will order parts from our old molds
until Master Fab completes the new ones." The next Tuesday, Dad had good
news. Texas Coach and National Van needed new molds and a bunch of new
parts built from these molds. Trashy Van continued to order parts at their
normal rate. As Family Fiberglass struggled, I made my final corrections on
my thesis and applied to the physics departments at Notre Dame University,
University of Kentucky, Cincinnati University, and Kent State University. I
was rejected at Notre Dame, Kentucky, and Cincinnati. Kent State gave me a
tuition scholarship. I accepted the scholarship at Kent state and found a room
in Leebrick Hall. After I accepted my scholarship at Kent State, I graduated
from Arlington State University with a master's degree in Physics.

After my Arlington State University graduation, things were getting
serious at Family Fiberglass. Trashy Van's orders were trickling to a standstill.
National Van and Texas Coach had just placed their orders to build molds and
patterns. Family Fiberglass laid off most of its production and repair workers.
They hunkered down on the patterns. For three weeks, Tom built the patterns,
and I assisted where I could. Family Fiberglass hired a friend of Tom's named
Bill Ashley. He was ugly, fat, and short. His mean spirit made him a bad
worker. I tried to make molds with Bill Ashley's assistance. I succeeded with
much stress, heartache, and Tom's help. On a record hot June day, Bill
demanded that I buy him a pop. I declined because I did not have enough
money. We returned to the break room to finish waxing a mold. About half way

through the waxing, Bill said, "I feel dizzy and weak." I replied, "Go to the office and get ice water." Bill stumbled to the office, sat in the air conditioning and drank a quart of ice water. As Bill cooled off, I sluggishly finished the coat of wax on the first big Texas Coach mold. Throughout the summer, I struggled with Bill, as Family Fiberglass struggled to survive the summer.

On that same day in Cleveland, my future best friend, Billy Glassman, worked as a dismantler at his Dad's Junkyard, Auto Parts Galore. He was a tall person with long, curly, and black hair. He was a little bit grubby at times. He was childlike but intensely loving. He enjoyed making his friends feel good and laughed when they were happy. On this bad day, Billy worked in the hot sun and drank a lot of fruit juice. At 10:00 am he came into the air conditioned store and guzzled a big glass of fruit juice. Billy said to his Dad, "It is hot as hell outside. Could I take a fifteen minute break?!" His Dad said, "You are a good worker, so take a half hour, and drink plenty of water." Billy asked, "How often may I come in today." His Dad said, "Whenever you feel thirsty." Billy said, "Thanks." His Dad said, "It will be so hot out there that you could die if you do not take breaks and drink plenty of liquids, so please take plenty of breaks and drink lots of water or juice." Billy took his Dad's advice and happily clocked out at 5:00 pm. He worked there for the rest of the summer to earn money to finance a trip to California with his friend, Mike Ichabond. Like many of his generation, they wanted to see the world.

Around August 15, 1988, Robert and I had a meeting to discuss my future at Kent State University. I opened the meeting by saying, "I am proud of your performance at Big RV Plastics, Sherman, and Arlington." Robert asked, "What are the high points of each victory?" I replied with pride, "At Big RV, we outsmarted and defeated Ted Monsterman from Fiberjunck, the Monster of the North in the Gainesville dreams." Robert asked, "What about Sherman?" I replied, "We rebuked the Occult Community of Ardmore, Oklahoma. This ended the Oilstring hex. We put two sorcerers out of business in the process." Robert curiously asked about Arlington, "What did we do in Arlington?" I replied, "Witches harassed Ron Christman and other members of Intervarsity Christian Fellowship, but we, including Intervarsity Christian Fellowship, prayed until Ron was safe in St. Joe." Robert replied, "It seems like I was the brain trust behind thwarting the Oilstring Hex and the Abomination of Fiberjunck." I replied, "Jesus Christ delivered Johnny, but your brains helped to keep us in line with God's will." Robert asked, "Whatever happened in Valley View?" I replied, "I prayed concerning Valley View until Jesus told me in a still soft voice to stop praying and let the teenage witches get caught by the Texas Rangers. The Rangers took them home to their parents."

Robert asked "How is Johnny?" I replied, "Johnny is fine until I lose my righteousness at Kent State University." Robert asked, "How is this possible?" I replied, "There is a statement in the Kent State Graduate School Catalog concerning the May 4th shootings. This statement implies that the May 4th issue is completely solved, and any May 4th supporter is a rouge dissident." Robert asked, "How does this threaten your righteousness?" I replied with great fear and worry, "If I wrongly assume that this statement in the catalog is the truth, I will show hate to the Kent State liberals and fall into sin with God. If I wrongly assume the innocence of the Kent State hippies, these hippies will have the chance to brainwash every choirboy east of the Rocky Mountains." Robert replied, "God will keep our choirboys!" I replied, "But what about our unsaved friends?" Robert replied, "I believe that the Church can effect protective prayer for them. This seems to work for friends in the Church, such as Rodney Elight, Gerard Chrispeace, or Tom Chrisgood," I replied, "What about Johnny Oilstring, Jason Shoemaker, Steve Mercado, or Jimmy Woodman. If I fail in Kent, their souls are in jeopardy of falling to Alister Crowley or Anton Lavey. I seem to be the only one capable of praying for them." Robert replied, "Christians in their families can pray for these unsaved souls." I replied with grave concern, "Jason Shoemaker and Jimmy Woodman have no Christians in their families strong enough to pray for them against Alister Crowley or Anton Lavey. Without my prayers, they will almost certainly lose their souls." Robert asked, "Does Johnny and Steve have a chance if you go down in Kent?" I replied, "Johnny has a Baptist Mom, Betsy Oilstring, who proved to be no match for even the occult community of Ardmore. Steve, Johnny's brother-in-law, has only Betsy to pray for him if I go down." I asked, "How could she stand against Alister Crowley or Anton Lavey? Who else could pray for Johnny?" I paused and said this emphatically, "Bottom line, one mistake at Kent State University, and we lose Johnny Oilstring!" Robert replied, "You know that the administration is lying." I replied, "I wish that we knew this! If the hippies are right about this, we must side with them, and God will be with us!" Robert replied, "If the issues involving the May 4th shootings are not resolved, embrace the liberals, and love them as good friends. God will be with you, and the administration will face God's judgment. If these issues are resolved, these hippies are rouge dissidents, maybe even communists. Bash the liberals, and bash them mercilessly! If your perpetual motion machine falls into Russia's hands, America's future is questionable. If America falls, Christians will face persecution worldwide. This endangers the Church. Assume until proven different that Kent State's catalog is complete truth. Bash the truth out of the liberals. Become their friends only if they are proven right."

After this meeting with Robert, I reflected upon what he said concerning the Kent State liberals. I thought, "Robert is awfully harsh concerning Kent State's liberals. Perhaps, I need to investigate the liberals before bashing. Even they are innocent until proven guilty. Perhaps, Robert is concerned about national security. Couldn't most of the liberals be good Americans even if one or two are communists. Perhaps, I failed as his commanding officer. I maybe should have given Robert a month to think this dilemma through. Perhaps, I should give Robert credit for being the first Pentecostal Christian in

Gainesville to acknowledge that there may be a cover-up in Kent concerning the May 4th shootings. This situation may need investigation. My Christian friends seem to label all hippies as pure evil. Perhaps, God would want me to lovingly correct them with the Word of God in hand. I will consult my other two analysts, Johnny Oilstring, who I do not respect because he is a hippie, and Myron Chrisgood, who trained Pentecostal Missionaries serving around the world."

ODA Johnny Oilstring and ODA Myron E. Chrisgood strongly disagreed with Robert. Johnny said, "Kent State University and Robert Elight's "bashing order" are a test of your character." I asked, "How so?" Johnny replied, "You preach that one must love their neighbor as themselves." I replied, "Yes, I do." Johnny said emphatically, "Then you must treat them as friends as long as they accept you, and they are not communists. The only reason for the restriction against communists is that you are working on a perpetual motion machine. If that machine falls into the hands of the Soviets, American security is compromised. I really am leery of restricting your friendships against communists, but national security could be compromised." I asked, "Does this mean that I should investigate the Kent State hippies before I bash them?" Johnny said, "Investigate first. If you cannot prove they are communists, be their friends." I asked, "Should I be their friends even if they wish to burn the American Flag?" Johnny replied, "They are standing for their beliefs. You should be their friends even if they disagree with you." I asked Myron the same questions that I asked Johnny. Myron said, "If these Kent State liberals are not communists, you should be their friends." I asked, "How do we determine that the Kent State hippies are not communists?" Mr. Chrisgood replied, "Investigate the truth of the college catalog before bashing the liberals. If issues concerning the May 4th shootings are not resolved, be their friends. If these questions are resolved, talk to me before bashing. We may be able to be their friends even if they are communists." I replied, "Thanks for the advice. Pray for God to give me guidance. See you later." The battle lines were drawn for the final battle concerning Johnny Oilstring's hex. Could Billy Glassman, a Kent State hippie, actually be a hero in this battle?

CHAPTER 8

THE BATTLE OF KENT STATE

I headed for Kent State University victorious with an A- average and a master of science degree from Arlington State University. When I arrived in Kent, I met with the chairman of the physics department and scheduled my classes. I registered for my room, moved in, and relaxed for a while.

A little later on that same day, I met my next door neighbor in the dorm. He was a liberal style, long haired, and medium build person. I introduced myself. I shook his hand and said, "My name is Kevin Moody." He said, "My name is Timmy Feldman." I asked, "What is your major?" Timmy replied, "English." I said, "I am a physics major." Timmy said, "Tell me more about yourself." I replied, "I am a Pentecostal-trained Christian." I feared I offended Timmy and asked, "Oh! Did I scare you?" Timmy replied, "I have an open mind and do not offend easily." I replied, "I am a real Christian and believe that I must love my neighbor and be kind to people of all generations." Timmy asked, "Are you sure that you accept liberals as friends?" I replied joyfully, "I accept any non-communist who will accept me." Timmy said, "I know where you are coming from." I said, "Tell me about yourself Timmy." Timmy replied, "I am the vice president of the Kent Interhall Council and an English Major." I asked, "What does The Interhall council do?" Timmy replied, The Interhall council is an elected group of people who advocate issues concerning students living on campus. I replied, "Interesting work. Need to get going." Timmy asked, "Would you meet me at the Loft, a bar in downtown Kent, at 11:30 tomorrow night?" I replied in a joyful voice, "I'll meet you at the Loft tomorrow night at 11:30. See you."

The next day on Friday, I went to the Student Center to the job fair. There, I applied for a job as an employee of the Kent State Food Service. I asked the manager for an application. I filled out the application and stressed my factory experience. The manager asked, "Can you work as a pot scrubber 3 pm to 8 pm Monday, Tuesday, Thursday, and Friday?" I replied, I will gladly take this job. The manager replied, "See you at 3 on Monday." The manager I spoke with was attractive and friendly. I headed back to my dorm rejoicing that God had given me a second chance after my failure to pass the qualifying exam in Morgantown.

That evening, I headed to the Loft, to meet Timmy Feldman. It was so crowded that I could not find Timmy for a half of an hour. When I saw Timmy, I shouted, "Hi, How are you doing." Timmy replied, "Fine." He then asked, "How would you like a pop and some pizza?" I replied, "I am hungry and would love to eat." Timmy introduced me to some of his friends, and we all enjoyed the pizza. After we all had a good time for an hour, I headed back to the dorm. Though we had a good time for the night, Timmy would prove to be only a friendly acquaintance for the moment.

In the Leebrick Hall elevator, I met a conservative person named David Pillarman. David was a friendly and attractive person of medium build. I said, "I am a Christian who believes that a Christian should love his neighbor as himself. My name is Kevin." David replied, "My name is David. I am also a conservative. I feel out-of-place on this campus." I replied, "I am also looking for good friends who will accept me." David asked, "Are you sure you will not become a liberal?" I replied, "Hippies cannot change my views unless the May 4th issue is not resolved. This does not seem likely to me." David replied, "Glad to meet somebody who will be my friend." We said goodbye with a good feeling.

The next day on Monday, I headed to my Quantum Mechanics class. There, I met a very intelligent and long haired liberal. I said, "Hi! My name is Kevin. What is your name?" Chris replied, "My name is Chris Peaceman. I am from Connecticut." "I hope I do not scare you off," I replied. "I am a Christian from Texas. I believe that God wants me to love my neighbor as myself even if we don't always agree on politics or culture." Chris replied, "I am glad to see an open-minded Christian." Chris said, "I will be glad to get to know you." I replied, "Class is starting. See ya later."

I headed to my math physics class and then to the food service. There, I met the head pot scrubber. Her name was Sally. Sally was a middle aged woman who stressed perfection. Sally had me rinse off the pots to make them easy to scrub. I quickly learned how to rinse pots. She then had me put pots in their proper places. I learned their proper places in 2 hours. The dinner rush came to the food service, but 3 scrubbers came to help scrub pots. One scrubber was the manager. One was a cook. The last pot scrubber was a friendly liberal girl in old fashioned glasses named Tammy Peacekid. Tammy said, "My name is Tammy Peacekid." I replied, "My name is Kevin Moody." I added, "I am a Christian graduate student majoring in physics." Tammy gave me a strange look and asked, "Do you hate liberals?" I replied, "I believe that my duty to God is to love my neighbor as myself. I will be friends with anybody who will accept me for who I am." Tammy curiously asked, "Is bashing liberals part of who you are?" I answered with a smile, "I am your friend if you will be my friend." I explained, "I accept disagreement and treat friends with respect." Tammy asked, "Should we build our military?" I replied with concern, "The US should build the military to prevent the communists from taking our freedom." Tammy answered me by saying, "We need a freeze on all nuclear weapons." I replied with respect, "I never met a treaty the Soviet Union kept." Tammy asked, "What about the Helsinki Accords?" I replied with resentment toward the Soviets, "My friend, Tom Chrisgood, went to jail in Kishinev for smuggling Bibles. They kept him in jail for four days, took all of his money, and kicked him out of the country." Tammy asked, "Wasn't Tom violating Russia's law by smuggling Bibles?" I replied, "Tom was enforcing the Helsinki Accords the Soviet Union chose to violate. He should have been able to mail these Bibles to his Pentecostal friends in the Soviet Union. That is why I am conservative, and why I think we need to build our military." Tammy asked with concern, "What about the victims of the May 4th shootings?" I replied with conviction, "The college catalog implies that the administration and the students have settled their hostilities. The establishment had better treat those victims with respect. If I find differently, I will join the May 4th Task Force and stand up for them as a Texas conservative. This kind of hate is a stench in God's nostrils." Tammy replied, "Nice to meet you. I am glad you believe we are good people. See ya."

Meanwhile; back in Cleveland, Billy Glassman and his friend Mike Ichabond departed for California. Mike was a friendly person like Billy Glassman. On the way to California, They stopped at Kent State University, so Mike could say goodbye to his girlfriend. At Kent State, Mike's girlfriend had a friend named Jill Beckley. Jill was a compassionate, friendly, and attractive woman. Mike said, "This is Jill Beckley." Billy replied, "Nice to meet you. I am on my way to California. I look forward to camping and meeting new people." Jill replied, "I would love to come along, but I have to study in Kent. I admire your sense of adventure. Tell me about your trip when you get back." Billy replied, "I will gladly talk with you when I get back." Billy felt he may have found a new friend. Mike said goodbye to his girlfriend and they departed for California.

The next day in my math-physics class, I had another conversation with Chris Peaceman. I said, "Hi! How are you doing?" Chris replied, "Just fine." Chris asked, "So you are an open-minded Christian, have you heard of proposals to freeze nuclear weapons?" I replied, "I think such proposals are not workable because the Soviet Union breaks treaties at will whenever it is convenient." Chris asked, "What treaties have the Soviets broken?" I replied with passion, "The Soviet Union broke the Helsinki Accords by violating human rights!" Chris asked, "How so?" I replied, "My friend, Tom Chrisgood, was caught smuggling Bibles to his Pentecostal friends in the Soviet Union. The Soviets put Tom in jail for four days, took all of his money, and kicked him out of the country." Chris replied, "Tom broke Russian laws, and he had it coming." I asked Chris, "Why did Tom have to smuggle Bibles to his Pentecostal friends?" I said, "According to the Helsinki Accords, Tom should have been able to mail these Bibles to his friends." Chris replied, "If we do not control nuclear weapons, mankind will destroy the world." I replied with great concern, "Without America's nuclear weapons, the Soviets will destroy either democracy or the world. We cannot trust the Soviets with a wooden nickel. They will give it back to us radioactive." Chris said, "We cannot trust the United States to do better than the Russians." Then, the professor came into the room to start class. I said, "We better let the professor speak, so let's continue this discussion later."

That evening, David Pillarman introduced me to some of his conservative friends. David said, "This is my girlfriend, Janet Mercules." Janet was a plump but attractive Greek woman. I replied, "Nice to meet you." Her brother Bill Mercules replied, "My name is Bill Mercules. Bill was heavy set but looked casually businesslike. David's friend, Mitch Fryman, replied, "My name is Mitch Fryman. I am an economic Republican. Economic Republicans believe in unregulated capitalism." I chose to overlook his ugly appearance and overly aggressive personality because we had something in common. I replied, "I believe Milton Friedman. He believes that government should not interfere with the economy. I am primarily a moral conservative." Bill replied, "I am both a religious and economic conservative." Janet said, "Dad is a patriarch of the Greek Orthodox Church." I replied, "I have met some sincere conservatives today." We talked for three hours and liked each other's company.

After class the next day, Chris and I resumed yesterday's discussion. I asked, "Could you show me that the US government cannot be trusted with nuclear weapons?" Chris replied, "President Nixon ordered break-ins at the Democratic Party headquarters in the Watergate Hotel." I replied, "Congress forced President Nixon to resign. He almost went to jail." Chris replied, "He appointed Gerald Ford Vice President, so he could be pardoned." I replied, "At least we kicked the bastard out of office and slowly cleaned it up." Chris replied, "Nixon should have spent time in jail." I replied with conviction, "I wish Nixon had gone to jail! It took Ronald Reagan to restore America's confidence in government." Chris replied, "Ronald Reagan illegally traded Iran weapons for cash to support the Countras in El Salvador." I replied emphatically, "Nobody ever proved this charge! He is innocent until proven guilty!!!" Chris asked, "Are you sure you want to trust the government with nuclear weapons?" I replied, "I am not totally sure that I trust this government completely. If I discover that the May 4th issue is not resolved and the hippies are not respected, I will question the integrity of the entire government." Chris said, "You should question its integrity now. The May 4th question in irrelevant." I replied, "The May 4 question is everything. If I cannot trust the government with the small issues, I certainly cannot trust them with things like nuclear weapons and big budget deficits. I pray that the May 4th issue is completely resolved." Chris replied, "I know that May 4th is not resolved." I saw the clock, panicked and said, "I am running late for my job, so we'll continue this later." I headed to the food service thinking, "If only he could prove these charges against the government concerning May 4, 1970, I would join the May 4th Task Force as a Texas Republican. I need the evidence to make a commitment to the hippies. Friendship with these Kent State hippies could stop me from getting needed security clearances for many jobs in physics, but these hippies are people too. If the May 4th is not resolved, I fail to love legitimate American liberals of Kent State the way Christ instructed. I compromise my ability to pray for Johnny Oilstring. If the Kent State liberals are legitimate Americans, I must show the Kent State liberals the love of Christ and try to be their friends. No excuses allowed. Maybe, I could ask Chris for proof tomorrow."

At the food service, Tammy asked in a friendly way, "How are you doing?" I replied, "I am doing fine," I said, "I hope to do a good and fast job scrubbing pots today." Tammy asked, "How do you scrub pots so fast?" I replied, "I rinse off the loose food on the pan and let the pots soak in the dishwater." I explained, "Soaking softens most of the burned on food which sticks to the pot." Tammy asked, "Where did you learn this about pots and pans?" I replied, "My parents made me do the dishes at home." I explained, "Mom taught me to soak pots and pans to make them easier." A new worker came into the room. She said, "Hi. My name is Dawn Peacegood." Dawn was an attractive and friendly woman with a businesslike look. Tammy said, "Hi. My name is Tammy Peacekid." I said, "My name is Kevin Moody." Dawn asked, "What is your major Kevin?" I replied, "My major is physics. I am a graduate student in that major." Dawn asked Tammy, "What is your major? Tammy said, "I am a general studies major, and a member of the Progressive Student Network, sometimes called the PSN." Dawn asked, "Do you believe in equal rights for gays and lesbians?" Tammy replied, "We believe in equal rights for all people including gays and lesbians." I replied, "I am about to scare you away from me because I am a Pentecostal Christian." Dawn replied, "I have an open mind, so I am not prejudiced against Christians." I replied, "I am an open-minded Pentecostal. I believe that God instructed me to love my neighbor as myself. He makes no exceptions for homosexuals, but He expects me to have no sex outside of marriage." Dawn asked, "Does this mean you will fight for equal rights for gays and lesbians?" I replied, "This means that I will be friends with any gay or lesbian who will be my friend, but for me, romance with them is not possible. I can be friends with a homosexual, but I cannot have sex with anybody." Dawn asked, "What about equal rights for gays?" I replied, "I don't know what the government should do about this issue. The Bible gives the government the authority to punish evil doers and reward good doers. Homosexuality is sin, and I am not sure that government should give sinful behavior equal rights." Dawn replied, "Then how does a Christian be friends with a homosexual?" I replied, "I don't know what the government should do with homosexuals, but Christians are instructed to love them as friends." Dawn asked, "What do you mean by loving them as friends?" I replied, "I will go places and do things with them. If I have an opportunity to hire somebody, I will give homosexuals a fair chance at the job. I cannot force this behavior on others, but I will treat all people with respect." Dawn asked, "What about these Christians who try to kill us in the name of Jesus?" I replied, "The Bible says in Matthew chapter 7 verse 1, "Judge not lest ye be judged." Christians do not have the right to condemn or kill homosexuals. Jesus requires his followers to love their neighbors as themselves. No exceptions!" "What does this mean for a homosexual? Asked Dawn. I replied, "Jesus died on the cross for the forgiveness of all possible sins of mankind. This includes homosexuality. If you do not believe me, remember the story of the adulterous woman." Dawn interrupted and asked, "What is that story?" I replied,

In Jerusalem, there was an adulterous woman. The people started to stone her to death. Jesus saw the town stoning the adulterous woman and asked the crowd, "Why are you stoning this woman?" The crowd said this woman is adulterous and the law says to stone her. Jesus started marking in the sand and said, "He that is without sin, cast the first stone." Everybody in the crowd left. Jesus asked, "Where are your accusers." She noticed that they were all gone. Jesus said, "Go and sin no more."

Dawn asked, "Does this mean that Christians should forgive and love everybody?" I replied, "Yes. Christians should respect everybody with no exceptions!" Dawn asked, "What do I say to those Christians who bash gays and want to kill them?" I replied very seriously, "You will get to heaven before these hypocrites. Tell them that a Christian with a good reputation warns them to stop bashing people. It is about 8:00 pm. I'll see you later." Dawn said, "Had a nice conversation. See you later." I thought, "I can't understand why an attractive and friendly woman like Dawn is a Lesbian. She could find a man. It seems like gays and lesbians come in all shapes and sizes."

On the next day, at Math Physics class, I forgot my concern about May 4th and resumed the discussion with Chris Peaceman over the evil Soviet Union. I reminded Chris about how little the world can trust the Soviets. Chris replied, "We cannot trust the US government any more than we can trust the

Soviets." I replied, "We are better dead than red. The Soviet Union will ban Christianity all around the world. This will result in God's wrath. God will not tolerate world-wide Communism." Chris replied by asking, "What gives America the right to impose a better dead than red philosophy on the whole world?" I answered, "America has enough nuclear weapons to destroy the world and should destroy it to stop Communism. Either America destroys the world in the defense of right or God will do it himself. The Soviet Union is a stench in God's nostrils." Chris asked in defiance, "Why do you bring God into this argument? Why do I need to believe in God? Wouldn't a loving God stop disaster from happening?" I replied, "Even if you do not believe in God, the temperature in hell will not change one degree." Chris replied angrily, "Stop preaching patriotism to me. I will never believe in God, and I think you are dumb for being a Christian. Let me know when you are willing to talk with me intelligently." I replied, "I take it that we are no longer friends because I am a Christian." Chris replied, "I'll see you when you become a liberal." I replied, "That will probably be never!! See you later!!!"

One week later in my math physics class, I said to Chris Peaceman, "Sorry for offending you a week earlier." I explained, "We simply have different views of the world." I pleaded, "I hope you will still be my friend." Chris replied, "You are forgiven." I replied, "Thanks, it is good to know you accept me as a Christian conservative." Chris asked, "What is your stand on the Arab-Israeli conflict?" I replied, "I believe that America should unconditionally support Israel because they are God's chosen people." Chris replied, "Your God must be a racist." I replied, "My God is not a racist. He just does not want other nations to persecute the Jews." Chris asked angrily, "What about the Arabs?" I replied, "Ronald Reagan's foreign policy adequately deals with the Arabs. If the Arabs give us trouble, we should bomb them. If they give us enough trouble or embargo their oil, we should nuke them." Chris asked, "What about Israel?" I replied, "We should not attack Israel unless they attack us first. If we go to war with Israel, the Jews may repent while we attack them. If this happens, our troops face the possible wrath of God. I do not support putting American troops in this danger." Chris asked, "What do you propose to do about Israel if they get out of hand?" I replied seriously, "God will certainly be their judge if they choose to do evil. Put Israel in God's hands and cut off military aid. This will keep us from committing any evil Israel may impose upon us." Chris asked, "Why don't you let God judge the Arabs?" I replied, "To the Arabs, we are the boss. The Queen of England declared Israel to be an independent state. It is our job to enforce her decree." Chris replied, "We will never have peace in the Middle East as long as we have a double standard for Israel and the Arabs. This double standard is why the Arabs hate America." I replied, "We should still bomb the Arabs whenever they make us angry." Chris replied, "This will cause the Arabs to embargo their oil, or the Soviets to attack our country." I replied, "We should bomb the Arabs mercilessly if they embargo their oil! I am not afraid of the paper tiger called the Soviet Union or of the dirt poor Arabs. Bomb the Arabs! They are Evil!" Chris replied, "Here comes the professor. I am glad to end this stupid argument."

About a month later, I was sitting in the classroom about fifteen minutes before class. As I was waiting for Chris Peaceman, I thought, "I will say "Build more bombs! Build more bombs!" This will make Chris mad. I will call him a communist." I saw Chris enter the room and chanted with passion, "Build more bombs! Build more bombs! Build more bombs!..." Chris chanted in response, "Ban the bomb! Ban the bomb! Ban the bomb!..." I replied with passion, "Reagan says we need to build more bombs, so we should mass produce bombs!" Chris asked with passion, "Why do we need these bombs?" I replied, "We need those bombs to discourage attacks by foreign countries." Chris asked, "What types of attacks by what countries?" I replied, "Libya sponsored the bombing of a diskotec in Germany and the hijacking of the cruise ship Achilles Lauro. These events killed nearly 100 people. President Reagan ordered Tripoli bombed in retaliation. Khadafy has been quiet since." Chris replied, "We should have negotiated with Libya. We killed Khadafy's child and many innocent civilians." I replied with passion, "That is Libya's problem! It serves Libya right to lose those people. They pay taxes to that evil country." Chris asked, "Is it right to kill those innocent Arabs?" I replied, "It was right for Reagan to defend our country by bombing Libya." Chris asked, "Won't you ever admit that Reagan can make a mistake?" I replied, "Reagan made a mistake. He hit Libya with the wrong kind of bombs. He should have nuked 'em." Chris replied with anger, "America should not play God with Arab countries! Nuclear weapons would have killed millions of Libyans!" I replied, "We should have blown Libya off the map. This would have discouraged terrorism." Chris replied, "I am not blood thirsty like you are. Class is about to begin."

Meanwhile, Billy Glassman and his friend Mike stopped in Kent on his way back from California. Mike Ichabond talked with his girlfriend. While Mike Ichabond was talking with his girl, Billy Glassman became friends with Jill Beckley. Jill and Billy Glassman talked about the trip to California and Jill's life in Kent. For the moment they were close friends. Billy stayed with Jill for two weeks until Jill's roommate kicked Billy out. Billy moved in across the hall and continued his friendship with Jill. After a couple days out of Jill's dorm, The RSA (resident Staff Adviser) caught Billy in the residence halls without a required escort. The RSA said, "You must have a resident with you when you are in the dorms. Get out of this hall." Two days later the RSA caught him again. The RSA said, "If I catch you in this hall again without a resident, I will kick you out of the halls permanently." Two days later, the same RSA caught Billy again. The RSA said, "Billy, get out and never come back." Then a student yelled, "He is with me!" The RSA said, "I am sorry." Billy said to the student, "My name is Billy Glassman. Thanks for letting me stay in the dorms." The student responded, "Hi! My name is Freddie Justman. I am at Kent State University on an art scholarship. You can stay with me. We young people stick together." Freddie was a long haired, bearded, and grubby looking person who was loving and very friendly. Billy and Freddie became the best of friends and roomed together for the rest of the academic year. Jill and Billy would eventually go their own ways but remain friends.

I met David Pillarman in his dorm-room. He said, "James Avonman, Chairman of the May 4th task Force, and Alan Peacemaker, Director of the Kent May 4th Center, are very mean liberals. They complain about the May 4th Memorial being scaled back. They say that President Schwartz is not even trying to raise money for the memorial. President Schwartz calls Alan's effort to raise money for the original memorial unethical. Look in the school newspaper at the article. Whenever Alan does not get his way, the hippies complain. They all act like little kids." I ignorantly replied, "They seem to fight unnecessarily over the size if the memorial. Their protest is totally unwarranted." Little did I know that the administration was failing to show legitimate American hippies and their families reasonable respect concerning the May 4th shootings. I should have investigated this problem. The controversy constantly appeared in the school newspaper. I feared losing David Pillarman as a friend if I dared question the Kent State administration.

I worked and studied in Kent until the end of the semester. I went home and worked at Family Fiberglass until the second semester began. I enrolled in Nuclear Physics, Quantum Mechanics, and Thermodynamics.

About one month into the new semester, a local bank handling Family Fiberglass's line of credit and checking account got nasty with the company. They bounced checks for a one dime overdraw, and required funds sufficient to cover payroll be on deposit for at least one business day for Dad to pick up payroll. One day, my Mom went to the bank to pay the mortgage on the building. To her surprise, It was paid! Joe Dogman, the bank's loan officer, took money out of my grandpa's account to make this payment. He carelessly mistook my grandpa's account for Dad's. Dad learned about this and was furious. He arranged a meeting with the bigwigs at the bank to discuss this issue. Dad confronted the bank saying, "You messed up royally by stealing Dad's money to pay a mortgage payment that I was about to make." Tom, Joe's boss, said, "Could you forgive us and explain to your Dad?" Dad replied, "You need to explain this to my Dad because you made the mistake." Tom replied, "I will explain this to your Dad." He asked, "How can we be of help to your business?" Dad left the meeting with a feeling of victory and a sigh of relief.

Meanwhile, at Freddie's dorm, Freddie introduced Billy to his art. Billy asked, "What is that painting you are creating." Freddie replied, "This is modern art. I am putting colors together to make a cool design." Billy replied, "I could learn to do that." Freddie said, "Go ahead." Billy and Freddie made two beautiful psychedelic designs. After they completed their paintings, Billy asked, "Can I learn to paint a beautiful woman?" Freddie replied, "With a little patience and teaching, you can learn to create anything artistic that you want." Billy asked, "Would you like to show me how to paint a scene in the woods that God created? Freddie replied, "I can teach you how to paint pieces of God's creation." They both went to the woods. They proceeded to paint a scene in the woods and liked it. Billy said to Freddie, "Art can be fun." They had a good time sharing art and nature.

Meanwhile, David Pillarman, Janet Mercules, Bill Mercules, and I went out to eat at the David's favorite Itialian restaurant. David found our seats, and we ordered our food. I ordered spaghetti and meatballs. David ordered Fettuccini. Bill and Janet ordered Alfrado and salad. After we placed our orders, we talked. David said, "We conservative students need to organize." Janet said, "We should start a chapter of Right to Life on the college campus." Bill said, "We also need the Conservative Frat Man's Club." David said, "I'll bet our friend Mitch Fryman can lead the Conservative Frat Man's Club." I said, "I am busy, but I support you in principle. I wish that they treated the students with respect. It is awful to have all of these security regulations because these liberals were violent twenty years ago." David said, "I will see what I can do to get a voice for conservative students." We talked and enjoyed our food for an hour and returned to our dorm happy.

Sometime in April of 1989, I saw Tammy Peacekid in the Student Center cafeteria pot scrubbing department. I said, "Hi Tammy! How are you doing?" Tammy replied, "I am doing fine." I said, "I believe that prejudice is evil, but the government should not enforce affirmative action." Tammy asked, "Why should the government stay out of the issue of racism?" I replied, "Government regulation will make the problem worse and decrease the efficiency of our businesses." Tammy asked, "How so?" I replied, "A Nobel Prize economist named Milton Friedman said that discrimination is evil, but government should not interfere." Tammy asked, "What happens to businesses that discriminate?" I replied, "I am greedy, so I will make the biggest profits by hiring the best man for the job. If I hire blacks and train them well, I can lower my pay scale and make even more money. Eventually, other companies will hire minorities and force their pay up to standard rates." Tammy replied, "That is greed!" I replied, "Greed makes the capitalist system work. The government's job is to keep people honest and protect their rights according to the Constitution." Tammy asked, "If the free market works so well, why do businesses still discriminate against minorities?" I replied, "The free market takes time to work. Government needs to create equality in education. If minorities are well educated, businesses that hire minorities first will get rich. Businesses which refuse to hire the best man for the job will eventually go bankrupt." Tammy asked, "Do you really believe Friedman?" I replied, "Friedman is correct. See you later."

One week later, I was laying on my bed watching the news. On that TV, a report came. The May 4th Task Force was protesting the compromised design of the May 4th Memorial. Chris Peaceman appeared on the TV and said, "I am mad because Kent State University promised to build the memorial according to the Bruno Ast design!" Chris said angrily, "They broke their word!"

Meanwhile, Billy Glassman said to Freddie, "It is a nice day. Why don't we go on a nature hike. I see beauty in the woods." Freddie replied, "I also like to hike and camp." Billy and Freddie walked to Towner Woods and walked down a trail. Billy said to Freddie, "These are wild raspberries." Freddie asked, "Are these safe to eat?" Billy replied, "These are safe to eat, as are many berries in the woods." Freddie asked, "Are there other edible berries?" Billy replied, "I have a book showing many types of edible berries, but some berries are poison." Freddie replied, "We could survive in the woods for a long time if we desired." Billy said, "Let's take a rest and listen to the birds sing." They both watched nature in action and loved it. Billy and Freddie loved their time together in the woods.

On the next day, I saw Chris Peaceman in my Quantum Mechanics class. I asked Chris with serious concern, "Did The Kent State administration really break an important agreement with the May 4th victims and their families?" Chris replied, "The administration really did break their agreement to build the memorial. May 4th is not resolved. The liberals are justified in their protest." I asked, "Can you prove this." Chris asked in disbelief, "Why are you even interested in our rights?" I replied, "Failure to resolve issues concerning May 4th is an abomination unto the Lord." Chris asked, "Do you really believe liberals are human?" I replied, "Liberals are human, but many are criminals who hate America, and some are communists." Chris replied, "I can prove the liberals were mistreated." "How?" I asked. Chris replied, "Talk to the May 4th families and members of the Progressive Student Network, also called the PSN." I asked, "Where can I meet them?" Chris asked, "Can you meet me at this Wednesday's PSN meeting?" I replied with fear, "I have to work that night." Chris asked, "Can you meet me at Thursday's May 4th meeting?" I replied, "I have to work that night as well." Chris asserted, "You do not really want to give us a chance." Chris speculated, "You must be afraid to enter the wolf's den to talk to us." I replied, "Can one of you meet me this weekend at Elight Island in the Wheeler Creek housing development in Gainesville, Texas." Chris asked, "Why Texas?" I replied, "I need to talk to my Scriptural Analyst, Robert Elight, to decide about the liberals." Chris asked, "What if we are found wrong by Robert?" I replied, "We will bash the liberals mercilessly." Chris replied "If you are really sincere, you will take time off of work to meet us at one of our meetings and face the wolves." Chris said hoping to end the discussion, "Here comes the professor." I replied, "I hope the administration hears this. If I find out that the liberals are being mistreated, I will join them as a Texas Republican."

A week later, I saw Tammy Peacekid of the Progressive Student

Network. She asked, "How are you?" I replied, "I am fine." I asked, "Is the administration really lying concerning the May 4th memorial?" Tammy replied, "The lies concerning the May 4th memorial are just the tip of the iceberg. The US Government tells lies whenever it is convenient." I replied, "If the government is lying about the May 4th shootings 20 years after the fact, they are lying about many other things. Trusting the government will be impossible if they are lying about these kids. How do you suggest that a Christian handles this?" Tammy said, "We are taught that we should never trust the government. We should always register and vote our conscience. We should always ask questions and hold the government accountable for its performance." I replied, "It sounds like I should be a good citizen and speak out against evil in the government." Tammy said, "Democracy requires us to be actively involved in the governmental process. Vote and join a political party. Consider running for office." I replied, "Some of the liberals, in Kent, seem to be good US citizens." Tammy said, "We are nice people, and some of us love our country." I asked with astonishment, "Can you show me?" Tammy asked, "Can you come to the SDS reunion two weeks from this Friday?" I replied, "I will think about it. See you later."

On May 5, I attended a Leebrick Hall banquet and dance. There I met my good friends, David Pillarman and Janet Mercules. I asked, "How are you guys doing?" David said, "Fine. Why don't you eat some of that fried chicken and potato chips?" He added, "Meet us at Table 5 after you get your food." I took a heaping plate of chicken, some potato chips, and 3 big cups of pop. I met David and Janet at the table and started eating. David left and said, "See you a little later." The rain started falling and the thunder clapped. I said, "I hope that lightning strikes the Kent State SDS and kills them." Janet said with respect toward God, "Shame on you. You should never wish God's wrath on anybody." I replied in my defense, "I am not totally serious." I explained, "I am frustrated because we have to pay for the violence committed 20 years ago by the SDS." Janet asked, "How so?" I replied, "We always have to escort our guests to our rooms in the residence halls. We cannot have gatherings of more than ten without permission from the university." Janet said, "Mitch and David are protesting the SDS reunion on the plaza." She asked, "Why don't you join them later?" I said enthusiastically, "I will consider, but I wish to over-eat this chicken and stay a little while for the party." After I partied hearty, I said, "I have to get going to the protest." Janet said, "Good for you. Go ahead and get active politically." I said, "See you after the protest."

The Conservative Frat Man's Club was protesting old members of the SDS having a reunion at Kent State. They were mad that the SDS burned down buildings and disrupted learning in the 1970's. Many of them resented security regulations stemming from the actions of the SDS in Kent. They feared the liberals would again cause a riot. I agreed with the Conservative Frat Man's Club, so I joined them in protest.

I met Bill Mercules and Mitch on the Student Center plaza. They showed me the signs to be used at the protest and met some people near the Student Center entrance. One person was an older Vietnam veteran. Mitch said, "We should honor all war veterans because they served America in its time of need." Bill said, "Congratulations on your military service in Vietnam. My name is Bill." The veteran replied, "My name is Tom." Mitch said, "My name is Mitch. I want to honor you for your military service. I wish to warn you that the SDS is in the Student Center plaza." Tom said with a glazed and hostile look in his eyes, "You conservatives do not get it." Tom explained, "I did not support the War in Vietnam, and I wish to support the peace movement and to support the SDS reunion." Mitch said to me and Bill, "We booked a room next to the SDS reunion." He asked, "Why don't we go there and disrupt the SDS reunion." Bill and I agreed. We all wanted to get out of the rain. On our way up to the room, we met the manager of the Student Center. He asked, "Where are you going with those signs?" Mitch replied, "To Room 246 in the Student Center" The manager told the Conservative Frat Man's Club, "You had better remove all of your protest signs and belongings from that room at once. It is not a good idea to let the Conservative Frat Man's Club into a room next to the SDS reunion. If you want, I can assign you to another room." Mitch declined. As we exited the building, we ran into a Kent State hippie named Kathy and her 11 year old girl. Kathy's 11 year old girl saw our signs and said, "It is against the rules to show those signs in the building." I said to Mitch and Bill, "We should reconsider this protest because God does not appear to be with us." Mitch replied, "Don't worry, everything will be all right, so let's do this protest for right." We also met Tammy Peacekid. She invited us to the SDS reunion. Mitch said, "We will think about it later."

We moved all of our protest signs outside and started to protest. Mitch and Bill started to chant, "SDS, You're a mess. You're a bunch of terrorists! SDS, you're a mess! You're a bunch of terrorists!......" All of us raised signs and chanted for ten straight minutes. Then, Bill said, "If you have any children, I would not enter the Student Center. The SDS is in there, and they are terrorists." I then chanted, "Child killers! Child killers! The SDS kills children." Then we all resumed the chant, "SDS, You're a mess! You're a bunch of terrorists! SDS You're a mess! You're a bunch of terrorists!..." About ten minutes later Bill yelled, "Alan, get a job!" I yelled, "McDonald's is hiring!! The food service is always hiring!" Bill yelled repeatedly for ten minutes, "Alan, Get a job! I repeatedly yelled after Bill said his piece, "McDonald's is hiring!" After ten minutes, the rain became heavy, so we decided to visit the SDS reunion.

On the way to the reunion, Mitch said, "Let's be nice to the hippies until they say something stupid." Bill said, "Let's eat them out of house and home." At the reunion, I met James Avonman, Chairman of the May 4th Task Force. James was plump and long haired, but friendly. James said, "Hi, My name is

James." I replied, "My name is Kevin Moody, a Texas Republican and a former student senator from Arlington State University." James replied, "I am a student senator and chairman of the May 4th Task Force." "Hi, my name is Alan, one of the nine wounded students from the Kent State shootings and May 4th Center Director." Alan was a well-known advocate for the liberal culture in Kent. He had a little gray hair, was well-built, and looked his age of 40. I replied, "The moral case for the Ohio conservatives looks shaky." I asked, "If I join your cause, who would be a friend to a Pentecostal Christian like me?" James replied, "We are friendly people. If you treat us with respect, we will respect you, and you will have friends." Alan said with passion, "We no longer believe in violence. Violence begets violence." James said, "I agree." Mitch came to me and said, "We had better take our place on the sidelines." He explained, "Their speaker is about ready to speak."

Their speaker, Tim Peacegood, said in his speech:

America lost the war in Vietnam. It served the arrogant United States right. Americans massacred the North Vietnamese and lost a lot of their own for a South Vietnam whose people did not want the Americans there to fight for a corrupt government. I am happy that the United States lost this war. As for the bombing of the math building at the Wisconsin University, We (the SDS) warned the authorities that we were going to bomb the math building. The government said the building was evacuated. When we blew the building up, we thought the building was empty. A person happened to be there to die. Does anybody have any questions?

Tim was a short, professional looking 40 year old communist. He was the 1968 president of the Kent State SDS. I asked Tim, "If the United States and the Soviet Union went to war, whose side would you be on?" Tim replied, "I will let you answer that question." I thought, "Everybody in the audience knew that the Soviet Union had thousands of nuclear missiles pointed at the United States, and the Soviet Union was a communist enemy of the United States. Everybody knew that North Vietnam was a communist ally of the Soviets. I just successfully insinuated that their speaker was a communist." For a few minutes, Tim answered questions from the liberals in the crowd. After the question and answer session, I went up to talk to Tim. He ran. One liberal came up to me and said, "You don't understand what May 4th was like." He cried, "You never lost a close friend in a political struggle." I replied, "I have some idea of what it is like. My friend, Tom Chrisgood, got caught smuggling Bibles into the Soviet Union. The Soviets held him in jail for four days. They took all of his money and kicked him out of the country. All this was done in violation of the Helsinki Accords. That is one reason I am a tough conservative." The liberal asserted, "At least Tom is alive. You can still visit him and have good times with him. We can't do that with the four dead students." I replied with sympathy, "I apologize for their deaths." The liberal said, "I don't believe you." Another liberal said, "Tim's father would be proud of what he said today." I replied, "My dad would be proud of what I said today. My dad's friend, Bob Faucenaught, died when the SDS bombed the Math Building at the University of Wisconsin." This second liberal said, "You will have to make up for what you did tonight. You bashed our speaker. You insinuated he was a communist." I thought, "We are so much alike. Someday soon, we could be friends with a little patience. We both suffered loss for our respective causes."

After the speech, the May 4th Task Force, The Progressive Student Network, and the Conservative Frat Men drank punch, ate crackers, spinach dip, and rye bread. Another Conservative Frat Man and candidate for the Catholic Priesthood, Jim Godman, talked one on one with the former president of the national office of the SDS, James Dough. James said, "It was all right for the SDS to burn buildings to the ground." Jim replied, "Violence is never right. There are some wars that are not justified. Jesus Christ commands that we be at peace with our fellow man whenever possible." James asked, "Does this mean that the Vietnam War was not justified?" Jim replied, "It may not have been. I would need to study its history to know." James said, "I believe that the hippie culture violence was justified because they were fighting for their freedom." Jim said, "You fought the wrong way because America is a free country." James asked, "What about the Army of God?" He said, "They blow up abortion clinics." Jim replied, "I sympathize with their cause, but their violence is wrong. God says we must make fighting a last resort."

As my friends and I were leaving the party, I met a 70's style hippie named Dennis. Dennis was friendly and well-built. Dennis showed his name tag and asked, "How are you doing, Kevin?" I replied, "Fine." I asked, "Are you liberals all communists, and do all of you hate America?" Dennis replied, "We are not all communists, and some of us love America." I asked, "What about your speaker?" Dennis replied, "You will have to excuse Tim. His Dad and uncle are leaders in the Communist Party. We liked Tim because he fought hard with us for world peace. We did not like Vietnam." I replied, "My best friend's uncle is the President of the International Ministerial Association. This organization runs many Oneness Pentecostal Churches around the world. I am a staunch conservative partly due to Robert's influence. I can forgive you for the SDS if you can accept me as a holy roller." Dennis said, "Let's accept each other." I replied, "I agree. See you later."

On our way home, I asked Jim, "Why does the administration lie about the May 4th shootings?" Jim replied, "Any time the government has to shoot to restore the peace, there is a cover-up." I asked with a small amount of righteous indignation, "Can you give me other examples in our history?" Jim replied, "When the government put down a riot at a West Virginia coal mine in 1921, There was a cover-up of the shootings necessary to put down that riot." I replied, "I will give the Kent State administration and the Ohio Republicans one more chance." I explained, "If I see one more dirty play by Ohio's Republicans or Kent State's administration, I will join the May 4th Task Force." Jim replied, "I understand because they are accountable to God for their actions."

At 9 o'clock the next morning, in the Kent State food service, I saw Tammy Peacekid. Tammy asked, "Hi. How was the reunion?" "I bashed a former SDS president as a Conservative Frat Man," I replied, "I called him a communist." Kim replied, "Shame on you. You should know better." I replied, "I am sorry. I won the argument, but I may have bashed Tim in error. The PSN and May 4th Task Force proved that May 4th is not resolved." Tammy replied, "Tim is not scared by you, the Conservative Frat Man's Club, or any other basher." I replied, "Tim does not have to be scared of me. I was wrong for bashing him and am leaving the liberal bashing business before I sin against God again. Please forgive me." Tammy replied, "I forgive you, but you need to apologize to Tim." I asked, "How do I do that?" Tammy replied, "Tim does not leave until 1 pm and you get off at 12 pm." She explained, "You might be able to catch him before he leaves." I replied, "I will not get off until 12 pm. To see Tim, I must go home and shower and change these stinking clothes. It will take me until 1 pm to see Tim if I am lucky." Tammy replied, "I understand because I really think you are sorry." I replied with gratitude, "Thanks for understanding." Tammy said, "I knew there is a lot of good in you." I said, "You will be happy to hear this." "What?" asked Tammy. I replied seriously, "I have found that the May 4th issue is not resolved. They are nice people. They are not all all communists. One more dirty trick by Ohio Republicans or Kent State's administration, I will join the May 4th Task Force as a Texas Republican." Tammy replied, "The Kent State administration is not scared of you." I replied, "The Kent State administration does not need to fear me. I can not do anything to them without God's help, but they had better fear the God of Israel that I serve." Tammy asked, "What can God do to President Schwartz?" I replied, "God can take the kingdom out of his hands and replace him with somebody better." Tammy asked, "Are there examples in the Bible?" I replied, "God took the kingdom out of the hands King Saul, Israel's first king. God also took the kingdom out of the hands of Belchazzar, The King of the Babylonian Empire. The Babylonian empire oppressed the children of Israel." Tammy asked, "Can you give me one more example of a powerful king being destroyed by God?" I replied, "God overthrew Ninevah and the Nation of Assyria because they intimidated the Kings of Israel, most notably the righteous King Hesakia." Tammy asked, "If God throws Schwartz out, who will replace him, another scoundrel as bad as him?" I replied, "If his replacement is as bad as President Schwartz, God will replace him. He will continue this process until the right person is in office." Tammy asked, "How long will this take?" I replied, "God will solve this problem in his own time." Tammy said, "President Schwartz is only going to play his evil games again." I replied, "Then, his days as President in Kent will be numbered." I asked, "If God be for me, who can be against me and win?" I declared, "I guarantee God is mad about the unresolved May 4th issue."

The next day on Sunday, I gloated in the pride of bashing a hippie who helped to bring down President Nixon and end the Vietnam War. I called my Mom and Dad, "Last Friday night, I bashed the 1968 President of the Kent State SDS," I said to Mom and Dad, "He gloated about how the United States lost the Vietnam War. I insinuated he was a communist by asking him for whom he would fight for if the United States went to war with the Soviet Union. He declined to answer and ran." Dad said, "These hippies are not as smart as they look." My Mom said, "I always knew that you should have joined the debate team in high school or college." Dad said, "Good luck on your finals. See you this weekend." I replied, "See you Saturday." I called Johnny. I said, "I bashed the 1968 president of the Kent State SDS." Johnny replied in a friendly but scolding voice, "Shame on you." I asked, "Why?" Johnny said, "You are a great Christian. I am disappointed that you would bash anybody." I replied, "I am sorry. I should have shown better judgment." I asked, "Will you forgive me?" Johnny said, "I forgive you, but you need to ask God and the Kent State hippies to forgive you." I asked, "Will you still treat me like a friend?" Johnny replied, "I will be happy to see you, but I will be busy with two jobs." I asked, "When and where do I meet you next Saturday?" Johnny replied, "Meet me at the Dangas Station on US 82 near the Gainesville City limits at 11:30 pm this Saturday night." I replied, "See you then!"

At the Dangas Station station, Johnny asked, "How are you doing?" I replied, "I am doing fine, I hope you still respect me after I bashed the liberals." Johnny replied, "You are a good friend even if you are not perfect." I said, "Looks like you have a customer." Johnny said, "I'll serve the customer and talk to you afterward" Johnny served about ten customers in a row and invited me to talk with him as he measured the gasoline in the underground tank. Johnny got out a ten foot long stick graduated in gallons. Johnny said, "This is the ruler I use to measure the gas in the station tank. First, I remove the lid on the parking lot gas tank. Then, I put the measuring stick in the tank vertically until I hit bottom. Finally, I remove and read this measuring stick, and I put the lid back on this tank." I replied, "Managing one of these stations must be simple." Johnny replied, "Managing this station is simple if you can put up with the long hours and the paperwork." I replied, "School is paperwork and long hours. This summer I need to study for my candidacy exam." Johnny replied, "Good luck with your exam. See you tomorrow at noon." I replied, "See you tomorrow."

On that Sunday, I met Johnny at his house. Johnny asked, "How is it going?" I replied, "I am doing fine." Johnny said, "My work hours are long and in the evening, so I will be busy." I asked, "Are you mad at me for bashing the SDS?" Johnny replied, "I still accept you as a good friend, but I am disappointed that a big time Christian like you would bash the hippies of Kent State." I asked, "When can we get together?" Johnny replied, "You can meet me at the Dangas Station on Friday and Saturday nights at 11:30 pm." I asked, "Do you want to go to my favorite restaurant in Gainesville?" Johnny replied, "I will be glad to go." At that restaurant, I asked Johnny, "How do we handle the SDS?" Johnny replied, "Apologize to the hippies you hurt. They may seem tough, but they have feelings. They hurt the same way that I hurt. They can be good friends like me." I replied, "I can put US Physics in danger by being friends with these hippies." Johnny replied, "You may need these hippies to get project Texhoma past America's big energy companies" Johnny said, "Treat the Kent State hippies like you treat me, and we both win." I replied, "I will think about what you said, so let's be good friends." The waitress said, "I can take your order." I ordered fried chicken and 2 servings of French fries. Johnny ordered fried chicken and smashed potatoes. Janie ordered turkey and stuffing. We ate our dinner and went home good friends.

Throughout the summer, Johnny and I shared a good friendship, and I studied for my candidacy exams. In the middle of that summer, I was working on molds when Tom said, "Somebody from South Carolina claiming to be a witch put a hex on Texas Coach, all of its suppliers, and all of Grayson County." I thought for a moment and replied, "A witch cannot put a hex on Texas Coach and all of Grayson County." Tom asked, "Why?" I replied, "There are thousands of Christian cowboys, Pentecostals, Evangelicals, and Catholics in Grayson County. If just two of these Christians pray for Sherman, Grayson County, and Texas Coach, this hex is finished." Tom asked, "Can quality hurt Texas Coach?" I replied, "A quality problem can bankrupt Texas Coach without a hex." Tom asked, "Will Texas Coach correct its quality problems if it has them?" I replied, "Texas Coach's president will correct any quality problems quickly." I further emphasized, "He may fire a few bad people, but he will solve Texas Coach's quality problems." Tom asked, "Are those firings the worst that will happen at Texas Coach?" I replied, "The worst that will happen is the firing of those few bad people." We completed our work day and went home.

That evening, I had a meeting with Occult Defense Analyst Myron E Chrisgood. We exchanged greetings, and I said, "History seems to favor your opinion concerning Kent State." Mr. Chrisgood asked, "Is May 4th resolved?" I replied, "May 4th is not resolved." I further emphasized, "One more hostile move against the Kent State hippies, and I will join their protest concerning May 4, 1970." Mr. Chrisgood said, "I believe your move concerning Kent State to be a good one." I asked, "What do you think about the Texas Coach hex that made the news this morning?" Mr. Chrisgood replied, "This hex is almost impossible to execute because there are too many Christians working for Texas Coach." I asked in response, "Does this mean that this hex will not work because many of these Christians will pray for God to provide for them?" Mr. Chrisgood said, "Just two Christians, in Sherman, praying for their needs will stop this hex in its tracks." I asked, "Why don't we break this hex now by praying for Texas Coach and Grayson County." Mr. Chrisgood replied, "Let us pray." I prayed:

Lord Jesus, Please protect Texas Coach, its suppliers, and all of Grayson County from this hex. I pray especially for Texas Coach Supplier Family Fiberglass, which is our family business. In the name of Jesus we ask this. Amen.

Mr. Chrisgood prayed:

Lord Jesus, Please protect Texas Coach, its suppliers, and all of Grayson County from this hex. Remember Family Fiberglass and Sherman Bus' Texas plant where our Christian brother draws his retirement. In the name of Jesus we ask this. Amen.

I said, "This will guarantee the Texas Coach hex to be a failure" Mr. Chrisgood replied, "It is good to nip this hex in the bud before it causes a lot of problems." I said, "We'll worry about our moral dilemma at Kent State knowing that Grayson County is safe. See you later."

During that summer vacation, a horrible thing happened. I was staying with Johnny Oilstring's brother, Jimmy, in LaPorte, Indiana. On Jimmy's television, I heard that Lou Holtz paid players while he was the head football coach at The University of Minnesota. It was alleged that Holtz gave Gardner $500 to give to a football player. As of July of 1989, Cordelli and all of Holtz's assistants at Minnesota denied knowledge of payments to football players. Little did I know, later in 1989, Pete Cordelli, Notre Dame's Quarterbacks coach, changed his story to say that Holtz paid Roselle Richardson. Later, Cordelli said the payment was $200. Lou would later say in his defense that he paid Roselle Richardson $20 for losing his wallet. This payment to Richardson was a minor violation of NCAA rules in either case. The NCAA will have found Holtz guilty of 2 minor violations in 1991. Notre Dame was innocent. Why did Pete Cordelli accuse Lou Holtz of paying Richardson and hurt Notre Dame? The media said that Pete Cordelli interviewed for a head coaches position at Kent State University. Johnny and I were stunned that Holtz or Notre Dame could do any wrong.

Pete Cordelli had just accused Lou Holtz of paying Richardson. This hurt Notre Dame's image. Even Notre Dame's greats were fighting for the spotless reputation of their football program. Nobody at Notre Dame could stop Cordelli from hurting Notre Dame's image. Thank the Lord! The NCAA would clear Lou Holtz of all but two minor violations! Notre Dame was innocent. Notre Dame was busy defending the their football program at a critical time concerning the May 4th Memorial. Kent State's administration had a big incentive to minimize publicity concerning the May 4th shootings in 1970. Cordelli interviewed for a head coach's position at Kent State in 1988. Ara Parsigian and Lou Holtz were great public relations men. Father Hessburgh spoke out against the Vietnam War in the 1970's. What a coincidence!!! Cordelli, a future head coach at Kent State, changed his story about Holtz paying Richardson at a critical time concerning the Kent State Memorial in 1989!!! This action demoralized the Notre Dame Athletic Department and hurt its credibility. What if somebody from Notre Dame spoke out about Kent State's May 4th controversy? Johnny thought that Notre Dame was unfairly attacked, but I thought that Notre Dame could take it without damage to their football program. Little did I know that I was wrong.

I returned to Kent State to study physics. During the first week of the academic year, student organizations recruit members on the Student Center plaza. I encountered the Progressive Student Network's recruiters there. I asked, "What is your stand concerning the environment?" Kim was manning the booth. She was a medium height, clear complected, brown haired, attractive, and friendly woman with a ring in her nose. Kim replied, "If something is not done about air pollution, we will have global warming." I asked, "Is our water any safer?" Kim replied, "Last year, used and infected syringes from New York's hospitals washed from the ocean on to the beach of Jersey City. This is a way to spread infectious diseases to millions of people." Kim further emphasized, "The water and food from that water is slowly becoming poisoned." I asked, "Where do we put all of our garbage?" Kim replied. "We put too much of it in landfills. The Progressive Student Network's environmental committee proposes that trash should be recycled." I asked, "Does this organization propose selling-out the nation of Israel?" Kim replied, the Progressive Student Network proposes that the Palestinians should have their own independent state." I replied, "The Jews are God's chosen people. America must not betray Israel, or it will face God's judgment. I cannot betray Israel and join the Progressive Student Network."

Meanwhile, Billy Glassman, and Freddie Justman enrolled in classes at Kent State University. A few days later, Billy saw a woman on the Student Center plaza. Billy said to the woman, "Hi, my name is Billy Glassman." The woman replied, "My name is Mary Cutman. Nice to meet you" They talked for a few hours and became friends. Mary was a dark complected, plump, and very friendly woman. Later Mary introduced Billy to her friend, Malinda Free. Malinda was a light complected, plump, and friendly woman. Billy, Malinda, and Mary talked for a few hours and became friendly. A few days later, Billy saw a woman in his anthropology class. Billy said to that woman, "My name is

Billy Glassman. I would like to know you." Katie replied, "You are a very nice and friendly young man. Let's be friends." On Wednesday, They all went to the PSN and decided that they liked the meeting. They all joined and became liberals in Kent.

One week later, Janet Mercules asked me to join Right to Life and help fight abortions. I joined. At the first meeting, I met the President of the Kent State chapter of Right to Life, Sally. Sally was an attractive, young, friendly, and businesslike woman who looked the part. Sally said, "Welcome to the Kent State Chapter of the Right to Life Society. My Name is Sally." I replied, "My name is Kevin." Sally said, "Our organization is fighting to stop abortions. We aim to make abortions unlawful and encourage pregnant women to seek other alternatives." I replied, "I am a Christian who believes it necessary to love his neighbor as himself. Trying to save unborn babies from abortions is a good cause." Sally brought the meeting to order and asked everybody to study the literature. I noticed the picture of unborn babies and said, "Unborn babies have a right to live, so we must do what we can to protect these babies." Sally replied with urgency, "We must try to outlaw abortions and talk pregnant women into putting their unborn children up for adoption." I replied, "This sounds like a plan." Mitch said, "We must take this message to the PSN and try to convince those women to put their unborn children up for adoption." Sally called everybody to attention, called a meeting next week on Tuesday, and dismissed the meeting.

At the next Right to Life meeting, Sally and Jim announced two protests concerning the abortion issue. One was an Operation Rescue protest at an abortion clinic in Akron. In this protest, they were going to block the entrances to the clinic and go limp if the police tried to arrest them. This protest occurred this Saturday, when I was going to Texas to visit Johnny. The other protest was three weeks from this Saturday. It was a peaceful and legal march concerning abortion in Columbus, Ohio. In this march, we were marching with signs on the sidewalks of the streets near Ohio's state capitol building. The Right to Life Society had all of the needed permits to march down the streets of Columbus. Sally said, "Anybody interested in going to Columbus please sign up today or next Tuesday." She asked, "Please bring $15 by next Tuesday to cover the cost of the charter bus if you wish to march in Columbus." I signed up for the march and paid my $15.

Meanwhile, Billy and his three new friends were hanging out on the Student Center plaza. They were discussing their beliefs. Billy said, "I believe that we need to start a recycling program in the dorms." Mary said, "I can haul recyclables from my floor in the dorms to the nearby recyclable center." Malinda said, "Katie and I can do the same in our dorms. Billy said, "I can haul trash and label trash cans for recycling. Let's start tonight!" Billy and his three friends all agreed, and they started a recycling program that changed Kent forever. Men and women often worked together for liberal causes, and sometimes they became good friends through the process. Though Billy became close friends with Katie, Mary, and Malinda, they would never become romantic.

Three weeks later on Saturday, I met the Right to Life group at the Student Center bus depot. Jim said, "Thanks for standing up for the rights of babies today. May God bless you today." A friendly man with long red hair, a beard, and a fit medium build, named Tom, joined the group. He said, "Many of the people in my political science class, including the professor, are pro-choice liberals, so I fear academic reprisals, but support Right to Life." I replied, "There is an appeals process dealing with unfair teachers. Let me reassure you, your professor will tolerate your views and treat them with respect." Tom asked, "What if my professor does not respect my views?" I replied, "We will hold him accountable." Jim said, "There is our bus." We all boarded the bus and headed toward Akron to pick up more anti-abortion protesters. We picked up the protesters and headed toward Columbus. Most of us enjoyed the scenery for two hours. When we arrived in Columbus, we picked up our signs and started walking down the streets. Well into our walk, we noticed the police watching. They were friendly. They just asked us to stay on the sidewalk, so traffic could flow freely. Jim said, "The police are friendly because some of them support our cause and know that we will not cause trouble." Towards the end of our march, we were tired and getting cold. We happily boarded the bus to Kent, and we were proud of our day's work concerning the abortion cause.

On that next Tuesday, at about 6 pm, I contacted Johnny. Johnny said, "You're always on Joe Sinc's case concerning his non-Christian behavior." He asked, "Why don't we fast and pray for Joe Sinc's salvation?" I replied, "Good idea, I will fast for Joe Sinc starting at midnight tonight." I headed to a Kent Interhall council meeting with great joy. After the meeting, I returned to my dorm and turned on the TV. San Francisco just had a major earthquake! I started my fast at midnight and prayed and fasted that whole day. At about 9 pm on Wednesday, God led me to drive to Cleveland. This still soft voice lead me to pray for people working at Cleveland Stadium (Map 10). This Stadium was nicknamed "The Dog Pound" by many football fans of the day. After I performed my mission in Cleveland, I returned to Kent. On my way to the dorm, I asked God, "Am I doing everything possible to please you?" The still soft voice of God replied, "The Devil is strongly located in one of two places: The Kent State administration or the Kent State May 4th Center." I asked God, "How will I know which power to oppose?" God replied in a still soft voice, "You will know which power is good by the resolution of issues concerning May 4, 1970. I will reveal this resolution in the next few weeks." I asked, "What shall I do while I am waiting?" God replied, "Wait until I reveal the truth to act concerning May 4th."

One day later, I went to Gainesville to see my friends and family. When I arrived in Gainesville, the power was out for the second straight day and trees and power lines were down. Dad said, "A tornado knocked out the power yesterday, but we hope the power will be on when we get home from work tomorrow." I replied, "I'll put on an extra blanket and make due with what we have." Dad said, "Your Grandma Esther does not have too much time on this earth. Could you please visit her this weekend." I asked, "Where is she hospitalized?" Dad replied, "She is at a nursing home named the Peaceful Resthouse. This nursing home is located on Grand Avenue with a big sign out front." I replied, "I will see her this Saturday." We worked Friday, and the power was on when we arrived at home.

On Saturday, I visited Grandma Esther at the nursing home. Grandma was a skinny 74 year old who looked 40. She had a loving heart. I asked, "How is my favorite grandma?" Grandma replied, "I am doing fine." She said, "I hope to be on my feet soon." I asked, "Do you remember some of the fine Christmas and Thanksgiving feasts we had at your house?" Grandma replied, "I enjoyed having the family over for the holidays. It was fun to see my grand-kids happy when they got their favorite toys." I asked, "Do you remember that Christmas at our house on Greenacre when you gave me that transistor radio from the Sears catalog that I really wanted?" Grandma replied, "It made me happy to see you happy in that house on Greenacre." "I remember another Christmas when we came to visit you from Indiana," I replied, "I got to see my friend Tommy Woodman, had a nice Christmas, and watched Notre Dame win the national championship in football." Grandma replied, "I enjoyed seeing all of you that year." I said, "I want to make sure that if something happens that you will be in heaven." Grandma replied, "I have committed my life to Jesus, and I have made right with him." I said, "I hope to see you at Christmas and to have a good time. Love you. See you at Christmas."

On Sunday at about 2 pm at the California Road stop of Dangas, I met Johnny for a friendly conversation. I asked, "Johnny, How are you doing? "Johnny replied, "I am doing fine." I said, "I just want to see my best friend a few minutes before I head back to Kent. How is the station doing?" Johnny replied, the station is doing fine, but I hired Becky and have feelings for her." I asked, "What about Janie?" Johnny replied, "Don't tell Janie because she will be mad because I even considered hiring her. I don't even talk to her and pray that God will work this problem out." I said, "I will pray that God works this out. I need to tell you something. Two hours after we declared fasting and prayer concerning Joe Sinc, a major earthquake hit San Francisco, and a day later a tornado hit Gainesville." Johnny asked, "Could Joe Sinc be without all of this bloodshed?" I replied, "We do not know that this is the judgment of God, but God had a purpose in the San Francisco earthquakes and the Gainesville tornado." Johnny replied, "I was just giving you a rough time. See you later."

Meanwhile, Billy and his good friends were hanging out on the Student

Center plaza. Malinda said, "I believe that a woman has a right to get an abortion and should be treated with equality." Mary said, "A woman has a right to do with her body what she wants." Katie said, "I agree." She asked Billy,

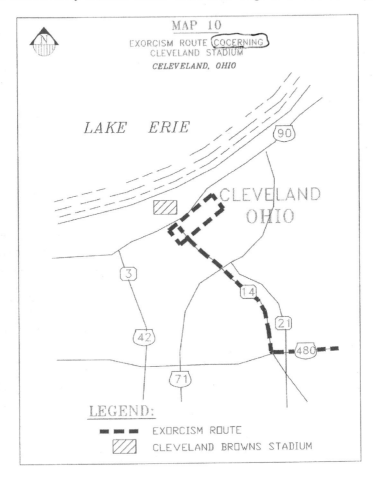

Map by Dan Eaves

"Do you think a woman has rights?" Billy replied, "I believe that every person has rights and should be treated well. You are all my friends." Malinda asked, "What are we going to do about those mean Conservative Frat Men?" Mary added, "They bash us mercilessly!!!" Katie proclaimed, "Their leader Mitch called me a Nazi!!!!" Billy said, "Maybe God will help us become friends with one of those Conservatives." Malinda said, "I hear that one of the Conservative Frat Men is suspicious of the failure to resolve the May 4th issue." Billy said, "If I run into him, I will try to be his friend. We should try to be friends with everybody." The others all agreed. Billy said, "I like all of you. If any of us get bashed, let's stick together." They all agreed.

On the Tuesday before Veterans Day, Dad called Kent to tell me about Grandma Esther. Dad said, "Grandma is barely conscious and cannot talk to anybody. She may die soon." I asked, "What hospital is she in?" Dad replied, "She is not in the hospital or receiving medical treatment." I asked, "Why not?" Dad replied, "Grandpa George will not give his permission to send Grandma to the hospital." Grandpa George was a fat, selfish, and retired truck driver. I replied, "This is ridiculous. Call your lawyer and fight for Grandma." Dad said, "I already called him, and the case goes to court tomorrow morning." Dad explained, "My lawyer says we should have our court order by 4 pm tomorrow, but Grandma may be dead by then." I replied, "I will pray for Grandma. Perhaps, you should bug the nursing home until 4 tomorrow. If she dies, this is not your fault." Dad replied with sorrow, "I love my Mom and do not want to lose her. It hurts to see her die in pain unnecessarily." I said with compassion, "Just do your best and put this matter in God's hands. Perhaps God is calling her to heaven. Heaven is a much better place than this earth. Grandma will be happy there." Dad replied, "I love my Mom. I am mad about how she is being treated. See you later."

Right after Dad hung up the phone. Dad called my Uncle Larry. Uncle Larry was a plump but very friendly and popular car salesman. They met at the nursing home. Dad asked the front desk, "When are you going to send my Mom to the hospital!?" The clerk at the front desk replied, "As soon as her husband authorizes it." Uncle Larry angrily replied, "That could be never!" He asked, "Do you want her blood on your hands!!?" The clerk replied, "I can do nothing, but I will get you the manager." The manager came to the front desk and said, "I cannot send your Mom to the hospital without George's approval." Dad said, "Come to her room and look at her." The manager said, "She looks bad, but I cannot call an ambulance without George's approval." Dad said angrily, "You will be speaking to my lawyer!!!! I love my Mom! Your treatment of her makes me sick to my stomach! Her blood will be on your hands! You will be sued!" Uncle Larry said, "When I get home, I will call the state! They will shut you down!" The manager said, "All right! All right! I will call the ambulance." The ambulance arrived five minutes later and took over Grandma's care. They gave her an IV she badly needed and took her to the hospital. The ambulance driver said, "Your Mom is in our hands. We are the boss until she gets to the hospital. She will get the best of care." There, Grandma received the care she needed, but it was too late. She died.

At about ten after four in the afternoon, Dad called me in Kent and asked, "Could you come to Gainesville for Grandma's funeral this Friday?" I replied, "I will hit the road tomorrow at 3 pm"

At about 8:00 pm Thursday, I arrived in Gainesville. Dad was heartbroken. He asked, "Why did Mom have to die without dignity." I replied, "I do not know why nobody cared about Grandma during her last days, but we can thank the Lord that she is going to heaven. She told me she made her heart right with God when I saw her three weeks ago." Dad replied, "I just wish she were here with us now." I replied, "We all loved her and would want to see her if we could, but we can be happy that she is in a happy place now." Dad replied in his defense, "We are all a bit selfish. I hope you understand. I will be with you at the funeral tomorrow."

At about 2:00 pm Friday, we all met at the funeral home. Kim was a friendly and attractive sister. Lefty was a quarterback at Arlington College in the 70's. He was short haired, bearded, and overweight but well-built. My sister Kim and her husband Lefty went up to Grandma's casket and cried. Kim said in a crying voice, "I will miss our loving and goodhearted Grandma. I wish she were with us for Christmas." I replied, "I wish she were around, but I rejoice that she is in heaven." My brother Kris also cried, but I told them Grandma was in heaven. Aunt Gloria, and my cousins, Kirk, Carla, and Craig, cried, but rejoiced that Grandma was in heaven. Aunt Gloria and her children were all rich and attractive Christians. Uncle Larry and his children cried about losing a good Grandma. Uncle Larry and Dad were mad at Grandpa George for the way Grandma died. They laid Grandma to rest at about 5:00 pm. Dad and Uncle Larry left the funeral mad at Grandpa George. Our family never spoke to him again.

Upon my return to Kent, I picked up a copy of the *Daily Kent Stater* and read about the May 4th controversy. After nearly one week of hearing how my Grandma died without dignity, this May 4th controversy made me sick to my stomach. I was angry that those liberal kids died with less dignity than my Grandma. Later that day, I met Jim Goodman at his dorm. I told him, "I am mad at The Kent State administration for denying the families of the four dead May 4th victims their dignity. They failed to resolve May 4, 1970 and lie to the world about it." Jim replied, "The government always lies when they do something wrong." I said with great sorrow, "If I continue to support these lies, I am putting Johnny Oilstring's soul in danger of a hex killing him." Jim replied, "I take it that you will be a May 4th supporter." I replied seriously, "I am not going to lose Johnny." I explained seriously, "If I confirm these lies this Wednesday at the May 4th educational presentation in the Tri-Towers Lobby, I will be forced to join the May 4th Task Force." Jim replied, "I guess that you must join the hippies. This could cost you your career in physics." I replied, "I must obey God or lose Johnny." Jim then gave me this advice, "The liberals are some of the nicest people you will ever meet." He added, "I hope you meet a liberal smarter and nicer than Johnny Oilstring." I asked, "Is this possible." Jim replied, "I know a Kent State May 4th supporter named Steve Colburn and respect him as a best friend. We just happen to disagree in many areas of politics. You will like these liberals." I replied, "I hope that you are right." Jim said, "Need to study. See you later."

On Wednesday, I saw Jim in the tenth floor lobby of Leebrick Hall. He said, "Go downstairs to meet your new friends." I replied hoping to save face with my conservative friends, knowing that May 4th is not resolved, "They will be my friends only if May 4th is not resolved." Jim replied, "Good luck at finding God's will." I replied, "See you later." I proceeded downstairs to the Tri-Towers Lobby. There, I saw the May 4th liberals. Remembering my bashing of Tim Peacegood, one of these liberals asked, "What is your problem?" I ignored that liberal, and I said to Alan trying to look like a conservative but knowing Alan was right, "Sorry to seem intimidating, but I have a question." I asked, "Why should we build that stupid memorial!!? Why do we bother Kent with a stupid detail?" I said, "If you answer this question and convince me you are right, I will join your group." Alan moved me to a private place and answered, "We need to build this memorial to help resolve tensions at Kent State." I asked, "What tensions?" I said, "The college catalog implies that there are no tensions." Alan replied, "Oh Really?" I replied, "The school newspaper tells of these tensions almost daily. President Schwartz should have read the school newspaper before publishing the catalog" I asked in disappointment, "Are we looking at a stench in God's nostrils?" Alan replied, "You are the expert concerning God's law." I replied disgusted and disappointed with the administration, "Oh! We are looking at a stink in God's nostrils. I am very disappointed with the administration. They should have resolved the May 4th issue long ago. Let's be friends." Alan replied, "Let's go to the lobby to watch the movie." When I arrived at the lobby, James Avonman met me, shook my hand and asked, "How are you doing?" I replied, "Fine. Alan just convinced me to join your organization." James happily replied, "I am glad to have you as a friend and a supporter. You are invited to come to our educational party at 3 pm on Saturday. Let's watch the movie." I watched the movie, met other prospective friends, and returned to my dorm.

On Friday, I had second thoughts concerning the party. I was walking home and asked God, "Should a Christian such as me have hippie friends such as James? Should I go to their party?" As I arrived at the dorm, I went to see David and Janet who were experts concerning God's law. They were gone! I went to see if Bill Mercules was home. He was gone! I even went to see Jim. Even he was gone!! I checked again fifteen minutes. They were all gone!!! I asked the Lord to give me guidance and checked a half of an hour later. They were all gone!!!! Panic set in. All of my Christian friends were gone. God called to my remembrance that they were all leaving town that night. I frantically checked for them every fifteen minutes only to panic even more. "Tell me what I should do!" I cried out unto the Lord, "I am scared! Please spare Johnny!!" I gave up and returned to my dorm. I cried out unto the Lord,

"Tell me what I must do!! I want to go to heaven, and I love my friend Johnny!!!" I prayed earnestly with fear and trembling before God for a half hour. Suddenly, the phone rang. I thought, "It must be Johnny!" By a great act of divine providence, It was Johnny! I asked Johnny, "How are you doing?" And I said, "I am glad to hear from you." Johnny replied with his own hurt, "I may be coming to see you tomorrow. Janie found out about Becky working with me, and she was mad." I replied, "I will always be glad to see a good friend." I asked, "If you come, when would it be?" I said, "I need to know if I can attend a party thrown by Kent State's famous liberals." Johnny replied, "Call me at 8 am to find out if I am coming." He said, "If I am coming, I will meet you at the party." I asked in a serious tone, "May I ask you a couple questions?" Johnny replied, "Go ahead and ask." I said with great concern, "I have been invited to party with the Kent State hippies tomorrow at 3 pm." I asked, "If you were in my place as a Christian, would you go to the party?" "You know me," replied Johnny. "I would go to their party." I asked, "In my place, would you feel that you had to go to the party?" "You must love your neighbor as yourself," replied Johnny. He said, "You must go to their party and be their friend." I replied, "Thanks for clearing up a serious moral dilemma." I asked, "Will you be coming tomorrow?" "Call me at 8 am," Johnny replied, "If I am not home or if I say no then, I am not coming. Otherwise, I am coming. See you later." Johnny applied the basic principles of God emphasized in the BSAT developed by Robert and me in 1983. With these principles, Johnny resolved a big moral dilemma concerning Kent State's hippies.

I called Johnny at 8 am and discovered that he was not coming to Kent. I got cleaned up and bought pop and potato chips for the party. I arrived at the May 4th party at Kathy's house and met Billy Westman at the door. He said, "The party is next door." I replied, "James Avonman gave me this paper saying that the May 4th party is here." I asked, "Did he make a mistake?" Billy replied, "The May 4th party is here." He said, "I thought you were looking for that head banging party next door. Come on in." I entered and said, "My name is Kevin Moody." I added, "I am a member of Right to Life and the Conservative Frat Man's Club." James replied, "You are a lot better than most students." He added, "You care about what is happening in this world." I said with great humility, "I am sorry that May 4th is not resolved." James replied, "You did not shoot these students. The Govenor Rhodes is responsible for these shootings." I replied with righteous indignation, "These unresolved shootings are a stink in God's nostrils. The administration ought to be ashamed to allow this to go on." James replied in a friendly manner, "I agree with you, but I would like to get some punch and spinach dipped bread. Be back shortly." Billy Westman came into the room. Billy was a short standing, well-built, long haired, friendly liberal. Billy sat down beside me and said, "They killed my friends on May 4th and lied to the world about it." I replied, "They should be ashamed. God will hold them responsible." Billy continued to say, "They covered up the shootings and humiliated the wounded students along with their families." I replied, "Gainesville will be interested in this abomination. You should have sued those idiots!" Billy replied, "We did sue them and it was a hassle. Ohio state law did not allow for the state to be sued. We had to sue them in federal court to get the right to sue Ohio." I replied, "What a mess!" Billy continued to say, "When we were finally heard in court, Kent State decided to build a gym over part of the site of the shootings (Map 11).[5] [6] This is why we camped out on the site of the gym for 6 months in 1977. Building this gym would bury the evidence concerning the shootings." I replied disgustedly, "What an injustice. If I did that, I would have been thrown in jail." Billy hopelessly replied, "These people involved in the shootings seemed to be above the law. Nobody would prosecute Governor Rhodes for the murder of our four friends." I replied, "They deserved jail time." I asked, "What happened with your civil suit? Billy replied, "We got tired of fighting." He added, "We settled for about a half million Dollars" I asked, "Wouldn't this be enough money to give each of you a good nest egg?" Billy replied, "It just barely paid Dean Kahler's medical bills." I asked, "Exactly what are you currently protesting?" Billy replied, "The administration promised us a nice memorial costing $1.3 million Dollars. They did not hire a professional fund-raiser and failed to raise the 1.3 million Dollars needed to build the original memorial. They said nobody cared. They claimed they had to scale back the memorial to a $100,000 memorial. This scaled back memorial has less meaning to us. We say they made a half-hearted effort to build the memorial they promised us. We deserve better." I replied, "They should be ashamed of themselves for making an effort to fool the world concerning their efforts to respect your friends and make peace with them. They could have found a good fund-raiser. Churches and charities successfully do this every day." Kathy came into the room and said, "I am Kathy." I replied, "I am Kevin." I added, "You remind me of a spirit-filled young Christian from Morgantown, West Virginia." Kathy replied, "I am from Beckley, West Virginia." I replied, "God even has his people in Kent's liberal culture." Kathy said, The Bible commands us to love our neighbor as we would want to be loved." I added, "Including Kent State hippies." Kathy corrected me saying, "Kent State liberals." She added, "We welcome you with open arms." I happily replied, "I accept my new-found friends." Kathy replied, "We are nice people. We will be good friends to you." I said, "I must be going." James said, "Remember Tuesday's May 4th Task Force meeting." I replied in Earnest, "I will be there. See you later." Kathy was a good looking though middle aged liberal woman of good character.

---

5   See Kraus vs Rhodes 1979 in Federal Court in Cleveland, Ohio

6   Pamphlet by Glen Frank, Thomas Hensley, and Jerry Lewis. "The May Fourth Site;" Kent State University, 1980

On Monday, Mitch from the Conservative Frat Man's Club sent me to observe a PSN protest on the Student Center Plaza. He thought that I was still a loyal Conservative Frat Man and wanted to spy on the PSN. The PSN was

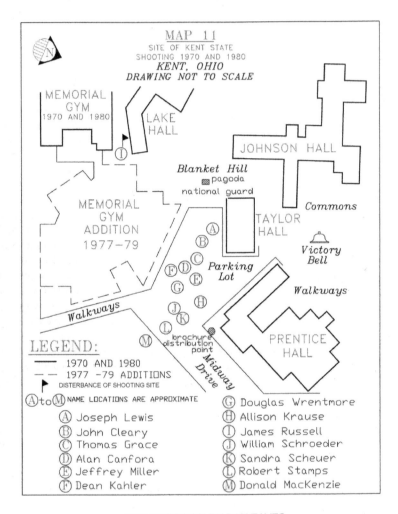

MAP BY DRAWN BY DAN EAVES
SEE FOOTNOTE 6 FOR THE SOURCE OF
INFORMATION FOR THIS MAP

protesting the CIA recruiting on campus. As I looked on from a distance, I saw two signs that got my attention. One told of the CIA installing the oppressive

Iranian Shah in 1953. The other sign told of six Jesuit Priests being killed by the CIA in El Salvador. "The United States is reaping what it has sown in Iran," I thought, "We oppressed Iran in the 50's and 60's. Now, Iran is one of America's worst enemies." I thought concerning the six Jesuit priests, "Catholic priests are no threat to national security, so they did not deserve to die." On that evening, I met Jim Goodman and asked him, "Did the CIA kill six Jesuit priests?" Jim said, "The CIA killed six Jesuit priests recently." He added, "I am surprised you did not hear that on the news." "I hope the President did not order this," I said, "If he did, and he does not explain the threat those priests posed to national security, I will have to support his impeachment." Jim said, "I hope you would want justice done concerning those six priests." I replied, "Anybody, including President Bush, associated with those deaths should be fired and thrown in jail." Jim replied, "Those responsible will likely get away with these killings because the CIA will cover it up." I replied, "We don't have the money to support such stupid missions! The government should cut the CIA's budget." Jim said, "I have to be going. See you later."

On that Wednesday, I said to Chris Peaceman, "I opposed the PSN's protest this last Monday, but I think I was in error." Chris asked, "How so?" I replied, "The CIA killed six Jesuit priests." I asked, "What threat did they pose to national security?" I declared, "Somebody should get fired and go to jail." Chris said, "I am glad to see you questioning the government. This scrutiny is what makes a democracy work." I replied, "I oppose the persecution of Christians and Jews. No excuses!" Chris asked, "Why does it always take Christians getting hurt to cause a cry for social justice?" I replied humbly, "Many Americans are Christians. When one of us hurt, we all hurt. When we hurt due to injustice, we get mad and try to hold the perpetrators accountable." Chris asked, "Why don't you Christians get mad when a non-Christian gets hurt by injustices?" I replied, "We don't get hurt when a stranger gets hurt because we are human and do not feel that stranger's pain. If we were perfect, we would be mad at a lot of injustices. Please forgive me for being human." Chris replied, "I accept you for who you are." I replied in a friendly manner, "Thanks. In my case, I got upset with the Kent administration when they persecuted those kids hurt by the May 4th shootings. I caught them red-handed lying to the world that these shootings are resolved." Chris said with a smile, "You really do stand for a better world. Let's be good friends." I replied, "Let's be good friends." Chris said to me, "Got go. See you later good friend." I replied with a good feeling, "See you later."

Our family celebrated Thanksgiving despite Grandma Esther's death. On the day after Thanksgiving, at about 2 pm, I stopped at Johnny's gas station. There Johnny said, "Kevin, long-time no see." I replied, "Glad to see my best friend." Johnny said with a smile, "I am having a great day because we sold $2000 worth of food and $3000 worth of gas." I said happily, "Looks like you will soon be district manager." Johnny replied, "Sales rose from $1500 a day to $3000 a day since I started managing the store." I replied, "They should soon give you a big raise." Johnny said, "I wish they would. I don't have enough money to buy fuel oil to heat my house. I feel sorry for my brother, Jimmy. He lives in LaPorte, Indiana and cannot afford to buy heating oil either. Please come into my office." I replied, "I need to talk to you about something." Johnny said, "Wait in my office until I serve these customers in the store." Johnny rang up twenty customers for fifteen minutes while I waited in the office. Johnny came into the office and asked, "What do you want to talk to me about?" I replied happily, "I need to talk to you about my new-found friends, the Kent State hippies. Some of the environmentalists may prove useful in marketing my perpetual motion machine." Johnny replied with the authority of his generation, "Just be their friends for a while. Do not include them in Project Texhoma until you get to know them." I asked, "Should I wait until I know their character and abilities concerning science or security work?" Johnny replied, "Some environmentalists could contribute to the test run or the design of the machine. Some old-time hippies could contribute to your security work. Some may be able to do both. Some may have the talent to work for US Physics but not the character. Good things come to people who wait." I said, "Need to get going to Gainesville. See you later." Johnny replied, "Stop at my house at 7 pm tomorrow. See you then."

At Johnny's house on Saturday night, Johnny greeted me by saying, "Hi! How is my favorite Christian friend doing?" I replied, "Fine." Johnny said, "I am glad you have some liberal friends in Kent because their influence is good for you." I bluntly said to Johnny, "I will need your advice concerning their culture, or I will be a flop in Kent." Johnny said with a smile, "Be yourself. The hippies accept anybody that will accept them. They need love just like you." I asked Johnny, "Will they really take me as a Christian?" Johnny replied, "They need you as a Christian. Show you are for real, and they will respect you. I do." I asked with astonishment, "Do you mean to say that the word of God is missing but useful in their political causes?" Johnny replied with this insight, "Obedience of the Bible will cause you to be a good friend to all of them. They love good friends. They will love you for it." I asked with great astonishment, "Are these people this easy to be friends with?" Johnny replied like a good hippie teacher, "You are one of us. We all love you. It is that easy." I replied, "Thanks for the advice." I asked, "May I talk to you if their culture confuses me?" Johnny replied, "I will be there if you need me, but you should find the Kent State hippies to easily be your best friends." We talked and partied all evening. I left Johnny's house with a good feeling concerning Kent.

On the next Tuesday, I attended my first May 4th Task Force meeting. At that meeting, I faced a rude awakening. The Kent State administration could not even agree with the students on a time to dedicate the May 4th Memorial.

James Avonman told the task force, "The administration wants to hold the dedication luncheon at noon. This conflicts with our traditional 12:24 pm bell ringing in the commons to remember the victims of the Kent State shootings." I addressed the meeting asking, "Don't the dead and wounded students get any respect in this joint?" Alan Peacemaker replied, "You and the progressive students are the only people in this place that give us any respect." James went on to say, "Do I hear a motion to propose to hold the dedication luncheon at 1:30 pm on May 4, 1990. Kathy said, "I move to make the proposal to hold the dedication luncheon at 1:30 on May 4, 1990." Billy Westman said, "I second the motion." James then said, "All in favor say aye." The whole group said "aye." James said, "All opposed say nay." Nobody responded. James picked Kathy to write the letter and approach the administration. James then went through the rest of the meeting and adjourned it. After the meeting, I said with hope, "I pray this proposal will solve the problem." James replied, "I hope that it solves the problem." I replied with grave concern, "It had better solve the problem, or God will be mad. This kind of disrespect is what gives us Christians a bad name! I say that this disrespect is an abomination unto the Lord!!" James replied, "You give Christians a good name. Look forward to seeing you at the next meeting." I replied, "See you later."

At the next meeting a week later, I read, in the agenda, that the administration did not resolve the problem. James said, "The administration will probably wait to make the decision to reject the compromise and hold the dedication luncheon during the traditional ringing of the bell on the commons." Alan said, "If the administration plays games with our traditions, they will have hell to pay." I said with righteous indignation, "This kind of performance is a good reason to go straight to the polls to vote a straight ticket to vote the rascals straight out of office!! Messing around with the traditions of people hurt by their organization is an abomination unto the Lord!! The administration and Ohio's politicians will reap what they have sown!" James said, "Throwing the rascals out of office is good revenge, but it does not solve the immediate problem." I replied, "Fear of being tossed out of office may cause the politicians to pressure the administration to do the right thing." James replied, "Thanks for caring about us. We may just try to expose their wicked games if they disrespect our bell ringing ceremonies." We discussed other orders of business and adjourned the meeting. After the meeting, I said to James, "I am not sure that I will be back for the next semester. Could we exchange phone numbers, so we can keep contact?" James said "Yes." We exchanged phone numbers and he invited me to a May 4th movie at Kent State University's assembly hall, known as the Kiva, and a party in an on campus bar, called the Rathskeller. I accepted his invitation and headed back to the dorm. Little did I know that Alan's and James' commitment to keep protests legal and peaceful would be tested to the limit by the administration's disrespectful policies concerning the scaled back memorial and the memorial luncheon during the

12:24 bell ringing on the commons.

At the Kiva on Friday, "I watched a movie about May 4, 1970. In that movie they showed the May 4th shootings in their gory detail. One thing mentioned in that movie was a rumor that the Kent State SDS was considering the possibility of putting LSD in the water supply. After the movie, I asked Alan, "Were you guys really going to drug the water supply, or was the media exaggerating a bad rumor?" Alan said in defense of the group, "We were really angry about Vietnam, but we were not even considering LSD in the water supply. We were a peaceful people." I replied with love for Alan's generation, "The media can be vicious with rumors. I apologize for Ohio's conservatives." Alan replied, "You helped promote these shootings." I replied, "I was a grade school student in South Bend, Indiana, and I learned about these shootings on the news." Alan said, "You are a Republican, and your party ordered these shootings." I replied in defense. "As a Texas Republican, I disapprove of the May 4th shootings and the subsequent cover-up. I am a Texas Republican and have many friends in the church who hate killing and lies. There is no excuse for those murderers and crooks in the Republican Party. They are criminals who belong in jail." Alan said, "They are above the law and will never see a day in jail." I replied with a sense of justice, "They are not above God's law! They had better repent, or they will go to hell!" Alan replied, "You really are my friend. Let's go to the Rathskeller and enjoy the rest of the night."

I arrived at the Rathskeller, but I did not meet my friends from the May 4th group. I found a seat and watched the show. After about fifteen minutes, a waitress said, "Hi, May I get you anything?" I replied, "Could you get me a coke and some popcorn?" The waitress replied in a friendly fashion, "I will get you your coke and popcorn. Just a minute." The waitress returned with two cokes and a big container of popcorn and said in a friendly way, "My name is Malinda Free. I see you are alone." I replied with discouragement, "No liberal wants to be a friend to a Christian May 4th supporter." Malinda replied in a friendly fashion, "It is wonderful that a Christian wants to listen to us. I want to be your friend." I replied in that same friendly fashion, "I already like you. You will make a good friend." Malinda asked, "What do you intend to do for the May 4th cause?" I replied, "Try to convince my conservative friends that doing right by the four dead and nine wounded students is the right thing to do for my God and my country." Malinda asked with great curiosity, "How do you intend to do that?" I explained happily, "Connect the May 4th cause to the Golden Rule and the Ten Commandments. After all, May 4th liberals are people, and Jesus tells us to love them as ourselves. No exceptions." Malinda said with a smile, "Nice meeting you. I will make my rounds and see you in a little bit." She made her rounds in about five minutes and came back with a big coke and a lot of popcorn. Malinda said, "Have as much as you like on the PSN." I asked, "What do you do in the PSN?" Malinda replied with great love, "I am an environmentalist, and I am on the woman's committee of the PSN." I replied, "I believe that we must do everything reasonable to protect the environment." Malinda asked, "Does that include tuning up your car and recycling?" I replied, "And not littering too." Malinda replied with due respect, "You really get it! I must do my rounds again." After another five minutes, Malinda came back with more food and fifteen minutes of great friendship. She repeated this friendly service three or four more times and made me feel like I made a best friend.

On the next day, I had an attack of the munchies and went to the Giant Eagle Super Market. On my way into the store, my new friend Malinda said, "Hi! How is my good Christian friend?" I replied happily, "I am doing fine." I added, "You liberals are really good friends." Malinda replied, "We enjoy making you feel good and try hard to do so." I replied with great joy, "I need to get my groceries, but enjoy talking to you a lot. See you later." I picked up 6 cans of tuna, 3 bags of potato chips, 6 boxes of macaroni, and a 2 liter bottle of Mountain Dew. I paid for them, and Malinda said with a smile, "Hi, Kevin. Could you give us a ride home." I replied gladly, I would love to give four good friends a ride." The only man in the group said, "Hi, my name is Billy Glassman." I replied, "Something tells me you will be a great friend." Billy replied in a friendly way, "I am like Malinda. I am happy when you are." The tall and heavy set woman said, "My name is Mary, and I am pleased to meet you." She added, "Malinda said you are a good Christian who loves us." I replied, "These PSN hippies seem to make very good friends, so I look forward to being your friend, Mary." I asked, "Who is this short friendly woman?" The short friendly woman replied, "My name is Katie." She added, "I really look forward to your friendship." I replied with great joy, "All of you seem to be great friends." Billy said, "That is what we want you to think because it makes it easier for you to have a good time with us." I replied, "I sure look forward to having you as my friends." Billy asked, "What is your major?" I replied, "I am a graduate student in the Physics Department." Billy replied, "You are really smart. I wish I had your brains." I replied, "Just apply yourself to your studies and in a few years you could be smarter than me." Billy asked, "Really?" I replied, "My brain has been damaged since I was four years old. If I can be smart, you can learn to be smart if you try." Billy replied, "Thanks for the ride and seeing good friendship in all of us." I requested of Billy, "Pray I pass my candidacy exam at the beginning of the next semester," Billy replied, "I wish you good luck on your candidacy exam. If you fail, you can contact us at our dorms and we will be happy to see and hear from you. I think you will see us for at least a semester either way." I greeted my four new friends by saying, "I am glad to have four great new friends." All four of my new friends said, "See you later and look forward to seeing you." I returned to my dorm with joy in my heart.

Six days later at the end of my last final, I met Chris Peaceman on the way out of the physics building. Chris asked, "How are you doing?" I replied,

"I am glad to be done with finals, but I am not sure that I am PhD material."
Chris replied, "At least you have a good master's degree, so you should do well
in life." I replied, I have many good friends." I added, "Some of them are
conservatives, and some of them are liberals." Chris replied, "Some of us have
influenced you." I replied, "I am a May 4th supporter and an environmentalist.
The lies concerning the May 4th shootings are a stink in God's nostrils. I am an
environmentalist because life on this planet will be history if we do not slow
down our cycle of wasting and polluting." Chris asked in a friendly manner,
"Would you like to take a walk with me to the PSN office?" I replied happily,
"Yes, I would like to get to know my new-found friend better." Chris replied,
"Since you caught the Kent State administration red-handed lying about the
May 4th victims, you have come a long way." I replied, "My basic values have
not changed, but my perception of Republicans has changed." I explained, "I
have learned some conservatives can and do lie when convenient." Chris
replied, "You have become an environmentalist and a peace activist, and I am
proud of you." I replied, "Unless the US and its allies change their ways, the
earth will be ashes." I added, "Hypodermic needles on the coast of New Jersey
is ridiculous." Chris asked, "What about world peace?" I replied, "My
Christian friends and I require our leaders to keep The United States at peace
with the rest of the world whenever possible." I added, "No American leader
will provoke a war if he is serious about getting my vote." Chris said, "I have
to get a few things out of the PSN office." I replied by asking, "They gave you
a key?" Chris replied, "I am the treasurer. I will be a second." Chris picked up
five or six envelopes and asked, "Would you want to walk to Brady's Cafe
with me to meet some of my friends?" I replied, "Yes." Chris said, "It is
beginning to snow outside." I replied, "I heard we are supposed to get a
snowstorm tonight." Chris replied, "You should spend the night in the dorm
and be safe." I replied , "I heard everybody had to be out of the dorms by eight
tonight." Chris replied, "If you ask, they will let you stay until morning." I
replied, "I will ask." Chris said, "Everything will be all right." I asked in a
serious manner, "Are you a representative of the Kent State PSN?" Chris
replied, "I am the second ranking officer." I replied, "I would like to ask the
PSN if it is OK to ask God to cause a blizzard to bury Kent on the second
weekend of the next semester?" Chris replied, "I would not mind having snow
so that I can ski." I asked, "Does God have your permission to hit Kent with a
blizzard if He exists?" Chris replied, "You have my permission if you ask God
to make sure that nobody dies or gets hurt from this blizzard." We arrived at
Brady's Cafe in downtown Kent to hang out with Chris' liberal friends. We had
a good time for two hours. I went to my dorm and packed my bags. I left for
Gainesville in the morning.

Once in Gainesville, I tried to contact James Avonman unsuccessfully 3
times on Saturday, But I arranged to take Johnny to my favorite Gainesville
restaurant on Tuesday. I tried again on Sunday and Monday to contact James,

but I was unsuccessful. I met Johnny at his house at 5:00 pm on Tuesday. Johnny asked, "Would you watch Hank while I am gone for about a half hour." I replied, "I will keep Hank busy until you get back."

Just as Johnny left the house, Hank asked, "Can you keep a secret?" I replied, "It depends on the secret." Hank replied, "You must not tell this secret to anybody including Dad." I asked, "What is the secret?" Hank said with great fear, "I saw the Devil at Dad's bedpost." I asked with great curiosity, What happened next. Hank said with great relief, "Dad asked Jesus to tell the Devil to go away. The Devil left Johnny's room instantly." I told Hank, "I am thankful that the Lord was there to fight for Johnny while I was struggling in Kent." A bad thought came to me, "The Kent State administration insinuated in their catalog that May 4th was resolved. This misinformation caused me to shun hippies for fifteen months and disobey the God's rule of loving my neighbor as myself. My prayers were hindered due to this shunning of Kent State's hippies. Johnny could have been hexed and killed." I was wrought with the Kent State administration.

Johnny came into the house and asked, "Are you ready to go to the my favorite Gainesville restaurant?" I said happily, "I am ready to eat chicken and French fries." Johnny said, "Let's go!" We all got into my car and headed to the restaurant. At that restaurant, I asked Johnny, "Can our new-found friends help with Project Texhoma's security?" Johnny asked, "Are the Kent State hippies environmentalists?" I replied, "They seem to be very dedicated protectors of the planet." Johnny replied, "Some of them will be great assets to the security at US Physics." He explained, "They will be able to hide the prototype until the day a famous rock band can run a rock concert off of the machine." The waitress came and asked for our orders. I ordered a chicken dinner, Janie ordered spaghetti, Johnny ordered fish, and Hank ordered hamburgers and French fries. The waitress took our menus and I asked Johnny, "Can some serve as mechanical technicians in the lab?" Johnny replied happily, "They are as good as me or Robert." He added, "Some can even serve in the Occult Defense Command." I replied with great astonishment, "Wow! You really love young people!" Johnny replied, "I am young. I love my own generation." Johnny and I enjoyed our dinner. We talked for a half hour. We went home.

Meanwhile, I still kept trying to contact James. I kept trying for a week straight, but with no success. On my last try, James placed a spooky message saying, "I will haunt all callers." on his answering machine. I figured he no longer wanted to hear from me, so I stopped trying. I prayed to the Lord in discouragement, "Lord, should I even bother to return to Kent? James Avonman does not seem to want me. Do the other hippies want me? I have little chance of passing the candidacy exam. Do I have a purpose in Kent?" The Lord replied in a still soft voice, "I shall give you a dream concerning what you are to do concerning Kent." A peace descended upon my soul, and I fell asleep.

The next morning, at around 5:30 am, The Lord gave me a dream. In that dream, I was in the Kent State Student Center on the second floor overlooking the Student Center plaza. There, I came up to a drink stand. On that drink stand, there were two drinks offered. One drink was May 4th orange juice, and the other drink was June 2nd blueberry juice. I drank a glass of the June 2nd blueberry juice and found myself in the Dangas Station at the intersection of California Road and Fair Avenue in Gainesville, Texas. At that gas station, Johnny Oilstring was waiting for his car to be fixed. Johnny and I spotted the same drink stand I saw in the Student Center. There Johnny asked, "Would you like some Hi C orange juice?" I replied, "Yes." I drank a glass of the May 4th orange juice and found myself in James Avonman's office in Kent. I woke up with the understanding that the dream symbolized an alliance between Johnny's friends and the Kent State hippies. June 2, 1985 was the day the exorcism raids of the Battle of Sherman were planned. The day we planned the exorcism raids was important because the day we planned the exorcism raids was the day we began to pray for Johnny in our hearts. Johnny always liked to go to the Blueberry Festival in Plymouth, Indiana, with his brother, Jimmy. Later, I would find out that May 4th Center Director Alan Peacemaker's hometown, Akron, Ohio, would have the Orange Blossom Music Festival every year. I knew that God wanted me to go to Kent and be friends with the hippies.

I returned to Kent to try to qualify for a PhD and to be a friend to Kent State's hippies. On Wednesday, I attended a PSN meeting in Kent. There, everybody was friendly. Chris Peaceman asked, "Why are you here?" He explained, "You should be studying for tomorrow's Candidacy Exam." I replied, "I have been studying for months and should be as prepared as possible. Studying tonight can only make me more nervous. Being with my friends can only help me tomorrow." An attractive and well-built woman sitting in the president's seat said, "Hi, How are you doing?" "I am doing fine," I replied, "My name is Kevin." I asked, "What is your name?" The Woman replied, "My name is Gabriella Free." She said in a friendly manner, "I am the President of the PSN. Welcome Kevin." I asked, "Does your organization accept a down on the farm Christian environmentalist and May 4th Task Force Bible lawyer?" Gabriella replied in a friendly fashion, "We accept anybody who will give our ideas a fair chance, so you are welcome here." I asked my friend Malinda, "How are you doing?" Malinda replied in her own friendly way, "I am glad to see you in Kent. I look forward to seeing you this semester." I replied, "I look forward to your friendship." Malinda replied, "I will be with you at protecting the planet and showing the Kent liberals support concerning May 4, 1970." Gabriella brought the meeting to order and discussed many issues including President Bush's invasion of Panama. Everybody seemed mad about this invasion. After an hour of lively discussion,

Gabriella adjourned the meeting. I went to see Gabriella only to see Billy Glassman. I did not recognize Billy because he grew his hair since I last saw him. I asked, "What is your name?" Billy replied with astonishment, "My name is Billy Glassman. You met me at the Giant Eagle super market." I replied, "You grew your hair since I last met you." I added, "Sorry. I did not recognize you." Billy replied, "You will see me a lot. You will know me as one of your best friends." I replied, "I would like to party with you sometime." Billy replied, "Just give me a little time, and we will be best friends." Gabriella said, "I must lock the room up soon." I said to Billy, "See you at the next meeting." Billy replied, "Look forward to it." I headed back to my dorm with a happy feeling.

The name of Billy Glassman seemed very familiar. I forgot that I mentioned him by name when I prophesied a major occult war ending at Kent State nearly six years ago in Robert Elight's presence. Billy was to be a Kent State hippie who was a hero. Little did I know that he would introduce me to the Kent State hippies and help me make peace with the Conservative Frat Man's Club.

The next meeting of the May 4th Task Force discussed the same problems as before, but the liberal members seemed less distraught. They started to plan the 20th anniversary of the May 4th shootings. As I was a Christian Republican, I could only watch and learn. One thing I spotted in the May 4th literature was a quote, "Long live the spirit of Kent and Jackson State." I asked James, "What happened at Jackson State?" James replied, "Two black students were shot at Jackson State at about the same time that Kent State's students were shot. We think the black students at Jackson State deserve the same recognition as we have at Kent State." I read the other literature and was moved concerning the Kent State hippies.

The second meeting of the PSN proceeded in a similar fashion, but I was wrought concerning the Satanic torment of Johnny's eight year old boy, Hank Oilstring. "I am going to join the PSN," I said to Gabriella, "Johnny's eight year old son, Hank, is facing demonic torment because my prayers were hindered. My prayers were hindered due to the my failure to show friendship with Kent State's hippies. I was afraid to be friends with Kent State's hippies due to the administrations misinformation concerning the May 4th issue. I am looking for an excuse to join the PSN and fight for the environment and for my good friends in the May 4th Task Force. Children do not deserve Satanic torment. First excuse, I join." Billy Glassman replied, "I believe you will have that excuse before the next meeting." Gabriella replied happily, "I hope Billy is right. I will look forward to seeing you at the next meeting. Need to lock up. See you."

After the second meeting of the May 4th Task Force, I prayed for the guidance of God. God laid this thought on me, "You will jeopardize Jimmy Oilstring's life if you ask God to put a blizzard on Kent." "The Devil is trying to tell me that a blizzard hitting Kent must go through South Bend and LaPorte Indiana," I thought, "Johnny's brother, Jim, who lives in LaPorte, does not have enough money to buy fuel oil to heat his house. If this is true, Lord please don't hit Kent with a blizzard. It would endanger too many innocent people between Chicago and Pittsburgh along the Toll Road." The Lord replied in a still soft voice, "A blizzard would kill too many innocent people. I will fight for the Kent State hippies in a way that they will love. The administration will know that I am the Lord." The Lord added in an angry but still soft voice, "The Kent State administration and its allies shall feel my judgment for the lies they told the world! For they have sown the wind, and they shall reap the whirlwind! For their wickedness, I have taken the university from their hands!"

On the next Sunday in the late afternoon, I received a call from Mitch Fryman of the Conservative Frat Man's Club. He said in a raspy voice, "Hello, (cough, cough, cough) This is Johnny Oilstring. I am saying you should not join the PSN. (cough, cough, cough.)" I was wrought with the Conservative Frat Man's Club. They did a poor and slanderous imitation of Johnny Oilstring. I wondered whether Johnny was still my friend and was depressed that anybody would interfere with our friendship. I called Johnny and asked, "Did you call me just a few minutes ago?" Johnny replied, "I did not call you a few minutes ago." I replied, "I just wanted to confirm that the Conservative Frat Man's Club tried to imitate you. They are harassing us. They had me a little scared that you may have quit being my friend." Johnny said, "I am your good friend, and the hippies are proving to be your good friends," I asked in response, "Does this mean that I should join the PSN." Johnny said, "You have a good reason to join the PSN. Go ahead and join." He added, "They will be good friends." I replied happily, "Thanks for the advice. I am glad to know you really are my friend. See you later." I thought, "Perhaps Johnny's advice concerning loving Kent State's hippies was scaring the Conservative Frat Man's Club. This was their best answer to Johnny Oilstring's advice."

On Tuesday, I heard that President Schwartz was terminating the flight training program. This made everybody mad. Many who had degrees in this program wondered about their value. Some Conservative Frat Men were offended. My friend, David, said, "my dad, W.P. Pillarman, has a friend who teaches in the flight training program. David's dad said angrily, "I have a friend in the flight training program. I am angry that he is losing his job and getting hurt because of President Schwartz's arrogance. Since May 4, 1970, this place has not been the same. I am not donating to Kent State any-more." Can the PSN or May 4th task force help?" I replied, "I will talk with the progressive students and let them know that President Schwartz has hurt Conservative Frat Men also." David replied, "Thanks. See you later." I returned to my room with a feeling of hope concerning Kent. Little did I know, The Conservative Frat Man's Club was setting a trap for me and the PSN.

On Wednesday, I approached Kim at the pro-choice Booth in the Student

Center. I said to Kim, "One of my friends, David Pillarman of the Conservative Frat Man's Club, is really mad about President Schwartz terminating the flight program. His dad is one of Mr. DeBartelo's lawyers, W.P. Pillarman. We have common ground with Kent's conservative students. Would the PSN and May 4th task force be interested in defending the flight program?" Kim replied, "We would be interested in defending the flight program." I replied, "This will help to heal Kent State and may soften DeBartelo's heart concerning some of his mall building." Kim replied, "We are interested in helping with the flight program, but we don't need DeBartelo." From nowhere Mitch popped up and said, "You Nazis!" I asked in disgust, "Why don't you fight this Right to Life battle by playing by the rules? Why do you bash liberals?" I said to Kim, "I am sorry that some in the Conservative Frat Men choose to play dirty." Kim replied, "That is all right. You like us." I replied, "Dirty players like Mitch give us Christians a bad name." Kim replied, "Nice talking to you. See ya later."

At the PSN meeting on Wednesday, Gabriella congratulated me concerning my membership in the PSN. I replied, "I believe that God requires us to care for His creation, the Planet Earth." Billy said, "I also want to help save the planet." I asked, "What can I do to help save the planet?" Billy asked, "Do you keep your car tuned and perform proper maintenance on it?" I replied, "I will start to maintain my car better." You can also walk or take a bus whenever possible," added Billy, "God gave me my excuse for joining the PSN," I told Billy. Billy asked, "What was that excuse?" I replied, "The Conservative Frat Man's Club called. They imitated Johnny Oilstring. They made Johnny sound like a pot head and sound like he said not to join the PSN." Billy replied, "You do not have an excuse for joining the PSN. You have a good reason. Friends are important, and the Conservative Frat Man's Club spat on your best friend." Mary added, "I am glad you are fighting for the environment." Malinda asked, "Want to walk home with us." I replied happily, "I will be glad to talk with my good friends for ten or so minutes." Billy said, "I am glad you value good friends enough to quit the Conservative Frat Man's Club for their sake." He asked, "Are we your best friends?" I replied, "You, Mary, Malinda, Katie and Johnny Oilstring are all my best friends." Billy replied, "Let's all be best friends." We all agreed. Billy said as a good friend, "We all have to be going. We all look forward to seeing you." I replied, "I would like to party with you." Billy said in response, "You soon will. See ya." I returned to my dorm happily that night.

On Thursday night at 6:00 pm, I attended the PSN's environmental committee meeting. There, I saw Billy and all of his friends. Katie Said, "Hi. How are you?" I replied happily, "I am doing fine. I believe we had better clean the environment while we still have a planet." Billy said, "I heard that you are working on a pollution free machine that consumes no fuel." I replied, "You heard correctly. I need all of the support I can get." Billy asked, "How can I help?" "Can you find me cheap junk generators or electric motors?" I asked. Billy replied, "I can get you as many car alternators as you need from Dad's junkyard in Cleveland." I asked, "When can you take me there?" Billy replied, "Meet me on the Student Center plaza tomorrow, and we can discuss this further." Malinda heard this conversation and said, "I am glad to see that you and Billy are working together on an important environmental project." I replied with great hope, "Maybe, we can get this invention past the large oil companies and market it." Malinda replied happily, "We will do anything we can to help." Kim, The chairperson of the environmental committee, heard the conversation and said, "I am Kim. I heard you talking with Billy about your environmentally friendly invention. Let's talk after the meeting.

The meeting went smoothly. Kim adjourned the meeting and said, "Thanks for defending us when Mitch bashed us. I heard that Billy is getting you alternators so that you can work on a pollution free generator or electric motor." I replied, "I have found an inconsistency between the laws of electrodynamics and conservation of energy. If I am correct, this machine will operate perpetually off of its own electromagnetic energy." Kim asked, "What can we do to help?" I replied, "For now, just be my friend. If this machine works, I will need help with security. Getting by the oil companies will take all of the help I can get." Kim replied, "We will be friends with anybody who accepts us." She added, "When you need our help, we will do what we can to help." I said, "I need to be going. See ya later."

At 8 pm, that same night, I attended the May 4th Task Force meeting. That night, God's judgment of President Schwartz began. Sandy Scheuer's Mom called Alan. She was outraged that President Schwartz would hold a luncheon concerning the compromised memorial at 12:00 pm. This time conflicted with the bell ringing on the commons at 12:24 pm This was the time the May 4th Task Force students traditionally ring the bell on the Commons in mourning of the four students killed in the shootings. Alan distributed copies of the letter President Schwartz wrote to the families [7]. President Schwartz publicly denied that he planned a dedication luncheon at the same time as the ringing of the bell on the Commons. This demoralized the May 4th Task Force greatly. I felt the hurt, as Alan said angrily, "They are so insensitive to us! We are very angry! This means demonstrations and protests on May 4th!! The Young Communists said they were coming to support us!! The whole world will know that the May 4th supporters are wrought with our administration!!!" The May 4th Task Force all felt the pain. After the meeting, I told Alan, "God will raise a standard against President Michael Schwartz!" Alan replied in frustration, "God better act fast! Time is running out!" I replied, "God always acts on time because Jesus loves us." Alan replied almost hopelessly, "I pray

---

7   See the letters President Schwartz wrote to the wounded students and the families of the dead students and the response from the Scheuer parents on pages 194-196 (letter 1)

204-206

you are right. I need to get going. See you later." I headed back to my dorm with a sense of righteous indignation. I thought, "The administration chose to scale back the memorial and they chose to disrespect the May 4th task force's tradition of ringing the bell on the commons at 12:24 pm to remember the victims of the shootings. To make matters worse, They made fools of the Scheurer parents because they complained about the memorial luncheon interfering with the traditional 12:24 bell ringing. This tested the May 4 Center's ideal of keeping protests peaceful and legal to the limit!!!"

On the following Monday, I went to the PSN's office to say hi to the members there. There, I met James Avonman's former girlfriend, Annie. She said, "I fear for my safety on May 4th. There could be riots on the campus that day. Pray that our culture can avoid the violence according to our ideals." I replied, "What can I say? The Board of Judges of Texas is considering the possibility of rebuking the Kent State administration in the name of Jesus for its disrespectful scaling back of the memorial, for its attempt to use the memorial luncheon to interfere with the May 4th bell ringing on the Commons, and for its disrespect they showed the Scheuer parents for speaking out against the disrespect of the May4[th] bell ringing on the Commons. This may be the only way to stop this impending riot or major and possibly illegal protest." Annie replied, "You are a lot like James." I replied, "The way to beat President Schwartz is to hit him hard with the power of the pen!!! Expose his evil in the press!!! Hopefully this will bring peace on May 4th, as you hippies and I both want!!!!!"

After my conversation with Annie, I headed to the Student Center bus stop discouraged by the events concerning May 4th. By some twist of fate, I saw James Avonman. I said in a discouraged manner, "It looks like Dr. Schwartz has discredited the May 4th families as liars. He is the biggest liar around. It looks bad for the future of the memorial." James replied, "All hope is not lost. Read the letter written to the May 4th families and wounded students very carefully. See what this letter says to the Scheuer parents who spoke out." I replied, "I will read this letter again very carefully. Pray for God to give me guidance." James replied, "I wish you the best of luck."

I returned to my dorm and read the letter carefully. The letter from Dr. Schwartz had me convinced that he intended to hold the luncheon concerning the dedication of the May 4th memorial at 12:00pm on May 4, 1990. This luncheon conflicted with the 12:24pm time the May 4th Task Force traditionally rang the bell on the Commons in remembrance of the 4 dead students. Technically speaking, Dr. Schwartz did not say that he intended to hold the dedication of the memorial during the bell ringing on the Commons, but President Schwartz was a master of the English language and ceremonial protocol. He worded this letter in a way that caused casual readers to assume that he intended to violate the bell ringing on the Commons. Exact words did not clearly make that point. Lawyers and English majors know how to play

Ardmove
Oklahoma

such tricks. I asked Pastor Lion, Pastor of the Second Apistolic Church in ~~Gainesville, Texas,~~ to read this letter. He thought Kent State was going to dedicate the memorial during the bell ringing. In his anger Pastor Lion asked, "Was this letter written to the families of the dead students!?" I replied, "This letter was written to all the May 4th victims and their families." Pastor Lion replied, "Do what you have to do!! President Schwartz should have known better!!" I asked Janet Mercules, daughter of a Greek Orthodox patriarch, to read this letter. She agreed with me that President Schwartz intended to make the Scheuers look like fools. I read this letter to Occult Defense Analyst Myron E Chrisgood. He taught Pentecostal missionaries the fine points of word of God during Apostolic World Christian Fellowship conventions held at his church, The First Apostolic Church in Gainesville, Texas. He agreed with me perfectly. Technically, the letter said there was no conflict between the memorial dedication and the bell ringing, but he believed that Kent State intended to make a fool of the May 4th supporters.

I examined the letter further. In the tradition of White Fiberglass, I picked this letter apart like Dad picked pattern makers and mold repairmen apart. I noted the administration's insensitivity to the families and his intent to deceive the world concerning the Kent State May 4th Memorial. In righteous indignation, I wrote a rough draft of the following letter to the editor of the *Kent Stater*, Kent State University's school newspaper.

I am concerned about the integrity of President Schwartz concerning the Kent State memorial. One of the Ten Commandments say, "The Shalt not lie." President Schwartz wrote a letter to the families of the four victims of the May 4th shootings. The Scheuer family thought that this letter said that the dedication of the memorial and the bell ringing on the commons would both be held at 12:24 pm. I read the letter and believed the President intended to hold the dedication when the students normally held the bell ringing. Three other conservatives agreed. This sinful administration lied to cover their mistakes. This is just another blot on President Schwartz's already bad record concerning May 4, 1970.

Concerned Christian

Kevin Moody

Graduate Student Physics Department.[8]

---

8   See a copy of the letter that published in the *Daily Kent Stater* 0n p197

207

On that Wednesday, I met Billy Glassman at the PSN's environmental committee meeting. Billy asked, "How are you doing?" I replied, "I am doing just fine." Katie shook my hand and said, "Hi." Billy said enthusiastically, "I can go with you to get those alternators this Friday." I asked, "When and where will we meet? Billy replied, "Meet me on the Student Center plaza at 11 am this Friday." Mary and Malinda said "Hi." Kim called the meeting to order. Kim said, "I am negotiating a plan with the Kent State administration to have recycling at Kent." Malinda said, "Good luck negotiating with the administration." She added, "I have been trying for two years." Billy proceeded to the back of the room and started to put recycle labels on trash cans. He wanted to help the environment now. Kim suggested, "Why don't we put those trash cans in each of our dorms." Billy replied, "I will volunteer to deliver the trash cans to the recycling center." Kim asked for three more volunteers. Malinda, Katie, Mary, and Malinda volunteered. Kim proceeded through the rest of the meeting and adjourned. After the meeting, I reminded Billy, "See you at 11am. Friday to pick up those alternators." Billy replied, "See ya Friday." Kim asked, "What do you have to do with the alternators?" I replied, "I will measure the armature and field magnets. On each electromagnet, I will measure the wire gauge and count the number of turns. I will then enter this data onto a computer and calculate the efficiency of the redesigned alternator. If the efficiency is at least 300%, I will build a prototype of this design and hope that this alternator is about 300% efficient. If this alternator works, I will need security to patent and market this machine." Kim asked, "What will the plan be?" "If this machine works, we will build a machine big enough to run a rock concert and show it to the world," I replied. Kim said, "I am impressed, but I must get going. See ya." I replied, "See ya later."

Meanwhile, at the May 4th Task Force meeting on Thursday, I showed the rough draft of my letter to the editor to Billy Westman. I asked him, "Is this a good response to President Schwartz's hostility toward the Scheuers?" Billy W. asked, "Do you think this letter is good?" I replied, "I think the letter is a good response. A writer always thinks his work is better than it is. That is why I always seek a second opinion." The chairperson called the meeting to order. They discussed the commemoration and started planning the impending demonstration. They sounded very stressed out and demoralized. She dismissed the meeting. Afterward, I asked the chairperson, "What do you think of this draft of my letter to the editor?" She read the rough draft and said, "If you think this letter is good, submit it to the newspaper." I replied, "Thanks. see ya later." I left the task force meeting feeling just as demoralized as the other members. I thought, "These normally mellow people are being tested to the limit concerning their ideal of peaceful and legal protesting."

On the next Monday morning, I printed out my final draft of the letter to the Stater and called Gainesville (Texas) Wheeler Creek Security Council

Chairman, Johnny Oilstring, and said, "Either we rebuke President Schwartz in the name of Jesus, or we risk a riot in Kent on May 4, 1990." Johnny replied, "I stand ready when duty calls." I said, "I will read a rough copy of my letter to the *Kent Stater* to you." I asked, "Will you critique my letter?" Johnny said, "Read me your letter." I read Johnny the letter, and Johnny said, "Print the letter as it stands. It sounds good." I signed the letter and submitted it to the *Stater.* The person receiving the letter at the *Stater* seemed impressed. If Johnny had not remembered the basics of the word of God on September 22, 1984 or not remembered the basics when I needed God's guidance concerning friendship with the Kent State hippies last November, I would not have been there to rebuke President Schwartz when the hippies needed me.

Later that day, I met Billy Glassman on the Student Center plaza at 11am to go after those alternators. "Go to the Music Library and wait for me," said Billy, "I will meet you in fifteen minutes." Twenty minutes later, Billy met me in the Music Library and said, "I am ready." Billy and I proceeded toward the Physics Department parking lot. Just as I arrived at the Student Center exit, Tim, a conservative student, asked in an angry voice, "What are you doing on the plaza hanging out with those animals from the PSN?" I replied in righteous indignation, "I am doing what thus saith the Lord, loving my neighbor as myself!" I asked in disgust, "Why aren't you out there with me?" Tim replied, "God does not want you to hang out with those animals." I replied, "Those hippies will make it to heaven before you will." I said with a loving heart, "I pray Jesus will save your soul. Good day sir." I met Billy, and he said, "That's telling him." I replied, "Thanks for understanding." Billy replied, "That is what friends are for." I replied, "I am sorry that people find it necessary to mock God by harassing PSN members. You will make heaven before they will." We got into the car and headed to Cleveland. Another conservative could not answer Johnny Oilstring's advice concerning loving my neighbor.

On the way to Cleveland, Billy and I were looking forward to seeing the alternators. I asked Billy, "How is your recycling program going?" Billy replied, "The program is going just fine. Three floors of my dorm are participating in the program. Six people are taking recyclables to the recycling center." Billy asked, "How are your computer simulations going?" I replied, "I have one thousand designs simulated, and will soon be sorting that batch." Billy replied, "I am glad to be of help doing these simulations." I replied with great hope, "Maybe one of these alternators will be a cheap working model of my invention." Billy said, "Take the Ohio 94 exit coming up." I took the exit and a few turns. Then, I found myself at Auto Parts Galore, the junkyard owned by Billy's Dad.

Billy introduced his Dad and two of his brothers by saying, "This is Dad, Vernon, and my two brothers, Tommy and Jim. I replied, "My name is Kevin Moody." Vernon replied by asking, "How did you meet Billy?" I replied, "I met Billy through the PSN. Billy will be an asset to my research project concerning perpetual motion." Billy said, "I am getting alternators to help with his research project." I said with great hope, "Maybe, your son Billy will help to heal Kent from the wounds concerning the Kent State shootings." Vernon said, "I hope you are right." Vernon asked, "Would you and Billy like to eat a large pizza with us?" I said, "I do if Billy wants to." Billy said, "I want to eat a large pizza with you and my family." Vernon ordered the pizza, and Billy asked, "Do you want to get the alternators?" Billy took me into the junk yard and got me eight alternators. He said, "All of these alternators work." I replied with great hope, "I will be able to get my data and may be able to machine one of these alternators to build a prototype." Billy replied, "Let's put these alternators in your car." We loaded the alternators and went into the customer showroom waiting for the pizza. The pizza arrived, and we enjoyed eating it. After we ate the pizza, we talked with the Dad and his family for an hour. Then, we headed back to Kent.

On the way to Kent, Billy and I talked about our lives, our roles in the PSN, and the Board of Judges of Texas. I praised Billy by saying, "Thanks for the alternators. They may help to save the planet by reducing our dependence on Arab Oil." Billy asked, "Will cutting oil help world peace?" I replied, "They may help world peace. Armageddon is said to start in the Middle East. A fight for oil can start such a conflict. Pray for my invention." Billy asked, "How did you decide to join the PSN?" I replied, "The decision was not easy. I could not do anything I wanted concerning the Kent State hippies. I had to follow Jesus or risk losing my best friend, Johnny, to a hex." Billy asked, "How did you know this was a hex?" I replied, "This story started when twenty horoscopes correctly predicted events concerning my friendship with Johnny. When the horoscope told me and Johnny would fight, we fought. When the horoscope said we would be friendly, we were friendly. When the horoscope said nothing about our friendship, nothing happened. This happened for about three weeks straight from April 16th to May 4th in 1985. On May 4th of 1985, the horoscope predicted the end of my friendship with Johnny. I was to call Johnny to arrange to see him at noon. I prayed concerning my upcoming conversation with Johnny and told the Devil, "Get out of Johnny's house, or I will ask God to throw you out!" The get-together with Johnny went as planned." Billy asked, "Could this have been a coincidence?" I replied, "The probability of these events occurring in nature is somewhere between one in a billion and one in a trillion." Billy replied, "Lightning strikes, and people win the lottery." I replied, "Lightning seldom strikes any person and the lottery is intelligently designed. These kind of events concerning common people in common situations almost never occur." Billy asked, "Did the story end there?" I replied, "The hex continued. On May 6, Johnny went on nights at Texhoma Box and Crate. He told me to contact him at two o'clock on Sundays. I contacted him or had other arrangements for three weeks straight. On the fourth week, Johnny's assistant, Doug had me come to see him. When I arrived, Johnny needed me immediately. His wife left him in the worst way possible. Johnny asked me to pray for him. I told Johnny that I was going to McKinney to see Robert and that when I reached the US 75 overpass in Sherman, Texas that his hex would cease to exist. On Tuesday, I drove to the overpass, and God stopped the hex. This caused a war concerning Johnny's soul." Billy said, "I need to get to my dorm. See you tomorrow at the plaza." I replied, "Thanks for the alternators." Billy said, "Any time I can be of help, call me. See ya."

The PSN meeting was the same old same old. At the May 4th Task Force meeting, Morale was extremely low. Alan said, "The Young communists are definitely coming to town on May 4th." Kathy, a student who once led the victorious fight to keep former Governor Rhodes from becoming governor in 1986, wrote a letter to the editor asking President Schwartz to go easy on the May 4th supporters for the sake of peace on the campus. I conceded that my letter to the editor may never be published. We all found it difficult to focus on the commemoration we were planning. We all felt like giving up and planning a big and mean protest for May 4th. I left the meeting praying for God to help the May 4th victims peacefully. I thought, "These May 4th supporters were being tested to the limit concerning legal and peaceful protests.

On Monday of the following week, I met Billy and his friends on the plaza for a quality get-together. Malinda challenged my pro-life stand by saying that, "A woman has the right to choose what she does with her body." I replied, "Ideally, we need to give a woman her freedom, but a baby has rights too." Malinda asked, "Should we keep unwanted babies alive from poor black neighborhoods?" I replied, "God tells us to value all human life even if it is handicapped. Who can judge what a human being can accomplish? Only God can." Malinda asked, "What about pregnant victims of rape?" I replied, "I believe we can let those moms abort their babies. I would be happy if we could just eliminate birth control abortions. That would cut the abortion rate by 90%. If I were convinced that education by Christians could cut the abortion rate by close to 90%, I would support pro-choice and teach that abortion is the wrong choice by God's standards." Malinda said, "In Sweden, they have choice and the abortion rates are low." I replied, "I wish Planned Parenthood would cooperate better with the Church. If Planned Parenthood would allow Christian counselors into abortion clinics, I would support choice. Abortion rates would drop like a bomb, and many pregnant teenagers would be saved by the Blood of Jesus. Unfortunately, Planned Parenthood does not allow Chriastian Counselors into abortion clinics." Malinda said, "Me and Mary will promote a debate with Right to Life because we are your friends." Mary said, "You may not agree with us on everything, but you treat all of us with respect and are a good friend to all of us." I replied, "I like all of you and wish the best for all of you." Billy asked, do you want to walk with us for a while?" I replied, "I would enjoy that."

We all walked across the campus to a point close to Prentice Hall. There Billy and I chose to mellow out. We saw people playing Frisbee. Billy noticed some women he thought were beautiful. Billy said, "Many people in the dorms now take their trash to the recycling center." I replied, "I bet they use the trash cans you and your friends provide." Billy replied, "We are running our own recycling program. We provide trash cans and take them to the recycling center. We figure that the only way Kent will recycle is if we do it ourselves." I replied, "Shame be upon the Kent State administration. Everybody must try to keep this planet clean. The administration should set an example." Billy replied, "The young liberals are the only good doers on this campus." I replied, "There are also a few good conservatives." Billy replied, "Sorry, I am just angry because only few people seem to care." I replied, "I think I understand." Billy and I watched the sunset and went to the Student Center.

We ate burgers at Wendy's and headed to Katie's dorm in Stuart Hall. We all had a good time in the style of the hippies. Katie asked, "Kevin, what kinds of things are you into?" I replied, "I am doing research into a possible perpetual motion machine. I cannot guarantee that it will work, but I have an idea that it will solve the energy crisis. I like to go to restaurants and eat fried chicken and French fries. I am lousy at games and sports." Katie asked, "What about sex?" I replied, "I never think much about it." Katie asked, "Why?" I replied, "I am just too busy. I am a Christian, and the thought of dating and marriage scare me. I really think of sex as a bedroom subject, and I am not adequately prepared to discuss it. Hope you can still like me." Katie replied, "Sorry to hear that dating scares you, but I still want to be your friend." I replied, "Thanks. Many young people hate me for not being romantic." Katie replied, "I want to be friends with anybody who will accept me as their friend." I replied, "I accept you." We all had a good time until midnight. At midnight, Billy asked, "May I take your exam that you give Scriptural Analysts." I replied, "If you pass, you will have the respect of an officer of the Occult Defense Command of the Board of Judges of Texas." We said goodbye to Katie and her friends. We left her dorm-room.

Billy and I proceeded to leave Stuart Hall. When we arrived at the lobby of Stuart hall, we stopped and talked at a decorative fountain in that lobby. Billy said, "I would like to take your exam for Scriptural Analysts." I asked, "Do you think you are ready?" "I am ready," Billy replied, "Just give me a chance." I said, "This exam will consist of two oral essay questions." Billy asked, "What is the first question?" I asked, "Tell me why a person loving his neighbor as himself would not steal?" Billy replied, "I would not want somebody to steal from me. I worked hard to earn money to buy my possessions. I enjoy using what I own, and I hate to lose it. If I steal from somebody, I will cause them the same pain that I hate." I asked the second question, "Why should a person never kill another who loves his neighbor as himself?" Billy had difficulty answering, so I gave him this hint, "Does not killing send your neighbor to hell?" Billy replied, "I should not kill because it may send the victim to hell, but that is not the only reason. I fear death. Sometimes when somebody is murdered, death does not occur instantly. When death does not occur instantly, a person is in great pain until his death. A person in that pain may get right with God, but the pain is terrible. If the person died, their families are sad for a long time. If I love my neighbor as myself, I would not want to send him to hell, cause a painful death, or cause sorrow for my fellow man. I would hate to suffer any of those things." I replied, "You made a 100 on the exam. That is an 'A'. You pass. If you take an oath you will be a Commissioned Occult Defense Analyst." Billy replied, "I am loyal to you and your friends, so I will take the oath." I administered the Oath by saying, "Repeat after me. I, Billy Glassman, promise to uphold the law of God, Defend the Board of Judges of Texas, and defend officers of US Physics and their friends." Billy repeated the Oath and said, "I do." I replied, "You are now a Commissioned Occult Defense Analyst." I added, "You are a hippie that I like and respect." Billy said, "I must be going home." I replied, "See ya later." I thought, "If Johnny Oilstring had not told me to love my hippie neighbors, I would not have never known Billy Glassman. I would have missed out on a good friendship.

On that Wednesday, The PSN meeting was routine, and Thursday's environmental meeting was the same. I was expecting the May 4th Task Force meeting to be boring, but it was a victory celebration. Alan said before the meeting, "Good work on that letter to the editor." I was surprised that my letter was published and replied, "God must have helped me to write that letter.[9] My research adviser said that I couldn't write. Thank the Lord for his help writing this letter." Alan replied, "Ding dong the witch is dead! God must have helped you write that letter! You defended the Scheuer parents! The administration will never bash us again!" I replied. "My hippie friend from Ardmore, Oklahoma, Johnny Oilstring, heard the letter as I read it to him. Johnny said, "Print the letter as is." I followed his advice." Billy Westman added fuel to the fire by saying, "This is another blot on his record. The President should resign. They should replace him with somebody better." The faculty adviser, Dr. Mason, said, "Congratulations on your work for social justice." I replied, "Thanks."

As I returned to my dorm, I thought these hippies were happy with me because I was a conservative who listened to them. That article did not solve the memorial issue but it gave them something they wanted. They wanted somebody representing the establishment to listen to them. The article proved that I listened to them. Little did I know that Alan firmly committed to keeping the protest of the scaled back memorial legal and peaceful partly because I listened to them and stood up for them. He also became a lifelong friend. With

---

9   See my Letter to the editor on p(197)

2o₵

Alan's support, all of Kent State's hippies supported a peaceful and legal protest. They all will have served as peace marshals on May 4, 1990 to ensure a peaceful protest. A riot became very unlikely.

I returned to my dorm to find the Conservative Frat Man's Club angry. I figured that I can't please everybody all of the time. Johnny Oilstring's advice concerning loving my neighbor paid off again for the hippies. It resulted in my letter to the editor. It greatly reduced the chance of an illegal protest or even a riot.

On that Friday, I called Johnny and asked, "How are you doing?" Johnny replied, "I am doing fine." Johnny asked, "What's happening?" "I am calling to tell you that the letter to the editor you helped me to write was published, and the May 4th Task Force was happy," I replied, "The morale of the Kent State hippies instantly improved. They thanked me in no uncertain terms. I gave Jesus Christ and you the credit. Alan Peacemaker became my friend. They have stopped talking about rioting or illegally protesting, and they are focusing on the 20th anniversary commemoration." Johnny asked, "Will they still protest the memorial peacefully? I replied, "There will still be a peaceful protest concerning the memorial, but they will probably emphasize keeping it peaceful and legal." Johnny asked me in a kind voice, "Could you do me a big favor?" I asked, "What is that favor?" Johnny asked in a kind but desperate voice, "Could you go to the Akron-Canton airport and get me tickets from Indianapolis to Dallas?" I asked, "Why do you need a one way ticket from Indianapolis?" Johnny replied, I am moving to Indianapolis to find a job." I asked, "How much do these tickets cost? Johnny said, "They cost about $200." I asked, "Will I ever see you again? Johnny replied, "You will see me at Steve's wedding on March 24. There, we will exchange contact information. Steve will be happy to see me. I hope you will send me the tickets." I replied, "I will go to the airport this Monday and buy the tickets." Johnny asked, "Can you get these tickets to me by next Monday?" I replied, "I will buy these tickets and mail them straight to you. I will call you next Friday to make sure you received the tickets." I asked, "Will this be Okay?" Johnny replied, "I should receive these tickets by next Friday, but you may call me to verify that I received these tickets." I replied, "I will call you next Friday." Johnny said, "See you later." I went to my Quantum Mechanics class very disappointed to hear of Johnny leaving.

Throughout the next week, the Conservative Frat Man's Club harassed me, but I took it all in stride. I bought Johnny's tickets on Monday and called him on Friday. I asked Johnny, "Did you get your tickets?" Johnny replied, "I received the tickets, and I thank you." I asked, "Will I ever see you again?" Johnny replied, "You will see me at Steve's wedding." I asked, "Will you tell me your new phone number and address there?" Johnny said, "You are a very good friend, so I will keep contact." I said, "The May 4th Task Force likes me, but the Conservative Frat Man's Club seem to hate me." Johnny said, "Those hippies are your good friends, but the Conservative Frat Men are using you." I asked Johnny, "How do you make that judgment?" Johnny replied, "The hippies love you for who you are, but the Conservative Frat Men hate you the minute you disagree with them. Your true friends will accept you regardless of money, popularity, intelligence, or politics. A really good friend will be your friend even if you are poor and a communist." I replied, "I will just associate with my good friends and forget the others." Johnny said, "Good idea, but I will see you at Steve's wedding." I replied, "I will be glad to see you at Steve's wedding, but I will see you later." I went to my physics class praying for Johnny.

Later on that Friday, I headed home to the tenth floor of Leebrick Hall. There, I met my conservative friends. David said, "Hi. How are you doing?" I replied, "I am doing fine." David said in an aggressive voice, "You should quit the PSN and the May 4th Task Force. You should rejoin the Conservative Frat Man's Club." I replied, "I cannot betray my new-found friends in the PSN, and I cannot support the sins of Ohio's conservatives." "Why not?" asked David. I replied, "These sins are flagrant. These sins are so serious that my ability to pray for Johnny Oilstring is compromised. The Bible says to love my neighbor. Joining the Conservative Frat Man's Club forces me to hate Billy Glassman and all of my liberal friends. I cannot undertake such an ungodly act." David said, "I am no longer your friend." I replied, "I will pray for you, but I must stand by my liberal friends." Janet heard her boyfriend David and said, "I am not speaking to you until you apologize to Kevin!" David said, "You caused me to lose my girlfriend!" Janet said, "Kevin is a human being, and you should treat him with a little respect." David replied, "When Kevin quits the PSN, I will be his friend again." Janet replied, "You should be ashamed of yourself!" I said, "See you later." Janet said, "I am your friend and hope David will come to his senses." On Monday, David apologized, and we were still friends.

Later on that Monday, I met Billy Glassman at the Student Center Plaza. I asked Billy, "How are you doing? Billy replied, "How is Project Texhoma doing?" I replied, "I computer simulated 100 motors yesterday." I asked, "How is the recycling effort going?" Billy replied, "Three floors on my dorm are recycling their garbage." I replied, "I am glad you are making progress, but I must tell you that the Conservative Frat Man's Club is harassing me." Billy replied, "I will be your friend no matter what happens." Mary said, "The PSN will likely debate The Right to Life Society concerning abortion rights." Malinda said, "Mary and I think that the conservative students have the right to be heard." Mary said, "We will fight for the pro-lifers to be heard because you are a good friend to us." Malinda said, "We will be with you to the end." Billy said, "I will be with you no matter what the Conservative Frat Man's Club does." I said happily, "I am glad to have such good friends." I said, "Must get to my Electricity and Magnetism class." Billy said, "See you later."

On that Wednesday, Mitch and Sally Peacegood put my friendship with

Billy and his friends to the test. Billy, Mary, Malinda, Katie, and I were having a good time in the Music Library when Mitch and Sally showed up to test my friendship with Billy and his friends. Mitch said, "Kevin is real good friends with me." Sally said, "He is also a good friend of mine." Malinda said, "Kevin is also our good friend." Mary said, "His friendship will likely allow a debate with the Right to Life Society." Mitch asked, "How do you know that Kevin is your friend?" Malinda replied, "We will have to ask him." I saw Mitch and Sally talking with Malinda, Katie and Mary and said to Billy, "It seems like Mitch is trying to break up our friendship." I asked, "What should I do?" Billy said, "You need to tell us why you joined the PSN in front of Mitch and Sally." Billy and I went to Mitch, Sally, Malinda, Mary and Katie. I told them all, "I joined the May 4th Task Force because the administration lied about their relationship with the Kent State liberals." Billy asked, "What about Johnny Oilstring?" I answered with conviction, "I joined the May 4th Task Force because I could not risk losing my power to pray for Johnny. The administration reneged on their word concerning the May 4th Memorial and bashed the May 4th supporters. This conflict started with the arrogance of Governor Rhodes in 1970 and has never ended. Ohio's Republicans should do right and end this conflict." Mitch said, "We tried." I replied, "You tried hard enough to get attention and quit before you got the job done. You Republicans could have been successful at raising the needed $1.3 million Dollars for the original memorial if you hired a professional fund-raiser and risked a little publicity." Billy asked, "What about the environment?" I replied, "Nobody in the Ohio's Republican Party seemed to care." Mary said, "There are some Republicans who believe that careless pollution is the price of progress and support the smokestacks for that reason." I replied, "That is why I joined the PSN." Malinda asked, "Are you friends with that creep, Mitch?" I replied with conviction, "I used to be his friend until he started harassing me for joining the PSN. A good friend will accept me for who I am. I could be his friend if he would respect my right to be a PSN member and respect my friendship with you people." Billy asked, "What about Sally?" I replied, "Sally is the President of Right to Life, so she is my friend." Billy said, "You are friends with some conservatives and some of us liberals." I replied, "I am friends with some conservatives, but, Billy, I am friends with you and all of your friends. Johnny Oilstring's advice, concerning loving my neighbor, allowed you to be my friends, and I am happy that I followed it." Malinda, Katie, Mary, and Billy agreed that we were all friends, and I was happy.

On Thursday, I attended the May 4th Task Force meeting. They started discussing the 20th commemoration in earnest. They talked about who would speak, about having the May 4th Task Force members take peace marshal training, and other routine things. The morale was not the type that would cause a riot. After the meeting, Alan, his friend, and I would talk. Alan said, "That letter to the editor makes you a part of the team." I replied, "I learned how to write such letters by standing up for Johnny Oilstring." Alan asked, "How so?" I replied, "In 1978 Johnny had a bad accident which killed 3 children. The people of Johnny's hometown in Oklahoma wanted to hang him. The local newspaper ran articles about his accident for three weeks straight. At Johnny's trial, it was shown that Johnny was sober and was guilty of no more than a traffic accident. As a result of this, Johnny was convicted of a misdemeanor and was ordered to serve weekends in jail for 1 year. The local newspaper published letters to the editor concerning the accident until 1985. Around Halloween of 1985, I spotted such a letter in the local newspaper. I wrote a letter to the editor calling him an irresponsible journalist. The families wrote back and said that they did not mean to harass Johnny, but they only wanted teenage drivers to be careful. That was the last time that Johnny was harassed by the newspaper." Alan replied, "That man really suffered." I replied, "With God's help, I stopped the harassment." Alan said, "I would like to meet this Johnny Oilstring." Alan's friend said, "Johnny Oilstring may have helped to stop a riot or an illegal protest in Kent." Alan said, "Thanks for helping us keep our ideals of non-violence and obedience of the law when it was very difficult. Sorry. We almost blew it." I replied, "Integrity, justice and kindness often stop violence and generate respect. You were almost driven to violence by lies and serious disrespect. Frustrations such as the scaled back memorial and disrespecting the bell ringing tradition on the commons could have driven me to wrath if I were in your shoes. Sometimes, listening and kind words by the right person stop a group's wrath cold." Alan replied, "A Texas conservative listened to us and helped to calm us down. Without Johnny Oilstring's advice concerning how that Texan should love his neighbor, he would not have been there to help us." I replied," I understand." Alan replied, "I am glad you understand."

We walked a few minutes on the Kent campus talking as friends. I said, "Kathy's organization, Students United Against Rhodes, may have helped to save Johnny's life." Alan asked, "How so?" I replied, "Occult Defense Analyst Robert Elight had a fear that politicians could destroy Johnny Oilstring and the Occult Defense Command. The enemies of the May 4th supporters and Johnny's enemies may have connections high in the occult. The Oilstring hex may have connections to the currency traders in New York or Europe. Richard Nixon had access to the most powerful witches in the United States. The Occult Defense Command had no viable defense against political attack. Robert was not an expert on politics. If Johnny's enemies in the occult allied with Kathy's political enemies, The Oilstring hex could have been successful." Alan replied, "Kathy's organization eventually became the PSN." We talked for a half hour and I returned to my dorm.

On Friday, I met Billy and his three good friends on the Student Center plaza. I said, "The Conservative Frat Men are harassing me as normal." Billy asked, "How is Project Texhoma coming?" I replied, I simulated 500 motors on the computer. Billy asked, "Will you use those alternators?" I replied, "My first prototype will be a generator." Billy asked, "Will your computer generate the design of the prototype from those alternators." I replied, "I will build a generator prototype from one of these alternators." Billy replied, "I am glad to see my alternators are so useful." Malinda said, "I have more good news." I asked, "What is the good news?" Malinda said, "This Tuesday evening the woman's committee will decide whether to debate the Right to Life Society concerning abortion." I asked, "What are the chances of this debate?" Malinda replied, "It looks like the PSN will debate the Right to Life Society." I replied, "Hope you are right." Mary said, "We all love you as a good friend." Katie said, "Me, Mary and Malinda are 3 of the 7 votes needed for the PSN to participate in this debate." Malinda said, "The other votes are all my good friends and will likely agree with me, Mary, and Katie." I said, "Tell me how the vote comes out." I said to the group, "See you later." I thought, "Kind words and friendship often solve unfair situations. It was unfair that the Right to Life Society could not be heard because the liberals blocked expression of their views by university regulations. My friendship with Mary, Katie, and Malinda may have helped to right this wrong, though the methods may seem unfair.

On the following Wednesday, Kim said at the PSN meeting, "Tonight at 8:00, The PSN and May 4th Task Force needs to present their case for funding the May 4th activities." I asked, "Why do we need to be there?" Kim replied, "We need to make our case to fund the 20th anniversary commemoration of the May 4th shootings." I asked, "Does this funding also help the Earth Day programming?" Kim replied, "Teamwork between the May 4th Task Force and all of the PSN's causes will benefit everybody." The Secretary of the May 4th Task Force, Sandy, said, "The May 4th Task Force made their request for funding later than usual, so we need to support the May 4th Task Force even more." I asked, "Do you want me to attend the meeting and pray for the May 4th Task Force to get their funding?" Kim replied, "If you think that prayer will work, pray for us." I replied, "I will be there to pray for the PSN and May 4th Task Force tonight."

At the Student Senate meeting, I met Alan, Kathy, and Billy Westman. Kathy was worried that the May 4th Task Force would not get their funding. I asked Alan and Kathy, "Would you like me to pray that you get your funding?" Kathy said, "We can use all of the support we can get." Alan said, "Pray for us." Kathy said, "Look across the room." I replied, "The Conservative Frat Man's Club is making a case to fund one of their speakers on May 4th." I emphasized, "The Conservative Frat Man's Club is one of the dirtiest organizations on campus." Malinda asked, "How so?" I replied, "They bash liberals mercilessly, break up their friendships, and harass me and my friends." I said, "Let's concentrate supporting the PSN and May 4th Task Force." The Student Senate meeting was called to order. After reading the minutes and discussing other issues, the motions to fund the May 4th Task Force were brought up. The President of the Student Senate asked for arguments for funding the May 4th Task Force's programming. I told Alan, "I need to pray concerning this need." I prayed to the Lord Jesus:

Lord, Help the May 4th Task Force to get their funding. Many of the victims and their families still hurt from these shootings. They cry for respect and justice. Jesus, Hear their cry. At stake is the healing of Kent State University. Help the May 4th supporters to see that you love them and provide their needs. A good task force presentation will go a long way in healing Kent State and the United States. Lord, we ask again, that you show the May 4th supporters your love and give them their funding. In the name of Jesus we ask this. Amen.

As I was saying my prayer for the May 4th Task Force, The Chairperson of the May 4th Task Force said, "We may have been slow to present our funding requests, but the May 4th presentation this year is the biggest program on campus." A conservative student senator said, "Our Student Senate has a deadline of February 1 for most funding requests." Another senator asked, "Why should we change our deadlines for you?" The Chairperson replied with conviction, "We should not let a stupid rule be an excuse for disrespecting our fellow students who were shot because they opposed the Vietnam War. The best way to heal Kent State is to show respect to your former fellow students. You do this by funding the May 4th commemoration." Kathy said, "Please do not let a stupid rule stop this important commemoration and give us our funding." The Student Senate voted to fund three out of four requests. This caused the May 4th Task Force to rejoice.

The next order of business was the proposal to fund the Conservative Frat Man's Club's May 4th speaker. I prayed the following prayer:

Lord, These Conservative Frat Men harass everybody that opposes them. They bash the PSN and tried three times to break up my friendship with Billy Glassman and his friends. Lord teach these Conservative Frat Men a lesson. Deny them their funding and teach them to play by the rules. In the end, save their souls and show them your love. I ask this in the name of Jesus, Amen.

As I was praying for the defeat of the Conservative Frat Man's Club, James Avonman blasted the Conservative Frat Man's Club for supporting the bashing of homosexuals. He told those present at the meeting that the written platform of the Conservative Frat Man's Club supports bigotry. He claimed that the Conservative Frat Man's Club should not get their funding because their national organization promoted prejudice in violation of tolerance of diversity. I rejoiced that the Conservative Frat Man's Club got blasted because they forgot one of the most important teachings of Jesus Christ, The Golden Rule. Mitch replied, "We don't bash gays on the campus." James replied, "You should not get your funding because your national organization supports gay bashing." James said, "We believe that you bash gays because your national organization supports it." As a result of James' blasting, the Student Senate denied the Conservative Frat Man's Club their funding. After the meeting, I said to Alan, "We got our funding." Alan said, "Thanks for praying for our funding." I replied, "God cares about you and your friends." Alan said, "God punished the Conservative Frat Man's Club." I replied, "If the Conservative Frat Man's Club does not change their ways, they will cease to exist." Alan replied, "Better not say it too loudly." I asked, "Why?" Alan replied, "Mitch will hear you and get mad." Mitch did hear and angrily said, "You have not heard the last of this." I replied. "God will punish your organization." I said, "See ya later." Mitch said angrily, "I will bite you back later." I headed back to my dorm a little fearful for the future.

At the May 4th Task Force meeting on Thursday, we all felt the effect of the Conservative Frat Man's Club biting back. Alan said, "I saw a political cartoon posted showing Fidel Castro saying, "I have nothing to worry about because I have friends in the May 4th Task Force and the Kent State Student Senate."" I replied, "I wonder what the Conservative Frat Man's Club will do next." Billy Westman said, "The Conservative Frat Man's Club members are mad because they didn't get the funding for their May 4th speaker." Alan said, "This harassment is sour grapes, and it shall pass." I replied, "I am a good sport. I feel like writing a vicious cartoon about the Conservative Frat Man's Club, but I do not want to stoop to their level. The Board of Judges is a clean organization." Alan said, "Let's be there for each other no matter what happens with this harassment." I replied, "That is a good idea." I headed to my dorm feeling better.

On Friday at about noon, The Conservative Frat Man's Club members all approached me on the Student Center plaza. Mitch proposed, "If you quit the PSN and the May 4th Task Force and rejoin the Conservative Frat Man's Club, you can head a research project concerning the environment and global warming." The red-bearded libertarian said, "This is an opportunity of a lifetime." I hesitated and asked God for an answer. The Lord replied in a still soft voice, "You are being offered the world to betray Billy Glassman and Johnny Oilstring and sell your soul." I thought, "If I accept this deal, Johnny Oilstring would die in Indiana and Billy Glassman would cease to be my friend." I thanked the Lord that he counted me worthy to face Jesus Christ's greatest temptation. I told Mitch and his friends, "I cannot accept your generous offer." Mitch thought I was crazy and asked, "Why do you turn us down?" The red-bearded libertarian said, "This is the opportunity of a lifetime." Mitch said, "We know what is best for you." I replied in a serious tone, "I cannot rejoin the Conservative Frat Man's Club because doing so would endanger Johnny Oilstring and betray Billy Glassman and all of my good friends in the PSN." Mitch replied, "You betray David and I by joining the PSN." I replied, "I betray Johnny Oilstring and reject his advice concerning loving my neighbor by tolerating the lies and hatred of the Ohio Republicans. You can still be friends with me, but I must put the Lord and all my friends first." I headed back to my dorm feeling victorious over the Conservative Frat Man's Club.

On Monday at noon, I met Billy Glassman and his three friends on the Student Center plaza. There, Billy asked, "How are you doing?" I replied, "I was in the battle of my life with the Conservative Frat Man's Club." Billy asked, "How so?" I replied, "The Conservative Frat Man's Club offered to fund research concerning the environment for betraying you and all of your friends and rejoining the Conservative Frat Man's Club." Billy asked, "How did you reply?" I replied, "I turned them down because I loved you, your friends, and Johnny Oilstring enough to turn down their bribery." Billy replied, "We know that you are a great friend and give you all of our support." Malinda said, "I have good news for you." Mary said, "The PSN women's committee has decided to hold the debate with The Right to Life Society." I replied, "This is good news!" I asked happily, "When is the debate?" Malinda replied, "We still need to set the date, but it looks like around April 15th." I replied, "This news is better than being tempted to betray my friends and the PSN." Billy asked, "Did the Conservative Frat Man's Club get you to join?" I replied, "Though I was tempted like Jesus Christ to betray you and your friends, I turned the Conservative Frat Man's Club down." Billy congratulated me by saying, "I knew you were loyal to us." Mary said, "You got the Right to Life Society their debate because you love us." Malinda said, "You are what a good Christian should be." Katie said, "Christians like you make me want to join the Church." I replied happily, "I am glad to be well liked somewhere." I went to class happy to know that I have four good friends.

On Wednesday following the PSN meeting, I met David and Janet at David's dorm-room. I asked Janet, "Would you like to be considered for Robert Elight's old job of Commanding Analyst of the Occult Defense System of the Board of Judges of Texas?" Janet said, "I would love to be the Commanding Occult Defense Analyst of Gainesville Security Central." I said, "There would be some challenges to this job and some great rewards." Janet asked, "Could you give me two examples?" I replied, "One such challenge would be earning the respect of the Elight's and the Chrisgood's at Fort Riblet Security Central in Gainesville." Janet asked, "Are the Chrisgood's and Elight's open-minded and tolerant to differences of opinion." I replied, "They are very non-judgmental and will treat you with respect." Janet asked, "Could you give me another example?" I replied, "You could face moral choices concerning national security." "Give me an example," requested Janet. I replied to the request, "You may have to help hide me and my prototype until it can be demonstrated at a rock concert." Janet replied, "In that case, supporting rock music to solve the energy crisis is a good work for both the Church and The United States." I said, "Let's discuss this position in detail." Janet asked, "Would 4 o'clock Friday afternoon at the 10th floor lobby be good." I replied, "See you at 4 o'clock on Friday in the lobby." I headed back to my dorm-room with hope that Gainesville Security Central's security system would be intact.

On that Thursday, Alan said at the May 4th Task Force meeting, "President Schwartz has resigned effective when they find a replacement." Billy Westman asked, "Was it over the May Fourth issue?" Alan replied, "President Schwartz says it was not because of May 4th, but I wonder." I replied, "May 4th may not have been the direct reason for his resignation, but his pride was a big factor in his fall. God has taken the Kingdom from his hands."

On Friday, I met Janet at 4 o'clock in the lobby. I asked Janet, "Could we take a walk?" Janet asked, "Why don't we?" We entered the elevator and I said, "To execute this project, an alliance with the PSN and the May 4th Task Force is necessary." I asked, "Can you become friends with some of the PSN and May 4th Task Force members?" Janet replied, "I like David Kruger of the May 4th Task Force and Billy Glassman of the PSN." I asked Janet, "Are you aware that Billy Glassman is the Commanding Occult Defense Analyst of Kent State University?" Janet replied, "I think that it is great that you love and respect the PSN and the hippies of Kent State. It is nice that you give a hippie a voice in the Occult Defense Command." We exited the elevator on the first floor and Janet warned, "There is Mitch spying on us from the stairwell!" I said, "Let's go outside." Janet warned, "David is behind the shrubs." I told Janet, "We will have to finish this interview later." Janet said, "I understand. Mitch and David need to respect our friendship." I asked Mitch and David, "What is the meaning of this!!!?" Mitch said, "Stop corrupting Janet with your friends in the PSN." David asked, "Do you have a new car? I replied, "Yes." David said, "We may scratch that new car with a key and make it look bad." I replied, "Get caught, and you will go to jail for vandalism." David asked, "What is somebody from the PSN scratched your car?" "I would make them fix it," I replied. David asked, "Why wouldn't you give us the same respect?" I replied angrily, "The Conservative Frat Man's Club on this campus deals in harassment and intimidation." David said, "I need to get going." I said, "See you later." David said, "Think about what I said" I went back to my dorm disappointed that I could not complete Janet's interview that day.

On Monday, I met Billy Glassman in the Student Center plaza. There Billy asked, "How is my good friend?" I replied, "The Conservative Frat Man's Club interrupted my interview with Janet Mercules." Mary asked, "Why are you interviewing Janet?" I replied, "I am trying to find an Occult Defense Analyst to replace Robert Elight?" Malinda asked, "What happened to Robert?" I replied, "I have not heard from him in over a year." Billy said, "That is awful." Malinda said, "We can take his place as your good friends." I replied, "You are all good friends." Billy asked, "Are we as good as Robert?" I replied happily, "You are all best friends!" Billy said, "We are happy that you like us." Malinda said, "The Conservative Frat Man's Club will respect us more after we debate the Right to Life Society concerning Abortion Rights on April 25th before finals." Mary said, "Remember Earth Day this Sunday on April 15th." We all prepared for Earth Day on Wednesday at the PSN meeting.

On Sunday, we all enjoyed the Earth Day festivities and learned about nature. Late on that Sunday, I met Tim Johnson on the Commons, and we discussed Janet Mercules as a possible replacement for Robert. Tim was a slender, long haired, well-built, and very friendly liberal leader in Kent. I said, "Janet Mercules is the daughter of a patriarch in the Greek Orthodox Church." Tim asked, "Can she respect PSN and May 4th Task Force members?" I replied, "Janet is friends with Billy Glassman and her conservative brother Bill Mercules is friends with Steve Colburn, who sold tie-dyes in Kent." Tim asked, "Does she impress you with her knowledge of the Bible?" I replied, "She could even teach me a thing or two about the Bible." Tim replied, "Let's listen to the speaker." We listened to the speaker tell us that we should junk our air conditioners for a half hour. After the speaker was through speaking, I told Tim, "The Conservative Frat Man's Club spied on my interview with Janet." Tim asked, "Why is that so important?" I replied, "To take Robert's place, Janet needs a security clearance. Her loyalties seem divided between the Conservative Frat Man's Club and our vital interests concerning Kent State's liberals. Should the spying of the Conservative Frat Man's Club hurt Janet's Security Clearance at Gainesville Security Central?" Tim replied, "Janet's close affiliation with the Conservative Frat Man's Club damages her credibility, and Janet should fail her security clearance examination." I said, "See you later." Tim said goodbye, and I headed back to my dorm feeling like Tim understood the problems at Gainesville Security Central and really cared.

Meanwhile, the Conservative Frat Man's Club started to harass me badly. On Monday night, they knocked on my dorm-room door at 2:15 am and drenched me with water. On Tuesday night, they ordered pizza in my name at 12:30 in the morning. On Wednesday, they called me at 12:30 am and kept me up until 2:00 am On Thursday night, they drenched me with water again at 2:00 am I got mad and called the campus police. Mitch got warned and approached me the next day. He promised to stop if I debated on the side of The Right to Life in next Tuesday's debate. I replied, "I will always support the rights of the unborn child because they are people too." Mitch said, "Let's be friends for your last two weeks even though we disagree about May 4th." replied, "Let's be friends who disagree on a few points of politics." Janet said, "I will attend the May 4th vigil in a week." I replied, "We have done more to heal Kent today than President Schwartz did in eight years."

On that Tuesday at The Right to Life Vs PSN debate. I met Billy, Malinda, Katie, and Mary fifteen minutes early. I told Billy Glassman, "I will be debating on the side of the Right to Lifers tonight because I do not believe in abortion, but I will do so as your friends." Billy Glassman replied, "I understand and love you as a best friend." Mary, Malinda and Katie agreed. I replied, "All of you have done more to heal this school than President Schwartz has done in eight years." My conservative friends, David, Janet, Mitch, Bill Mercules, and Sally said "Hi." I said to Billy Glassman and all of his friends, "I must be seated on the conservative side for this debate." Billy Glassman said, "Let's get a pizza after this debate." I agreed.

The debate began. Malinda asked, "Why do you show pictures of that dead fetus?" I replied, "We mean to remind the public that the fetus is a baby dependent on its Mom's umbilical cord and deserves to live just like any May 4th supporter." Mary asked, "How do we outlaw abortion without wrecking a young woman's life?" Sally replied, "We propose that a woman have the child and put him up for adoption or have help from her parents raising the child." I added, "There are many couples who would love to have a baby, but they have a medical condition blocking a pregnancy." Bill Mercules added, "There is a shortage of babies up for adoption." Janet added, "Adoption enables the woman to have the child without wrecking her life." Malinda said, "In Sweden, a woman has the right to choose and abortion rates are still low." Mary asked, "Why can't we have both choice and low abortion rates in this country?" I replied, "I wish we could have both choice and low abortion rates in America, but Planned Parenthood makes this impossible." "How so?" asked Katie. Janet replied, "Abortion clinics want to make money and do not allow Christian counselors to have the opportunity to encourage the pregnant teenager to put the child up for adoption." Bill Mercules asked, "Does the system really allow a woman to explore all options before having an abortion?" Billy Glassman replied, "We must improve choice so that a woman knows all of her options, but I pray that we can give the woman a right to choose." I replied, "Maybe, if this system would improve, some Christians could support a woman's right to choose." I added, "We must reduce abortions by 90%." Malinda added, "Some of us also want to reduce abortions." Katie added, "I would not want an abortion, but want a woman to have that right." We continued this friendly debate for an hour and were all friends. Janet said to Billy Glassman, "I will be at the May 4th vigil." Billy Glassman replied, "I will be glad to see you there." We disagreed about politics, but we were all friends. All of us participating in this debate went to eat a pizza and had fun. By becoming friends, both sides won this debate.

One week later on Monday, I met Kathy and Billy Westman in the PSN office. There, they were preparing signs for the protest on May 4th. One of Kathy's signs read, "BUILD THIS MEMORIAL RIGHT." She was referring to the half-hearted effort to raise money to build the $1.3 million memorial they promised and the scaled back version of the memorial which resulted. Another sign said, "LONG LIVE THE SPIRIT OF KENT AND JACKSON STATE." I greeted them by saying, "How are all of you doing?" Kathy replied, "We are doing fine." She added, "We are getting ready for the big march on Friday." I asked, "What little thing can I do to help?" Kathy asked, "Will you be there for the May 4th vigil on Thursday and on May 4th for the march and the commemoration? I replied, "Unless I am sick, or unless something terribly unexpected comes my way, I will be there." Kathy replied, "Being there for us is what you can do to help." Billy Westman added, "Would you pray for a sunny day on Friday?" I replied, "I will pray for a sunny day and for a peaceful protest." I added, "Keeping the peace is my first priority, but I will pray for both." Billy replied, "We really want a sunny day." He added, "We will keep the people in line. Remember that all of us are peace marshals." I replied, "I will place this matter in God's hands." I added, "God will work this out for the best in the long run." I said, "I need to get to class, so I'll see ya later."

On that evening, I met David and Janet near my dorm. Janet said, "I will attend the vigil on Thursday." I replied with great joy, "I am glad to see that you are trying to understand the May 4th victims, their friends, and their families." David said, "Now you corrupted my girlfriend, Janet." I replied, "She is showing Jesus' love to the liberals making her a good Christian." Janet said, "I like you and David Kruger as friends." She added, "I will be at the vigil." "I will be there," I said.

On Wednesday night, I attended a PSN meeting concerning the protest on May 4th. I had a cold and thought nothing of it. As the meeting progressed my cold got worse. Toward the end of the meeting, I was coughing so much that Billy Glassman asked, "Are you all right?" I replied, "I just have a little cold, but I am all right." Billy suggested, "You should go home and rest." I went home and went to bed.

On the next morning, I felt sick and called in sick at my job in the food service. I rested until 2:30 and went to the Kent State Health Center. They said that I had walking pneumonia. I told Billy and Katie that I could not make the vigil and possibly the protest because I had walking pneumonia. I felt bad, but went home to rest.

On Friday, I felt better as, I watched the May 4th special on the Today Show. By 11:00 am, I felt good enough to attend the protest concerning the scaled back memorial. I took a sign and joined the protest. At the protest, Tim Johnson cried out, "They raped the Memorial!" Tim also said that violence would dishonor the four dead May 4th victims. He said that a peaceful protest was the best way to show their anger. They rang the bell in the Commons at 12:24 and returned to the dedication of the memorial. At the dedication, Ohio Governor Dick Celeste said that he was sorry for the May 4th shootings. I rejoiced that Ohio's Democratic party had just made themselves right with God. The governor said that he could be proud to be an Ohioan. The rain started to fall. At the end of the dedication about two hours later, the protesters marched to the Memorial Gym and called it quits. At the Memorial Gym, I met

Malinda. "Would you like to come to listen to the Conservative Frat Man's Club's speaker tonight?" Malinda asked. "I should go home and rest this evening," I replied, "I was lucky to attend the protest, but I will attend the weekend events." Malinda replied, "I know that you were sick." Malinda added, "Thanks for attending the protest. Hope you are feeling better soon." I replied, "See you this weekend."

On the way home, I met three people from out-of-town who were supporting the May 4th protest. One person introduced himself as saying, "I am Barry from the PSN at the University of Chicago. I support the May 4th *() Space* protesters because the administration opposes recycling at the University of Chicago. I sympathize with the May 4th supporters who have run into a brick wall in Kent. Another hippie said, "I am Linda from the PSN at the University of Minnesota. I sympathize with the progressive students in Kent as well." Another out-of-town hippie said, "I am Bob from the PSN's national headquarters in Iowa City, Iowa. I understand why Kent's progressive students are protesting the May 4th issue. They are frustrated that they get no respect." I returned to my dorm thinking, "These young people all stick together. When one hurts, they all hurt." I rested in my dorm, for the night.

Throughout the weekend, I attended PSN and May 4th events. One event at the Memorial Gym stood out. There they had an event like a pep rally. There they cheered, "Beat back the Bush attack! Beat back the Bush attack!..." Later on they cheered, "Arrest George Bush! Arrest George Bush!..." After that Pep rally, I rested for the night and attended an event where everybody formed groups and discussed issues concerning their rights and encounters with law enforcement. I found myself in a group which had a Young Communist. This Young Communist told of recent encounter with the FBI. He said that the FBI planted evidence that an officer of the Young Communists betrayed them. I said, "I have a friend who was hurt by the Soviet Union." The Young Communist asked, "How so?" I said, "He got caught trying to smuggle Bibles into the Soviet Union." The Young Communist asked, "Did he go to Siberia?" I replied, "No. They held him in prison for four days and kicked him out of the country with no money." The Young Communist asked, "Why was he stupid enough to smuggle Bibles into Mother Russia?" I replied, "According to the Helsinki Accords, my friend, Tom Chrisgood, should have been able to mail those Bibles to his Pentecostal friends in the Soviet Union. The Soviet Union forced his Pentecostal friends underground, forcing their friends in the free world to smuggle Bibles to them." The Young Communist said, "Tom should not have broken Russia's laws." I replied, "Brezhnev violated the Helsinki Accords making him a war criminal!" The Young Communist said, "I understand your anger toward the Soviet Union." I replied, "I think I understand your anger toward the United States." The Young Communist said, "The FBI violated our free speech and persecuted our people." I replied, "We do not have the money to waste persecuting dissedents!" "I am glad you stand for right in America," replied the Young Communist. I replied with sympathy, "When the Soviets persecuted my Christian friends, I wanted to burn the Soviet flag in LaPorte, Indiana's town square. I love America and cannot burn

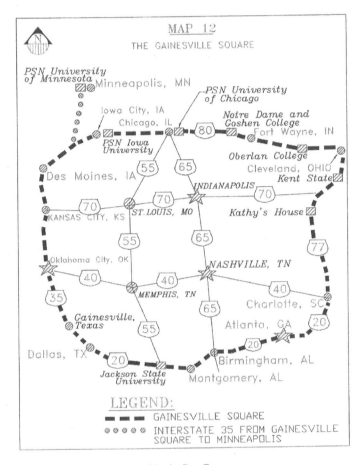

Map by Dan Eaves

the American flag. I can and will call my congressman to task concerning the FBI's violation of our laws and waste of taxpayer money. I understand why you may wish to burn the American flag."

After my encounter with the communist hippie, Billy, Malinda, Katie, Mary, and I had a deep conversation. Billy said, "I am glad that a Christian like you loves us. All we want is for you older people to accept us and to listen to us. Tell your friends that we are nice people." Malinda, Katie, and Mary agreed. I replied, "God intends for all of us to be friends. We are all in this

MAP 12 A

HUMOUROUS
REPRESENTATION OF
NORTHEASTERN OHIO
1970-1990

MAP BY BRUCE
GROSSMAN

world together." Billy said, "Preach it brother! Preach it!" I said, "Did you know that Interstate 80 connects Kent State to the PSN in Kent, Chicago, and Iowa City which also support the May 4th cause in Kent? It also connects Notre Dame, where Father Hessburgh defended the peace movement in the 1970's, to the PSN and May 4th Center in Kent. Furthermore, Dallas, Gainesville, and the PSN in Minneapolis, also represented here, are all connected by Interstate 35. Jackson State, where police shot two black students in their dorm-rooms, is within 20 miles of interstate 20 which passes through Dallas. Interstate 20 connects to Interstate 77. Interstate 77 connects the PSN's founder, Kathy Peacegood's, hometown of Beckley, West Virginia, Alan Peacemaker's home town of Akron, Ohio, and your own hometown of Cleveland, Ohio." Billy asked, "What does all of this mean?" I replied, "Note that all my interests and these of Kent State's hippies lie within 20 miles of the square formed by these highways or on one of these highways (Map 12). Perhaps God is saying that we should love each other because we are all connected. In other words, we are all in this together. We are all Americans. We all love our freedom. Thank a World War II veteran or a Christian that we are not speaking German. Thank a hippie for helping to keep our country free. Nixon had a plan for taking our freedom." Billy said, "You really get it. We love Christians and older people who appreciate us." I said, "I accept any American who will accept me." Billy said, "I accept anybody who accepts me." Malinda, Mary, and Katie agreed. We were all happy and close for the moment. Although we are close but politically opposed, many concerned with Kent still fight, and some conservatives still play dirty like Nixon or the Vietcong (Map 12A). We should pray for God to show them the right and peaceful solutions for this country. Let us be close. Let us be friends for life. Let us set an example all concerned with Kent State and our country can follow. Billy, Malinda, Mary, Katie, and I agreed.

2014 After my lesson in tolerance of diversity and love of Billy's generation, it was time to say my good-byes to my liberal friends in Kent. I walked around the campus and said goodbye to Alan, Gabriella, and Tim. I saw Billy and Katie. Billy said, "Give me your phone number, and I will call you." I gave Billy my phone number. He would call me and keep contact with me. He kept contact with me to this day in 2013. My perpetual motion machine would prove to be a failure in 1991. I saw Kim. She said, "I like your results, but disagree with your methods." I said, "Let's exchange phone numbers and keep contact." We exchanged contact information and said our good-byes. Symbolizing our new-found friendship, Kim and I hugged each other as we said goodbye. I left Kent victorious over the Oilstring Hex and found a group of friends for life. I returned to Gainesville, collected my $200 from Johnny, and saw him in Ardmore. Johnny and I continued that friendship until 2005.

THE END

APPENDIX PART 1

HISTORICAL BACKGROUND FOR THE BATTLE OF FORT ROCK

This novel is based on a true story. This story is fiction mainly because I changed the names of most characters and changed the name of my hometown, names of some universities I attended, and locations associated with my hometown. I also used literary license to depict a few events that I theorized or did not witness. Unlike the novel, this background is not fiction. There really was a Project Texhoma, a crisis with the US Dollar, an extremely bad influence in the fiberglass industry, The rock band Kritikal Kondishun, a vicious hex that felt like Pearl Harbor, or striking coincidences appearing to be that hex, and a May 4th controversy that almost caused a riot or an illegal protest in Kent in 1990.

THE MAY 4th SHOOTINGS, SUBSEQUENT COVER-UP, AND NOTRE DAME FOOTBALL

On May 4, 1985, my best friend, fictionally depicted as Johnny Oilstring, had just suffered from a vicious occult attack. My Christian friend, fictionally depicted as Robert Elight, and I could get prayers answered as far away as Kishinev, Russia. In October of 1983, Iran threatened to block The Strait of Hormuz. Much of the oil needed by the free world flowed through the Strait. The powerful Soviet Union had backed Iran. The world was in danger of World War III. I commanded in The Name of Jesus that Satan leave the Strait of Hormuz. Perhaps, other Americans prayed for the same thing. God answered this prayer. There was peace in the Strait until 1987 when the Soviets were too broke to help Iran. In 1980, Robert Elight, and I defeated what we thought to be the most powerful Satanic influence in the fiberglass industry. In October of 1978, I prayed and fasted for the US Dollar. The Dollar had plummeted almost daily. I feared another Great Depression. Three days after the fast, The Federal Reserve started buying Dollars on the Foreign Exchange Market. God had given the government guidance, and the fall of our Dollar stopped for a month. The Dollar stabilized. Because of these and other prayers, I thought that the organization, fictionally depicted as the Board of Judges of Texas, was invulnerable to the occult. This May 4, 1985 occult attack felt like Pearl Harbor.

On May 4, 1985, Kent State University was supposedly healed, and the May 4th shootings were supposedly resolved. The Kent State hippies and the Kent State administration celebrated. I wished that I could share in their happiness as I saw them on TV that day.[10] They were happy, but I was mad at the devil. I prayed that God would give me friendship with Kent State's hippies. The still-soft voice of the Lord said, "You will be friends with these hippies, and you will like it." These hippies had an agreement to build a memorial. A contest was held to find a design for the memorial. Bruno Ast's design won. [11] This design would cost a half million dollars to build. Now came the challenge: raising money to build the memorial.

To raise the money for the memorial, President Schwartz contacted prospective corporate sponsors and large donors to the university. The university could not even start to raise the half million dollars necessary to build the Bruno Ast design. President Schwartz tried to raise the money on his own, but only raised a small fraction of the money needed for the memorial. Then, the bottom fell out. In June of 1986, the American Legion publicly called the proposed May 4th Memorial "a memorial to terrorists." Kent State University had a big incentive to minimize publicity concerning The May 4th shootings. In the 1970's some of Ohio's officials were being investigated by the

---

10   Associated Press. "Kent State Students Set Vigil;" Dallas Morning News, May 4, 1985.

11   Stoffel, Jennifer; Kent State Journal. "Terrible Event Echoes in Dispute on How to Remember it;" New York Times, December 14, 1988.

Feds for possible criminal offenses connected with the May 4 shootings.[12] During that same decade, The victims were suing about the May 4th shootings.[13] As of 1990, The administration wanted to settle the May4th issue with or without respecting the May 4th victims and their families. They wanted to move on as a university,[14] [15] Consequently, The Kent State administration became much less aggressive at raising money for the May 4th Memorial. They did not even find a professional fund-raiser.

Over the next two years, the debate between the Kent May 4th supporters and the administration escalated. Former governor James Rhodes ran for governor of Ohio. Rhodes ordered the National Guard into Kent a few days before the Kent State shootings. This angered the Kent State hippies. They felt that Rhodes, who ordered the Kent State shootings, was not fit to govern. I agree with the hippies. The Kent State shootings could have been avoided. This governor at his best showed poor judgment in Kent on May 4, 1970. The hippies said that Rhodes murdered four of their friends. Perhaps, the hippies were right!! For this reason, the hippies worked aggressively to defeat Governor Rhodes. Praise the Lord; Dick Celeste beat Rhodes!!![16] President Schwartz was half-hearted about his effort to build the memorial. A professional fund-raiser had not been hired. Kent had something big to hide!!!

Early in 1988 Notre Dame's Assistant Coach Pete Cordelli interviewed for the head football coach's position at Kent State. Dick Crum got the job.[17] Pete may have learned of the May 4th controversy in Kent. Later in 1988, Joe Walsh, guitarist for the Eagles, publicly supported the building of the memorial.[18] He

---

12   Associated Press. "KSU Probe Opens." The Reporter Dover-New Philidelphia, Ohio; May 13, 1970, page 1.

13   Associated Press. "Kent State Jury to begin deliberations." Journal News; Hamilton, Ohio; Page 21.

14   "Legion may oppose Kent State Memorial as Insult to Vets;" Los Angeles Times. Los Angeles California: July 11, 1986. p.2.

15   Walker, Crystal Williams, "Schwartz is praised and criticized for letter." Akron Beacon Journal, Akron Ohio, April 6, 1990,.

16   Love, Steve; "Kent State Shooting Victim Working to Defeat Rhodes;". Akrom Becon Journal, October 3, 1986.

17   Seaburn, John. "Crum Set to accept Kent State Job," Akron Beacon Journal, January 18, 1988, page d5 Sports Section.

18   "Joe Walsh Can't Forget Ohio;" Chicago Sun Times February 18, 1988, p. 18

did an annual benefit concert for the Kent State Memorial that year. No more benefit concerts were held. Alan Peacemaker and Joe Walsh likely did not communicate well because they were both extremely busy. Perhaps, President Schwartz 's closing of the fund-raising effort stopped this effort. I read of the closing of the fund-raising in the school newspaper in November of 1988. This end of fund raising resulted in a shamefully scaled back memorial. Some of my friends who were campus conservatives hinted that they would stop being my friend if I joined the hippies. Peer pressure stopped me from doing the right thing.

Over the next semester, my conservative friends kept me from joining the hippies. Despite a friendship with a liberal, fictionally depicted as Tammy Peacekid, in the Kent State Food Service, I remained an Ohio Republican. The person, fictionally depicted as Chris Peaceman, went on TV and said that Kent State broke its word concerning the memorial. I feared losing any security clearance I needed to work as a physicist. I feared losing all of my conservative friends in Ohio. I even thought that I could lose some friends in my hometown, fictionally depicted as Gainesville, Texas. As depicted in my fictional novel, "The Battle of Fort Rock," I engaged Chris Peaceman about joining the hippies, but I made an excuse to back off. I feared losing my career in physics and losing 75% of my friends. My friend Tammy Peacekid invited me to the Students for a Democratic Society (SDS) reunion. Students for a Democratic Society was an organization that protested the Vietnam war on many college campuses. Sometimes the SDS was violent. I almost went as her guest. I was busy that night at a party in Leebrick Hall. At that party, my conservative friends got me to attend their protest of the SDS reunion. I bashed the 1968 President of the SDS, fictionally depicted as Tim Peacegood. I insinuated that he was a communist who would betray his country. My friends, Tammy Peacekid and Johnny Oilstring, held me accountable.

In the summer of 1989, something horrible happened. I heard on a South Bend station that Holtz paid players while head football coach at The University of Minnesota. It was alleged that Lou Holtz gave Gardner $500 to give to a football player. As of July 1989, Holtz and all of his assistants denied knowledge of football players at Minnesota getting paid. Little did I know, later in 1989, Pete Cordelli, the Quarterbacks' Coach of Notre Dame's national championship football program, changed his story. He accused Lou Holtz of paying Roselle Richardson in 1985 while Holtz was the head coach of the football program at The University of Minnesota. Holtz later said he paid Roselle Richardson $20 because he lost his wallet. Cordelli would later charge Holtz with paying Richardson $200. These allegations hurt Notre Dame's reputation and stressed out many people in Notre Dame's Athletic Department in 1989. Holtz's payment to Richardson, whether it was $200 or $20, was a minor violation of NCAA rules. Cordelli made allegations about paying Roselle Richardson against Lou Holtz and stuck with his details even after

Holtz admitted he was wrong.[19] [20] In 1991, Lou Holtz was found guilty of 2 minor violations by the NCAA. Notre Dame was innocent. After the NCAA hearings, Lou claimed that Pete Cordelli changed his story about Holtz's payment to Roselle Richardson seven times. Holtz also said that the scandal at Minnesota and against Holtz hurt the Notre Dame Community from 1988 to 1991.[21] Why did Pete Cordelli persist against Lou Holtz and hurt Notre Dame's Football program? Pete Cordelli interviewed for a head coaches position at Kent State University in 1988. Pete Cordelli accused Holtz and hurt Notre Dame at a critical time concerning Kent State's May 4th Memorial (1989-1990).

Kent State University had something big to hide. They failed to keep their promises to the May 4th victims and their families. My Aunt Gloria (Gloria Jean Moody Knight) was friends with Virginia's governor in 1970. Virginia's governor was friends with Governor Rhodes or somebody who knew him. She said that the Kent State shootings could have been avoided. Many other people agree with Aunt Gloria. Notre Dame's former President Theodore Hessburgh spoke out against The Vietnam War. Notre Dame's Former Head Football Coach, Ara Parsegian, was an expert in public relations. What if Hessburgh, Parsegian, or some other public figure from Notre Dame learned of the ongoing May 4th controversy in Kent? Would they have spoken out and exposed the truth of the controversy concerning The May4th Memorial?

Meanwhile, back in Kent, I started my academic year at Kent State. I was looking for an excuse to join the hippies, but their stance about an independent Palestine scared me off. I joined the Right to Life Society and the Conservative Frat Man's Club. Little did I know, God would tell me to quit the Conservative Frat Man's Club. My best friend, Johnny Oilstring, got me to pray and fast for fictionally depicted Rock Star Joe Sinc of the fictionally depicted band The Pee Weas. God's answer was to wait on Joe Sinc and investigate Kent State's May 4th issue. If the issue is not resolved, and the administration is at fault; join the hippies as a Republican from my home state. Then, my Grandma Esther died. Grief from this death caused me to take one last look at the May 4th controversy. I challenged Alan Peacemaker to explain the memorial to me. When he did, I became very disappointed with Kent's Republicans. They did not even try to resolve May 4th. The hippies invited me to a party on Saturday

19   Looney and Yeager, Under The Tarnished Dome, Simon and Shuster, New York, 1993, PP 183-186.

20   Patrick Reusse, "Plan Goes Up in Cigar Smoke".Star Tribune: Newspaper of the Twin Cities, September 30, 1989

21   Tybor, Joseph; "Irish Coach Criticizes NCAA Staff". Chicago Tribune, March 28, 1991, p1 sports.

November 19, 1989. That Friday I had second thoughts about their party. I asked God, "Should a Christian like me go to a party with hippies like them?" That Friday night, I tried to talk with my conservative friends for one last time, but nobody was there for the weekend. I wept and cried unto the Lord, "Lord tell me what to do about the party with Kent State's hippies. I want to go to heaven, and I do not want to lose Johnny Oilstring." I wept and cried for more than an hour. Then, as if by divine providence, Occult Defense Analyst Johnny Oilstring called. He told me his problems, then I asked Johnny, "In my place would you go to a party thrown by Kent State's famous hippies?" Johnny replied, "You know me. I would go to their party." I asked Johnny, "In my place would you feel that you had to go their party?" Johnny replied, "You should love your neighbor as yourself. You should go to their party and be their friend." I went to their party and became their friend.

Little did I know, Kent was in danger of a riot on May 4, 1990. The administration tried to plan a luncheon at about noon on May 4, 1990. This interfered with the tradition the Kent State hippies had of ringing the bell on the commons at 12:24 pm on May 4th of each year to remember the May 4th shootings. The members of the May 4th Task Force and The May 4th Center were outraged about this disrespect for the families and friends of the victims of the May 4th shootings. Sandy Scheuer was killed in the May 4th shootings. Her parents spoke out about this disrespect. To make matters even worse, President Schwartz tried to make fools of Sandy Scheuer's parents by lying about this disrespect publicly.[22] This disrespect even outraged some of my conservative friends. The Board of Judges had a tough choice. They either rebuke President Schwartz in The Name of Jesus of face the possibility of a riot in Kent on May 4, 1990. I wrote a letter to the editor of the school newspaper, *The Daily Kent Stater*. This letter rebuked President Schwartz. I lacked confidence to send this letter, so I showed this letter to members of the May 4th Task Force. They were so demoralized that they could give me little support. I asked Gainesville Wheeler Creek Security Council Chairman, Johnny Oilstring, for advice. He told me to print the letter as it was. A week or so later, this letter published in the *Kent Stater*. When the hippies saw this letter in the newspaper, their morale spiked. This caused the hippies to plan their commemoration in a more peaceful and constructive way. Everybody in Kent's counter-culture wanted and had a peaceful protest about the scaled back Memorial as they ideally wanted to do. Everybody in Kent's counter-culture, including my fictionally depicted best friend, Billy Glassman, served as a peace marshal on May 4, 1990 during the protest to ensure this peaceful protest.

Meanwhile, back in South Bend, Notre Dame was occupied with defending the honor of their football program. Why did Kent State hire

22   See letters 1, 2 on pp 194-197 209-20

Cordelli? Pinkel had better qualifications than Cordelli. An *Akron Beacon Journal* sportswriter picked Pinkel over Cordelli. Pinkel had good rapour with Kent State's fans and could have been a factor in rebuilding the program by both selling more tickets and giving Kent State a good football team.[23][24] Last time I heard in 2008, Pinkel was The Head Coach of The University of Missouri Tigers, a BCS contender in the Big 12. Cordelli could run an offense as well as Pinkel, but he took Holtz to the NCAA to dispute how much money Holtz paid Roselle Richardson. In 1991, Lou Holtz claimed that Cordelli changed his story about Holtz's payments to Roselle Richardson seven times. Cordelli had no proven rapour in Kent. Cordelli's payment dispute generated controversy concerning Notre Dame and the University of Minnesota. Notre Dame was a university with a history of its president supporting the peace movement [25]. Controversy associated with Cordelli occurred at a critical time concerning Kent State's memorial (1989-1990). What if somebody from Notre Dame spoke out concerning the scaled back May 4th Memorial? An athletic director associated with Schwartz, Amodio, gave Pete Cordelli a one year contract extension in December of 1991.[26] This extended Cordelli's contract through the 1994 season. His record as of December of 1991 was 1-10. In November or December of 1992, Amodio gave Cordelli a contract extension through the 1995. As of December of 1992, Cordelli's record was 3-19.[27] For a similar two year record of 2-20, and for a better overall record of 7-26, Head Coach Dick Crum was fired in 1990.[28] Unlike Cordelli, Dick Crum caused no controversy at Notre Dame or Minnesota. In 1994, Kent State President and

---

23   Alexander, Elton. "Cordelli New KSU Coach". Cleveland Plain Dealer, December 4, 1990

24   Seaburn, John. "Pinkel Has Edge at Kent." Akron Beacon Journal, December 2, 1990

25   "Hessburgh Bids Catholic Schools Learn Form Youth." New York Times, April 13, 1971, p.20.

26   Alexander, Elton. "KSU football Coach Pete Cordelli and Akron Basketball Coach Crawford Both Receive Contract Extensions." Cleveland Plain Dealer, September 24, 1992, Page 6 Section d.

27   Alexander, Elton."Kent Extends Cordelli's Contract". Cleveland Plain Dealer, November 24, 1992 p. 6e
28   Love, Steve. "KSU Misreads the Signals Firing is Bid to Recapture the Illusion of Having Arrived," Akron Beacon Journal, November 18, 1990, Page A1 Sports.

May 4th supporter, Carol Cartwright, fired Pete Cordelli for abusing football players and his losing record. Cordelli's record was 3-30. This process cost Kent State's Athletic Department the $172,000 that it took to buy the two remaining years left in Cordelli's coaching contract, all due to the questionable contract extensions.[29] Schwartz or somebody from Kent State's administration, please explain Cordelli's hiring and Cordelli's contract extensions.

Did the Cordelli controversy hurt the Notre Dame Football program? Since 1988, Notre Dame had not won a national title. In 1994, Notre Dame Athletic Director Dick Rosenthal retired from Notre Dame University because he wanted to be with his family.[30] Two big scandals in three years concerning the integrity of the Notre Dame Football program is very stressful for any Notre Dame athletic director. I would have wanted to spend time with family and friends in that situation. I would have retired. Looney and Yeager's book was likely to occur no matter what Kent State did in 1990. Looney and Yeager's book was done in poor taste. Cordelli's controversy was morally outrageous. Kent State please explain Cordelli's hiring and contract extensions for a record of 3-19.

This resignation marked the beginning of the mediocrity of Notre Dame's football program. Notre Dame lost at least 3 games a season until September of 2012. They were even a second rate contender for the national title that year. They lost the National Championship game with Alabama 42 to 14. Looney and Yeager attacked Notre Dame with league-wide problems. They attacked Notre Dame for secret steroid use by football players.[31] Looney and Yeager complained about Notre Dame players playing hurt.[32] Many people who were good enough to play at Notre Dame hated to miss practice and football games. They had the personality to play slightly sick or hurt because of their pride. Mr. Looney or Mr. Yeager, why didn't you suggest that the team doctor work directly under the athletic director or the university president as a NCAA policy for all college football programs? Mr. Looney or Mr. Yeager, If you had a solution for the secret player steroid use, why didn't you publish it? Many American companies could have stopped employee drug use years ago. Mr. Looney and Mr. Yeager, what you wrote did not result in the NCAA finding one major violation on Notre Dame football. Kim Dunbar embezzled money

29   Alexander, Elton; Kent State Fires Coach Cordelli, Cleveland Plain Dealer, February 22, 1994, p. 1D, Sports.

30   " Notre Dame Athletic Director announces Retirement," The Telegraph, Alton, Illinois, August 2, 1994, P. 18.

31   Looney and Yeager, Under the Tarnished Dome. Simon and Schuster, 1993, pp. 33-48.

32   Looney and Yeager, Under the Tarnished Dome. Simon and Schuster, 1993, pp. 49-72.

from a local contractor, joined Notre Dame's Quarterback Club, and entertained Notre Dame football players with the embezzled money. The NCAA found Notre Dame guilty of a major violation of its rules due to Kimberly Dunbar's actions. This violation was the first and only major NCAA violation in Notre Dame's history as of August of 2013[33] [34] I find no record of this violation in your book, Mr. Looney and Mr. Yeager. Please explain why you chose to pick on Notre Dame rather than exposing all of college football. Mr. Cordelli, what was the big deal at Notre Dame and Minnesota? Mr. Cordelli, you gave Notre Dame bad publicity and a lot of stress over a minor NCAA violation Lou Holtz committed at the University of Minnesota. Notre Dame was innocent. Shame on you!!! President Schwartz, Paul Amodio, or somebody in the Kent State administration please explain two contract extensions Cordelli got for a losing record of 3-19. Please explain Pete Cordelli's hiring over Pinkel. Please explain why a letter of recommendation from Lou Holtz should override a proven rapour that Pinkel had in Kent!!!! We, in South Bend, Indiana and the taxpayers of Ohio have the right to know!!!! Kent State President and May 4th supporter Carol Cartwright was absolutely right in firing Pete Cordelli. She actually judged employees on the basis of merit. Thank the Lord for Carol Cartwright!!!!

Did Notre Dame Football's mediocrity hurt the South Bend Tourism Industry? It is the opinion of many people in South Bend that Notre Dame's mediocre record of the last generation slowed down the tourism industry. During Notre Dame's good years, business at South Bend's restaurants and bars increased.[35] This means that business declines at bars and restaurants during bad years. Two restaurants that closed due to a decline in business are Bennit's Buffet in Roseland and Peaberry's cafe in downtown South Bend.[36] [37] These restaurants closed due to reduced business late in 2001or early 2002 during a recession. Notre Dame's football team had losing seasons two of the last three

---

33   "Notre Dame's Pedistal Not So High Now." Herald-Palladium, St.Joseph, Michigan, December 18,1999, News section.

34   Modrowski, Roman; "Dunbar Might Provide Details Involving Players, Former Notre Dame Booster Pleads Guilty." Chicago Sun Times, Chicago, Illinois; August 14, 1998, Late Sports Final Edition, Sports Section, Page 116.

35   Schroder, David; "Fans ready for Notre Dame Football," Fox 28, August 7, 2010, 8:39PM.

36   Prescott, Heidi. "Bennit's Buffet Will Close after 29 Years in Roseland," South Bend Tribune, December 14, 2001, Buisiness section.

37   Prescott, Heidi. "Peaberry's Cafe in Downtown South Bend Closing its Doors." South Bend Tribune, April 12, 2002, Sports Section.

years as of late 2001. Due to slower business, several other nearby restaurants and bars were likely hurt in late 2001 or early 2002. The College Football Hall of Fame is moving to Atlanta due to disappointing attendance at the hall. Notre Dame Football was mediocre during most of the 17 year tenure of the hall in South Bend, Indiana[38]. Kent State please explain Cordelli's hiring over Pinkel and contract extensions for a losing record of 3-19.

Kent State needs to explain its hiring of Cordelli over Pinkel and the two contract extensions they gave Cordelli. They need to explain the disrespectful treatment they gave the May 4th victims and their families. Enough honor has been lost over the Kent State shootings and questionable actions concerning them. May 4th should be solved on the football field. Knute Rockne was depicted to propose that college football could be an alternative to war in the movie, *Knute Rockne All American*. Issues concerning the May 4th shootings have not been solved by years of public debate, by lawsuits in court, by illegal protest, or by years of peaceful protest. Notre Dame, you should challenge Ohio State University to a series of football games sufficiently to raise the money necessary to build the original Bruno Ast design of the Kent State Memorial and to give veterans groups an equal amount of money that is given to the Kent State May 4th Memorial. A negotiated percentage of the game's profits should be given to the veterans and to the May 4th Memorial. Ohio State University, Your university is called The Ohio State University. I challenge your football team to defend the honor of The State of Ohio. Should you accept, your football team will not only defend the honor of the State of Ohio, but they will restore your state's honor. Let's restore the Notre Dame football program's reputation and ensure its renewed winning tradition. Let's restore Ohio's honor. The hippies and Christians should ultimately forgive the Kent State shootings and the peace movement's protests, so this country, The United States of America, may be healed of the wounds caused by the Vietnam War. In the Name of Jesus Christ, I propose this. Amen.

---

38 "College Football Hall of Fame in South Bend Closed For Good." WSBT TV, Mishawaka, Indiana; December 31, 2012

13 Ten Point Spaces

APPENDIX PART 2

2 Ten Point Spaces

LETTERS AND PICTUERS

LETTER 1
THE SCHWARTZ AND SCHEURER LETTERS
MY HAND WRITTEN COMMENTS PICKING
PRESIDENT SCHWARTZ APART[39]

← Normal
10 pt
Letter

A Stench in God's Nostrils

No Sensitivity to the families and wounded students

"Woe Unto them that decree Unrighteous decrees and that write grievousness .which they have p—
Isiah 10:1

---

39 I received this copy of these letters at a May 4th Task Force meeting in February of 1990

LETTER 1A *[cut Space*

THE SCHEUER LETTER IN LARGER PRINT

Michael Schwartz
President's Office   Jan. 30, 1990
Kent State University
Kent, OH 44242

Dear Mr. Schwartz,

At this time, we would like to respond to your recent letter of invitation to visit the "memorial" site, attend the "memorial" dedication program and your "luncheon" after the dedication program.

First, we decline the invitation to visit the "memorial" site prior to May 4, 1990. Secondly, we will later decide our personal schedules for May 4, 1990.

As you may be aware, for many years now, we annually have attended the meaningful May 4 Task Force commemoration programs at noon on the KSU Commons. Of course, we again plan to attend the May 4 Task Force commemoration at noon on May 4, 1990, and so we must decline your invitation to attend your "luncheon" at noon on that day.

It is our opinion that your attempt to sponsor such a "luncheon" during that noon hour is very insensitive and inappropriate. If you had a child killed on May 4, 1970, at Kent State, would you feel like eating lunch there during that hour?

Those are sacred moments which we choose to observe with the students and others on the KSU Commons in memory of our daughter, Sandy. During those solemn moments at noon on May 4, during the annual ringing of that bell, we always pause and remember our beloved daughter with a silent prayer.

Your attempt to sponsor a "luncheon" is an attempt to divide our families and supporters. We will therefore not join you.

Sincerely,

Martin Scheuer   Sarah Scheuer

LETTER 1B

← Cut Space

THE SCHWARTZ LETTER IN LARGER PRINT

Office of the President
(216) 672-2210

Kent State University
Kent Ohio 44242-0001

January 25, 1990

As you know, one year ago Kent State University broke ground for the construction of the May 4th Memorial designed by Bruno Ast of Chicago. The construction is now virtually complete, and we are planning the formal dedication of it on May 4, 1990 at eleven o'clock in the morning. Former Senator George McGovern has agreed to speak at the dedication. I expect the ceremony to last about one hour.

I have watched the construction of the memorial almost daily since the ground breaking, and I find it a stirring work of art. I hope that you will join the university community for the dedication ceremony and that you will join us at a luncheon for honored guests following the ceremony.

In addition, I would be very honored if you would visit the memorial with me at any time before May 4th in order that you may see it privately, without the media and others present. I can and will arrange such a visit at any time, at the university's expense, if you wish it. Please let me know. And, if you will be able to be with us on May 4th, please do let me know. That visit, if you are able to be with us, will also be at the university's expense.

I am looking forward to hearing from you, hoping that you will accept these invitations.

Sincerely yours,

Michael Schwartz
President

MS:jd

LETTER 2
MY LETTER TO THE EDITOR OF THE KENT STATER[40]

Student appreciates Scheuers' strength

Editor, States,

I commend the maturity and character of Sarah and Martin Scheuer, parents of the late Sandy Scheuer, who was slain May 4, 1970.

They apologized even when President Michael Schwartz made a mistake at their expense. They spoke out against Schwartz's luncheon because they had good reason to believe the luncheon was at noon.

I read a copy of this letter casually and thought Schwartz had planned a luncheon at noon during the May 4 Task Force's commemoration. Three other conservatives agreed.

Therefore, I believe Schwartz changed the time to 2 p.m. to escape public criticism. Let's congratulate the Scheuers for speaking out against a sinful KSU administration and then giving this administration the benefit of the doubt.

I would not have apologized for that letter if my child had died in that way. Schwartz should be ashamed of another blot on his already bad record of insensitivity concerning May 4.

Kevin L. Moody
Graduate Student, Physics

---

40 Moody, Kevin. "Student Appreciates Scheuer's Strength." Daily Kent Stater; February 22, 1990; p2

PICTURE 1
THE WORKINGS OF AN ELECTRIC MOTOR

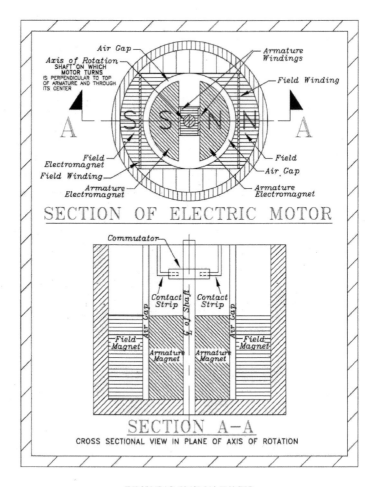

DRAWING BY DAN EAVES

PICTURE 1A
SCHEMATIC DRAWING OF ELECTRIC MOTOR

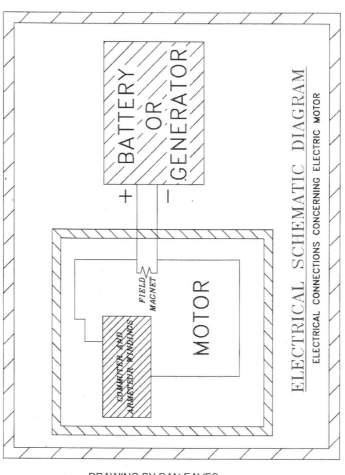

DRAWING BY DAN EAVES

PICTURE 2
FIBERGLASS AIR BUBBLES

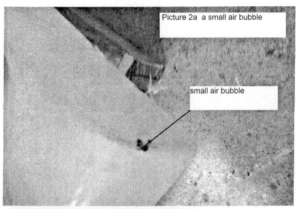

Picture 2a a small air bubble

small air bubble

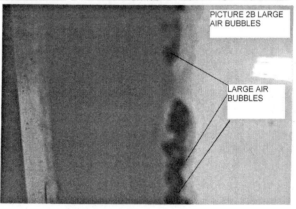

PICTURE 2B LARGE AIR BUBBLES

LARGE AIR BUBBLES

Proof

Made in the USA
Charleston, SC
03 December 2013